All's Fair

*Book Seven
of the Souls of
the Saintlands*

Tonya Adolfson

Published by Fantastic Journeys Publishing,
Boise, Idaho
PUBLISHING HISTORY
E-Book released through Kindle
Soft Cover trial edition June 2017
Mass market edition/ XXXXXX

Cover art: Photo of fabric by John Farmer
Created in Gimp 2.6 by John Farmer
Cover Art copyright by Fantastic Journeys Publishing
Interior Art by Lorraine Barraras and Suzette Urbano
Edited by Bri DeMaree, John Farmer, Gwen Bradley, and Stephanie Reese
Content copyright ©March 2017 Tonya Adolfson.

Published in the United States of America.

ISBN: 978-1-941276-02-0

The characters and events portrayed in this book are fictitious. Any similarity to real persons, living or dead, common or deific, is coincidental and not intended by the author, unless, of course, I know them.
No Augustinians were harmed in the making of this book, though a few folks were roughed up a bit.

<u>*Reviews for the Souls of the Saintlands Series*</u>

Thine Enemy's Eyes

"I loved it I stayed up late several nights because I had to know what happened! It's a great read with excellent pacing and such entertaining and rich characters. I loved the rich world she created and the details used to make it stand out. I cannot wait to read the second book to learn more about the characters and places mentioned! I highly suggest this book."
Maryanne Durant, Amazon Review

"I cannot wait for the next book, and hopefully, subsequent books to follow."
Steve Nunez, Dragonfleet Studios

"Tonya Adolfson's debut novel is incredible! Full of intrigue, wildly imaginative characters and set in a medieval fantasy world of such authenticity it blew me away. I would heartily recommend this to anyone, and can't wait until the second novel comes out!"
I. J. Smethurst, author of the *E.D.F Chronicles*

"The plot has interesting twists and turns to keep you going straight through the book. When it ends, it leaves you wanting more."
Shelley Wolf, Amazon Review

"…good political intrigue… good action scenes… Not to mention one of the heaviest cliff hangers I've seen in a while."
The William Jones Review

"This is a very well written book, and has more plot twists and turns then I could count, but each one made me all the more eager to keep reading and see where the story would end up."
Durin Boge, Amazon Review

"I've read and reread this book 5 times now, it's easily one of my favorites! The characters are well developed, the twists and turns of the story kept me guessing, and the story line easily kept me wanting more."
Chalyse Padigimus, Amazon Review

"I'm a busy professional without a lot of time to read and this book absorbed my free time quite enjoyably for the past week. It has a touch of the almost magical within an imagined realm akin to medieval Europe. It has romance without focusing overly on the tawdry details as she has better things to do with the plotline. She develops several characters including their background in succinct but inviting storytelling and she juggles all of these characters' knowledge gaps about the current situation of court intrigue quite well. I'm really curious to see what book 2 has in store for me."

Sheila Harmon, Amazon Review

"Some trouble trying to make sense of the geography at first; however, not sticking to a real-world atlas got me over that hurtle. The story itself is very interesting with a nice twist at the end."

Rold DeDog, Amazon Review

"Tonya Adolfson has a way of drawing you in to make you feel like you are right there with the characters. I could not put this book down because I was so in love with the characters, I had to see what was coming next. She keeps you guessing until the very end. At times, I found myself a little sad for a particular character and then later rejoicing with them. I strongly recommend this book and cannot wait to see what happens next in book two."

Kayla, Amazon Review

"This is the first book from Tonya Adolfson I have read and believe me, it won't be the last. She caught my attention for the first page and held it through all the plots and conspiracies. The setting is wonderfully imagined and the characters fully realized, and believable. A brilliantly written fantasy tale filled with exciting intrigue. I'm glad I bought this and the second book together!"

Samuel Sturkie, Amazon Review

"Tonya has definitely found her place on my bookshelf. Now have the first 4 books! Can't wait for the next one!"

Spencer Maschek, Amazon Review

"This is a fantastic beginning to a fantastic series. I could not put it down. An amazing world full of detail."

Adam Wells-Grube, Amazon Review

"Ms. Adolfson has woven a web that will catch you while you're not looking. The characters are dynamic, with relationships we can relate to

and an intrigue so deep that I could not put the book down until it was over; and I was begging for more. There are few books that I have found that suck me in the way this one does."
Hannah Therrien, Amazon Review

An Unpolished Gem

"In a perfect follow through to Thine Enemy's Eyes, Ms. Adolfson continues to illustrate just how sticky the politics and personalities of her world really can be. She never lets go of you, even after the book is done. Just when I think I have a character figured out, they surprise me; I can't even tell how many sides to this story there are. I can't wait for book three!"
Julien McBain, author *Ghosts of the Past*

"It is difficult for second books in a series to have the same weight as the first. This is the rarer case of the second book surpassing the first."
Christopher Garcia, editor of *the Drink Tank*

"This book is just as captivating as the first book in the series. Again, I was so enthralled with the characters, plot twists, and story line that I literally couldn't put it down and finished reading it in one day..."
Chalyse Padigimus, Amazon Review

"I love her writing style. She creates this world that becomes real to its readers. Oh, and then there are these great characters with such richness and depth you cannot help but to love and in some cases, hate them! She has written it in such a way you have no idea where or who, if anyone, the main character will end up with. There is such a depth in the story you just cannot put it down. I read it in a matter of hours. I know these are books I am going to read again and again throughout the years. It has to be a great book for it to have that kind of status on my bookshelf."
Maryanne Durant, Amazon Review

"Love the way the characters grow and mature. Can't wait for the next book!"
Shelley Wolf, Amazon Review

An Open Enemy

"I have flown through these books. I totally love the tangled story with so many twists and turns. These are written by someone who knows how to keep their audience captive and I cannot wait for the 4th book!!! I have been dying to know what happens! This is definitely and awesome read every true fantasy buff should have on their shelf."
Maryanne Durant, Amazon Review

"By the time, I reached this novel I knew I was going to be a lifelong fan. These characters hold pieces of the human experience that filled me with a sense of hope, left me speechless and at times exhausted me. An emotional journey filled with adventure that I will treasure and live over and again every time I read it for the rest of my life."
Anonymous, Amazon Review

To Thine Own Self

The whole series of these books are very cleverly written and very in depth with rich detailing and character development. I absolutely have read these books over and over again. There is a lot of action within the pages along with laughter and pain. The books tend to suck you in and show a world unlike any other.
Maryanne Durant, Amazon Review

Tonya Adolfson will take you further down the rabbit hole with this latest installment. There's only one problem. Nothing can prepare you for hitting the bottom. Riveting and jaw dropping twists that only add to the story are in store for all. Be grateful Book 5 is already out, for the wait would have been unbearable.
Steve "Warky" Nunez, Dragonfleet Studios

This series is 11 stars out of 10!
With some books, it's hard to read them again once you know the plot twists. But with Tonya, she weaves her stories with such sublime brilliance that you want to read them again and again. Whether you're caught up in the beautiful dream like dialogue between two star struck characters or breathlessly page turning during the heart pounding action scenes, you will love this must-have series! Spoiler Alert: The books just keep getting better and better!
Ethan Shaw

"To Thine Own Self" is a wonderful book full of love, sorrow, adventures, plot twists and turns, and everything you can imagine. Oh, how it ended! After finishing the first thing I said (with a smile) was "I need to go send 'hate mail' to Tonya." In the note, I told her "You're not my favorite Tonya right now." Now I wait patiently… well somewhat patiently, for book 5 to come out.

Stephanie Reese

"To Thine Own Self" is book 4 in the Saintlands series that Tonya Adolfson wrote. This is a wonderful series full of intrigue, adventure, love and magic of the medieval times. This book transports you into the lives of the people and the lands to the point where you don't want to put the book down to go to sleep. I can't wait for the next book to find out what happens next. Tonya has become one of my favorite authors and deserves to have all her books read and reread over and over again. Each book is really that good. Thank you so much Tonya for giving us the Saintlands series

Tish Firmiss

"To Thine Own Self" is a dynamic continuation in the "Souls of the Saintlands" series. A delicate balance of action that moves the story forward without feeling overwhelmed or bogged down. This book in particular adds great detail to both the land and characters that have been introduced. While this is the fourth book, she has not stopped adding new mysteries and plot changes that must only be resolved in the next book. I anxiously await the next release date so I might again join the world that has created and learn how everything is resolved. A truly wonderful book and series.

Krista Wells

I started this series wanting a good story, I'm now fully committed to this universe.

If you're this far along, you already know what a great story you've gotten yourself into. You know these characters are driven as only people can be, not just archetypes. What will stand out in this book is the attention to detail. It isn't just a dance, it's a dance you can visualize. It isn't just clothes, you can feel what the draping of the silk must feel like. Think of what your favorite characters and stories have come to mean to you over time. Now tell them to make room. By the end of this book, you will be hooked. There is no turning back.

Andrea Cortright, Animeland Convention Owner

Full of Sound and Fury

I have never felt such strong emotions from reading a book. I was immersed in this book so much so, that when a certain spoiler happens, I threw my book across the room and cried into my pillow.

After book shaming this title for a while, I had to know how this book was going to end.

Warning! The ending leaves you craving the next book, and sobbing into your pillow. People who buy this book should invest in some tissues as well.

All in all, I'm excited to see where all of the relationships are heading, especially Myrgen and Catriona. I want them to be together, but after seeing that the author doesn't rule out ANYTHING from happening, I'm on edge hoping and wondering what fate will allow.

Steve "Warky" Nunez, Dragonfleet Studios

I am already reading it for the 2nd time. I love this book. Tonya Adolfson has done it again, another great book in the series. It starts with where the last book left off so that you are right back into the suspense of it all. She will hold you spell bound by what happens next and, by the end of this book, you will be wanting the next to keep the suspense going. Just when you think you know what will happen next, she throws you a curve and you keep reading to see what will happen. I love her books and can't wait for the next one to come out. I don't care how long it takes her to write it, I want to continue living in this series. What a great place to immerse yourself in. Thank you, Tonya. Please keep writing this series.

Tish Firmiss, Amazon Review

The game is afoot!

We know what to expect from just about everyone, so nothing new on the characters. We've finally settled in to a few less surprises from our friends and focus more on moving the story along. And move it does!

The curtain is pulled back on the pantheons. We're getting A LOT more of the spiritual story than some might be comfortable with, but if people didn't see that writing on the wall by now, they haven't been paying attention. I like that it's ALL of them addressed pretty fairly, not just one or the other. And we're starting to see that no one belief is necessarily right or wrong (they're all right AND wrong), they all have their nuances. They have been part of the story the entire time. I'm happy to finally see them more prominent.

There wasn't the rip-roaring page turner that the previous books have been. I was able to sleep at night reading this one, but make no mistake: the blazing fire has only transformed into an intense smolder. The honeymoon is over, but the relationship is only just getting started!

Bring on book 6!!

Andrea Cortright, Animeland Convention Owner

Words can't even begin to justifiably escribe the sheer awesomeicity of this book series. Tonya builds a lore-filled world in a way that few others can achieve with masterful control of her characters. And just when you think you have a handle on things, she throws so many swerves, even Vince Russo would end up with whiplash. But everything that happens keeps you wanting to come back for more. Can't wait to see what she conjures up next.

Richard Englebert

To Gwen, because she allowed me into her heart to revive someone we all love. Thank you. I always knew you'd be a great queen.

Acknowledgments:

First and foremost, I'd like to thank all the people who were inspirations for this book:

Gwen for Gwen, John for Raven, Dartanian for Alexander, Jeff for James, Misha for Emmy, Morgan for Alan and Johannes, Rod for Xeno, Shanna for Fierah, Stephanie for Belladonna, Erik for Dom, Jared for Draethen, Dave for Octavius, Morgan Wolf for Morgan Wolf, Aaron for Duncan, Adam P for Ambroise, John for Myrgen, David for Henri, Jennifer for Ce'Nedra, Daddy for Thessius, Kim for Ysabel, Joe for Nicaise, Jenn for Flora, Aggie for Aggie, Allan Hobbs for Allen Hobbs, Andrea for Aislyn, and all the hundreds of friends and family that have been contributors to this book. Your work has been amazing and your lives inspiring.

A big shout out to the most amazing editors a gal could have: Gwen Bradley has helped with this project for over 15 years and still comments on the initial drafts to this day. Also thanks to John Farmer for always helping with the read throughs. And Stephanie Reese, you are beyond priceless.

Thanks to Shannon Galarneau for being my agent and helping me fulfill the dream of Fantastic Journeys Publishing. I'd also like to thank Steve "Warky" Nunez for all his enthusiastic support.

And finally, to my wonderful family: Morgan and Misha, for being so tolerant of Mommy's work; to my Daddy, Ray Lamar Manley, for inspiring me to tell stories for the sheer pleasure of my audience; to my Mom, Rosemary Virginia Manley, for reading historical romances; and to the Great and Powerful Todd, for being everything a Prince needs to be.

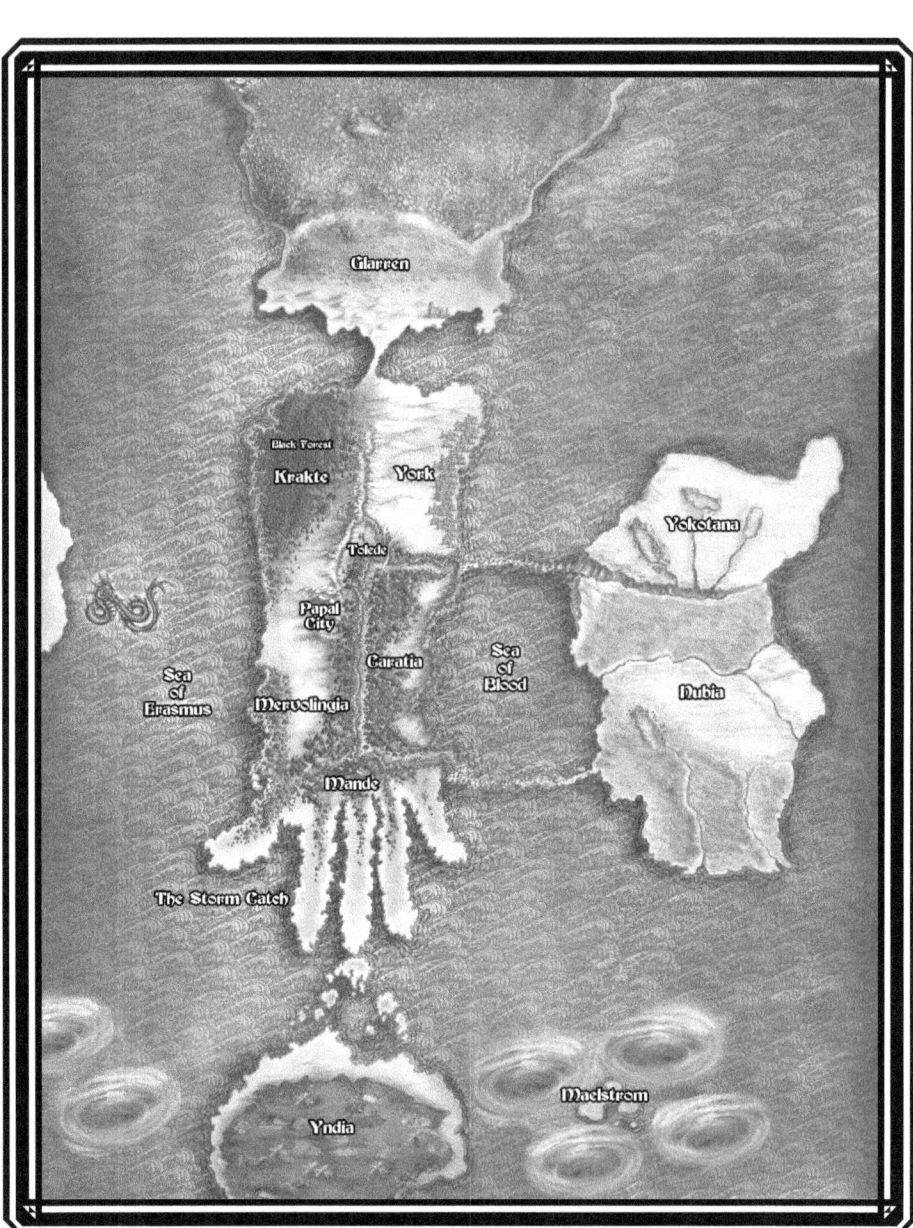

Summerland

The teachings of Fang and Claw penetrate deep in the savannas of Nubia. They are carved into the sides of trees, rocks and in the ground near watering holes. An oral religion, they pass the wisdom of their totem animals through rich poetry. The elders of a tribe sit around the fire after dinner and one will speak a single line. The next in the circle must add to the poem by adding another line. The third in the circle must then speak a line that changes the meaning of the first when coupled with the second. This pattern continues until the story is ended.

Book One

"The Tale is to the Listener as the air is to the lungs.
The voices of our hands speak to the fire."
(The story begins.)

You can no more win a war than you can win an earthquake.
-Jeannette Rankin

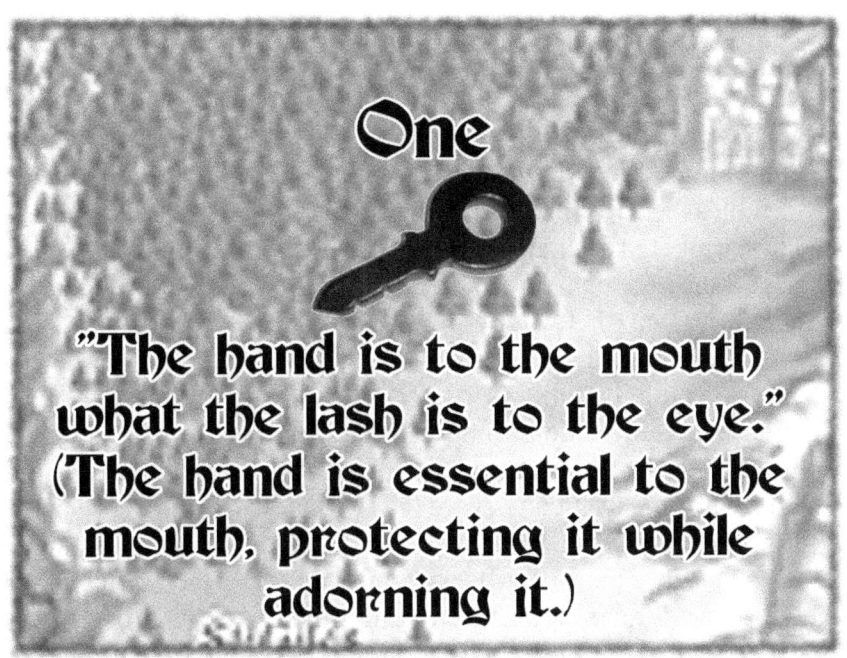

One

"The hand is to the mouth
what the lash is to the eye."
(The hand is essential to the
mouth, protecting it while
adorning it.)

"Archers! Light arrows and burn the Queen's table to the ground."

Bartolemaus Johner, the Voice of Command for the Midsummer King himself, expected his order to be obeyed and he was obliged. Three eagle-headed archers in Krakten royal livery ran forward from a nearby encampment, nocking arrows as they did so. They touched their arrows to a salamander in a campfire, setting the tips aflame.

They fired at the now empty dining table in Queen Sovereigna's greeting pavilion. Johner watched the flames spread to the coat of Tanglwyst's that the human king, Alexander, had worn.

The black sludge burned like lamp oil, as was its nature. Nothing that touched the shadow realm could abide the touch of fire, and this particular sludge was quite susceptible. Ogres ran up, grabbing buckets of water that were in nearby camps but Johner held up his hand for them to wait. They watched the fire almost as much as they watched him, eyes darting between the two potential disasters.

He monitored it until the last of the three rabbit-eared scouts was consumed before motioning to the ogres on standby with buckets. As the fires hissed out, Johner turned to a goblin messenger.

"Gather the lieutenants. They now report to me."

Catherine de Medici, Queen mother of Mervolingia, screamed her orgasm, unleashed from caring about society or decorum. Sovereigna joined her, triggered by the pleasure unleashed in the joining spell. They fell back on the bed, exhausted and happy.

"What was in that wine?" Catherine reached for their glasses, handing Sovereigna hers.

"Just a youth potion I use every day. It helps me stay sharp, something you need while dealing with Fae."

"Well, it kept *me* going! And the Joining Spell? That was glorious!"

"I have always wanted to share that with you."

"I want to give it as a wedding present to every person I know." She kissed Sovereigna, the lingering kiss of a love too long denied. Their bodies embraced, their clothes from a lifetime of captivity discarded as if they were in their twenties instead of almost six decades old.

"The ingredients grow in Krakte, in my personal garden. They are useful for negotiations."

Catherine frowned. "Oh, yes I guess they would be." She glanced around the room. "And now for the unpleasant part. Where is the Privy?"

Sovereigna smiled. "I'll show you."

They dressed sparingly, camp slippers and a Mandian surcote that could double as a gown, and exited into the noisy camp. They went to a latrine set up only for Sovereigna's use. A couple of guards nodded to the women as they approached and Catherine entered while the Queen of Krakte gave her the privacy of distance. Sovereigna noticed Johner standing near a sizable fire. Then she realized the fire was within the walls of her greeting tent.

Catherine came out as Sovereigna grabbed a guard, pointing to the fire. The ogres that were her personal detail realized the danger and called through the camp, grabbing water buckets set around for just this purpose. She rushed to Catherine, gathering her as she went towards the fire. They skirted the tents, getting to safety.

By the time her privy guards got to the tent, the fire seemed to be out. Sovereigna looked over Catherine, then herself, making sure no stray embers made their way onto the royal clothing. She was about to storm over to the Fae General when Catherine gripped her shoulder, stopping her. Catherine nodded to an area a little closer to the gathering group, while still in the shadows.

"Lieutenants, the enemy has attacked and retaliation is mandatory."

"Sir?" One of the lieutenants, a foxlike creature with clever eyes, glanced about at the now smoking furniture. "What happened?"

"A human working for Heaven has brought a weapon into this camp and left it here. It has destroyed three of our fellows. It seems Heaven is not above using the infernal shadows to fight this war." He looked at each leader. "Instruct your soldiers to surround the village and trap Heaven's Champion before more destruction is wrought. Once King Corrigan arrives, we will hear his orders and obey. It is up to the Midsummer King to decide their fate."

Sovereigna pulled back, then tugged at Catherine's hand, guiding her through the shadows, away from the meeting. The dinner with Alexander and Tanglwyst had ended the threat of war between their people. As a result, the army presence between the village of St. Giles and the Royal Encampment had thinned as warriors met in the valley to spread the word. They got out of ear shot of even the rabbit scouts before Sovereigna spoke, yet still she kept her voice low.

"I don't understand. Why is he declaring war?"

Catherine shrugged looking around the area. "I don't know. There aren't any human guards or bodies. Why did he say 'the enemy has attacked'? And Corrigan… Is… is that really…?"

Sovereigna nodded. "Yes, the Fae Lord of Summer. He's the Warlord of the Fae and commands the full might of their steel. I won't have control over my own army if he is here."

"What are we going to do?"

Sovereigna glanced back at the distant smoke from the dying fire. "We're getting you to your son. I don't know who attacked but I can tell for certain he'll be blamed."

Tanglwyst de Holloway sat at her desk, looking over her company's paperwork. She dragged her hands through her hair, worried about the amount of loss she was seeing in the documents.

The manifests from the shipment that arrived during the siege let her know what was donated to the town, and the loss of the vineyard and buildings set the cost very high. Even if she set sail tomorrow there would be no way to recover these losses. Her entire family might need to be relocated.

Sovereigna's offer to have her half-Fae army help rebuild was kind, but the Black Forest could not be harvested for supplies, meaning she would have to go to the forests around St. Giles on the Mervol side. That risked exposing Catriona's home and Tanglwyst was not willing to do that yet. The other option was to go to the south of the valley, into the forest there, but the amount of harvest required would expose all of Allen Hobbs's travel blinds, which had kept her and Alexander safe on their way to the village. She knew harvesting from the Disputed Forest, as her friend Tulio called it, risked angering the Fae that lived there and she had enough problems already.

Any other option was too expensive. She didn't know the resources of the Queen of Krakte, but she couldn't see a mundane option that didn't hurt people.

She stood and opened the window, giving herself a break. She smelled the smoke from the campfires and leaned on the sill to look down to the City Guards office, where she could see figures in the windows, talking.

Gomez and Alex. Probably telling him all about dinner.

One of the figures stood and came to the window to lean on it. It was Alexander, of course. He looked to her home and smiled, sneaking a wave at her. She returned it, the smile on her face there regardless of her will. Gomez stood up behind him, carrying two mugs to somewhere. They didn't have any way to speak, though she could feel Alexander's warmth through the connection they shared through the Power of Sovereignty. As one of the only ones who had ever given it up freely, she wondered if Charles felt the same connection to Alexander as she did because of it.

Alexander looked over his shoulder at something Gomez said, and he reluctantly pulled away from her gaze. Gomez went to the window, smiled and waved to her, then shut the glass. The lights were dimmed for sleeping and she nodded, understanding. It *was* very late. Before too long, the sky would start to move into dawn and they would be able to spend time together again. But that would happen *faster* if she went to sleep. Perhaps things would look better in the morning.

For the sake of her family, friends, business, kingdom, and heart, she closed the window and went to bed.

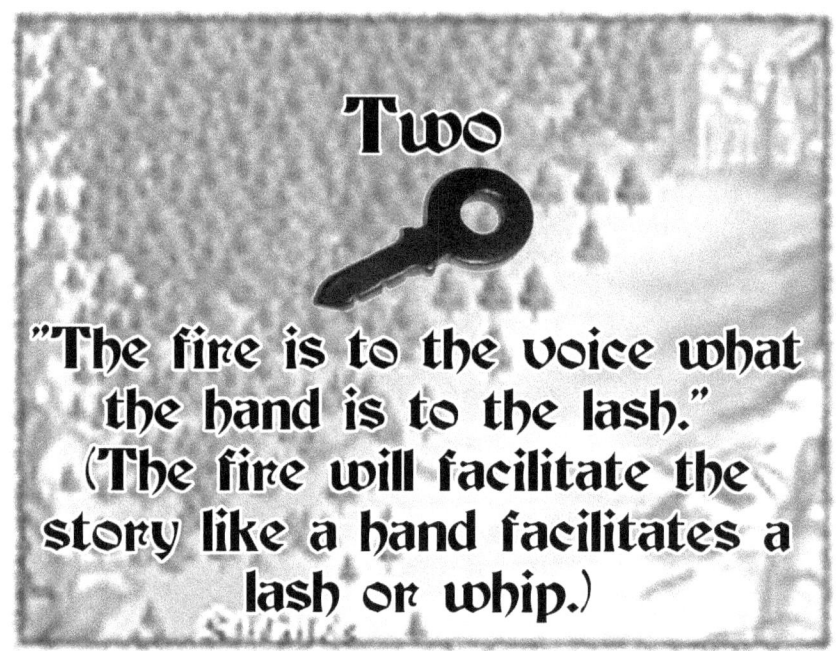

Two

"The fire is to the voice what the hand is to the lash." (The fire will facilitate the story like a hand facilitates a lash or whip.)

"Catriona?"

Catriona coughed blood onto Myrgen's chest, then fell to the ground. A massive bruise, the same color as the stones Raven had just shoved into her chest, darkened the skin around the broken sternum. Her chest was jerky in its movements and blood trickled from her mouth. Myrgen dropped to the ground beside her, cradling her. Her eyes were sharp with pain and fear.

Alistair grabbed Raven's shirt, his fists embedding in Raven's throat. *"Why did you do that?"*

Raven grabbed at Alistair's hands, needing the air Alistair was blocking. "I… need her to… die here..."

Alistair eased up on his strangulation, but he maintained his grip.

Lucifer turned to him, horrified at Raven's reaction. "You did this on purpose?" He gestured to the broken woman bleeding internally on the floor. "This isn't some accidental side effect?"

"Well, yes." Raven winced as Catriona coughed far too much blood onto her face and neck. Her entire windpipe seemed to be filling with blood and her body was trying desperately to keep her airways clear. "Though I really wasn't expecting this much of a mess."

Alistair threw Raven away from him and turned to Myrgen. "What do you need?"

Myrgen shook his head. "Help me get her up."

Alistair helped lift Catriona, and Myrgen picked her up and rushed out of the study. Raven started to follow but Alistair shoved him away from the door. Lucifer snagged Raven's arm and tugged him out of the way.

"I just…" Raven started, but Alistair raised his fist and Raven fell silent.

Alistair followed Myrgen out to the garden that overlooked Summerland. The man went directly to the wall and turned to Alistair.

"Hold her, please."

Alistair took the woman he loved when he was alive, and Myrgen climbed over the low wall. He then reached out for her. Alistair returned her to his care as she strained to pull in a wheezing, bubbling breath. Her eyes shifted to Myrgen and then closed as her breathing became shallow.

"Thank you." Myrgen shifted her to rest against his chest.

"Myrgen."

Myrgen turned to look at Alistair.

"What will you do with her?"

"Take her home." He glanced at a house within sight of the mansion where they now stood.

"For how long this time?"

Myrgen looked back at him. "Goodbye, Alistair."

Alistair watched Myrgen walk away.

Lucifer held Raven back until he heard the door at the end of the hall close, then he looked at the mage. "It might be wise for you to be on your way before they return."

"But I have to wait. I need to see what she turns into."

9

Lucifer cocked his head. "Wouldn't Caratia be a better place to do that? I mean, here, she'll just be herself. There, you'll see the fruition of your handiwork."

"Oh." Raven thought for a moment. "Yes, I suppose that's true. I won't get to ask what I need to up here."

Lucifer nodded. "No, you really won't. Here. I'll see you to the door." He walked Raven up the stairs to a door to a balcony.

Raven looked around. "Is this how I got in?"

Lucifer shrugged. "Actually, you got in because I asked you here. I wouldn't expect that again, not after…" He jerked his head in the direction of the downstairs study.

Raven nodded. "Ah. Because they might be upset with me?"

Lucifer blinked, his lips tightening into a hard line. "Uh, yeah."

Raven looked around. "How do I get back?"

"I can help with that." He walked Raven over to the edge and pushed him over the railing.

Raven gave a startled scream and was gone.

Lucifer walked back downstairs and into the study, poured a couple brandies, and walked out to the garden. He saw Myrgen carrying Catriona in his arms as he turned onto the street and out of sight in front of a house. Lucifer handed a glass to Alistair.

"How is she?"

Alistair took the glass and sipped the brandy. "Her breathing was all but stopped when she passed over the wall. I think her last gasp was there."

"Ah." Lucifer sipped his brandy.

Folks started gathering at the street in front of the house Myrgen went in. Alistair sniffed back some emotion, his eyes following a young, blonde woman.

"You okay?"

Alistair nodded to her. "That's… that's my daughter."

"The blonde?"

"Yeah. I…" Alistair shook himself out of the emotion. "Sorry. I wasn't expecting to see her and with Catriona and what happened just now…"

Lucifer decided to seize that. "She's been here before, right? Catriona?"

"Yeah. Usually, death changes her but not this time."

"*That* sounds like something to explore."

"And I have no doubt Myrgen will be doing just that. I know I would be. You never know if Raven might decide to do it again."

Lucifer let a moment pass. Their banter tended to be fast paced, a feature he adored, but this felt like something that needed to be carefully approached. "So, do you have any idea why your friend would do that in the first place?"

Alistair shrugged. "I don't know. Raven is... *difficult to understand* sometimes."

Lucifer had no trouble accepting that assessment. "What do you think will happen," he nodded towards the house, "with that?"

Alistair took a deep breath, thinking. "I suspect he'll find out how she returned unchanged last time and recreate that. If he can't, he'll die to stay with her." He turned to Lucifer. "Is it murder if he kills someone who returns?"

"If she decides not to, yeah."

Alistair sat on the low wall. "Is that what it takes? Just deciding not to return?"

"I don't really understand things on the Land side." Lucifer pointed at himself. "Archangel."

"Right. I almost forgot. Well, Myrgen is now a Land worshipper. It would be up to the Land to judge, I suppose."

A woman with long, dark hair laced with white walked out of a house on the far end of the street and stood, looking at the crowd. Alistair stood when he saw her.

"Hunh... She's still here?"

"Who?"

Alistair pointed. "The lady at the end of the street there. That looks like the First Dûcesa. But she died three hundred years ago. She should have moved on by now."

"Unfinished business?"

"For three hundred years?"

"Well, you've been around for three hundred years and never moved on."

Alistair nodded. "Well, not voluntarily." He looked around at the crowd. "No Second or Third Dûcesa. Not really unexpected with the Second though. She wasn't alive long enough to get anything to work out. Raven did her in too. That's probably for the best, really. It will be

11

pretty awkward for him to wander amongst people whom he's responsible for sending here."

"Well, I don't think we have to worry about that anymore."

"Why not?"

Lucifer took a sip of his brandy. "This mansion here is kind of a special place, you might say. I built it to touch nearly every realm. It's also very well protected. No one comes in here without my express, written consent."

"Wait, you mean the invitations and that note the first time…?"

Lucifer nodded. "And just now, I asked Raven to leave. Then I threw him off the balcony. He's unlikely to return."

"Wait, what? You mean you've sealed off the Afterlife somehow?"

"Kind of. I have a rider to my contract, so to speak, that says I don't have to interfere with the natural processes, but I don't have to leave them alone either. I built this place to touch every Afterlife I could, and I control access to it. Yeah, people can just die and go where they go, but if they have a chance at passing through *here*, I can interfere with that."

Alistair turned around and leaned on the wall. "Well, later, I'll take issue with that."

"Not now?"

"I'm a little pissed at Raven right now."

Lucifer smiled and leaned on the wall too. "I can live with that."

They sipped the brandy and watched the crowds of dead decide to return to their daily routines.

Myrgen put the wet, bloody cloth in the basin and took it back to the dresser. He took off his shirt and wiped down the blood Catriona had aspirated on his face and chest. She was sleeping for the moment and he didn't know how long the transition would take. He himself had not felt death claim him, but he was certain it must have. He was interacting with the dead in the Afterlife. It only made sense that they were both gone from the surface world.

He put on a fresh shirt and then pulled a chair over from the bedroom hearth. He sat beside her, waiting for her return.

He didn't have to wait long.

Her eyes fluttered open and she looked around, her hand going to her chest. He reached out and touched her face.

"Hey there."

She looked at him, relaxing, then sat up and looked around the room. "So. He really did kill me, huh?"

"Yeah. Are you okay?"

"Yes. The damage doesn't linger here." She looked at him. "Did he kill you too?"

"I guess you could say that. I brought you here from the mansion." He nodded to the window where he could see Alistair and Lucifer talking in the garden. "If I can interact with the dead…"

She nodded. "Then it only makes sense you are dead as well. Do you know why he did it?"

"All he said was that he needed you to die here. And he wasn't expecting the mess."

Catriona looked at her chest but her customary black clothing hid the blood. She touched her hair and frowned at the sticky red on her fingers. "It feels like a bath is in order but that is an awful lot of work."

"Maybe this time, I'll build one of those fountain things Xannu has in the Open Lotus."

"Oh! Yes, those are wonderful. I wonder what it takes to build here?"

"I suppose we can ask around." He hesitated, looking at their hands. "Are we staying then?"

"I suppose we should find out why Raven did this first or it may be a recurring thing."

Myrgen held her gaze. "I don't care why he did it. He was out of line. He doesn't get to decide when you die. He did that *knowing* it would change you. He did it *on purpose*. I don't really give a blood why. He had no right." He squeezed her hand. "You don't owe him anything."

"No, but I owe *you* something. I owe it to you and me to assess if he is a threat."

"He killed you. He's a threat."

She smiled. "Are you just going to assume that *every* time someone kills me?"

"Probably. I think it's a good rubric for such things."

"Do you know where he is now?"

Myrgen shook his head. "Don't know. Don't care."

13

"It might be important."

"Then you can talk to him if he comes by to visit."

She frowned. "You mean after he's dead?"

"Turns out that's not as final as it used to be."

"I'm pretty sure it is for most people."

Myrgen sighed. "Well, I don't know what's going on there. Alistair was pretty upset after he hurt you. If Raven is still around, I'd be surprised if he *wasn't* roaming the streets here, confusing bystanders."

"He's part Fae. He probably wouldn't go here. He'd go to Sovereignlumin."

"Good riddance."

"Myrgen…"

He stood. "I'm sorry Catriona, but I have no sympathy nor remorse over the people responsible for killing you. I don't have to. It's my job to protect you and every time someone succeeds in sending you here, I have failed. I don't know why you returned before without changing but I'm gonna find out before we go back." He moved the chair back to the hearth.

She stood and walked over to him, hugging him from behind. "How?"

He layered his arms upon hers and gave a quick squeeze. "I don't know." Her turned to face her, holding her. "But I'm not leaving here unless I know what I'm getting out there. I don't want to protect a stranger."

They embraced for a few minutes in silence, then she nodded to the window.

"That's going to be problematic."

Myrgen looked at Lucifer and Alistair chatting on the garden wall. "Do we need to get a curtain?"

"Or a large bush like they have at the palace in Patras." She looked at him. "You ready to go see them?"

"I can go talk to them while you clean up."

"What makes you think I want to clean up without you?"

He smiled and kissed her, then went to get a bath ready.

Catriona dried her hair and wrapped it in a towel. Myrgen finished drying as well, their bath draining into a pipe that carried the water to the garden. Catriona glanced up and saw Alistair and Lucifer in practically the same positions they were in when she looked last time.

"Does time not pass for those outside?"

Myrgen looked out the window and shook his head. "It passed for me. I went to York, stormed a fortress, and painted about sixteen paintings."

"You painted?"

"Mhm."

"Where are they?"

"In the Eastern tower at Ashstone."

She smiled. "That alone might get me back home."

"I'll paint something here. We don't need to leave if you don't want to."

She touched Myrgen's hand. "That's where our people are. I may not owe anything to Raven, but we *do* owe something to our people. You are their Stâpân."

"I am *your* Stâpân. I'm here to protect *you*."

"And they are a part of me." She kissed him. "You are too."

"And that's how I want it to remain. If you keep dying, that might change. *You* might change."

"But I didn't."

"Yet. I don't want to risk it." He stomped into his boot. "Any idea why?"

Catriona shook her head. "I just knew you were waiting. I *remembered* you."

He looked at her as he stomped on his other boot. "But I'm already right here. Do I have to be there to call you out?"

She shook her head. "I don't know." She nodded to Alistair. "But maybe one of them does. Let's go ask."

He kissed her hand and they left the house.

Alistair nodded to Lucifer. "I told you they would come back."

Lucifer turned to see the couple walking towards them. He waved. Catriona waved back. "Well, that's a good sign. She isn't holding your friend's actions against me."

"She's pretty good at sorting out what drives people. Had she known Raven was a threat, she never would have let him get that close."

"And now that *I* know he's a threat, he won't be allowed near her again." Myrgen nodded to his friends. "Is he still there?"

Alistair shook his head. "Nope. You're safe."

Catriona glanced at the mansion. "Why did he do it?"

Lucifer shrugged. "He didn't really say. Something about needing you to come back as part of this place."

She glanced away, sadder for the knowledge.

Myrgen saw this and sighed. "That's actually something we wanted to ask about. What are the parameters of her return? Do I need to be out there? How does it work? More important, does she *have* to change? She didn't this last time so, maybe she can stay the same?"

Alistair took a deep breath. "I'm afraid I'm not the person to ask. I met the Dûcesa during the War. I didn't get the chance to talk about things. That's… well…"

Catriona rolled her eyes. "That's Raven's skill set."

"Well, not exclusively." Alistair pointed to the house at the end of the street. "There's someone who can help you."

Catriona and Myrgen turned to see where he was pointing. An older woman with long black and white hair stepped out of the house and looked around. She turned her gaze upon Catriona and Myrgen.

"By the Stones." Catriona's voice held reverence. "The First Dûcesa." She looked at Myrgen. "I recognize her from the portrait from the study at Ashstone."

"That portrait is three hundred years old." Myrgen looked at Alistair. "How is she still here?"

Alistair shrugged. "I was just as surprised as you."

"Wish us luck then." Myrgen turned back to the village.

Catriona looked at Alistair. "Will you be here when we're done?"

Alistair smiled. "I doubt it. I need to check on James. Seeing Gwen earlier…"

She smiled, nodding. "I'll tell her you were asking about her."

"Can she see me here?"

"I don't know. But I can ask. I suspect our friend here," she nodded to Lucifer, "knows how to reach you if she would like to talk."

"Yeah, he has his ways."

She nodded and joined Myrgen in returning to the village.

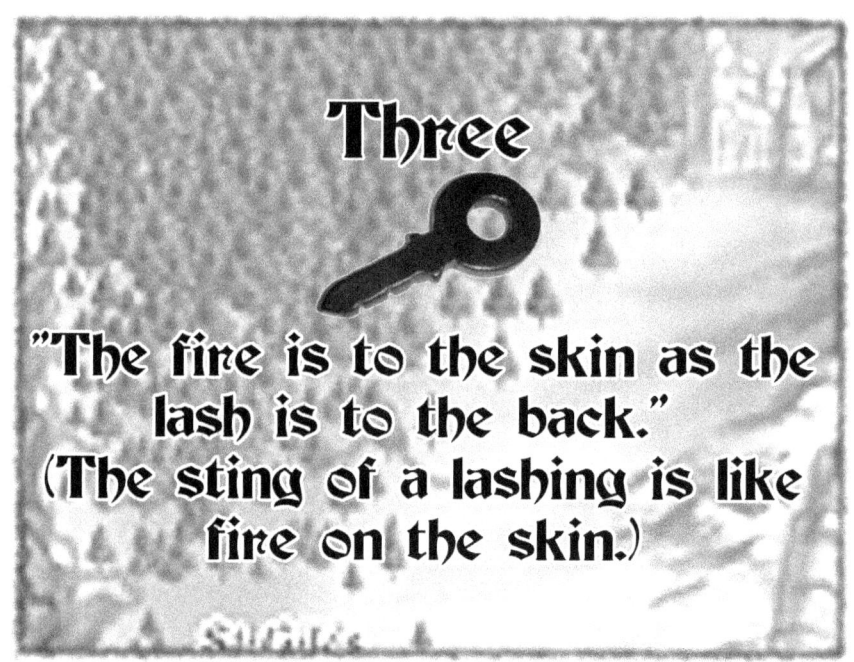

Three

"The fire is to the skin as the lash is to the back." (The sting of a lashing is like fire on the skin.)

Raven hit the ground before he realized he was falling. He had barely left the balcony railing when he landed, but it felt like he had plummeted a hundred feet. He heard bones pulverize and felt his skin rent by the shards. His throat filled with blood but he was on his stomach so the blood simply flowed from his mouth onto the dirt. He tried to figure out what happened, why his personal protection spells didn't go off. Then he realized his protection spells wouldn't go off if he wasn't in danger. A drop from a second story balcony wouldn't even warrant an air spell to slow his fall. Somehow, Lucifer had made his magic think he couldn't be hurt so it didn't protect him.

He looked around as best he could to try and assess where he was and determined he was probably in York, near Persephone. That was helpful at least. There, he had a place he could heal.

He tried to move and was unable to feel most of his body. He realized he had a broken neck. He closed his eyes and called out to Lauriel. An eternity later, the Fae wolf arrived. The wolf grabbed his collar and used his own Fae magic to move through the earth to Persephone. The ancient buildings were in pieces on the ground, the preservation spell warring with the foliage now consuming them.

Lauriel dragged him to his bed in the basement, then returned with water. While Raven sucked at the water, Lauriel used his Fae connection to speak to the plants in the tower. They wrapped Raven in vines to stabilize his broken bones and put life-sustaining sap to his mouth. Raven lifted his head enough to drink the fluid but that was the extent of his abilities. Without the use of his hands and voice, he couldn't even cast spells to heal himself.

Lauriel nodded, and looked around. There were no more servants here, but Catriona's time in the trap had at least restored the plants and animals to this area. Insects flowed into flowers and the trees were bearing fruit now. Raven fell asleep while Lauriel foraged.

He felt his consciousness slip and he realized he was dying. He sighed. It was not what he wanted, but he was okay with it. Lying in his marriage bed made him think of Wilgefortis and he almost smelled her in the pillows. He drifted into memory, where they danced and kissed, when he helped Merrick midwife the birth of his twins (by leaving the room), and where they nurtured their grandchildren after their son took the seat at Canterbury.

He remembered the loneliness he felt when he was helping the Third Dûcesa, and how he decided he was done after five years of not seeing his wife. He remembered finding out it had been over a decade and how she had not forgotten him like he had her. His heart broke anew when he went to her after another long absence to find she had stopped taking the longevity potions he made for her because they were causing her pain and damage. He had always fixed her after the potions but the last time, he had lost track of the years (again) and the tumors on her spine had sent her into great agony. By the time he came back around, her age had deteriorated too far and she had hung onto life only long enough to tell him goodbye. She had slipped away that night into real, final peace.

And now he would go to her. He wasn't certain she would still be in Summerland. She might have waited for him. She might have moved on already, having done her living while alive. He almost reached out to Alistair then, to ask him to look for her. Then he remembered the reason he was dying and dismissed the idea. He would find out soon enough.

He waited for the pain to end, but it didn't. He waited for the sensation that he was in another place, but it did not come. He smelled no new smells, felt no new light. Everything was numbness and cold. He tried to slip into the afterlife, into Sovereignlumin, but he felt *no connection at all to that realm.*

He panicked and opened his eyes. Lauriel lifted his head. He was lying beside the bed Raven had shared with Wilgefortis for over a hundred years. Raven was still wrapped in vines and still couldn't feel his legs but his throat felt better. He tried to speak and it came out as a croak.

"'Ow… long…?"

Lauriel shook his head. Apparently not very long at all. The healing sap was doing its job but if there was too much damage, it could take a while. He knew a spell with only a verbal component he could use to determine the extent of the wound so he used it. Sure enough, every bone was broken.

The vines surrounding him grew thicker and stronger, maturing visibly. Thorns seeping the sap pierced his skin deeper. This was a side effect of using his magic, something the local farmers had always appreciated. Being in contact with the plant as thoroughly as he was, it absorbed everything he gave off. He felt the skin around the piercings begin a slow burn, like he was just cut with a whip. He took that as a good sign. Pain meant he was alive, and that he was regaining feeling.

He tried to figure out what to do next. Was he *really* unable to die? If so, it meant Catriona *was* the Death Bringer, like he suspected. Missing for centuries and he managed to anger her enough to deny him access to any afterlife.

He moved his fingers a little and relaxed. When he got out of here, he would go to Caratia and apologize. He had a lot to apologize for, but the woman he owed those to was not in this realm. If he ever wanted to see his beloved again, he needed to make amends with the one overseeing her.

He closed his eyes again, and let sleep assist his healer.

Michael de Sablonierres lay awake on the straw mat on the floor. Rain had started falling just after dark and the smell of Trimelda's garden filled the room. After so long travelling in the wasteland of York, it was nice to smell vegetation again. The vision of the lion still haunted his dreams but being with Trimelda made them better. He knew the lion had something to teach him but he no longer remembered the language of Fang and Claw.

It was hard to believe he had been gone only a few years, but living with Myrgen felt like a lifetime per year. Sometimes two. This year definitely felt like it was taking several to tell its tale. It was only a few months ago that he brought the first tray of food and a dog to a small boy in a cell. Now, he was in the legendary house of a saint unrecognized by the Church, one watched over by a wise woman from his home country of Nubia.

He wondered how Myrgen was doing. He seemed to be on a better path than he had been in Patras. Intrigue and royalty were unhealthy bedfellows and Patras had enough to slay a legion. Michael was glad to be rid of it all. Still, he missed his friend.

James Douglas, his other friend, was off to the north telling his mother and father about the death of his sister, Gwen. Probably Alistair too, their uncle. So much tragedy. He had given his friend the space to break the news so his mother would not be distracted by having a guest to care for during a time of grief.

He understood this custom but didn't always agree with it. At home, if someone fell too soon, the entire village would come to the family so they would not be alone. They would commit the body to fire and send it to the sky. Then the ashes were sown into the ground to help the crops. Burning also repelled the animals that would feed upon corpses. Criminals were rarely burned, letting the animals and insects destroy a body too evil to become a part of food. Animals could process the evil of humans and were seen as the ultimate judges because they knew a wrong person when they smelled one.

He wondered if he was going to die from the lion. If so, it meant he was evil. He didn't really think he *was* evil, but if the lion did eat him, it meant he would be purified in the process. Either way, he would be a part of the world as he should be. He saw writings on papers hung on the wall. They were a story of a lion and a farmer, told in the way of the Fang and Claw.

The claw is to the heart as the fang is to the throat.
The blood is to the ground as the rain is to the crop.
The crop is to the mouth as the rain is to the well.
The stone is to the well as the plow is to the ox.

The story was there, difficult to understand if you did not know the way. As he read it, his understanding returned.

There was a farmer, using an ox to plow his field. The farmer used a whip to get the ox to move, but the whip cut the flesh of both. The blood called the lion and the lion saw the ox. But rain came, and the river flooded behind the lion. A flash flood drowned the lion, but the plow held the ox in place, wedged on the rock the farmer was trying to move. The river became the threat, and the lion was forgotten.

Was *he* the farmer? Or the ox? He hoped Trimelda knew. He wasn't sure anymore.

Movement caught his attention, but he didn't sit up this time. Trimelda had gotten up twice already to use the privy that night.

She shuffled to the door and left again. He heard her puttering in the rain, walking through the plants in the garden. When she came back in a few minutes later, she wasn't wet, despite the storm outside.

"Trimelda, are you magic?"

She looked at Michael, then chortled. "A magical Nubian? Psh."

"Then how are you not wet? And how did you know to cover the donated goods? How did you know to make the furrows deeper today through the garden to collect the rain?"

"I know where to walk so I don't get wet. My bones ache when it's going to rain, so I prepare. Since once I *get* wet, I get *cold*, I do my best to not get wet. Once I get cold, I have a hard time warming up. So, I extend the shade awning so it pours the rain from the roof onto the soil instead of the stone path. I cover the goods so they don't get ruined in the rain. And the deeper furrows carry more water to the roots of the plants to help them grow." She waved him off. "I'm not magic, young Michael. I'm old." She chuckled again. "Though I *can* see how the two can get confused."

She looked at him, then frowned. "What's *really* on your mind? Something has you awake at this hour and it ain't the rain."

Michael took a moment to figure out what was the trouble. "I guess it's that I don't know my role yet." He looked at the poem on the wall. "Am I the farmer? The lion? The ox? The river?"

"You might be none of those. You might be the whip."

He sat up on his elbows. "The whip?"

"It is used to motivate and to punish, to wound the Land and the animals, but it wounds the wielder as well. It is a tool more than an entity in the story."

"Is that all I am? A storyteller's tool?"

"I doubt that. I think you are more like the river. You carry all of the tools and threats away, but also the helpers. You leave behind the one you served after helping him live on. You saved him." She nodded to the poem on the wall. "One thing it doesn't truly go into is what happens to the ox after the water erodes the stone, freeing the plow. It is assumed that the ox dies, drowned in the swollen river. But oxen are strong swimmers. If he got his head above water in time, he lived."

Michael lay back down, lacing his fingers together to tuck them behind his head. This idea intrigued him. They didn't really know the fate of the lion either, which meant that story was still yet to be told. He let his eyes close and fell asleep to the thought.

Four

"The skin is to the fire as the smoke is to the meat." (The lash colors the meat when it is struck.)

Sovereigna and Catherine slipped into St. Giles and hid in the shadow of the church. The proximity made Sovereigna's skin itch and Catherine noticed her discomfort.

"Let me go on and find Alexander. You stay here."

"I'm afraid that won't do. The people here saw me torturing their families. I'm responsible for the deaths of several of them, including children. They won't give me sanctuary."

Catherine frowned, then saw the sign designating the home offices of the Tanglwyst Trading Company. "Then we'll take you there."

Sovereigna looked where Catherine pointed, and nodded. They avoided the windows and lit areas of the street, slipping up to the front door.

"Won't it be locked?" Sovereigna's whisper was fraught with nerves.

"Depends upon if my son is with her or not." She pressed the latch and the door swung silently open. Catherine arched an eyebrow. "Interesting. I wonder which one did the refusing?"

They slipped inside and locked the door. There were no other exits except the stairs at the back of the room, barely visible in the streetlamps. They went up them, the nightingale stair echoing a squeak throughout the upstairs room. A door was open in the southern wall and they saw a bed with a single figure in it. The figure stirred but did not get up.

"Did we wake her?" Catherine's whisper was low to keep from carrying like the stair had.

Sovereigna closed her eyes a moment, then opened them. "Yes. She is pretending to be asleep now."

"Probably hoping we are Alexander." Catherine cleared her throat. "Tanglwyst?"

The figure in the bed turned and sat up. "Your Majesty?"

"Majesties. You have us both."

Tanglwyst got up, putting a robe over her sleeping gown. "What's happened?"

Catherine restrained a smile. *The girl realizes there's a problem. Good. That saves time.* "Apparently, there was an attack on the Fae army encampment. There's been a call to arms and the Midsummer King himself has been alerted."

"By the Saints. What did Alex do this time?"

"I am not certain it was him. The General said Heaven attacked." She turned to Sovereigna. "I need somewhere for Her Majesty to hide. Can she stay here?"

Tanglwyst nodded. "Stay with her. I'll go get Alexander."

"Are you sure?"

Tanglwyst put on slippers. "Do *you* know where he's staying?"

Catherine blinked slowly, recognizing her defeat. "Be careful, then, young woman."

"Keep quiet. I'll be back."

She returned a few minutes later with Alexander and Gomez, both looking like they dressed in a panic. Alexander went to his mother and hugged her.

"Mother, are you alright? Tangl said there was something wrong." He looked at Sovereigna.

Tanglwyst gestured everyone to seats in the room, pulling her desk chair over as Gomez and Alexander sat in the chairs reserved for clients and the Queen Mothers sat on the sofa. Catherine and Sovereigna explained what they saw and heard.

Alexander slapped his forehead. "*The jacket.*"

Tanglwyst and Gomez sighed in realization.

Sovereigna and Catherine both looked lost so Alexander explained.

"Where did this sludge come from," Catherine asked, "if the strange man burned it?"

Alexander paused. "From a mistake. Johner fell on it and it began to eat away his armor. He already said he couldn't let it touch him or he would die. I wiped it off with the coat while Raven got the armor off him."

"So, Johner *knew* the coat was tainted when he let you into my home?" Sovereigna's voice was sharp as a headman's axe.

"I think he saw it as a protection measure he hoped I wouldn't use. I fear, Your Majesty, you were a rather prominent threat, to both myself and my Lady."

Catherine's eyes flicked to Tanglwyst at his possessive comment, and saw she also noticed, but let the comment go, for now. *That's going to come back on him later.*

Sovereigna exhaled, but said nothing more.

Gomez saw an opening and took it. "What did he mean by 'when King Corrigan arrives'?"

"Apparently, this assault on the Fae nation is not dismissible. Even though he allowed it into the encampment," Sovereigna turned to Alexander, "it killed someone and he is blaming you."

Alexander stood. "I need to go fix it then. Apologize, before more people get hurt."

Everyone protested but Sovereigna, who sat quietly.

Catherine led the charge. "You would be putting yourself forth as a hostage. I will not allow you to do that."

Gomez said, "If that happened, you know the city guard would be obliged to rescue you. That would leave the village unprotected with an enemy army right outside."

Tanglwyst nodded. "And the cost to the kingdom to have you returned isn't something we can afford right now. Not with the army being mobilized and the search for a bride."

Alexander threw his hands in the air. "Fine. I get it." He walked over to the window and looked out onto the street as the room quieted down.

Gomez looked at Sovereigna. "Can you re-erect the barrier? Stop the Fae from entering?"

"No. It is Fae magic. It won't stop a Fae nor any Fae agents."

Alexander straightened. "I know how to stop them." He turned and looked at Gomez. "The blacksmith's apprentice just walked by."

Gomez jumped up and looked out the window. He looked at Alexander. "Will there be enough?"

"We have them working non-stop. That basket had dozens of sigils in it."

Alexander and Gomez ran for the door.

"Get the guards awake. We're going to need their help."

Gomez nodded and rushed to the guard's barracks. Alexander went on to the church, where the blacksmith's apprentice was delivering the basket to the priest. The priest seemed simultaneously nervous and excited.

"Good, good. Put them there. We need these blessed immediately." The priest went to the font and picked up a sigil.

The apprentice bowed and turned to see Alexander. "Your Majesty!"

"Didn't mean to startle you... I'm sorry, what is your name?"

"Ais. Ais Dracon."

"Ais. Sorry. How many more are there of these?"

"Just this one for now. The alchemist and woodcutter got the pattern streamlined. I brought by the samples earlier but you were away." He pointed at a couple sigil discs on the altar. "Brother Robert said this was the best choice for what he needed."

Alexander looked at the samples and agreed that the ones chosen were the best. "How long are they taking now?"

"About an hour. We can do one a minute."

He looked at the basket. "There are that many in here?"

Ais nodded.

"How many do they have supplies for?"

"About five hours' worth, Sire."

Gomez stepped into the church and Alexander tossed a disc to him. "We need to figure out how far apart these can be. With any luck, we can surround the village. It won't keep out fire arrows but it can keep out the foot soldiers."

Gomez nodded. "Are these ready?"

Brother Robert shook his head. "I still need to bless them."

Gomez looked at the font by the door. "Is this blessed?"

Brother Robert blinked, then smiled. "*Yes. Yes it is.*"

A few minutes later, the guards were being handed wet wooden discs and told to surround the village.

Alexander checked the overlap of the barrier and had the discs buried just under the surface but about a building apart. It would take a little time, but Ais said he could keep bringing the baskets to the church for soaking, then return them to the next line of guards.

The orders given, Gomez stayed to oversee and assist while Alexander returned to Tanglwyst's office. The place was quiet when he entered and he stayed silent while he went upstairs, staying to the edge in case there was a creaky one. The bedroom door was closed but a figure was on the sofa, hidden under a dark blanket.

He went to the sofa and touched Tanglwyst's arm. She started awake, then relaxed when she saw who it was.

"The queens are in there. I wanted to wait for you so I sent them off to sleep as much as they could."

"You need to do likewise." He touched her hair.

"So do you but we can't all get what we want."

He smiled, then took a deep breath.

She put a finger on his lips. "No."

He frowned.

"I'm not going to go somewhere 'safe'."

He protested but she disarmed him with a kiss. Then she scooted over on the couch and pulled him onto it. He settled into it, and she lay down on him, snuggling into his chest. He knew he couldn't fight her, so he surrendered and fell asleep.

Five

"The meat is to the lash as the lash is to the hand."
(The use of a lash damages the hand that wields it.)

In Summerland, the time of day seemed fickle to Myrgen. It was always the correct time of day for whatever the activity was, and always the correct time of year. There was never snow on the ground, the crops were always just about ready to be harvested, the flowers always in full bloom. The temperature was hot enough to cool someone in the fountain in the center of town, but not so hot as to make the street stones painful for bare feet.

He noticed this especially as he and Catriona went to the house with the dark-haired woman. Children were waking up from afternoon naps, cats and dogs were lazing about after a full morning of playing. Bread was cooling on the window sills, ready for supper. Clothes hung to dry were absorbing the fresh afternoon scent that made him feel like he was home.

Except he had never noticed any of these things growing up. The smell of his clean clothes had always been outshone by the glint of coins or the shadows of intrigue. He never wanted to stand out so he colored and scented himself to blend in, be ignorable. Oh, he could shine when it was necessary, but he was equally good at disappearing into a crowd.

Now, being in the sun felt *right* and he didn't miss his old life at all. If not for his commitment to Catriona, he would be content to live out his days in this place, or see what the next place held…

He shook his head, like he was snapping himself out of a dream. Catriona looked at him.

"What?"

He swallowed. "I think I almost moved on."

Catriona gripped his shoulder. "Are you sure?"

"Not really. I've never moved on before so I really have no frame of reference. But I just felt… at peace. Like I didn't have anything else to reconcile."

She closed her eyes, nodding. "Yes, I imagine that is what it takes. According to the teachings of the Land, Summerland is for any unfinished work you have. If you died young, for example, you live out your life span. If you were working on a particular art piece, you get to complete it."

"What about the farmers in those fields? What are they waiting for?"

She shrugged and started walking again. "You'd have to ask them."

"Like we plan to do with her."

Catriona nodded.

The First Dûcesa was standing outside her home and bowed as they approached. They returned the gesture.

"Your Grace, we have come to speak, if you are available."

"You are the current Dûcesa." She turned to Myrgen. "And you are her Stâpân."

Catriona blinked slowly, processing this. She glanced at Myrgen, then back at the Dûcesa. "I have not acquired that title. I am the Stâpâna of Caratia."

She looked at Myrgen. "Then you are?"

"The current Hunter."

"Is that so?" She looked at Catriona again, appraising. "What can I do for you, Protector?"

"You were Dûcesa for many decades. Some say for over a dozen. In that time, did you ever die?"

"Ah." The First Dûcesa gestured to the inside of her home and Catriona and Myrgen followed her in. She took hot water out of a

30

steaming kettle on the hearth and poured it into three mugs. She added leaves to them and a few drops of honey.

"You ask because you want to know what happens?"

Myrgen cleared his throat. "She has been here already, and she... well... everyone told me she would change. But she didn't."

"And you want to know why?"

Catriona nodded.

The Dûcesa sat at her kitchen table and Myrgen and Catriona gathered two chairs from the room and sat across from their tea.

"When you returned, Stâpâna," she looked at Myrgen, "where were you?"

"In Caratia, at Ashstone."

"In the world then."

"Yes."

She looked at Catriona again. "And you remembered him?"

"Yes."

"That is the secret. You must *want* to return, and you must *want* to remain the same. If you doubt or desire to bring anything with you, it will change you. It may only change something small, but eventually, if you die often, you might be overwhelmed by the tiny changes. Without your Stâpân, you will forget who you were."

"So, he needs to be out there to bring me back?"

"It helps if one of you is outside. It can be either of you, to be honest. Slade... took more than one blow meant to fell me."

Myrgen looked around the room for the first time. Everywhere around them were carvings of a burly, handsome man with long, heavy hair. His eyes were intense and he looked capable of dethroning a mountain.

"Do you know why we come back?" Catriona leaned forward. "Why are we denied death until we beg for it?"

The Dûcesa shook her head. "That I never did find out. After a hundred and nineteen years together, neither Slade nor I ever figured it out."

Myrgen picked up his tea. "Do you know about the stones?"

"The ones with the gold flecks?" She sat back in her chair, picking up her mug. "Of course I do. We learned early about the memories. Eventually, I stopped shedding them. The stones are only dropped if the Dûcesa does not have a firm enough grasp upon who she is when she returns. But if she remembers where she wants to go, or where she was the last time she died, the stones don't appear."

Myrgen sighed. "That explains why I didn't find one before."

"I don't think there will be one this time either." Catriona looked back at the Dûcesa. "What happens if I touch memories from another Dûcesa?"

"You learn of her life."

"She doesn't replace me?"

The Dûcesa shook her head. She glanced at Myrgen. "You say you are the Hunter? What does that mean?"

"The Hunter…" He looked at Catriona. "Back before there were countries, the Life Giver and Death Bringer walked the world. One day, the Death Bringer met a man who became her companion and protector. His name was Hunter, because that was his job."

"How do you know this?"

"Because I found memories that were far older than any you experienced. And they told me who she used to be."

The Dûcesa frowned. "The Death Bringer? That was a myth, long gone from this world before I came along. Where were these memories?"

"In a cave where she and Hunter were murdered. Repeatedly. There were a dozen stones scattered on the floor of a pit."

She looked at Catriona. "And you have these memories now?"

Catriona blinked. "Yes, I guess I do."

"Then… you are the keeper of the afterlife. You can reach the other realms."

"I… don't know. I haven't thought to try."

"*Can you go to the Fae Realm?*"

Myrgen interrupted. "Why?"

The Dûcesa looked at him. "There are answers there that…" She looked away.

"Is this about Slade? Getting him back from the shadow realm?"

She cocked her head. "What do you know of that place?"

"I know that they sealed the Last Child and his army into it to stop the world from being destroyed. And I know Slade was drawn in too, protecting you."

"Do… do you have his memories?"

"No. But I know the tale from people who were there."

She relaxed. "Oh. I didn't think any of them still drew breath."

"There are a couple still around."

The Dûcesa closed her eyes, a thin line of tears wetting them. Catriona took Myrgen's hand and squeezed it. "We should be on our way."

The Dûcesa nodded. "Trust me on this: Spend the night together. The world is very demanding. Only in death can you get a moment's peace."

The couple nodded and left for their own home.

The Dûcesa let some time pass before she stood and went outside in the twilight. People were gathering in their homes for meals but she wasn't hungry. She looked at the field where the couple had been standing before they visited and decided to lay upon the hill to watch the stars come out. She walked up and sat down, closing her eyes as she lay back in the grass. She let the quiet settle her, listening to the sounds of families laughing in the distance.

Something fluttered in the air above her and landed on her cheek. She sat up, grasping it. It was a piece of paper, black with elegant writing in white upon it.

I'd love to chat with you, if you don't mind. Would you join me in my home for dinner?
~L.

She looked around and drew back as a gigantic mansion that was not there before dominated the hill. A handsome man in a white Mandian coat leaned upon a garden wall, holding a small glass with brown liquid in it.

He nodded. "My Lady."

She stood, looking around. "Where did you come from?"

He glanced at the sky. "That is an incredibly long story. Perhaps we could share it over dinner?" He reached out his hand to her.

She looked at the note, then back at her home. "Perhaps you should come to my home instead."

"I do not have that ability, I'm afraid."

"Are you a ghost?"

He narrowed his eyes in thought. "That is an interesting question, and one I have never thought of before." He gave his head a little shake. "But no. I'm an archangel."

She frowned. "What is an archangel doing here?"

"Inviting you to dinner."

The Dûcesa looked at the mansion. "Is that Heaven?"

"No. It is an in-between place. It touches all but does not become a part of any."

"Touches *all*?"

"Yes."

"Even realms that are sealed?"

The man blinked, cocking his head. "That sounds like a question looking for a very specific answer."

"It is."

"Then yes. I believe it can definitely reach a realm that's sealed. You might not be able to enter it and nothing can leave in…oh." He stepped back as she climbed over the low wall in a single swift move. "You're a nimble little thing, aren't you?"

"Yes, and I'm too old to waste time flirting."

"Is that what we're doing? Well, believe me, age is not a factor for either of us." He gestured to the door. "Shall we?"

She followed him to a study where a table and two chairs had been prepared. Beautiful linens decorated the place settings, embroidered with vivid colors and complex designs. The glass dishes mirrored the designs in intricate swirls that she was not certain were actually possible.

A sideboard nearby held numerous kinds of meats, cheeses, pies, breads, and vegetables and he brought over a sampling of each. The hot things were still hot when she tasted them, and the flavors were better than fantasy. She knew she ate every day because she enjoyed cooking, but she also limited her joys and ate very little.

These foods were almost magical, but still she restrained herself. She was wary of this person, this place, and anything he gave her and with good reason.

"So, archangel? 'L.' That must mean you are Lucifer."

"Straight out of legend, my Lady."

"Purveyor of the Infernal."

Lucifer sighed, arching an eyebrow. "I fear that is likewise true, my Lady."

"Good. That's why I came."

Lucifer leaned on the table. "You are a plethora of surprises, my Lady." He glanced at the morsels of food she was consuming. "And let me help you with something. You are currently in neutral ground. You can't be taken from here. You may only leave here of your own free will." He nodded to her plate. "Besides, as wonderful as this food is, won't the memory of it and the lack of its presence in your own home be enough to keep you in Summerland?"

She frowned and almost left. Then she realized he was right, and indulged in the fare. He smiled at her and went back to eating as well. She pointed a fork at him. "You're very perceptive."

"I've spent time around someone recently who really has a knack for it. I get the feeling it rubs off on folks."

"So, what made you speak to me tonight?"

Lucifer took a drink of brandy. "You have been here far longer than anyone should be. Why?"

"I'm waiting for someone."

"Someone sealed in another realm."

She nodded. "I figure if anyone can open that realm, it would be the one tied to the infernal."

"What about the one who opened the realm? Or that sealed it?"

"Trapped in a dream from which she cannot wake."

Lucifer blinked. "How did *that* happen?"

"That is the question, isn't it? If it were self-imposed, she would have come out of it long ago. That means someone else put her in it and is somehow maintaining it regardless of how much time passes."

"What is powerful enough to keep a Fae Lord from waking?"

She stopped eating and looked at him, shocked that he seemed to know who she was.

He glanced up and waved away her look. "Of course, I know who you are and how you got here. And I know what realm you seek to look in to."

"Can you actually do it?"

"Yes. The spell had a divine component to seal away the infernal. But the question for you is do you really want to look in there? Slade didn't go into a better situation."

The visual that he would not be how she remembered him had summoned her tears for centuries now. It was one she needed when others had stopped working. "I feel as though seeing it will reinforce the image in my head."

"It can also bring an end to your suffering. You will know for sure he is not redeemable." He set down his glass.

"Have... have you already seen him?"

"No. I simply know I can do it."

"Would it take long?"

"No."

She looked at the ceiling, willing her tears to stay where they were. "I have lingered in Summerland for centuries on the fantasy that we might be together again. I pretend it is so, even though it hurts to hope. This... painful suspension... it must be like what he goes through. To know for sure..." Her hesitation carried into her voice against her will, but her companion politely ignored it.

Lucifer was quiet, letting her decide without external prodding or input. The candlelight on the table danced together in the ballroom of the colorful dishes. Eventually, she looked at him again.

"I think..." Her breath caught in her throat. She cleared it and went on. "I do wish to see him, yes. But I think I'm not going to tonight. It isn't the right time."

"You're welcome whenever you're ready."

She smiled. "I appreciate that. But I will not impose upon you."

He took her hand. "My Lady, it is an honor to be in your presence. You cannot impose when it is my truest desire." He kissed her hand and stood, drawing her to her feet. "But I'll not keep you against your will either. Not now, not ever."

She assessed that statement. "Are you sure?"

"Yes."

She rather liked how concise his answers were. He could be flowery of speech when he chose to, but he could also get to the point if it was important. "Thank you."

"Of course. But tell me, how long do you plan to stay in Summerland?"

She sighed. "That I cannot say. As long as Slade is absent, I'll wait. Oh, I know he's gone or he would have been back long ago, but unless he is by my side, I don't believe I'll ever move on."

"Forgive me for saying so, but that seems like a lonely existence."

She looked into his eyes and saw genuine care. *And by the Stones, he's handsome.* "I won't lie. It can be."

"Well," he patted her hand and released it, "should you ever need a friend or companion, please come by."

She arched an eyebrow. "You're certain you'll be around?"

"I am." He turned to the table. "Do you wish to finish dinner?"

She smiled. "I still have an incredibly long story to hear from you."

"And I am happy to tell it." He escorted her to the table and took away the dishes of food to make way for fresher fare. "Let me tell you how I got my wings."

When the tale was done, she sat smiling, the creases by her eyes thicker from the alternating laughter and tears. She drained her goblet for the fifth time and sighed.

"Thank you for giving me such an entertaining evening."

Lucifer nodded. "That sounds like a parting sentence."

She pushed back from the table. "I fear it is later than I planned and I should be on my way home."

"Then allow me to escort you, my Lady, at least as far as I can."

He offered his arm and they walked to the garden. The moon was high and bright, lighting the way across the meadow. The houses were all dark, inhabitants resting, possibly even moving on tonight having finished some task or hobby. It was peaceful.

He helped her over the wall and she turned back once more.

"You know, your tale was tragic and glorious and frightening, but it was also something else. It was *familiar*. I find myself looking at you as if I knew you in a past life."

"You and I both had at least one. But if it helps, I do not recognize you."

"No, I don't think you would. Every time I died, I took on the appearance of one who had my former self as a parent, and the other was a native from the region where I returned. For one thing, my eyes used to be far more green."

Lucifer looked into her eyes and suddenly realized he *knew* those eyes. They had once granted him the chunk of Land so he could make the connection between Heaven and Earth. It was the reason this place could touch every afterlife, and hide from them all. His smile faltered, but she looked away before he had to hide it.

"Please come back any time."

She bowed goodbye and took her leave.

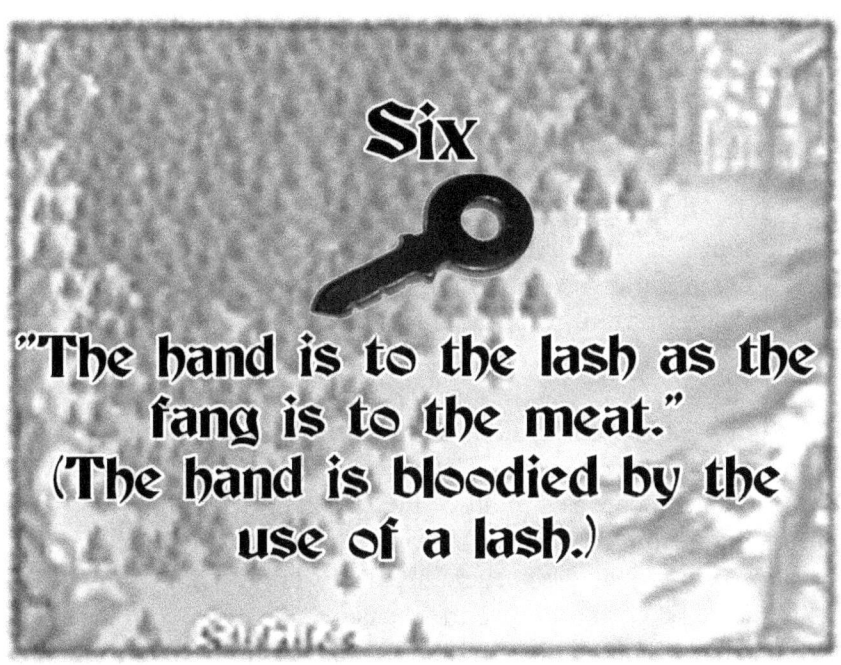

Six

"The hand is to the lash as the
fang is to the meat."
(The hand is bloodied by the
use of a lash.)

Lucifer watched the Dûcesa go, recovering from his realization. It was entirely possible he imagined the whole thing. Catriona's eyes were that clear, emerald green of the Bringer too and he had not decided *she* held the power of Death in her hands. Still, this woman was older than anyone knew and had put even more years between her leaving of the surface world and her entering it.

But that was long ago, and the tale tonight had reminded him of his daughter. He remembered loving her, but no longer remembered what she looked like. He knew she had come to this place, to Summerland, when she died but she had long since moved on. Perhaps she had met his wife and they had been allowed to know each other. His wife had died upon his daughter's birth, alone in the woods after being attacked by wolves. They had never even laid eyes upon each other.

Perhaps they were there, waiting for him now.

He closed his eyes and shook his head. *Down that path lies madness.*

He exhaled and pushed away from the wall, a final glance at his dinner companion before she walked out of sight behind Catriona and Myrgen's home. He went to the study and sat on the sofa they had shared. Servants came in and tidied up the room, removing all traces of the evening's activities. They had already been there multiple times during the night, setting up the table, cooking, cleaning up blood from the murder. Typical servant duties. He barely noticed or cared because they were mere constructs, like the rest of the mansion. Nothing was here that he had not made himself.

He had all the creativity in the world within Hell. It burned away from the souls, leaving them pure and translucent, but the darkness that left the souls in little wisps of smoke had collected on the ceiling of the room for thousands of years. He could create anything out of that suffering.

Suffering.

He got up and went upstairs to the attic area, knocking on the trap door in the ceiling. It opened and he ascended the spiral stairs to the Hand of Karma. The place was still all white, with a crystal pillar in the center of an elaborate marble table. Alistair sat looking into the Pillar, but turned to see his friend arrive, sending the Pillar into dormancy.

"Lucifer. To what do I owe the pleasure?"

"I just had dinner with a charming young woman. I came up to brag, of course."

"Well, by all means," Alistair gestured and another chair appeared, "I await with baited breath."

Lucifer sat and leaned forward, elbows on his knees. "So, I just spent the evening talking with that Dûcesa woman."

"The *First* Dûcesa?"

"Yeah. Interesting lady, though she did let me do most of the talking."

"Were you just too self-involved or what?"

Lucifer laughed. "Not this time. No, I was letting her relax for a while. Do you know what brings people to Summerland?"

"Besides dying?"

"Yes."

Alistair sat back, stretching. "Nope."

"*Suffering.* Suffering taints the soul. Doesn't matter if it's self-inflicted or done to them. Doesn't matter if it's just an awareness of the suffering of others. When you take in pain, you taint the soul. Giving pain can do that as well but after a certain point, that suffering puts your soul into Hell. If you are a Land worshipper, you go to Summerland.

"Remember when I told you about the souls getting more and more soiled? How I was guiding people to sin so they would come to me? That's just how *Heaven* works. The Land has a different approach. That suffering is sifted away by experiencing life in a joyful, fulfilling way. Look at that place."

He gestured towards Summerland.

"It's gorgeous, comfortable, peaceful. You can grow a garden, learn to paint, be with your loved ones. It is designed to help you *move on* and rejoin the souls to be born. As a result, the suffering is removed but the life experiences remain."

Alistair nodded.

Lucifer pointed. "That woman has been in that place, *that* place, for over *three hundred years*. Do you have any idea how unlikely that is?"

Alistair frowned. "I didn't really think about it. I figured you left when you decided to leave. I mean look at the First Dûces…"

Lucifer nodded. "Exactly. The reason you thought it was just a choice is because *she's still there.*"

Alistair nodded. "I know Gwen's still there but I didn't see anyone else I knew, outside of Catriona's family. But I know people from the War or that I've met from Glarren. *None* of them were there."

Lucifer sat back nodding.

Alistair crossed his arms. "So, how is she doing it? Slade?"

"Sort of. Slade is definitely a factor. She asked if I could show her that realm."

Alistair started. "You can't, can you?"

"Show? Yes. At least I assume I can. But enter? No."

"Don't."

Lucifer frowned. "Why not?"

"Because you might be wrong."

"We're in the afterlife here."

"Those things consumed *souls*. Instantly. They didn't go on to that Well you mentioned. They didn't go to Hell. They went *away*. All those folks in Summerland would disappear. Including your new infatuation."

"I wouldn't call her an infatuation…"

"Yes you would. Why else would she interest you?"

Lucifer pointed at Alistair. "It turns out *that* is the interesting part. Why is she hurting herself to stay there?"

"Well, like I said, Slade…"

"No. That's the tool she's using to hurt herself, and I have the feeling that's wearing out. That's why she asked to see him."

Alistair shook his head. "Then why?"

Lucifer nodded. "That is the true question. Is she avoiding the end, in which case that fear should be enough to keep her there just fine. Instead, she invokes a tragically lost lover. And here's another thing: She mentioned the Fae Lord that made the spell. Said she is in a slumber from which she can't awaken."

"That's true. Calpurnia hasn't opened her eyes since she cast that spell, as far as I know." Alistair frowned. "You know, at the mansion, when we went on break, Raven mentioned Sovereignlumin. He said that Sovereignlumen, the guy…"

"How do you tell the difference?"

"Uh, you have to see it written down. Sovereignlu*min* is the place, Sovereignlu*men* is the man. Anyway, Raven said the man was the one who imprisoned Persephone, who is the source of all Magic in the world, in that trap. And he suspected Catriona might be the embodiment not of Death, but of the Life Giver instead. Unfortunately, he decided to kill her in order to prove it and I don't get the impression she is who he thought. Still, he was under the impression she might be able to question him about what happened."

"Is he dead or is he, too, asleep and unable to awaken?"

Alistair shrugged. "I assumed dead but…"

Lucifer held up two fingers. "That's two people from that war interested in the same place."

"You think what is keeping Calpurnia down is the same thing keeping the Dûcesa in Summerland?"

Lucifer started to speak, then shifted his thought. "I don't know. But now, I'm not so sure they aren't." He looked at the Pillar. "Can you see if anything has changed?"

Alistair nodded. "I'm sure I can." He concentrated and an image of a woman on her side, sucking her thumb, came up. Both Lucifer and Alistair moved back, then moved closer. They exchanged a glance.

"Well, that wasn't what I expected."

Alistair shook his head. "Merrick likes to pose her."

"That sounds treacherous."

"Yeah, I'm glad no one who can paint is near her. That would be a problem if she ever wakes up."

"So, why hasn't she?"

"You think it has something to do with the spell? As long as it's operating, she can't wake up?"

"I don't know. But two Land Worshippers have now focused upon it after three hundred years. Why now?"

"No idea, but Raven said Embertwist is down as well. It's possible something is taking out the Fae Lords."

Lucifer leaned on the table. "Have you checked on Raven?"

"No." Alistair waved his hand at the Pillar and it showed him Raven in the bedroom at Persephone. He scowled at the vines wrapping the mage, thorns stabbing into him. "By the Balance, what the Hell did you do to him?"

"Pushed him off a balcony."

"Of what? The Papal Palace?"

"Don't worry. It's not like he'll die."

"Yeah, but he's not very helpful right now either." Alistair snorted. "I can make a trip down there, see how long it will take to get him functioning." He looked at Lucifer. "Remember how I said I would take issue with this later? That's now. Now's later." He nodded to the trap door. "Get out of here. I need to figure out how to help him."

Lucifer stood and walked to the trap door opening. "Keep me informed, if you would. I would like this woman to finally rest."

Alistair waved him off and disappeared.

Alistair opened the door into the basement of the main tower at the Covenant of Persephone. The last time he was here, Myrgen was rescuing Catriona. Alistair had already learned he could still die, even as Karma, so when they clashed with the oldest Servant of the Land, the danger had been real. Now she was in the trap that held Catriona and the debris from that battle had begun to gather dust.

He stepped over the onyx pebbles that used to be part of the great central tower. That was now in pieces in the courtyard, brought down by blessed cannonballs in the war. Raven and Wilgefortis' room was protected in the basement, a ceiling of one-way glass allowed light to stream through. Back in the active days of the Covenant, they had a whole ecosystem in this room. After the towers fell, everything died along with the rest of York.

In the decrepit bedroom, Raven was still wrapped in vines, barbs in his flesh. Alistair walked over and stood looking at him. Raven opened his eyes, then smiled, spitting out a small branch from his mouth.

"Alistair… I had an accident…"

"Next time, try not killing people."

"Okay."

"How bad is it?"

Raven lifted his head. "I can lift my head. That's good." He wiggled his fingers. "And those seem to be working."

"I take it this is news?"

"Yes…"

Alistair sighed. "Why did you do it, Raven? Did you really think killing her would somehow awaken something in her?"

"Has she returned yet?"

Alistair shook his head.

"Then we don't really know yet, do we?"

"What is the best-case scenario here, Raven? What exactly are you hoping will happen?"

"I… hope she'll be half in this world and half in the next, enabling her to walk between worlds at will. Then she can go to my grandfather and find out why he put his beloved Magic in that trap."

"And why will that be the best-case?"

"Because… because…"

Alistair waited for him to figure out what he was after.

Eventually, Raven shook his head. "I don't know. He loved her so much. I don't know what could have possessed him to imprison her like that."

"What makes you think he loved her?"

Raven looked at Alistair, ready to protest. Then he thought about it. "I've always heard… The legends say…"

"So, you put this woman and her beloved and me through the hell of her dying, after she had just died and returned, because a thousand-year-old tale told by humans said Sovereignlumen loved Persephone?"

Raven collapsed back onto the mossy pillow. "She seemed perplexed by his action too."

"Did she? Or do you *think* she should be and therefore, she was?"

Raven blinked. "I'm not any good at mental magics."

"You might have misread what she meant, Raven."

"I suppose that's possible. I don't read as much as I used to. I did spend several years as a cat."

Alistair just stared at him a moment, then shook his head. "How long before you're healed up?"

Raven looked at himself again. He closed his eyes and whispered, then opened them. "It's still pretty bad. The bones that were broken are mending well. The ones that turned to powder are the ones taking more time."

"Anything I can do?'

Raven frowned. "What sorts of powers does Karma have to heal things?"

Alistair thought about it, then shrugged. "Nothing short term. Things get balanced eventually, but I can't do much quick."

"Then I guess we have our answer."

Alistair looked at Lauriel. "Let me know if things go badly, alright?"

Lauriel wagged his tail and cocked his head.

"He wants to know how he's supposed to contact Karma."

"Say my name."

Lauriel nodded.

Alistair patted Lauriel on the head and left Raven to rest.

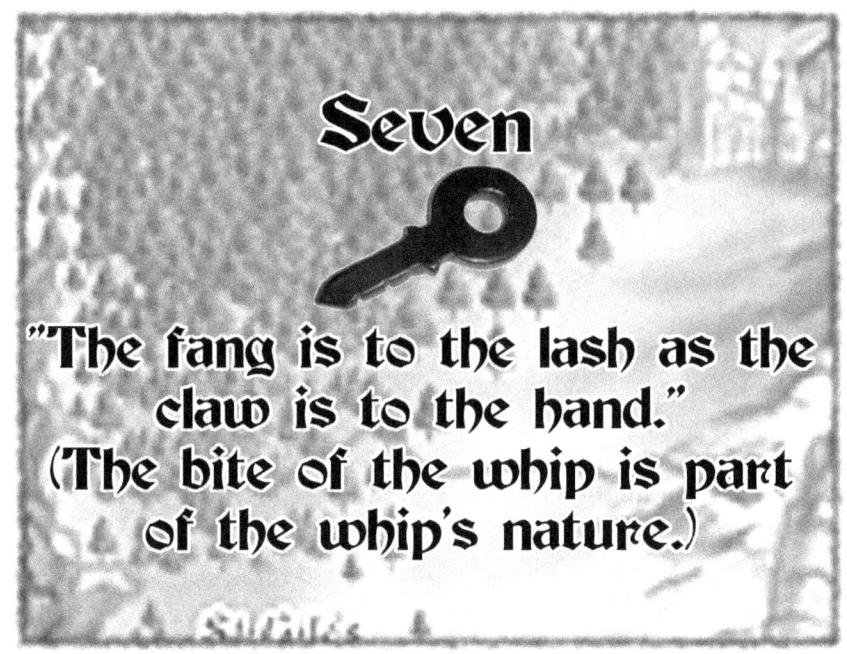

Seven

"The fang is to the lash as the claw is to the hand."
(The bite of the whip is part of the whip's nature.)

Catriona woke and looked beside her at Myrgen. He was looking at the ceiling and he turned to her when she stirred.

"Hey there."

She smiled. "Good morning." She glanced out the window at the mansion. "Any stirrings from the hill?"

Myrgen looked out as well. "Nothing I've seen. I don't think Lucifer lives there. He has a home."

"Yes. Hell. Where would you rather be?"

Myrgen shrugged. "To be honest, he's far different than the Church would have you believe. I wouldn't be surprised to find Hell isn't the nightmare they profess."

"He *did* tell us he was most assuredly the villain in this."

"Did you get that impression?"

She sighed. "I didn't read anything like that, except he definitely believes it's true. But he has been told his entire existence that he is a monster. After a while, you come to believe such talk."

He rolled onto his side so he could look at her. "Have you ever had that happen?"

"It's something I have prevented from happening a few times. Knowing someone is innocent of a crime, or that the crime for which they are imprisoned is one they acknowledge has given me some notable members of my crew…"

The silence creeped and lingered a moment. Sadness filled her eyes. "Thinking about Octavius?"

She nodded. "I take solace in the fact I haven't seen him here."

"Where do you think he went?"

"I don't know." She sniffed back the pain of the thought. "But with Estelle gone, he probably is doing what James is: breaking the news to family."

"Is he going to be okay?"

She shrugged. "I have no idea. They have been inseparable for almost a decade. And she's Fae, so there's that aspect. She would never intentionally hurt him, but he may not be able to do without her. Perhaps, once we are done here, we'll go to Galadorn and look for him."

Myrgen started to speak but then his throat closed down. He cleared it and the difficulty showed in his face. "Do you… do you think you'll sail the *Enigma* again?"

Catriona closed her eyes, like she knew the subject had to be addressed and had been putting it off as long as she could. She let her tears flow, not bothering with trying to impair them. "No. It would be like setting a corpse up at dinner. The *Enigma* has died. We need to scuttle her and send her to Calista."

They sat quietly for a few moments, holding each other's hands in comfort. Myrgen had grown so much on that ship and he could barely contain his sorrow. He could not imagine the pain the rest of them were going through.

"What will you do after that?"

She took a deep breath, steadying herself. "Talk to the crew. See what they want to do."

"Do you think they know?"

"That the ship was a living thing?" She shrugged, stabilizing. "Honestly, no. They worship Calista. The ship has always belonged to the sea for them." She smirked. "They probably don't even realize I'm dead right now."

"You think your crew, *your crew*, don't know you're *dead* right now?"

"Let's hope not. If they do, there will be a lot of trouble. They *do* know the ship is in dry dock right now, especially if they know Octavius has gone. Most of them will have left to visit their own families for a couple months. When they return…," she looked down at their hands, her face releasing some of the pain it was holding, "maybe there will be a new ship to board. The shipwright in Zara did a good job taking care of her all these years. He may have a new design he wants to explore."

He watched her, then stroked her face. "You seem ready to return then."

"Not… yet…" She nestled into his arms and took a few minutes to grieve.

Hours later, after a bath, they went to say their goodbyes to their family. Gwen hugged them both, then took Catriona aside into a shadowy area. A slender woman was almost invisible there.

"Catriona, this is the Sinister Glove."

Catriona bowed. "The lieutenant of Embertwist?"

The Glove nodded.

"But your presence *here* means…"

"Yes, I'm human. We all are." She glanced towards the hill. "I saw you and your friend there come from that area. There's a mansion or something we can sometimes see. Last night, the First Dûcesa disappeared into it and was gone for hours. She returned well after midnight. What's up there? And should we be worried?"

Catriona looked at the mansion. She could still see it which meant her invitation was still valid. "The owner built it to border the worlds of the Afterlife, but you can only get in with his express, written invitation. That might explain why it's not entirely real to you."

"Whose is it?"

Catriona glanced at Myrgen, who was enjoying a few words with Drake and Anika. "Lucifer."

Gwen put her hand on Catriona's arm. "Hell's Lucifer?"

"I'm afraid so."

The Sinister Glove glanced at the hill. "The ruler of Hell has set up a mansion which requires an invitation to enter and touches every Afterlife. I feel *very* uncomfortable with that."

"And you were *invited there*?" Gwen didn't sound comfortable either. "Do I need to be worried?"

Catriona smiled. "It couldn't hurt. But keep an eye on the First Dûcesa. Don't let her go there too often."

"How are we supposed to stop her?"

The Sinister Glove smirked. "Oh, I have ways if we need to. But I don't have a way to *retrieve* her if we must. I'd better work on that."

Catriona nodded. "Let me know if you need help."

"How are we supposed to do that?"

Catriona thought a moment, then shrugged. "Ask the Land. It will know where to find me."

Myrgen walked over and waited out of earshot. Catriona walked to him and took his hand.

"How did *you* get out of here last time?"

Catriona looked around. "I don't remember. There was…" Then she saw the horizon glowing and smelled the stones of home. She pointed. "There. That's where I sensed you were before."

He took a deep breath and they walked towards the light.

"What is it, boy?"

Lauriel sniffed at Raven's arm, then looked at him.

Raven nodded. "You sure she's back?"

Lauriel nodded.

Raven examined himself again. His bones were whole in most places. He had a few weak spots in his ribs, which took the brunt of the damage. His shoulder joints and hips weren't quite what they were before, the pain reminiscent of what he was told arthritis was like. As a mage as well as part Fae, his bones were unlikely to contract the ailment so he could only go on hearsay, but the stories described his current state. He still had fractures in every bone in his feet, which, it turned out, was a lot of bones. His hands were good though. One benefit to not knowing he was falling was that he did not throw his hands in front of himself to brace his fall. That spared his hands the damage done to the rest of him.

This made casting more complex spells possible, though he had not been much of a "spell-writer-downer" (as he thought of it). Every spell he remembered now was simply gestures, maybe a few words. He had always found it important to have a few escape-oriented spells that were unvoiced and didn't require hand movements. Over the last three centuries, that had simply become the norm. This would mean he could function without too much effort.

The biggest drawback to fixing body damage magically was the duration. It was effectively a cosmetic fix. The body had to heal naturally, and using magic to fix the body was assembling it with papier-mâché. Eventually, the façade broke down and, while the spell was in effect, no natural healing took place. If one didn't maintain the spell, new damage could result. The only way to fix damage permanently was to make the body magical long enough to become whole and absorb the healing.

That's where the sap came in.

This was a source of *čaro* designed for healing. It had rehydrated since Catriona was imprisoned and was stronger than he remembered. That could just be a result of time left alone. *Čaro* built up, stockpiling. As long as nothing interfered it would fill to overflowing, consuming an area and making it more and more of a magical environment. These often became gateways to magical realms, which were great hideouts for mages.

He willed the vines to release him, and they did, growing thicker and stronger because of his magic use. He wiggled his toes. They hurt (everything did) but he could walk. He knelt by the bed, touching the ground, and prayed.

Land, please let Catriona know I would like to speak to her. I need to apologize. Please lend me your strength and connection to all to express my desire. I thank you and hold to your wisdom.

Lauriel cocked his head and glanced at the vines and the piercings in Raven's skin.

"You're right. I really should." Raven put up a spell of protection, covering himself with earth to keep him safe.

Lauriel cocked his head the other way.

"Oh." Raven wagged a finger at Lauriel, nodding. "You're right about that. Land magic won't really counter the Land, will it? Um... Okay, I know what to do." He also added a magic component. The best defense against a Land based attack was Divine magic, but Raven had no connection to Heaven and no way to get one. He instead used water to cushion his body. It was just that, a cushion, but it might help.

He looked around for a moment, then rubbed his grumbling stomach.

"Apparently, I'm hungry."

Lauriel nodded.

Raven looked up at the now broken sunroof. The trees in the courtyard were bearing fruit and his magic use had caused some of it to ripen. He bent the branches down, and pulled a couple pears off. He tossed one to Lauriel, who ate it in one gulp. Raven admired that. He could not accomplish it in his present form but wouldn't do any better as a cat so he just ate it like a person. Sometimes he wondered if thinking of doing things "like a person" made him less of one.

He barely got the first bite swallowed before the earth opened and consumed him.

Catriona and Myrgen entered the glow together but once inside, the Land separated them. Catriona felt her clothing burn away but the flames never touched her. Then she felt the warmth enfold her and cradle her, embracing her with energy and health. There would be no sickness or pain or even fatigue when she emerged. She felt happy and alive.

Air cooled around her, and she discovered she was in a ball on the ground. She unfolded, already on her feet, and stood slowly, adjusting to her surroundings. Warm air wafted through her hair, not hot, despite the almost lava-like surroundings. She saw the veins of red pulsing through the stones and knew she was home.

She also realized she was nude.

This might be awkward.

There was a presence behind her and she turned to face it. Kneeling before her was a giant lava beast. It did not lift its head when it spoke, emitting no sound, only thought. Her eyes shifted to a clouded dark jade. She nodded.

"Bring him."

The ground opened before her, blowing her hair behind her, but she did not move. A figure was spit out onto the ground to lie at her feet. She looked down at him as he writhed in pain at his expulsion. Her voice carried enough weight to crush the world.

"Raven."

Raven groaned in pain and looked around. He frowned. "Where am I?"

"Not where you were."

Raven looked up at her and paled. He groaned getting to his feet and furrowed his brow at the bowing lava beast. He took a similar posture before her.

"What do you want?" Though it was phrased as a question, Catriona said it flat, like a statement. The impact of it showed on Raven.

"I… uh… want to apologize?"

"Then do so."

Raven blinked. "Oh! Yes. That sounds like a good idea. Let's… let's try that. I'm sorry I murdered you so you would be half dead."

She looked at him, unable to keep the ire and disbelief from her expression. "Why would you do that?"

"Because I need to know what happened at Persephone." He pointed at her. "You're not just some human with a weird title. You *replaced* the source of all magic in a trap that only went after powerful folks. You're something else."

She folded her arms. "And what do *you* think I am?"

"I think you are not Stâpâna or Dûcesa. I think you might be *the* Dûcesa though. But not the Fourth or anything. That feels too weak. But it might be too weak but now it won't be because I killed you and now you're back!" He smiled like he had achieved some sort of victory.

"And why is that important?"

"Because I want you to help me talk to the dead."

"As you wish."

She formed a dagger out of stone and thrust it into Raven's chest.

Eight

"The claw is to the heart and the fang is to the throat." (The smell of blood has called a predator.)

Raven gasped, surprised. *Why are people killing me all of a sudden? I've lived over three hundred years and have never been killed more than I have of late.*

He fell, twitching, onto his back. The light faded on the edges of his vision while getting brighter in the middle. He saw Summerland and reached out towards it. Then, he was propelled back to the room with nearly the same force as when he was thrown from the balcony. He hit and felt renewed pain and loss, but at least this time, he had his protections up.

Water splashed all around him, sending up a cloud of steam. The earth barrier protected him from the extreme temperature and he waited a moment for it to dissipate.

He pulled the dagger from his chest and leaned forward, clutching the wound. It took some concentration, but he managed to put aside the pain so he could cast a repair spell. As his heart began to knit together, he glanced again at the lava golem that knelt there. It had not moved, not shifted its averted gaze.

He looked at Catriona again. "Ow."

She looked moderately surprised. "You have been denied death."

"Yes." He coughed, rubbing his chest.

"Because of your attack on me?"

"Apparently so." Raven blinked. "Wait… *you* didn't deny me this?"

She just watched him puzzle through it, not interjecting.

"If you didn't do this, maybe you aren't the Death Bringer after all." He raised his hand and dropped his gaze. "Not that you aren't the Pain Bringer Pleasedon'tstabmeagain."

Her eyes became less clouded and she took a step back. A chair of lava-laced stone rose around her and she relaxed into it. "Tell me what you want me to find."

Raven nodded. "My grandfather is Sovereignlumen. He… *Legend has it* that he loved Magic, so much so that he wanted to join with it. She could and did become a physical entity so they could couple and create the Fae and all the magical realms and sources." He waved his hand. "That… Don't try to visualize that. Anyway, she was the one that was in that trap that killed you the first time. It grabs the most powerful thing in the vicinity and it spit her out and grabbed *you*. Not me. Not my dog. *You*. And if you aren't the Death Bringer, then you are still pretty important to the world. More than Magic."

"And how was killing me supposed to clear that up?"

"Before you died, had you ever been to Summerland? Or any other realm?"

She shook her head.

"And yet," he gestured with both arms towards her, "here you are." He rubbed his chest as it whinged at the effort. "Ow."

"What did you want from me?"

He frowned and took a deep breath. "I want you to find out why."

"Why I'm back?"

"Why he did it. According to legend, their love was the reason the world is a great place, full of beauty. He changed and well, Fae don't have a lot of free will to change, which means he was tricked into it. To betray her and put her in a trap that would power a spell…"

Catriona held up her hand. "Wait… what?"

"What?"

"What do you mean, 'power a spell'?"

"What do *you* mean, 'power a spell'?" He eyed her suspiciously.

She blinked, thinking, then turned to the lava beast. "Are there any other mages in the world that can explain what he means?"

The beast looked at her and nodded. It gestured and a crystal pillar rose from a pool of liquid stone. Images formed within it, showing a man and a woman walking through the countryside. They crested a ridge and saw hundreds of fires from a huge army. The smoking ruin of a huge tent sat near the northern border.

"Oh. I guess things with Mervolingia's king didn't go so well."

Catriona looked at Raven, then at the beast. "Where is my companion?"

The beast stood and gestured. Catriona stood, the chair melting away as she left it. Raven looked at them both.

"Should I go with her?"

The beast put a massive hand upon Raven, covering his entire body with a fingertip.

"Let him come."

The hand retracted and Raven realized what had just happened. That creature wasn't just really large and very far away. That was a physical embodiment of the Land.

The Land is taking orders from her.

Catriona stepped out of the meditation chamber and met Myrgen as he was arriving at the doors. He handed her a long coat. Also in his hand was a sealed missive.

"This just arrived by *Tevethetlan Madar*."

She looked at him. "The infallible bird? From where?" She pulled on the sleeves.

"*The Drum and Nightingale*. Tomas and Symonne."

"Open it."

Raven came out of the chamber. Myrgen glanced at him, then back down at the missive. He read the letter aloud.

"*Stâpâna,*

An army holds the Bordeaux Valley. It appears to be Fae.

T and S"

Raven glanced at the missive, still rubbing his chest. "Oh, the war thing. I guess everybody knows about it. Then again, wars aren't really peaceful or quiet."

Myrgen looked at Catriona. "Why is he here?"

"Land brought 'im."

"Ah. What are we going to do?"

She frowned. "I don't understand this. Why would the Fae army be attacking?"

"No idea," Raven pulled his shoulders forward to stretch them, "but someone named Dom used an amulet to bring someone named Elizabeth to St. Giles, which was held hostage by someone named Sovereigna who would be angry that someone named Alexander would use a Fae-killing poison. But that's stupid because I burned all the Fae-killing poison except for maybe the part that got on Tanglwyst-somebody's coat. But it didn't matter because it was all human politics and Johner really should leave before Corrigan shows up."

Myrgen blinked. "I understood exactly half of that."

Catriona swallowed. "And I caught the other half. Come on."

"Where are we going?"

"To the stables. I need to get eyes on this problem."

Raven pointed to the chamber. "Why not just use the pillar thing? That's how you just saw it before."

"Saw *what* before?" Myrgen's voice was showing his thinning patience.

Catriona felt something almost catch, almost surface. But then it was gone, leaving a trace of itself, like a scent after bread has left the kitchen. She looked at Raven, then at the chamber. "I don't know what you mean."

Raven waved them forward and walked back into the chamber. He walked past the glowing stone wall that hid the rest of the room from the doorway, then stepped back into the main chamber. It was hot, and glowing orange and heavy and empty.

Raven spun around. "What… where is everything?"

The effort caused him to wince as his bones protested the fast movements. He held his chest again, focusing on his breathing.

Catriona put an arm around him. "Where is *what* 'everything'?"

"The lava and the stone guy and the throne, although you did dismiss the throne. *And the Pillar*, the thing we came in here for."

Catriona looked around. "This is how this chamber looks."

Myrgen nodded. "Yes." Then he frowned. "Although…"

Catriona looked at him. She read him and saw he, too, had some recollection of a difference. She nodded. "Yes. Exactly."

She looked at Raven, then gestured them all out. "You are injured still. You should be at home, resting."

"Yeah, that isn't happening."

Myrgen touched her shoulder. "What do you want to do about the letter?"

"We need to get to the pass. Quickly."

"For what?" Raven's pain still etched his face.

"To see what's happening there, like I said."

"Look, say you go to the pass. What can you see there? Think."

She closed her eyes. "The town."

"And?"

"The Valley."

"Are you sure?"

"Yes I…" Then the vision of the actual area came to her. "Wait…no. There's a forest there. It stretches for miles."

"Exactly. Unless you go to the valley itself, you can see anything. Even from the top of the pass."

Myrgen nodded as she opened her eyes. "He's right. I forgot about the woods, but they obscure the entirety of Bordeaux, even from the pass."

"What should we do then?"

Raven leaned against the wall and Catriona and Myrgen both noticed the blood at once. They caught him as he started to fall.

"Where to?"

Catriona nodded towards the stairs. "The family surgeon. Second floor."

They took him to the medical room, mindful of his protests through clenched teeth. A thin, blond man there named Selig rushed to them as they entered.

"Selig, help." Catriona was worried. The blood was starting to soak Raven's shirt.

Selig's husband, Charles, guided them to the bed and Selig got Raven's shirt off him. The wound there was closing, but was still nasty.

Selig looked at the couple. "What happened?"

"I don't know. He just started bleeding."

Charles and Selig started cleaning the blood and Myrgen and Catriona stepped into the hallway to let them work.

"*Do* you remember what happened?" Myrgen searched her eyes.

"I stabbed him with a sword. I think."

"*In the chest*?"

"Apparently. But it was in the transition time, after I returned. I have trouble remembering what happens in the chamber. I always go in when I return home, to commune with the Land after being so long at sea. It gets rid of my sea legs so I'm not nauseated for a week."

"And yet?"

She nodded. "When he said that, I felt a memory trying to surface. But then, it left. Do you remember anything from when I was gone before?"

Myrgen nodded down the hall. They walked. "I remember you dying. I remember Raven saying someone could help you. Merrick. We went to Sovereignlumin through the wall of the vault in Persephone. But while he was looking for this Merrick person, I felt you slipping. I wanted to take you home. Alistair said he could get us here from there. We came out in the chamber.

"But it was… different somehow. There was stone, of course, but there was also…lava?"

Her emerald eyes showed her confusion. "*Lava*? Like orange-yellow molten rock?"

"Yes," he gestured to the grey stones with the red veins all around them, "but not anything like these. I saw a painting in a book in Yndia of a volcano. The Meditation Chamber looked like the painting of the fire stones flowing through the jungle. But it wasn't impossible to be in. I went there every day to see if you were back and it… became *normal*. That room has vivid pools of orange molten rock."

"Except just now, it didn't."

Myrgen nodded. "No, you're right. It didn't. And at the time, it didn't seem strange. I think that room makes the inhabitants of it feel like that is normal."

He opened the door at the end of the hallway and climbed the spiraling staircase that was nestled in the wall.

"During the attack by Mande, I hid the household in there. They never once seemed to notice the appearance. I thought I'd have to answer questions, but no one asked any."

"You went in there every day?"

"Yes. Just in case that was the day you returned. I had almost lost hope. That was why I was glad I had this."

He unlocked the door at the top and opened it. Light streamed in from the early morning sky, dust dancing through the showers of sun. The room was populated with paint jars, bottles with corks, and cups with paintbrushes with their bristles displayed. Against the east wall, her eyes looked out at the empty room, canvas after canvas demonstrating experiments or angles. On the west wall was a disheveled bed, several burnt out candles missing chunks of wax sat next to sealed jars half or one-quarter full of pigments. There were paint smudges dried on every surface, and crusting cloths that echoed the painting in the center.

There, Catriona looked into her own eyes, the sea behind her stretching out into the night. A large moon lit the subjects like the railing of the *Enigma*, the deck, the crest of the waves. Her hair was fluttering out of its braid (like always), and her eyes glistened in a green so clear and deep, she felt she could cut them and make jewelry. The look on her face was delight and just a hint of infatuation. And she was pointing at something at sea.

"The *whale*."

Myrgen smiled at the awe in her voice. "Also, known as the moment I fell in love with you."

She started to reach out, but stopped. "Is it dry?"

He frowned. "I don't know… I finished it right before you returned and I'm afraid I can't tell you how much time has passed since then. We were in Summerland for at least a day but the paint takes a while. It might not ever completely dry. The portrait I did of Elizabeth in my prayer nave was able to be marked with a fingernail and I did that years before. After that one, I started mixing my own."

He walked over to the pigments. "I don't know for sure what these are. They were waiting for me and they were the right color. They mixed. At the time, I didn't care beyond that."

She turned to him. "What are you going to do with it?"

He looked surprised. "It will go in the study, beside the others."

"But…" she looked back at it, "Anika was before me."

He took her hand. "Anika hasn't come back."

She swallowed, but it was stopped by the lump forming there. She felt the tears come and didn't try to stop them. She tried to remember how happy Anika and Drake were, how happy Tib was, but it wasn't enough standing in the home they all shared.

She sat on the bed with Myrgen and cried wordlessly for an hour.

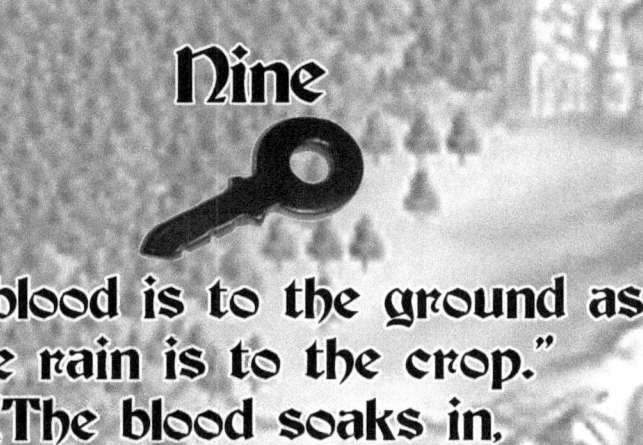

Nine

"The blood is to the ground as
the rain is to the crop."
(The blood soaks in,
unhindered by the surface, for
the land knows no difference.)

Gomez knocked on the wall by the stairs, startling His Majesty and his beloved out of their slumber. Tanglwyst fell off the sofa with an *oof* and Alexander scrambled to help her up. She laughed, sitting on the floor, and waved Gomez up.

"Your Majesty, the guards have set the discs as a barrier around part of the town. We need you to check it."

Alexander nodded. "I'll get on that. I need my mother and the Queen taken to the church, in case any of the Fae army get past the barrier. We need to act while it's still dark."

Gomez looked at the predawn sky. "That's less than an hour, Your Majesty. We need to get you to safety too."

"What do we do about the townsfolk?" Tanglwyst put her hand on Alexander's knee.

He glanced outside. "I don't know. Perhaps, in their homes…"

"They can't *stay*, Alexander. They'll be killed."

"The barrier…"

"Won't stop a flaming arrow."

Alexander sighed. "What do you propose?"

She knelt. "We put them on the ships in the harbor and get them away from here. According to Helen, there were several ships just outside the barrier. They had unloaded supplies onto the *Sulocco* when notice was given that Sovereigna was going to let it through. My Captain paid for the goods that were exchanged and several ships went on their way. The ships that were lingering on the edge of the harbor still have family here and refused to leave until they had to."

"So, they have room to take their families and friends?"

Tanglwyst nodded. "And any goods we wish to send to make sure they are taken care of. But gathering those goods might take a while. We don't know how long it will take for the Fae army to get here."

"I doubt they'll be here today."

Tanglwyst arched an eyebrow. "You sure about that?"

Alexander stopped himself from replying. Gomez knew they had seen enough strange things to be unsure about anything regarding the Fae.

Gomez took the opportunity presented by the silence. "What's west of here? I've heard there are islands in that direction."

Tanglwyst nodded. "One of the common, more lucrative ventures for ships that come to St. Giles is to try for the islands to the west. But I don't know that they would risk their families on the trip."

"Risk? What's there that's riskier than just sailing to Rouen?"

"Pirates. The islands have exotic fruits and woods. You can pack them in crates designed in Krakte to keep them fresh and they fetch a huge price in royal kitchens. Worth a year's trade if you can make the trip. It's how I built my fortune. The pirates don't want ships leaving the islands, and the ones coming in will be nearly empty to bring back as much fruit as possible. But they often have chests of money from royal chefs, and that makes them worthwhile. That's where Urien was last seen headed to, but no one has seen him or his ship since."

"How did *you* manage it?"

"Catriona's ships…" She stumbled over the mention of the woman, and Alexander squeezed her hand to encourage her to continue. "That fleet often ran protection for us on those runs. She would either drive the knowledgeable captains away from us, or destroy the ones who wanted to take her down. It was said that cannon fire could not penetrate the defenses of the ship. Something about you had to have been on the ship or invited or friend. I heard too many variations on the legend but the end result was that you couldn't sink it if you were an enemy. And a friend wouldn't fire upon it."

Alexander paled at the story, averting his eyes from this lady. The mention of the woman Alexander had pursued all spring seemed to be a sore spot, but Gomez was not certain Alexander wasn't under a spell. The last time he had seen his Lord, the man has been pursuing the mother of his child. Now, he was thoroughly with a woman Gomez *knew* to have a magical touch. He had seen it work with his own eyes.

Alexander had told him of the failed trip and the subsequent death of Gwen, even heard about the trip to the Papal City to rescue this lady. Still, the turn was so complete, he worried it was false. If she had bewitched him, the kingdom could suffer under a queen unworthy of it. If he was using the woman to get over Catriona...

Well, that just might be worse.

Tanglwyst kissed his hand, a reassuring gesture he followed with a pat on hers.

Gomez decided to reorient the conversation. "Will the fleet she ran be available to protect the townsfolk here if we get them on the ships?"

Tanglwyst shook her head. "I connect with them in Rouen. We're overdue. But being at sea is better than being in bow range. We need to hurry though."

She stood and gestured for the men to head downstairs while she knocked on the bedroom door. Gomez escorted Alexander to the main floor and the king stopped him in the darkened room.

"Gomez, what's it like out there? Any movement from the army?"

"I haven't seen anything. But all of this happened a few hours ago. They may not have plans to attack before dawn."

"I'll check the barrier. I need you up on a roof, checking the army's movements. You should be able to see the whole valley from the top of this building."

"Yes, Sire. And Sire?"

"Yes?"

He started to ask about his intentions with the lady but then thought better of it. In truth, if Tanglwyst went with her ship, Gomez would be able to see if this was real or just Alexander filling a void. "We need to make sure she leaves with her ship. She needs to be out of the battle zone. Too many people rely upon her."

Alexander glanced at the stairs. "I know. I just don't know how. It's not like I can shove a merchant ship out of the dock with my foot. Besides," he shook his head, "I promised I wouldn't try to work against her will when it comes to her decisions. I can't control her and frankly, I should never have tried in the first place."

He put his hand on Gomez's shoulder. "If she goes, she goes. If she stays, she stays. We'll deal with her presence or absence as she sees fit."

Gomez nodded and they walked outside.

Tanglwyst leaned against the bookshelf at the top of the stairs, smiling.

He got it. He finally got it.

Despite the direness of the situation, she couldn't help but smile.

The bedroom door opened and Catherine and Sovereigna came out. Their dressing gowns showed little rumpling, designed as they were to allow nursing mothers and noble women to receive guests without getting into corsetry. Tanglwyst was wearing hers as well, having used it to do business in this very room on more than one occasion. For the working woman, this was the uniform.

Catherine looked around the office. "Where did my son go?"

"Outside. He's checking the holy barrier around town."

"Alone?"

"He's not alone. Gomez is with him, and the guards are the ones placing them. But we have work to do. We need to get the people out of this town before the other army gets here. I have an idea how to do that."

She told the Queens about her evacuation plan.

Catherine glanced out the window at the brightening sky. "Are there enough boats for everyone?"

"I don't know. When the barrier came down, several people left with their families. They didn't want to risk them in the next situation. So I think, if we let people know the threat, they will go quickly and willingly. But we need to get the word out quietly."

Sovereigna nodded. "I can send a whisper to every human ear."

Tanglwyst shook her head. "Fae magic has already done so much damage, they'd never believe it. In fact…"

Sovereigna straightened, nodding. "I need to get away from here, *before* they realize I'm here."

"Yes." Tanglwyst glanced at the window as she heard a cock crow.

Sovereigna hurried to the stairs but Catherine stopped her. "I'll come with you."

That's either going to be a fight, or they will go off together. Either way, I'll give them their privacy.

She went into her bedroom to change and shut the door.

Alexander went to the nearest set of guards and nodded as they bowed to him. He looked at their feet where a basket of about twenty wet wooden discs sat on the ground.

"How is the barrier coming?"

The ginger guard nodded to the church side of town. "We started at that end as soon as the discs arrived and were blessed. Wanted to cut off the advance of those things on the dangerous side so we lay down a line of them across the road. That took most of the night to avoid getting caught by Fae patrols."

"What are you doing with these?"

"Putting them at the windows and doors of all the homes with people still in them. We figure that will stop the monsters from stealing the children or disguising themselves as a returned husband. There aren't enough discs to make a border so we are doing this instead." He nodded to the business next to Tanglwyst's office. On the windowsill was a disc. He saw another one on a door stop down the wall.

Alexander felt a hum coming from the basket and glanced around. Several houses also hummed, though not as loudly. He crouched beside the basket, listening. The barrier would have an almost audible component to Alexander but these men didn't seem to hear it.

"Good thinking. Are there any other baskets of discs?"

"A couple more people have a basket by the forest to the west. They're checking houses."

Alexander looked that way, worried. Catriona's cabin was out that way. "How far out?"

"Just outside town. There aren't enough to spread too far."

Alexander stood and looked south. He saw the red line painted on the ground on the road out of town. "That line, the one that marked where the Krakten Queen's barrier was, does it go all the way around the village?"

The guards looked at each other, then nodded. "Yes. We helped paint it ourselves."

Alexander looked at them again. "How much paint did it take and how long?"

A few minutes later, Gomez came down a ladder after the guards left Alexander. The guards were hurrying to the guard house.

"What's happened?"

Alexander nodded to the line. "That goes all the way around the village. I told them to get as many buckets of water as they could find, and have the priest bless it. Then they can pour the water on the same strip of paint they have already cleared. Cut out the second step of getting these wet and then placing them."

Gomez nodded the basket. "What do we do with those?"

"They were putting them on the houses to protect them from invasion. Won't stop a flaming arrow, but..."

Gomez nodded. "It will stop them from physically touching the house. That's brilliant."

"And they've already checked the houses for inhabitants. So only the houses with those discs on them have villagers still here."

Alexander saw movement at the downstairs window of Tanglwyst's office. It was his mother. He looked around for any other movement, and went to the door, opening it just enough to speak through.

Catherine glanced through the crack, looking around. "Sovereigna has slipped out the back door. She's got a spell that will keep her hidden."

"This building doesn't have a back door."

"It does now."

Alexander nodded. Gomez came over and recognized Catherine.

"Your Majesty."

"Grande Guard de Santander." Catherine looked over her shoulder, then stepped aside, opening the door. Tanglwyst came out, dressed for travel. She had a satchel hanging at her side, the strap across her chest at an angle.

"We need to get the people out quietly," Tanglwyst glanced down the street, "and the best place to start is there. The Wise Wench will have patrons there now and sailors from last night upstairs. They can spread the word. We might be able to get everyone moving out by noon."

Gomez nodded. "Where should I go? They don't like me at that place."

Alexander looked around. "Help the guards lay down the border. We'll get the citizens out of here." He looked at Tanglwyst. "I have good news. It involves these wooden discs."

Gomez went to help the guards and Alexander brought his mother out and explained the strategy of the guards. The three of them split up and started knocking on doors.

"Borders are secured, Your Majesty." Gomez nodded to Tanglwyst and Alexander. "How goes the evacuation?"

Tanglwyst gestured to the docks. "We've had a few ships fill up and head out. None of them are prepared for carrying people instead of cargo so they are only heading to St. Teresa, the next port south. It's very small, but it's on the other side of this valley. People are already planning on visiting family in other cities but there's been no time to alert them. No one is going to be properly prepared for this."

"What about *your* family, my Lady?"

Tanglwyst glanced towards the valley. "They are heading to Cliffside. There, they will head into the Disputed Woods. Osondrea understands the Fae and I told them to call it the Disputed Woods and seek the head of the bandits there, Tulio D'Or."

Alexander nodded. "I'm sure she'll be back by now."

Tanglwyst sighed. "I hope so. But I don't know if they'll be safer in the woods."

Alexander snapped his fingers. "The woman in the woods. What was her name? The Nubian woman who saved you from the barrier."

"Aislyn. She and her family were gone. Looks like things were packed hastily too. She probably left like a lot of people did, not drawing any attention to themselves. Most of the houses were empty when your mother and I checked."

Gomez folded his arms across his chest. "The guard did a pretty thorough job of checking all last night. The discs were carefully placed to save people."

"Anyone staying behind?" Alexander glanced at the dark buildings.

"A few, Sire. That jeweler has a satchel full of small anvils that she knows how to wield. Monique from the Wise Wench is another. Several others with businesses got creative with their tools. In the end, about fifty people are staying behind, and four times that have gone. The guards aren't sure where."

Tanglwyst nodded to the south. "A few families tried to leave via the south road but returned quickly when they saw the breadth of the army. They didn't want to risk being grabbed by the monsters. They are on the ships that left and are getting off in St. Teresa."

Gomez pointed to the woods. "What about the Black Forest? We know the Fae won't go in there."

Alexander turned to look at the foreboding forest. "It *had* crossed my mind. Had it been a greater emergency, I would have done that. The only trouble is that we don't know for sure there's no Fae blood in these people. With the woods that close, you never know."

Gomez saw a guard waving to them and he nodded acknowledgement. "Excuse me, please."

Tanglwyst smiled. "I should be checking on the *Sulocco*. It's going to get under way here soon. I need to say goodbye."

"I'll walk you down." Alexander took Tanglwyst's hand and they left the guardsman. Once out of earshot but within sight of the dock, he leaned to Tanglwyst. "I need you to take my mother to Patras."

Tanglwyst looked at Catherine, who was helping a woman and child get settled on the deck of the ship. "Why?"

"Because I'm going to be here, and I need her there, to protect Emmy. Plus, Mother has ruled as regent before during a civil war. We'll need her to authorize the building of the army if things go awry here."

"You'd make her fight her *lover*?"

"No. I'll do my best to see what we can do to diffuse this by working *with* Sovereigna. But I have to make sure Mother's at home to protect Emmy. We can't risk a noble deciding Emmy is a bargaining chip to gain the throne. Remember, I set her as my heir."

Tanglwyst sighed. "Alright. I'll send her on my ship."

"I need you to *take* her on your ship."

Tanglwyst frowned. "You're trying to get rid of me?"

Alexander kissed her. "Of course not. But Emmy needs *you* too. She's comfortable with you and trusts you. You're her friend and you know court." She scoffed but he continued. "Moreover, you know the catacombs to help her hide, or escape. There's a passage door in my room, in the prayer nave in case you need it. Even mother doesn't know how to navigate them like you do."

"I hate you."

He smiled, realizing he'd won. "I know." He kissed her more heartily this time. "Get what you need. We need to go."

She glanced back at the city above her, her hand on the satchel. "There's nothing back there I can't get later. Stay in my room. It's more comfortable than the barracks and more defensible."

"Thank you."

"And don't get killed."

He smiled broader. "I won't. You can keep track of me." He tapped his head.

He walked her up to the ship and watched her talk to Catherine. When Catherine looked at him, they exchanged a look and a gesture Tanglwyst didn't see, and they got the ship under weigh. They watched Alexander until the ship turned away from St. Giles and out of sight.

Alexander took a deep breath and hoped that would not be the last he saw of either of them. He turned back to the village. It was quieter and felt hollow with the people gone. He could still smell the campfires of the army and hear their drums and occasional battle cries. Even though he knew his mother and Tanglwyst were safely away from there, he felt less comfortable without them.

He chuckled. A week ago, he had been angry enough with his mother to threaten her. Now, he was entrusting his niece's life and the whole kingdom to her. A lot had changed in such a short time. He could barely believe less than a season ago, he had Catriona in his arms in his bedroom in Patras, falling asleep to her breathing. Now, she was so far out of his life, he couldn't remember what she looked like. He knew her description, her scent would probably trigger a memory, but everything else was a blur.

He saw Gomez and waved, then went up to the man he considered his best friend.

"Gomez, they're off. All the ships are gone and everyone is safe."

"That's especially true now, Sire." The ginger guard who was placing discs on the houses before walked up to them. He was wearing a large smile of pride. "Come, if ya would. I have something to show ya."

Gomez and Alexander exchanged a look and followed the guard into the main office. He took them back where the jail cells were.

"I think we're safe. The whole place is lined with iron bars."

The lone inhabitant of the only cell in the town was Sovereigna.

Ten

"The crop is to the mouth as the rain is to the well." (The crop is food, the well is water.)

"Leave us."

The ginger guard looked at Gomez. Gomez nodded. "I'll stay with them. Do as the King commands."

The ginger guard bowed and left, glaring at Sovereigna.

Alexander turned to Gomez. "I need to tell you something but it needs to be in private.

Gomez glanced at the Queen. "Understood. Where, sire? Can we be certain she hasn't cast a spell to listen everywhere?"

"Luckily, I know a place where she and the Fae have no power."

"The *church*."

"Exactly. Please make sure it's empty."

Gomez frowned. "Are you sure you'll be alright alone?"

"Yes. I…"

Gomez raised his hand. "Of course. You have the Power of Sovereignty and the holy touch of Heaven. Just stay back from the bars. She can still grab you."

"I'll keep my distance."

Gomez left and Alexander waited until he heard the front door close. He stepped close to the bars and Sovereigna leapt up from the cot where she had been sitting.

"What happened?"

Sovereigna rubbed her head. "I fell. Stepped in some blasted holy water. My shoes were repelled and I hit my head. Next thing I know, I was thrown on this cot and the door clanged closed. Where's Catherine?"

"Safe. She's on a ship to Rouen. She and Tangl will get to Patras and protect Emmy. Mother will send the troops, run the country, and be a formidable protector for Emmy."

Sovereigna relaxed. "Good. I couldn't bear the thought of her injured in all this."

"Well, no one knows about you two nor about the peace we struck before. To them, this is all just a continuation of yesterday's attacks."

"What are we going to do?"

Alexander ran his fingers through his hair. "First, I'm going to get Gomez to distract the guards. Then, we'll get you out of here. Wait here and just… be scary. That will stop anyone from hurting you. Can you do that?"

She waved her hand and a blue glow that looked like the barrier covered the inside of the entire cell.

He nodded. "That should do it."

"Be careful, Alexander. Catherine would never forgive me if I let anything happen to you."

He smirked. "I'm certain that goes both ways."

Alexander bowed and went into the outer office. Standing by the doorway to the jail cells was Gomez. Alexander didn't need the ability to read souls to realize he had just overheard the whole thing.

"Gomez."

Gomez held up his finger to his lips and Alexander stopped talking. Gomez gestured to the door and the two men went into the church next door. When Alexander was inside, Gomez took the king's hand and put it in the font of holy water.

Nothing happened.

Alexander looked at Gomez. "I'm not bewitched."

"Is your mother?"

Alexander looked around the church for the priest, but didn't see him.

"The priest is out at the road, blessing barrels of water on a couple of carts. What's going on?"

Alexander stood in the doorway where he could see the priest walking towards the wagons. "We don't have a lot of time, so I'll keep it short. I need to get Sovereigna out of here."

"Why?"

"Because Corrigan himself is on his way here, summoned by Johner."

"The Fae King of Summer?"

"I doubt there's multiple Corrigan's in the world."

Gomez ran his fingers through his hair, turning away from the king. "By the Saints, Alexander, they'll kill us all."

Alexander was surprised at the use of his name by Gomez, and he took that as a sign of the level of overwhelmed his friend was by this news. "I know. That's why we evacuated while you placed the discs."

"But not everyone left. And they still have their homes, their businesses here."

Alexander nodded. "I know. This is a major revenue stream for the kingdom. Peaceful relations with Krakte is the reason Elizabeth was married to Charles. It's a linchpin in our economy."

"What are we going to do?"

"I still want to talk to Johner. I need him to understand this wasn't intentional." He glanced at the road and saw the priest returning. "But I need Sovereigna free to do that."

"Why?"

"Because my mother will be in charge of my kingdom while I'm here. She can't restore peace with Krakte if they kill her beloved. Especially now that they are finally together. And I can't establish peace either if I don't have a sovereign to work with."

"That's not true. Emmy is the heir to the throne of Krakte. If Sovereigna dies, Mervolingia has instant peace."

"Not before my mother allows her killers to be destroyed by the Fae army."

Gomez stopped, stunned. "You really believe your mother would be so vindictive?"

Alexander sighed. He didn't really. Not anymore.

Gomez rubbed his forehead. "You can't let her go. She murdered people. Her spell killed *children* Alexander. One woman caught her toddler by the shirt as he started to fall into a fire. She rescued the child from being burnt. But then the spell came down and the child *burned to death* in his mother's hand. The woman *killed herself* because she couldn't get the smell of her child's roasting flesh off her skin. She threw herself into the barrier."

Gomez pointed at the jail house. "That woman *belongs* in there. She should be *burned herself.* You can't ask these people to let her go." He pointed at Alexander. "And you can't just release her back to her country. You'll be overthrown in an hour. These people, *your people*, deserve justice. I'm sorry as hell that your mother finally found love with the woman of her dreams but that woman is a real-world nightmare to everyone else."

The priest was almost to the church and Alexander nodded. "You're right, of course. But it must be handled properly or we will have a war on our hands that we can't fight. Besides, remember, she only invaded because of what happened to Elizabeth."

"Are you trying to tell me that the lives lost here *equate* to that of a dead, insane, murderous queen?"

"No." Alexander looked at the priest, who stopped in the doorway. "I'm saying that child's blood is on *my* hands, not hers."

The priest looked at the two men and sighed. He put his hands upon Alexander's shoulders. "Your Majesty, if I may be so bold, it is the Hero's Curse to blame himself for things a villain does. Whatever your wrongs, they are yours alone. You are not responsible for anyone else's evil." He looked at Gomez as well. "Every person has a choice about how they handle a terrible situation. You are right to accept your own part in this horrible war. But only accept that for which you are the villain, for your enemies will surely claim the times they are the hero."

Alexander frowned. "That is… *incredibly* insightful, Brother Robert. Thank you." He turned to Gomez. "I need to figure out what to do now. This is still a problem."

He left the church. His remembered how happy his mother had looked when they went their separate ways last evening. Now, he was in a terrible position. He went to the jail and went to the cell.

"I'm sorry, Your Majesty. I can't get you out of here."

"What? Why not?" She sounded either angry, scared, or worried, or probably a combination of all three.

"The... deaths... from before. When the barrier was up and the spell freezing everyone was in place, many people died. They are going to want justice for those deaths."

"But... you are their king. Simply command them to listen to you."

"And risk a coup? The Papal City is sealed off by Fae magic. I can't be confirmed by anyone except the Pope himself. If I go against the will of my people right now, some noble will come in and promise war just to get me deposed. Then I'll be killed and you will still be held accountable."

"Let them try." She stood to her full height, head raised. "My army..."

"Is being appropriated." He spread his hands, pleading. "Is there anything you can do if I let you out of here? Anything to *save* lives?"

She closed her eyes and dropped onto the cot. "No. Not really." Sovereigna put her face in her hands. "And Johner is as much at fault for that coat in the encampment as you. He *let* that thing in."

"And will that matter to Corrigan? Or will he trust his lieutenant over us? Will he blame you as well for escalating the situation?"

Sovereigna sighed, glancing at the floor. Then she looked up at him again. "Make some pretense for getting me out of this cell. I can escape if I'm not bound by iron. Or you can exile me to the woods. If I can make it to the Black Forest, no Fae will follow me. If they enter, they can't leave. Then I can get to Catherine..."

"Don't you understand? You can't *go* to Patras. You can't *leave* this room. Your presence in the capital city will be taken as an invasion after this. There hasn't been time for word to get out about the peace we made last night. No one in town even knows it. The last the kingdom heard, you were destroying Mervol land and killing citizens. There's no coming back from that."

Alexander ran his hand through his hair, turning from her to check the front area. The ginger guard was not there, undoubtedly off doing something for the town with the barrels. He trusted Gomez to keep the Queen in place and Gomez trusted Alexander to do likewise. For now, they were still alone, though Alexander did check behind the door jam in the office, just to be sure.

Sovereigna looked behind her at the small window. "You're right. This *is* the safest place for me. I have a barrier to keep out humans and iron to keep out Fae. Until this gets sorted out, I need to stay here. Besides," she sighed and looked at Alexander again, "if Corrigan is coming, I need to be here. Between Johner and I, we might be able to stop any fighting before it starts. I can keep the humans out of it."

"Are you sure you can do that?"

Sovereigna scoffed. "No. But you're right. *I* chose this path. I need to be held accountable. Now, if you'll excuse me, I have a few letters to write, starting with your mother."

Alexander's eyes were wet. "I'll get you some paper and ink."

"Sire, I have a message for you from the Voice of Command."

Corrigan Starshadow turned to the small orange and blue bird. "Speak it."

Johner's voice came from the tiny creature's throat.

"Your Majesty, the situation on the Black Forest border is dire. Heaven has implemented the use of shadow weapons against the Evil Queen's army. It appears Heaven has entered the war personally. What are your orders, Sire?"

Corrigan frowned. *Shadow weapons?* "It appears Heaven has chosen to end this this world. Messenger," the bird fluttered its wings, "alert our allies. Prepare for the final war with Heaven."

The bird broke into several identical birds and flew off in different directions. Corrigan turned to a gigantic stump in the woods around him. He waved a hand above it and the terrain of the world sprung up on the surface. Everything was to scale so he could determine the best course of action.

The cliffs crossing the knuckles of the main continent were the key issue. Had they been common mountains, Tooele would simply carve a road between them. The road would become impassable to humans afterwards, but for the army it would be an easy march.

But these were not common mountains. The cliffs around Caratia had been raised by the Land itself, sealing off the faithful from the Heaven worshipping scum. Since that time, the Church had sealed them with holy symbols, permeating the soil with blessed water and invoking the Archangels upon the valuable ores. The Land gave the humans gold and silver in threads throughout the cliffs, enough to make them protect the soil, but none of the weaponry ores ran through there. As a result, weapons for the human military were purchased rather than made.

The weaponry ores were exclusive to Land-worshipping areas and enriched in lava-fueled forges for centuries. Fae weapons were a part of each individual Fae, so none of their basic human spells would work upon the flesh of a Fae. This was difficult to understand for non-war Fae, but Corrigan's soldiers understood the weakness. They could heat the metal of armor and weapon to burn the hands and bodies of human armies.

Battling holy militaries were a different story though. Where divine magic was employed, metal didn't heat and arrows could slay his kindred in groups. There were a few battles he recalled before the issue with the Soulless Ones. His adversary, Michael, had fallen in battle during that war, and he had taken with him all tactics and skill. Worse, he had taken honor from the battlefield. Corrigan did not trust the brothers left behind not to be scoundrels and thieves.

He summoned his spies, simple creatures that took the form of cats or falcons. Their claws sent a truth serum into the recipient, causing them to tell the secrets of troop movements and supply runs. When finished with the mission, they could disappear into smoke and return to Corrigan on the winds.

"I need you to scout the area around here." He pointed to the Papal City. "Report troop movements and preparations."

They nodded. The cat creatures turned into kittens and the falcons picked up the tiny felines in their talons and flew off to the north.

He closed his eyes and reached out to Johner. A light formed on the map, next to the forest prison border. Divine magic formed the secret to the prison and legend had done the rest. Embertwist had been around that area, part of a covenant called Serenity. Welcomed by the human mages, he had learned much of their ways and secrets. If there were secrets to the Black Forest, he would know them.

Corrigan turned to a tree that stood wide in the forest and strode to it. It opened like a door and he entered the tower of Sovereignlumin. He went down the stairs to the Summer door and entered the tower proper. The lobby of the tower had four doors, one for each season. A week before, Corrigan had felt the change of the seasons fall to him, meaning Embertwist had spent all his energy for the year in a single burst. It was a month before Summer would even begin to show itself, and Corrigan waited for word from his brother as to why. No such intelligence had arrived.

He went to the flowering door and opened it. He climbed the spiraling stairs to the top. There, upon a bier like his sister Calpurnia, his brother lay as if dead. Corrigan was accustomed to his brother's tricks and he waited for the joke to be sprung. He looked around for the lieutenant but he did not feel her presence. As a human, she could not hide from him if he chose to look.

This is odd. She would not be away from his side if he is here and powerless. It is her duty as a lieutenant not to abandon him in his time of need.

Then he noticed what Embertwist was holding. It was a left-handed glove of fine black spider silk. The palm was torn apart and where it lay upon his chest, his clothing was the russet of dried blood.

Corrigan stepped back in horror.

Someone has slain the Sinister Glove? But how?

His brother's chest rose and fell with the rhythmic consistency of one in torpor. His sister Calpurnia, the Autumnal Monarch, had slept for centuries with the same appearance. Her human lieutenant Merrick waited upon her still.

Perhaps he has some insight into this.

Corrigan walked down the staircase and went to the cornucopia doorway. He climbed the stairs and found his sister upon her back, a book on her chest. An old man puttered near an alchemy table, glancing at an open book.

Corrigan drew his sword upon the stranger. "Thief! What are you doing in my sister's chamber?"

The man dropped his alembic and he raised his hands, turning to face the Midsummer King. "Corrigan?"

"Merrick?"

The old man nodded and Corrigan blinked, confused. "You've aged. This is not possible for a lieutenant, nor one in service to a Fae Lord."

"I am not in her service, Corrigan. I never have been."

"But," he gestured to the room and to his sister, "you attend her in her torpor."

"Yes. I will so long as I can."

Corrigan looked at Calpurnia. "How have you lived so long without her help?"

"I'm not without my own skills, Your Majesty. But my time is definitely waning. I can no longer leave the Fae Realm. To step onto mundane soil would cause my instant death."

"Have you determined what keeps her from us?"

"I never have, Sire."

Corrigan sighed, then turned to bow to Merrick. "Thank you for your vigilance."

"It is my honor to serve her for the rest of my days."

Corrigan took his leave of the ancient mage and returned to his own door. Autumn had always come to the world on cue and never fluctuated on strength since his sister fell into her slumber. Corrigan had always passed his power into her during the Ritual of the Seasons, and her body had released it in slow, even measure.

What happened with Embertwist was *different*. Corrigan had acquired all of his powers of the season in a single moment, the turning over of the world's growing season not being the gradual flow with which he was familiar. He knew beyond doubt he held not only the power of Summer, but the power of Spring as well. It added to his power in a way that he did not experience with Calpurnia.

So, although the two appear to be suffering the same malaise, their circumstances are different. It is not the same spell that affects them. Could this also be part of Heaven's war plan?

He had no idea whose council to seek for this and less idea how to manage the needs of Spring. He was Summer and all he could do was *be* Summer for longer. He had no option to be otherwise.

Perhaps that's the point of this: To force us to change, thus killing us.

But Embertwist was still Embertwist. He was simply asleep, expunged of his powers.

And alone.

This thought concerned Corrigan most of all. The Sinister Glove was no fool and beyond competent. She would not fall to anything other than... an Archangel.

That must be what happened. Johner said Heaven was interfering directly. Their goal must be to remove our lieutenants and render the Fae Lords into torpor.

He had to admit that was an interesting and untried plan. And from all appearances, it looked like it might work.

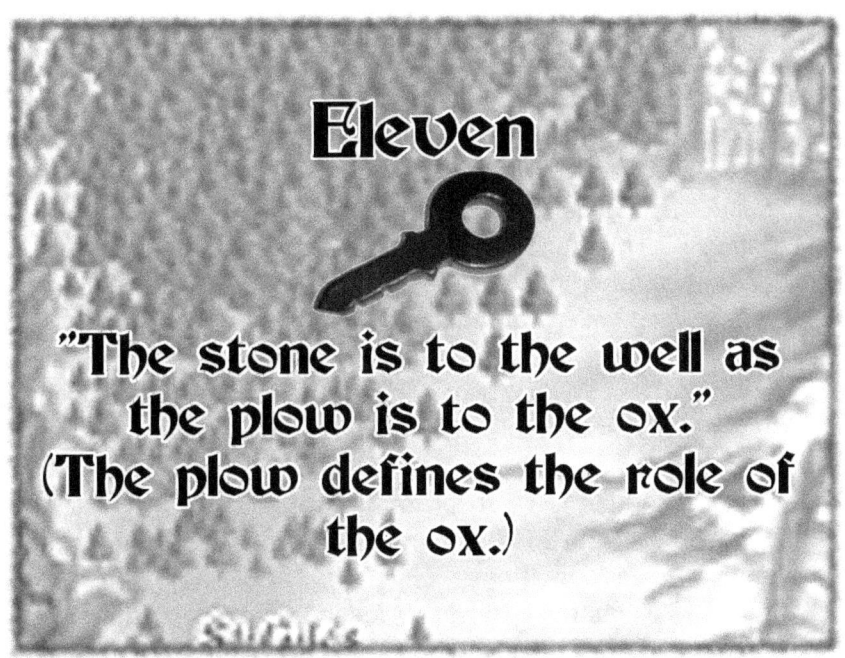

Eleven

"The stone is to the well as the plow is to the ox." (The plow defines the role of the ox.)

As Sovereigna settled in to do her letters, Alexander glanced outside at the silent town. He could hear the sound of a hammer on a chisel, undoubtedly cutting the discs, and the smell of burning wood from the brand. There was also a sharp scent of alchemy and iron. Truly, his subjects were working together to protect the town and their homes.

Will I do any less?

Alexander decided he would not. The threat to the town was still there and with their queen locked up, it was only a matter of time before they attacked. The discs were already around the town. He decided to take a page from Sovereigna's book and put up a barrier where the holy water and symbols were already present. He went to a link in the chain of discs and holy water and knelt. He felt for the essence of Heaven there, basically looking for the spiritual equivalent of the Power of Sovereignty. He found it easily.

He imagined all the non-Heaven-worshipping creatures out there and envisioned them repelled by a new barrier of holy light. Then he rethought the holy light and just made it a repelling sensation like the holy ground already possessed. He didn't want to draw attention to the barrier and have it seen as a hostile action. Especially not with the way things were going.

Once he felt the barrier strengthened, he waved over a couple of guards.

"Gentlemen, please take to the rooftops and keep an eye on things."

"Does this have something to do with the captured queen, Your Majesty?"

Alexander frowned. "You know about that?"

"Of course." The guard smiled with his companion. "We heard she was caught on the other side of the Wise Wench."

Of course the guards that found her would brag. "Yes. And we need an alarm system if they attack. So, I need someone on those rooftops." He pointed to the Wise Wench Tavern, Tanglwyst's offices, the barracks, and a two-story manor that served as the town hall and mayor's residence.

The guards nodded. "We'll spread the word, Sire."

"Find a bell or a pan and hammer. Anything to make a loud enough noise if someone sees something."

"Will do." The guards bowed as Alexander dismissed them.

The fatigue he had been holding off caught him and he felt his energy drain away. He rubbed his eyes and returned to the guard's office. He looked in on Sovereigna.

"How is it coming?"

She looked up. "It will take some time. You rest. I will let you know when I am finished.

Alexander tried to resist but the idea of closing his eyes was too enticing to deny.

"I'll be right in the next room."

She nodded and returned to her writing.

Sovereigna stood. "That should do it."

Alexander opened his eyes. He had heard her as clearly as if she had said it next to his ear. He was laying on the small cot in the Captain's office. He stood and walked over to the cell.

"This is for your mother." She handed it over. It was sealed.

"How did you seal it?"

She smiled and handed another one, also sealed, to him. "This is for the head of my guard. He's a large half ogre wearing a black and green sash. His name is Herrschaftlich Schutz Manfreid."

Alexander nodded. "Is he going to try and get you out of here?"

She nodded. "Yes."

Alexander nodded. "Okay then. I'll keep people out of the way."

"That would be wise."

He looked at her. "Was he going to come for you anyway?"

"I would expect no less. Wouldn't your red-haired friend do likewise?"

Alexander smiled. "If they are equivalent, then indeed he would." He tapped his palm with the letters. "I'll get these out right away."

She bowed and went back to her bunk.

Alexander went into the front office. Gomez was standing outside in the street. Alexander put the papers into his doublet and joined him.

"Your Majesty."

"Gomez."

"How is she doing?" Gomez's voice was concerned but his eyes were less so.

"She is proud, repentant, missing my mother. She wrote her a letter."

"Have you read it?"

Alexander shook his head.

"Don't. If anyone other than the appropriate recipient opens a letter from Krakte, they'll die. They've always bewitched the missives."

Alexander swallowed. "Right. I remember hearing something like that at the palace but I couldn't tell if it was just foolish stories meant to frighten nosy staff."

Gomez shook his head. "They lost a messenger who was new to the job a few years back. Opened a letter of congratulations on Elizabeth's pregnancy from a Krakten noble. The boy died within minutes." He glanced over his shoulder to the office housing the cell. "That was for a routine letter. Something important like a love letter would definitely sealed by magic."

"I'll remember that. Is there a way to break it?"

"Not that I've seen."

"Well, the trouble is that I'm not sure how to send it. The ships have sailed."

Gomez frowned. "And all messenger birds are dead now, lost to the barrier."

"None have come in from Patras?"

"The news of the barrier's drop would still be a day out from there at least. I didn't send word out because we never had a way."

Alexander sighed. "And I'll bet mother never told her messenger at the Friar she was leaving. He's probably shifting from furious to frightened on the hour."

"If she had a messenger, we might need to head over there. At the very least, it would get you out of here before you could be taken hostage."

Alexander thought about Tulio and his merry band. The woods were Fae claimed and he would be more vulnerable pinched between them and the occupied valley. "It would be smarter to get Charles, the messenger, to move south, but if the Midsummer King is coming, we don't want to lead him to any place inhabited. I'm tempted to flee to Krakte, into those woods."

"I doubt they'd follow you. They know that danger."

The blacksmith's apprentice walked by carrying a new bushel of wooden discs to the church. Alexander and Gomez watched Ais enter the building, then looked at each other. They spoke at once.

"I have an idea."

The priest at the church turned to the king and guard as Ais put the discs back into the bushel.

"Of course, we have plenty of fresh water and I can bless anything that comes in. As we determined from the occupation before, the Fae will avoid the holy ground."

"And we also know from the Queen's capture that her magic was affected by the holy line." Gomez was excited by the idea.

Alexander felt less sure of the idea but he also thought it might leave an opening for Sovereigna's man to get her to safety. They had not protected the area between the forest and the back of the town. There was nothing but the rectory and the deeper guard barracks between the forest and the jail. Her man could not enter the forest and leave again, but he could get her in there with no trouble and no one in St. Giles would pursue her.

The priest nodded. "But it will take barrels and barrels to line the valley. Any space would be a hole through which the enemy could escape."

Alexander nodded. "That's actually the point. We leave the only way out to be to the north, back to Krakte. Once they return home, we can release the Queen back to them."

Gomez flicked a glance at Alexander but did not question him before the priest.

"*Return her*? After all she's done?"

"Brother Robert, she only came here after her *valid* requests for her daughter's body went unanswered. The reason for the incident is my own arrogance. Returning her to her home unhurt is the first step to healing this horrible offense. The fault is mine and whatever the people need from me to make amends, I will do. It's the only thing I can do to make up for it."

Brother Robert frowned. "Perhaps confessing will help. You can get guidance from Heaven."

Alexander looked over Brother Robert's shoulder at the symbol on the wall above the altar. "I will do that once the town is secure. But it is day now, and I have something I need to do before noon." He turned to Gomez. "Continue to strengthen the protection on the eastern edge of town. And start getting the water and symbols stacked near the southern road. We need them ready to move."

Brother Robert arched an eyebrow. "And where will you be, Your Majesty?"

Alexander glanced at the priest and then at Gomez. "I need to stop a war."

He left the church.

Gomez followed him out. "That was dramatic."

Alexander nodded. "Well, I felt I needed to do something or I'd be in tears for an hour reliving every sin."

85

He walked towards the eastern road that lead to the Krakten army encampment. Gomez stepped in front of him, barring his way.

"Okay, why don't you tell me your plan now?"

"I'm going to apologize to Johner. I never meant for this to happen so I need to apologize and see if he'll let Corrigan know not to come here. If we can get Sovereigna back to Krakten soil, this whole war can be averted."

"You'll be sending a message to your people that the royalty are better than the rest of us. With the Papal City covered in thorns and a Fae army marching on Bordeaux, you'll be overthrown before you see Patras again. You don't have the backing of the Caratian army so you literally have no way to stop it if these people rise against you. I'm begging you not to release her."

"The deaths here were retaliation for killing her daughter."

"Which happened *after* she killed our king."

Alexander sighed. Gomez just wasn't going to let this happen. Alexander looked at Gomez and nodded. "That doesn't mean I shouldn't apologize to Johner."

"Fine. And what will *I* be doing?"

"You'll be setting up barrels of holy water along the road where our troops will come from. We'll need them safe when they come to St. Giles."

"Holy water will be a deterrent, but they will simply fire over the barrier. It's not enough."

Alexander looked around, then knelt by a symbol on the ground. He touched it and concentrated on the Power of Sovereignty. It flared and he glowed. That glow spread to the symbol, then to the holy water mud nearby. Alexander stood and the glow diminished and disappeared.

"That's my plan." He looked at Gomez again. "If I can get a connection of enough holy symbols and water lines, I can make a barrier that will drive them north again. No, it might not stop arrows. But it will stop troops and our people won't be harmed by it. And if anyone fights it, we shift the line to push them to the Black Forest."

Gomez blinked, then stroked his chin, nodding. "That could work. That could work just fine."

"But we need as much water as we can get to soak as many soldiers and armor as we can. Which means getting the holy water where the army can get to it. If they make an unbroken line, I think I can protect them even from arrows."

Gomez nodded. "I'll go take care of that. How long will you be?"

"I don't know. I'm going to ask Johner if he has a messenger he's using. He may have a way to get the missive to my mother. Since it's undoubtedly sealed with Fae magic, they will be less likely to be hurt by handling it."

"I want it on record that I don't like you going there alone. I also want it on record that I realize I can't stop you, as evidenced by me for several years now during your secret summer excursions."

"I'll tell a scribe."

Gomez pointed at Alexander. "See that you do."

Alexander glanced around. "Look, I know you think I don't understand how dire this is because I used to leave all the time. Trust me, I get it. If I'm captured, my enemies will say to let me pay for the sins that got us here. My allies will try to rescue me. The royal treasury will go to pay my ransom. I may end up married to bring peace. I get it. I do."

He put his hand on Gomez' shoulder. "If I *do* get captured, get my mother back here. No one can out-negotiate her. Even a Fae Lord."

Gomez looked at the encampment, then back at the Wise Wench Tavern. "Fine. I'm going to get on top of this building and watch your exchange with him though. If I get the feeling things are not going well, I'll alert the guards."

Alexander patted Gomez's shoulder. "See you soon."

They parted company and Alexander moved towards the Fae encampment. He saw the smoking ruins of the Queen's pavilion from the small rise in the road, then he saw a glint of shining metal armor.

Johner.

He started towards the man when a shout called his attention off to his left. A gigantic half ogre, wearing a black and green sash that would have been bed curtains on any other surface, bellowed orders to a group of scouts. Alexander glanced at Johner, then went for the ogre.

"Herrschaftlich Schutz Manfreid, I have word from the Queen."

The half ogre turned to Alexander, who strode with purpose, holding out the missive with *Manfreid* written on the outside. He took the letter in his giant hands, making it look like something a doll would hold. He waved his hand over it and it opened.

He read it, then glanced at Alexander. "It says you will know where she is being held."

Alexander fought to keep his gaze steady. "Uh, yes." He glanced at the missive that predicted his willing, or possibly unwilling, assistance. "There is a building on the other side of the church. She is in the back of that, against the western corner nearest the forest."

Manfreid looked Alexander over and he realized that his royal status would not stop one of those fists coming down on him. His nervousness threatened to flare the Power of Sovereignty and he steadied himself by forcing his breathing to slow. He felt nothing from Tanglwyst and reached out to her as Manfreid re-read the letter. She was asleep on the ship, and he smiled, glad she was at least getting some rest.

Manfreid turned the letter over to a scout who sniffed the letter, then the air. The scout looked like a normal person with a large nose but his actions reminded Alexander of a fox hound. The scout turned to Manfreid and nodded.

"He tells the truth. I can smell her that way. The church interferes with the scent but the letter has given me a connection to her."

Manfreid nodded. He looked over Alexander's head and Alexander turned to see Johner watching them from the road.

Okay, just breathe. Pretend you don't know there's been an escalation. In truth, the place looks just like it did yesterday. There will be no way to tell anything has changed since last night except that Sovereigna has been taken. Just come here with this news and assume that's the reason for the army being on edge. I mean, honestly, this just *happened a few hours ago.*

He breathed deep, nodded to Manfreid, and walked to Johner.

Twelve

"The plow is to the ground as
the lash is to the ox."
(The plow gouges the ground
like the whip gouges the ox.)

The barrels behind Tanglwyst shifted and she opened her eyes. The young girl on her lap was sound asleep, and so were Tanglwyst's legs. Daylight was in full force and the main sail was no longer able to spare her from the direct sun. She doubted it mattered. She would have slept all the way to St. Teresa.

Catherine smiled at her. "Do you need a break?" She nodded to the little girl.

Tanglwyst smiled. "If you don't mind."

Catherine knelt down and took the girl from Tanglwyst, then stood and was relieved of her by the girl's father. He bowed to the Queen Mother and took her away. Catherine turned to Tanglwyst, who was shaking her legs against the deck to get feeling back in them.

"Was it something I said?"

Tanglwyst looked at the man and his daughter, then smiled. "Probably when you said 'I do' to King Henri."

"Why do people always dwell on that one little mistake?"

Tanglwyst laughed before she realized the improperness of the act. "I see now where Alexander gets it." She looked at the dressing gown, which was starting to show wear from the ordeal. "I'm sorry I didn't have anything you could change into."

Catherine looked at her gown, sighing. "This is Sov…" She glanced at a family who stepped past, then at the nearby folks who were half asleep around them. "This is appropriate royal attire, but then again, we are not quite in royal surroundings, are we?"

"I'm afraid not. I have some spare clothes here."

"In my size?" Catherine shook her head. "My clothes need not be what you concern yourself with, my dear. I wore this kind of outfit at the Papal City throughout my duties."

"Were they this physically demanding?"

"No. But we do not have another option." She smiled then glanced at the captain on the helm. "The Captain said we would be in St. Teresa by noon. Why is there another port so soon?"

"Necessity. St. Teresa is a town that has several sawmills. They cut the wood in the forest around the Bordeaux Valley. It's the only sawmill in the valley and the Black Forest can't be harvested so it's the first stop on the way south from Krakte. Because it's such an important port for the northern part of the Kingdom, the citizens are very careful harvesting the wood. There have been no new houses built in St. Teresa in over a hundred years."

"How do they handle it when children grow up and get married?"

"Most move to St. Giles, which is why everyone there has family here. When one generation gets too old, they move up to St. Giles with their children and the next generation moves down to learn the trades. Wood cutters work the forests and have camps in the woods, but they winter in the city while other relatives run the mill. There has been talk of putting in a second mill in Cliffbase. It's possible this incident will cause many people to explore that option now."

The sailor in the Crow's Nest hollered out a call and the Captain nodded to him. The sailors started moving amongst the drowsing families, stirring them. Within a few minutes, a bustling extended dock came into view. There was a dry dock on the shore, set back into the cliff in a natural sea cave. Sizable petards were lowering stacks of wood to the catching deck below. A dozen people were waiting and, as Catherine and Tanglwyst watched, they got the wood unloaded to pallets and tied down to eye bolts set into the cliff wall.

Tanglwyst gestured to the set up. "We don't know who set the eye bolts but they have been there as long as the town has records. They never rust and there was a time when the church threatened to destroy the town because the bolts might be Fae in nature. The local priest convinced them it was the opposite, that the source was divine, so they let it be."

Catherine pursed her lips in disgust. "That sounds like the Church. When I was there, I met with plenty of disfavor and judgment. Yes, some was regarding the Massacre, but there were those who just didn't like *anything*. There was one fellow in the library…"

"Brother Fausto?"

Catherine pointed at her. "That's the one. You know him? Or know *of* him?"

"He's the one that attacked us in the basement of the Papal Palace."

She nodded, sniffing back her derision. "Oh that's right. Monstrous creature."

"Well, I'm sure he's paid the price." Tanglwyst looked to shore. "A lot of people are coming to help." A dozen people were on the docks, ready to help unload.

"Where are they planning to take them?"

Tanglwyst shrugged. "That I don't know. Like I said, the town is deliberately small."

The ship started to make port and everyone prepared to get ashore. It took another half hour to get the ship to dock and when the gang plank was set down, many disembarked. The dock workers moved people along to the shore, family representatives gathering their relatives into groups. The Harbormaster waved to Tanglwyst and she accompanied the Captain onto the dock.

"Hail Captain Nesbit."

"Harbormaster Mendoza." Captain Nesbit embraced the dark-haired woman who ran the dock. "How are you this day?"

She smiled. "Good to see you, Uncle David. Is everyone okay?"

"There was no trouble. The children were too tired to get sick and the parents were too frightened." He turned to Tanglwyst. "Cassandra, I don't think you've ever met the Lady Tanglwyst. Lady Tanglwyst, my niece, Cassandra."

Tanglwyst bowed. "I thought Christopher Sturz was the Harbormaster here."

"Ah, yes… Well, he was. But recently he…" She frowned, thinking carefully. "He…" She shrugged and took a deep breath. "He was having sex with a dolphin and drowned."

Silence.

"Excuse me?"

Cassandra gestured to the dock. "He has always had a love of the sea. He would walk out into the water and… and…"

"Couple with it," Captain Nesbit helped.

"With the *sea*? How?"

"None of us paid too close attention to that part." Nesbit rubbed the back of his neck, looking uncomfortable. "But we've all seen him."

Cassandra nodded towards the sea. "So, he was out there and a dolphin showed up. They are aggressive lovers with other dolphins and he, well, he was in the right place at the right time with the wrong way to breathe."

"Wow."

Cassandra pointed to the Harbormaster's office. "Rebecca Houseston is working on a portrait in the office now. Would you like to see it?"

He looked at Tanglwyst. "I don't know if the Lady has time…"

Tanglwyst nodded. "I think supporting artists is essential, especially in times a war. Who else will chronicle what occurs?" She turned to Cassandra. "Please, lead the way."

Cassandra bowed and the trio walked to the sturdy building at the end of the dock area. The building showed very little signs of wear, especially for being wood right on the shore. Ornate paints and carvings decorated the outside.

"Beautiful building! I'm surprised I've never noticed it before." Tanglwyst examined the painted columns flanking the doorway.

"You are often in with Lord Dominic working on the logs and manifests if we stop here. I usually pick up lumber on the way to St. Giles, so we don't see this port with you aboard until later in the season."

"Ah. Dominic. Yes. Well, he won't be travelling with us again." *Won't be traveling anywhere again. Good riddance.* Still, she had loved him. The amulet was the reason for his betrayals but she still felt that he could not have been so deeply corrupted if the seeds of it were not already there.

"Yes, I had heard he got a promotion. Kingdom Chancellor?"

Tanglwyst smiled at her captain. "News travels fast."

Nesbit gestured to Cassandra. "She got the bird with the message a week ago. It didn't come like the decree about the Princess, or you, but it did get out."

"Me?"

"There was a period of time when you were clearly no longer a suspect in the death of the king and became trusted enough to stand in for him for a while. He was King again shortly afterwards but you were obviously pardoned."

"Ah." *The transfer of the Power. Of course everyone felt it. That is the nature of the beast.* "Yes, he did pardon me. I was very grateful. I didn't like the light of distrust that could transfer to my household members. Too many nobles would leap at the chance to imprison them and take over their holdings."

Captain Nesbit nodded to his employer. "And yours. I kept the ship away from shore while you were being questioned. Just in case."

Tanglwyst smiled. *Away from shore* meant on an island they discovered almost a decade ago, west of Krakte. It faced a strange cave in the high center of the cliffs that were part of the Black Forest. The cave almost resembled a skull and there were often lights flickering in the eyes. The island itself was rumored to be the home of a storm giant centuries ago and that kept it safe. No one superstitious went there and that included the entirety of maritime workers by nature. Calista spoke in superstitious portents, validating the practice so her sea worshippers paid heed to them. Plus, the island frequently had storms surrounding it. There was but one way to sail into the island and that was discovered by Nesbit by accident last year.

Last year.

Has all this really happened in the span of a single winter? It seemed like years had passed since she and Nicolai had parted ways. So many things had changed in the last few months, she barely recognized her life now. For everyone else, the world had turned at its normal rate. There were people out there *bored* with their pace of life. She realized this effort here was a grasp at slowing things down, if only for that moment where she looked at a piece of art.

They entered the hut and a heavy woman with spectacles and a generous smile looked up from her painting. It wasn't large, less than two feet square, but it was being painted on a sheet of wood shaped like a wave. The man in the portrait was young, not quite thirty, with dark hair and laughing eyes. He was frolicking with a dolphin which stretched along the bottom edge. The woman was looking over the piece when they came in.

"Rebecca Houseston, this is Tanglwyst de Holloway. She wanted to see your portrait."

Rebecca stood and stepped back. "All that's left is the drying now."

Tanglwyst looked it over. "How did you get it done so fast?"

"Oh, he asked for it a month ago." She gestured to the window and the harbor. "Getting the paints to dry in a coastal town is practically impossible. It took this long just to have all the paints set. I brought it down a few days ago, but realized it needed an epithet so I added the dolphin."

They looked at the small, crisp words painted into the bottom edge of the dolphin's belly. *He died doing what he loved.*

Both the Harbormaster and the Captain snorted a laugh, which they quickly covered. Tanglwyst frowned at first, then got the joke. Though the laugh never made it out of her mouth, it settled in her eyes.

"Anyway, the people from St. Giles. What will you do with them?"

Cassandra nodded, sobering. "Their families have opened their homes. We built some temporary shelters when we heard of the trouble, just in case anyone escaped. They aren't much, just simple A-frames with hay bales for doors and stone stacks for a hearth. We haven't had to make any doors for so long, no one had the hardware."

Rebecca pointed out the window up at the cliff. "They are taking some folks up now."

Tanglwyst turned around and saw parents gripping their infants and young children tight as they were raised from the sand to the town at the top on a petard. The platform was sizable, easily holding twenty people, and there were fencepost walls to keep things from falling out. She had seen similar elevators for loading livestock on ships.

"How many shelters do you have?"

"Not many." Cassandra looked back at the lady. "Only about six. They take about a day to put together. But with the other people here, they might be able to build more than one at a time. The trick is not to work the wood too much so it can be dismantled to sell for ships. They are put together by sawdust putty and lashing ropes." She shrugged. "Like I said, temporary."

Tanglwyst turned back to the platform that was now reaching the top of the cliff. The families were offloaded and the petard sent back down for another load. It worried her that the shelters were being made temporary to preserve the wood for sale rather than to protect the children displaced by this incursion. If the structures fell apart in the rain, the inhabitants could get sick or die.

"What if I bought the wood for the shelters? Then you could build them more sturdy. We don't know how long the families will be here."

The Harbormaster shook her head. "They can't be made permanent. There's a law in place to protect the King's Forest. With the invasion, we assume the town's resources will be commandeered to support the incoming Mervol army. If we don't have spare wood, they'll dismantle the shelters for their siege engines."

Tanglwyst frowned. "You honestly think the army would do that?"

"Apparently, the Mayor has already received a bird."

Tanglwyst looked at her ship, already almost empty of the families from St. Giles. Suddenly, she no longer trusted that they were safe here.

"David, all the guardsmen stayed behind in St. Giles. Anyone here with their families might be conscripted into the army. They can't have had time to assemble if they are already sending out birds. And St. Giles couldn't send any out to explain."

Captain Nesbit looked out the window at the petard full of people. Several of the people on it were of fighting age, both men and women. The Mervol army did not discriminate when it came to protecting the country.

He folded his arms across his chest, drawing his mouth tight. "What do you want to do?"

"We have food and supplies. Maybe we need to take them *away from shore.*"

Captain Nesbit's mouth settled on a half-smile. "We know there's room."

Cassandra flicked her gaze back and forth between her companions. "Won't the army consider them deserters?"

Tanglwyst looked at her. "I don't know."

Captain Nesbit shook his head. "No one has been conscripted. There's no violation of law happening. However, the army will take anyone of able body. It won't matter that you have young children to care for."

Rebecca raised her hand, entering the conversation. "They'll surely leave one parent behind to care for the children."

"Not when the entire town of St. Teresa is related to them. The children will likely be left here in the care of any townsfolk that aren't also conscripted. Chances are that few of the locals will be taken since they run the sawmills on such a small crew. That means everyone else is up."

Rebecca frowned. "You sound like you know all this first hand."

Captain Nesbit nodded. "I served long enough to almost get a ship in the Mervol Royal Navy."

"Almost?"

"My wife fell sick, so I stepped away from the Navy to take care of her. By the time she passed away, the commission was given to someone else. I decided to retire and join the private sector." He looked at the other two women. "The point is that these people will be right back in the battle we took them from."

"Or make them fugitives in the meantime."

Tanglwyst looked at Cassandra. "Does anyone else know about the missive regarding the Army and commandeering the wood for the siege engines?"

Cassandra nodded. "I told everyone so they could make the shelters properly."

Captain Nesbit sighed. "Then yes, it would be desertion, or at least dodging the conscription. It would only have worked if we had not landed here."

There was silence for a moment. Then Cassandra glanced at her desk. "I'm not sure you have."

Rebecca looked at her, then at the petards. "Yeah. I'm not sure you have either. And I've been here all day. In fact," she stood, stretching, "I need to stretch my legs, Cassandra. Do you need anything from your house?"

Cassandra looked only at Rebecca. "Yes. I think my Harbormaster's log book is up there. Would you mind checking for it? I seem to have misplaced it so it may take *asking around* to see if anyone has seen it. I can't log any ship arrivals without it."

"Shame that recent storm cost us some supplies. Did you get those recorded?"

Cassandra smiled. "Why do you think I need that log?"

Rebecca left without acknowledging Tanglwyst or Captain Nesbit and Cassandra sat behind her desk and pulled out a Harbormaster's Log. She began writing down a few things like lumber, water barrels, and sacks of sawdust under a heading of "Storm Losses".

Essentially, everything necessary to make temporary shelters for about fifty families.

Tanglwyst and Captain Nesbit stepped out of the office and went to the ship. Rebecca was speaking to the petard operator and several people on the shore. He glanced at the ship, then nodded. He spoke to several other people in the platform preparing to head up. They all disembarked and those caring for children shifted back towards the ship. Quietly, Tanglwyst and Captain Nesbit got people settled for a two-day trip.

A few men went to the Harbormaster's Office and came out with a list a few minutes later. People were directed to stacks of lumber and oiled sacks that probably contained the sawdust. Supplies were loaded as more St. Giles townsfolk returned to the docks.

Tanglwyst felt a pang of concern from inside warring with the relief and joy at being able to help her friends and family. When the pang didn't recede, she focused upon it. Her eyes grew wide and she braced herself.

Alexander was in trouble.

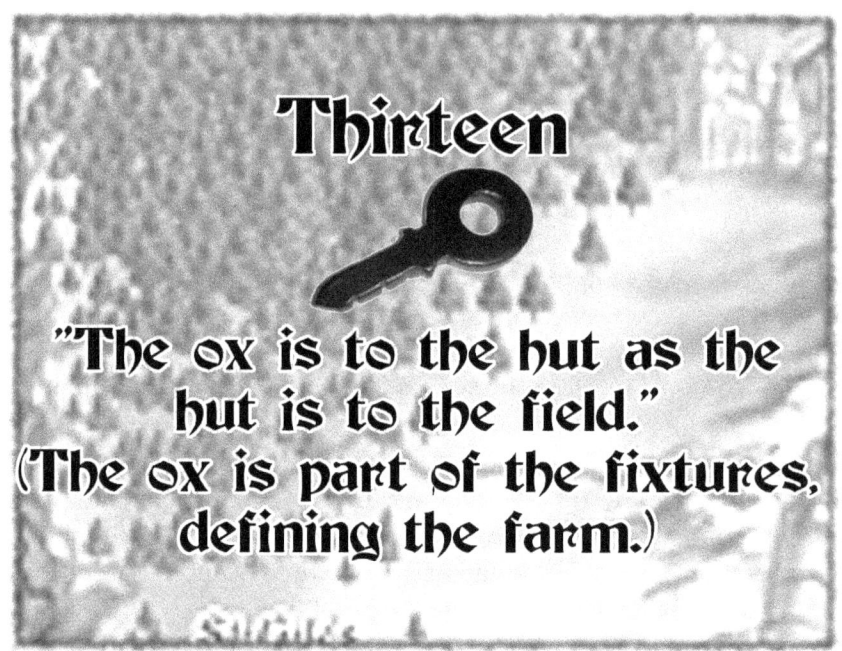

Thirteen

"The ox is to the hut as the hut is to the field."
(The ox is part of the fixtures, defining the farm.)

Alexander looked at the Fae general and bowed. "General."

Johner returned the bow. "What brings you to the encampment?"

"I left my jacket here last night. I wanted to retrieve it before any Fae went… near…" Alexander gestured towards the pavilion where the four of them had dined the night before. He was genuinely surprised to see the extent of the damage. He knew it was burnt, just not to what degree.

"I'm afraid you're too late." Johner folded his arms. "Fae lives were in fact lost to the coat. The garment and the residue from it were destroyed with fire."

The image flashed in Alexander's mind of the black sludge Gwen had become and the horror he felt when he realized he had destroyed her. The image caused a shudder and threw off his entire plan. He swallowed, closing his eyes against the memory. "I am so sorry. I…"

Johner gave Alexander a moment to recover before speaking. "Why don't you tell me what really happened instead of what you planned to say."

Alexander felt like he was a child again, trying to hide the fact he and Charles had slipped their guards and gone to see the notorious Giovanni. *He's a thousand years old. What did I really expect?* "When I left last night, I fear I was distracted. Freeing Tanglwyst was uppermost on my mind. We had also reached a peace with Her Majesty of Krakte. When I left, it was after one of the longest days I have ever spent on my feet."

He gestured to the burnt remnants of the grand pavilion. "I don't know how to make amends here. I almost returned when I realized I had left the jacket, but my mother stopped me. With the escalation and the shouts of orders from you taking control of the Krakten Army, she refused to let me come." He straightened, taking a deep breath. "But I'm here before you now. What do you need from me to make this right?"

Johner waved away Alexander's martyrdom. "This was not your doing, my friend. The coat never left my attention from the moment I saw it upon you. I had just spoken to a guard to keep all Fae away from the thing until you retrieved it. I had observers watching the entire exchange. Once your mother arrived, everything seemed to calm. That was when I set the guards to watch the coat, after you left your chair to move closer to the couple."

"So, you *knew* it was here and you let me leave it?"

"I wasn't about to touch it to return it and neither would any of the army. I don't know how *your* military is run, but our orders can't be denied. It is in the nature of the Fae soldier to always be a soldier. The coat would not have been touched.

"No, this was murder."

Alexander frowned. *"Murder?"*

Johner nodded. "Oh most, assuredly. I heard a trumpet sound right before the incident."

Alexander didn't understand. "A trumpet?"

Johner nodded. "Small, light, almost non-existent. But the rabbit-eared scouts heard it. I only knew something was happening because of the sense of the divine which seeped into the area. Otherwise, I simply would have assumed you were doing something with your townsfolk. By the way, are they all to safety?"

Alexander sighed. *Of course he knows about our efforts. He has archers that can shoot geese half a mile in the air and hear conversations on the other side of the valley. What was I thinking?* "Those that would leave."

"I approve of this. You did not have to hurry. I would have given you time to remove the non-combatants."

"I should have guessed that." Alexander shrugged. "I'm just not as good at this as you."

Johner smiled. "That is clear, and truly should have been expected. I am, after all, a bit older than you."

"I'll not underestimate you again."

"How far away are they?"

"Tanglwyst took them and my mother to the south. She didn't say where."

Johner arched an eyebrow.

Alexander squirmed, grimacing in guilt. "But I can sense them in the next village south, next to the cliffs."

"Then we shall keep our skirmish confined to the valley."

"Thank you, sir." Alexander shook off the sense of being chastised as he remembered what Johner had said. "You said you heard a trumpet?"

Johner nodded. "Yes. By the time I realized what was going on, it was too late. Since neither you nor your companions are really the trumpeting type, and you simply do not possess this concentration of divine energy, it can only be a direct attack upon us from Heaven."

Alexander felt his blood chill. Could his refusal to do Brigit's bidding be behind all this? He had to admit that Brigit's guidance towards Tanglwyst had been the right path, *and* he still felt this was a violation, especially since it cost some soldiers their lives.

By all the saints, Brigit, please tell me this was not your work.

"I will find out what happened."

Johner nodded. "Indeed you shall. But tell me, are there any more of those weapons amongst your people?" Johner motioned to the burnt-out husk of the tent.

"No, of course not."

"Good." Johner turned to the half-ogres nearby. "Seize him."

Alexander felt panic stab at him and he stepped back, preparing to flee. He felt Tanglwyst take notice of his state and tried to push the fear back. *If she returned because of this...*

The giant men reached for him and Alexander's shipboard instincts took a moment to manifest. The first one grabbed him but his Power flared and the creature drew back a burning hand. Alexander started to run for the town. He knew the church would keep him safe and that was where he needed to be to talk to Brigit anyway.

Several large half-Fae were crossing the road and the two guards behind him shouted in Krakten. They stopped, unwittingly causing a complete block of the road, and Alexander veered to the right. He ran through the tents there, leaping over a snarl of overlapping tent ropes. He came to a mess too high to hurdle and he looked around.

The Forest!

Alexander heard Tanglwyst's suggestion as if she were shouting it next to him. He nodded and ran for the woods.

He caught whiff of the nettles on the breeze right before a stabbing pain through his right calf toppled him to the ground. He fell, skinning his elbows and knees, and getting a gash on his cheek. He turned back to look and saw a hole gushing blood. Nearby, a headless arrow lay pegged into the ground, tip to fletching covered in blood. It wasn't even finished and it took him down.

He tried to get up and another hit the ground, penetrating the same hole. He screamed, pinned, as the half-ogre guards caught up to him.

Brigit, the patron saint of healers, opened her eyes. It was dark but she saw something she had forgotten and it took her a moment to understand what she was looking at.

Stars.

She thought about moving but that caused such great pain, she decided not to do that again for a while. Instead, she listened.

No sound reached her. No breeze. No bird. No insect. She determined she must be in Hell for there to truly be nothing around. No animals to chew upon her helpless body. She tried to move and was stabbed with a thousand swords of pain, but she took comfort in the fact that the effort emitted a sound as she groaned and the ground crunched beneath her.

She turned her head to the right and saw Giles and Clara in similar states. There were enormous clouds of dust still hanging in the air around the three of them but amazingly, there was no blood. Brigit tried to speak but her lungs held no air.

She did the only thing she could. She prayed.

George.

George, can you hear me?

It's Brigit.

But she felt no connection to Heaven at all. She had been cut off.

Good riddance.

She didn't know how she felt just then, or if this was truly her point of view now. She had been a Heaven Worshiper her whole life and for centuries after her death. She felt like it would take a lot to rob her of her faith.

Yeah, like maybe being cast from Heaven because a petulant angel wants to destroy the world?

Well, yes. That just might do it.

She heard the crunch of movement from the other two piles of flesh and turned to look at them. It took an eternity for them to move to look at her and when they did, they all made the effort to hold each other's hands. As the sky started to lighten, she heard a sound like a cart rolling over dust. A man came into view, about fifty-five years old, wearing simple robes of homespun cloth. He looked over her, then over her companions. He walked over to Brigit and pushed back the cowl on his head.

"Brigit?" He looked at the others. "Giles?"

He frowned, then settled into a crouch to look her over. "If this is what it looks like, you're all going to have to deal with a few things. First off, you're healing right now. If I try to move you, it would be like trying to move a sack of soup. You need to knit your bones back together. The good news is that you'll have time. Brace yourself. I need to make a few adjustments."

He ran his hands firmly along Brigit's entire body. Every once in a while, he shifted something, causing her to flinch. He pointed to her face. "That's good. That you can feel that is good. It means there's no permanent damage."

After he had aligned her entire body, he moved over to Giles, then Clara. After the sun was well above the horizon, he walked back to her and placed a large stone by her head. He put a second one on the other side.

"I can't do much, but this will help. It will rain soon. It always rains."

He put a piece of cloth over her mouth, poking a little into it so it touched her tongue. He did likewise to the others.

"Keep this off your nose, if you can. You won't die but you won't like it."

Then he got a shovel from his cart. He started digging around her and covering her in the dirt.

"This will protect you from the weather, but more important, it will keep you in place so you don't move and heal wrong. Trust me. You don't want to have to rebreak anything to get it to work right."

He got a light layer of dirt over her before it started to rain. He then moved a little quicker, trying to get the body cast formed before he was scooping mud. He didn't make it and before long, he was filthy.

The rag in her mouth collected water and she realized that she was, in fact, very thirsty. She let water collect in her mouth, then bit the cloth to swallow. The man saw what she did and smiled.

"That's smart. That's very smart. Hey, you two. When you want to drink, bite the cloth first. Then you won't swallow it."

Clara mumbled something and he leaned in, then straightened up.

"You're welcome, my dear." He stood and looked at the three of them. "We're going to be here a while but it's okay. I've been through this before. Though I have to admit, when it happened to me," he gestured to the crater around them, "it wasn't with this level of rage."

She tried to smile and even that hurt. But it was worth it to interact with the man saving her life. He knelt down beside her again and wiped some rain from her forehead.

"Don't worry. I won't leave you."

She started to cry. She tried her voice again and this time, it worked.

"Thank you, Raymond."

He smiled and nodded, then sat in his cart to rest.

Fourteen

"The crop is to the lion as the cloud is to the moon."
(The crop hides the lion.)

Catriona opened her eyes, surprised to find herself laying down in a strange bed. She turned to look around and saw the life-sized painting of herself near Myrgen's silhouette at the window. He looked at her as she shifted, coming over to sit beside her on the tiny bed.

"How are you doing?" He smoothed back a stray hair caught in her eyelash.

She frowned, sitting up. "I fell asleep?"

"Hard. When you started snoring into my shoulder instead of sobbing, I took it as a welcome change. You didn't even stir when I laid you down."

She wiped her eyes, finding them lightly crusted with salt. "Crying takes a lot out of you."

He smiled. "I know. Trust me. This isn't the first time that's happened in this room."

She smiled and then nodded to the window. "What were you looking at?"

"The town. I can still see the scars from the battle against Cipriano."

She watched his eyes and realized that view also looked onto the street in front of the church where Gwen had died. James had lit the toxic sludge that had once been his sister on fire to destroy it, burning away all trace of her.

Myrgen frowned. "What are you thinking?"

She glanced at the window, her brow furrowing. "Raven said that Dominic took Elizabeth somewhere with an amulet, and that there was 'Fae-killing poison' left behind."

"Elizabeth was part Fae." Myrgen closed his eyes. "I thought I almost understood him there but he was rambling." He looked at her again, shaking his head. "I thought I would ask him to explain it later but, honestly, I've never had a follow-up conversation with him that explained away a damned thing."

She nodded. "Dominic used an amulet to move Elizabeth's body to Alexander and he got some of her on Tanglwyst's coat. If he's in St. Giles, with the Fae army..."

Myrgen snarled. "How many Fae can he kill with that stuff?"

"All of them."

He thought for a second, then nodded. "Because it perpetuates."

She nodded, then looked away, pain on her face. "But Alexander wouldn't... would he?"

Myrgen stood and walked back to the window. He leaned on the sill. "There was a time when I would have said no. Alexander was a healer and would never hurt someone. But that's... that's not him anymore. Do you know who that 'Johner' individual was that Raven mentioned?"

"The Voice of Command. There are scrolls on the Fae Lords and their lieutenants in the study. He is the right hand of Corrigan, the Midsummer King."

"I know about him from Augustinian Mass. Michael the Archangel is his holy counterpart." He turned to face her again. "Catriona, there's a General who studied with my father in the Mervol Military Academy. His name is Aethelraed Rhydderch. The Northern Yorkish spelling was so convoluted, his teachers and colleagues had a lot of trouble with it. He eventually earned the name Blackheart because of his ruthlessness when it came to war games."

"He sounds like a monster."

Myrgen shook his head, folding his arms across his chest. "Quite the opposite. He was a very noble man, according to my father. But he would exploit any weakness to reach your surrender. When my father retired after my youngest brother was born, he would come by and play games with us. He was kind to us, but he would never give any quarter to my father in board games. Dad didn't mind. He said Raed would always temper the victories with spirits so my father lost graciously and Raed did likewise."

Catriona smiled. Myrgen felt genuine affection for this ruthless strategist. "You love him."

"Yes. He would not have been my father's friend had he been unworthy. It was him that made sure the woman who tried to break up my parents disappeared. I like to think she was simply sent away somewhere, but the truth is that she's likely either dead or a slave." He shrugged. "Last autumn, I would have said I aspired to be him."

"And now?"

He pushed off the wall and went to her, going on one knee before her. "I would not be where I am this second without his influence, but I'm happy to leave that behind to protect these people around us. I know, if necessary, I can be that ruthless against our enemies. I just have a reason now *not* to be." He kissed her hand. "Face it, Catriona. You saved my life."

She kissed him, a full, deep kiss that filled her heart. He gave as good as he got and she felt the sadness of her losses lessen just a bit. "Thank you."

"I'm pretty sure I'm the one in *your* debt."

She sighed, then turned serious. "So, this Raed Blackheart, you think he'll use the méreg against the Fae?"

"Méreg?"

"The sludge."

He nodded. "If he has a weapon that will defeat that army, he'll use it." He watched her eyes a moment. "What do you want to do?"

She paused, then took a steadying breath. "We need to talk to Raven. He was there with Alexander. He may know if the soldiers have arrived yet."

"And if they have?"

She frowned. "Then we are already too late."

Myrgen and Catriona entered the hallway and saw Selig sitting outside Raven's room. They looked at each other, confused.

"Selig?"

Selig looked up and stood. "Stâpâna, Stâpân."

Myrgen glanced at the closed door. "Is he asleep?"

Selig snorted. "I doubt it. Not that I think sleeping would in any way shut him up."

Catriona and Myrgen both relaxed. Myrgen opened the door and the couple went in.

"And then Aiden took the Soulless touch from me, and it, well, it actually killed *him*." Raven looked at Myrgen and Catriona. "Oh, hi there! I was just telling this little fella about the Soulless War." He gestured to a ladybug on the wall.

Myrgen blinked and nodded. "What did he say?"

"I don't think he believes I was there."

"It's a pretty big expectation that it should trust such a claim."

Raven frowned. "When I was a young mage, insects *believed* me when I told them things."

"Clearly, you've lost your credibility amongst their nation."

Catriona smirked. "Um, while you are trying to find where you had your misstep with the entire bug kingdom, can you tell me if there was a human army with Alexander when you saw him?"

"Human? No. He didn't even have his own tent."

That stopped the conversation for a moment as both Catriona and Myrgen tried to sort out the relevance of that comment. Myrgen recovered first out of sheer exposure.

"Did you hear anything about when they would arrive?"

Raven frowned. "Probably. But by then I was in York again." He looked up. "You were there." He pointed to Catriona with a knuckle. "And you," and to the bug, "and you…"

She closed her eyes and sighed. "I think I'm tired."

Myrgen nodded. "He does that."

"Wait." Raven looked at them. "Why are you asking about the Mervol Army?"

Catriona looked back at him. "Because they have that Fae poison you mentioned and someone willing to use it."

Raven sat up. "They do? I thought it was destroyed."

"You said some got on a coat."

"Well, yeah, but Alexander said he wouldn't…" Raven's brow furrowed in concern.

Myrgen folded his arms. "And you believed him?"

"Well, of course. I mean, he spoke to Clara in the church and everything."

Catriona stood baffled by the comment, stunned into silence. Myrgen just guided her away from the strange man, nodding to the bug.

"I think he asked you a question."

Raven looked at the bug. "I'm so sorry. What did you say?"

They left the mage to his conversation and headed to bed.

"You okay?" Myrgen closed the bedroom door behind them.

"Why do you ask?" Catriona started unbuckling her belt.

"You didn't say a thing coming from Raven's room. Does it bother you that he's here? Because I will drag his carcass behind a horse all the way to the border of York if he's a problem."

She smiled, shaking her head. "Thank you, but no. It is not necessary to remove him. He's not a problem for me."

"He's a problem for *me.*"

She stepped over and put her arms around his waist. "I love that about you."

"I lost you because of that monster."

"And you'll lose me again because of another. But now we know how to combat the change. You can't hold grudges like this. It will ruin you."

"Don't tell me who I can and can't protect you from." He softened the chide with a smile, and held her close.

"There will be far too many enemies in the coming months to waste time on one who is not a threat to us."

Myrgen kissed the top of her head. "Fine. But only because there are worse creatures in the world than him right now."

"And I can understand those when they speak."

"And we can understand those when they speak, yes."

She sighed and sagged into him. "I know why he did not stay as Stâpân. He had someone he loved, someone he wanted to be with when he died. To be the Stâpân to a Dûcesa is to become immortal."

She's remembering him. That's why she doesn't fear him. She's remembering when he was her Stâpân.

But the Stâpân alone was not immortal. It was only as the incarnation of Hunter to the Bringer that death could not claim them, but the truth was that he still found it all so large. He did not need to add more weight to the moment for either of them. He knew he was the Hunter, and he knew she was the Bringer, even if she did not want to say it out loud. The stones had disappeared inside her and had not reappeared. He had not checked the Meditation Chamber for them, but he somehow knew she still had them all. Raven had shaped them with magic into a single stone, combining a history of memories.

"How much more do you remember from your previous incarnations?"

She exhaled, stepping back from him. "I have not sifted through them. I know there are holes, gaps of darkness, but I also know all I have to do is concentrate to recover them. I simply…" She sighed.

"Don't want to?"

"Not yet. I know, when I need it, they will be there. I don't want to need it yet because it will change me. It may be temporary, or it may linger for eons. I am not ready to be that person yet."

"What person do you want to be now?"

She turned to him. "I want to be the person in that bed with you inside me."

Myrgen knew what she meant. They had been dead. Now they wanted to be alive.

He kissed her, drinking in her breath and giving her his. Their clothes barely survived the process of removal as the tone became more intense with each touch.

They made love, a pure, desperate coupling that pushed away the world for a single hour. Afterwards, they drifted to sleep, exhausted physically as well as emotionally.

When Myrgen awoke, Catriona was in a hearth chair by the fire. Her silhouette revealed she wore a robe and was awake. She turned to him as he sat up.

"Can't sleep?"

She shook her head. "I've been thinking. We are going to have to take the field against Mervolingia. The méreg will not affect our warriors."

"Are you sure your citizens will be willing to risk that? Gwen had a Fae connection that was hidden from the world. How many of your people have the same thing?"

"Citizens? Undoubtedly several. As Land worshippers, they have no problem with the Fae and a few innkeepers and millers have Good Neighbors."

"Is that a particular type of Fae?"

She nodded. "The ones that keep weevils out of your flour or keep the house tidy. If you notice them, they will flee so you leave out offerings and leave the place empty regularly. The kitchen below has a fleet of them, which is why it is always clean and smells like baking bread."

"So, why would they risk that to join the army? Or are you not planning on telling them the danger?"

"It will not matter to them."

"Are they so devoted to the country that they will betray their Fae friends?"

"Caratia does not conscript their people to fight their wars. That would be inappropriate."

He frowned. "My love, you are being cryptic. I have been here for a while and have seen no evidence of a standing army."

She smiled. Her eyes glittered emerald in the firelight. "That is because you have never been to the war room."

Myrgen and Catriona stepped out of her room and she led him to the study. They entered and she nodded to the doors. He closed them as she went to the hearth of the giant fireplace.

"There are reasons why the Caratian Army is undefeated in the history of the Saintlands. One, their armor is blessed by the Land. If the weapon is forged of ore taken from the soil, it cannot penetrate the armor."

She pressed her hand to a stone and a secret passage opened behind the hearth.

"Two, the army is part of one another. They share a bond that allows them to communicate, regardless of the distance separating them. Even obstacles do not interfere."

Behind the hearth was a stairway that led down into the castle. The stones ran with the thin line of lava, providing enough light to show the stairs but nothing else. After a moment, the stairs ended at a large chamber doorway.

As they stepped into the room beyond, the glow of Ashstone increased, illuminating row upon row of metal and stone statues. Some were on horses, some so heavily armored, it would be impossible to get up if they fell, and all with vicious looking weapons. The armor all looked like monsters of legend, from gryphons to dragons to minotaurs.

"And three, they are not human."

Every statue turned to look at her as her eyes turned to jade.

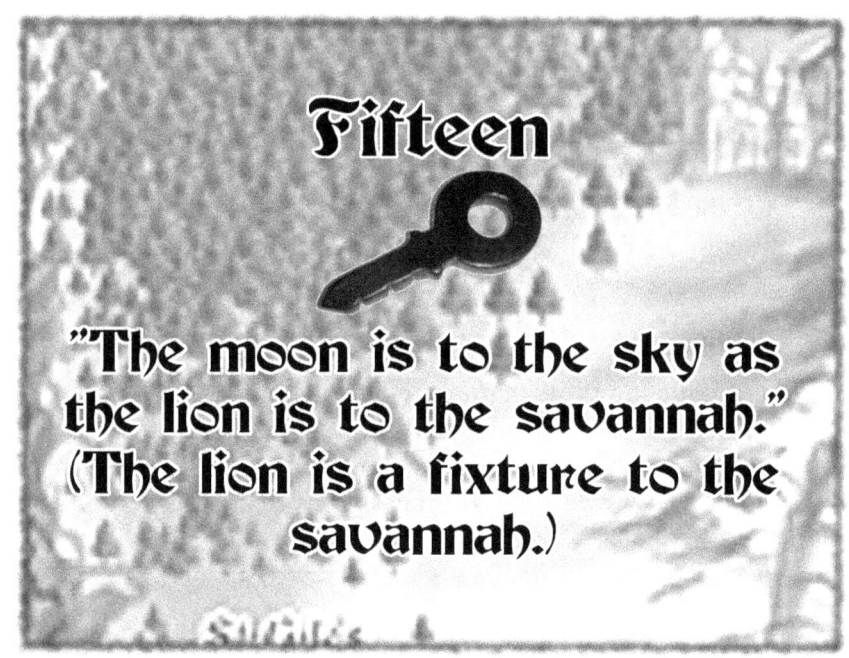

Fifteen

"The moon is to the sky as the lion is to the savannah." (The lion is a fixture to the savannah.)

Catriona closed the door behind Myrgen.

"I need a drink." He went up the stairs. In the study, he poured brandy into a glass and drank it without offering her any. He took a few deep breaths to steady himself before pointing at her with his glass and raised pinky.

"I've seen that before, you know."

"The army?"

"The *eyes.*" He poured another glass and downed it.

"I'm not sure that's the right way to drink that. You lose the flavor. Here." She went to another set of bottles and pulled one with a long, sweeping neck like a swan. She uncorked it and poured into a fresh glass.

He replaced the brandy glass in his hand and swallowed the fluid. "Don't distract me." He winced as the alcohol burn consumed him. His face flushed and his eyes got wet and shiny. He swallowed, which didn't seem to help. "Wow." He looked at the glass in his hand and steadied himself on the desk. "Has it always been this bright in here?"

"Well, that drink does amplify things. It helps you cope with difficult concepts."

"Like living stone monsters."

She raised her eyebrows and shrugged.

He frowned. "Glad to see you keep it handy. Clearly this is a common occurrence."

She rubbed the back of her neck. "Common enough that the kitchen has the recipe." She walked to the hearth stone and closed the passage.

He was silent a moment. When she turned back to him, he was looking at her again. "And they are on our side?"

"They serve the Land, just as you and I do." She walked over and poured herself a glass from the swan-necked bottle.

"And how are they activated? Is it a trait of the Dûcesa or what?"

"It is the action of the Stâpân or Stâpâna. You control them too."

He straightened, setting the glass on the desk. "Then why did they look at you?"

"Because I reached out to them first. And because I knew about them. You did not, so you did not know your role with them." She took a drink from her glass and gestured to the chairs by the desk. "But their purpose is the same as yours: To protect our people."

He glanced at the hearth now like it had betrayed him by hiding this secret all this time. "How many are there?"

"As many as needed to end the conflict. They do not have a number. The Land releases them as they are needed. It also takes them wherever they must go."

"And because they don't need to eat or rest, they don't stop. What happens if they are destroyed?"

"Another forms."

"And their armor?"

"Inherent."

"So it can't be removed and worn by our enemies."

She shook her head.

"Which is why no one knows about the armor's properties."

She sat, watching him. "Yes."

He gritted his teeth behind his lips, shaking his head. "I always wondered why there was never a single suit of Caratian armor *anywhere*. Countries had fought them before and been beaten by them, but there was never a trophy suit in a throne room or church. Allies didn't have any ancient suits like they did every other place in the world." He pointed to the north. "The Queen of York has a full armory on display of every kind of warrior including Yokotaman armor and *she* doesn't possess Caratian plate. There are very few illustrations of it either, mainly because of the lack of extant suits and survivors." He leaned on the desk, shaking his head. "I'm sorry. This is going against everything I have been taught about avoiding witchcraft."

She frowned with her eyes and smiled with her lips. "You met *Lucifer* last week."

"And that did not unsettle me like this is."

She relaxed and drank her liqueur, letting him muddle through it.

"How hard is this going to hit me?" He raised his glass.

"Not bad. The brandy will win that fight."

"Better boost its combatants then." He finished the glass. He walked around to sit beside her. "And they won't be affected by the méreg?" He nodded as she confirmed this. "Because the Land doesn't accept it into the soil, like the blood of the unworthy."

He looked at the hearth again, his body reading acceptance. He exhaled and looked at her again. "Your eyes changed. That isn't a good thing."

She leaned forward, her elbows on her knees. "It felt… different. I still knew myself, but I could *see* something more."

"What?"

She thought a minute, then closed her eyes, shaking her head. "I can't find it. I know it's in there but it is…"

"Was it from the Soulless War?"

"No. But it was *because* of it. The army is not one I have ever commanded, but Drake was alive the last time it was employed. Anika had to make a statement to some Papal threat."

"From the Pope before Gregory. I remember that. I was a boy but I remember Father had to go to war near Toledo. They fought the Caratian army on the desert of York."

"They thought our mountains contained gems."

"Do they?"

"Oh yes. But they are not the thing that the army protected. There are forging fires utilized by Toledo. The Church tried to appropriate them. The Land could not allow this. Turning the fires into holy beings would have either destroyed the forges or destroyed the bond between

114

the Land and the ore worked within them. The creatures of the Land would have been helpless."

"So, they made it about the gems to throw off the scent."

"It was Anika's idea. She had a wagon captured by the Papal forces that carried a chest of uncut gemstones. Once they were analyzed, it was determined this was how Caratia was paying for its weaponry. It changed the way they looked at the war. They no longer cared about the forges and focused upon the gems."

"They never tried again?"

She snorted. "They committed every soldier to this cause. They only now have enough people to protect their city, almost twenty years later. They had to raise their forces from infancy to restore their numbers and they could not recruit from the surrounding area. York worships Calista and Krakte worships the Fae. Their only hope was Mande and Mervolingia. Mervol forces had just taken many losses, and Mande takes care of Mande first. The barrier against *those* people was employed regularly in the ensuing decade."

Myrgen looked at his empty glass. "That's why they needed a new way in."

She nodded.

They fell silent, both feeling the absence of Drake and Anika right then. Drake's papers were still on the desk, letters he was writing when he and Anika returned from bringing Tib home. In their bedroom, Catriona knew Anika still had needlework half finished. There was a sense of loss again and Catriona drained her glass before she started crying.

"I am going to return to bed. Try to sleep again. Are you coming or staying here?"

"I think I'm going to stay here for a bit. I need to assess how this changes things." He reached out and took her hand. "I love you. I worry about you." He kissed her fingers.

"I love you. And thank you for worrying. But I think we are safe from you losing me again."

"I'm sure Slade felt the same way."

She had no reply for that, so she kissed him and went to bed.

"Lucifer?"

The First Dûcesa stepped into the hallway of Lucifer's mansion. Her voice carried throughout the building and a moment later, Lucifer's head poked out of the study where they had dined.

"My lady?" He stepped into the hallway, a glass of brandy in his hand. "Did you forget something?"

She nodded. "I believe I did." She went to him and kissed him.

He separated from her, stepping back. "Wait, what are you doing?"

She furrowed her brow. "I… thought…"

"That I was helping you to get something out of you?"

She blinked at him, her face solidifying into her own certainty. "What? No. I thought about the evening I just spent here. It was…"

Lucifer seemed to have learned his lesson about interrupting and waited as she muddled through her own thoughts. He gestured to the study, then raised his glass in a question, all without filling the air with commentary that would distract her. She shook her head.

She sat, putting her hands in her lap. "This evening was very pleasant. I wanted to thank you. You see, I have been in this place for a very long time. My activities have become routine to the point where they no longer work." She glanced at the ceiling, settling back a bit and stroking the sofa. "This is different. *This,*" she patted the furniture, "and that," she pointed to the brandy, "all of it had been different. Summerland is a paradise for those who die in service to the Land. We can be with our loved ones, fulfill our lifelong dreams, live out our lives. When we are done, we move on.

"But I don't move on. I have watched my loved ones come and go until I have no one left to recognize. Even my successor went on. But I have remained."

She gestured to him. "You have given me pause. I spent this evening with you and listened to your tale. It seemed to go on forever," she smiled as he gave her an embarrassed nod, and she reached out and touched his hand, "but it was new, and very welcome. So, thank you. But it made me realize I have been trapping myself here, hoping for something that simply can't happen. I'm never going to see Slade again. He won't be returning from that place and if he did, he wouldn't be the same. He can't hold me here anymore."

Lucifer nodded. "So, is this goodbye then?" He gestured to the doorway. "Is that what that was?"

She smirked. "Is that what it felt like?"

"Nope. It felt like you wanted to start something. I just wasn't sure what or why."

She nodded, tilting her head to look at him. "I've had people check on me periodically when they get here. They go around and meet everyone they don't know. I've formed friendships and been happy and sad when they have moved on. But none of that made me feel *different*. None of them changed my outlook. I simply kept prodding my own wounds, attempting to stay just miserable enough to never leave.

"This place is a little slice of something I have never encountered and it has turned my attention from just waiting, to wanting to explore. I want to *do* things. New things that have nothing to do with hurting."

"And what if those things make you move on?"

She took a deep breath. "Then I guess I move on. But until that moment," she shifted closer to him, "I would like to feel something other than pain."

Lucifer reached out and touched her face and she pressed into his palm.

"Far be it from me to deny a lady. Or a gentleman for that measure."

She laughed and her world felt brighter for it.

Catriona felt something grab her arms and legs, then lift her into the air. She twisted, trying to get free but whatever had hold of her took away all her leverage. Her limbs were stretched, pain filling them like she would be ripped apart. Right before her limbs tore, the pulling stopped, suspending her in the dark.

Then the pain started to fade. She tried to move, thinking she was going numb, but the restraints were all encompassing. Her pain didn't renew with her efforts like she expected and instead, she felt her pain and consciousness slipping from her. It ran up the restraints, carried away to something she couldn't perceive. She tried to cry out for Myrgen, but her voice sputtered less than a whisper before it, too, was gone.

She felt her body die and as her spirit left it, she felt something around her, connected to the restraints.

There was a darkness, and a light. Away. Beyond. There was no other word for it.

She reached out to it.

There was the briefest hint of contact.

Then she was in a room of lava and stone.

Before her was a behemoth and it was on a knee before her, head and body bowed in supplication.

She nodded to it from a place above the creature and it stood. Though it towered above the ground, it was never above her. All that was above her then was that other entity, the dark and the light.

She knew the behemoth's name.

It was the Land.

Catriona opened her eyes. The room was quiet and she was alive and alone. The room was still mostly dark, but she could see the beginnings of twilight shooing away the weaker stars. She sat up and tried to remember what the dream was about. There were very familiar aspects of it, but she did not remember ever having that dream before. The place of lava and stone were…

She flashed upon seeing a bier of rocks covering her son's body, but it was all normal Ashstone earth, stones provided for the purpose of protecting his body and waiting for her to return to commit him to the ground.

And then, it wasn't.

Superimposed over the image was the vision of a chamber of broken, jagged volcanic glass with orange fire and golden lava moving between them. The chamber was dark and had the feel of being buried beneath a huge amount of earth. The only light was that provided by the hot, flowing streams. Ash and sparks floated in the air and the smell was that of a forge, fire and metal in one scent.

Every time she returned home after sailing most of the year, she would spend time in the Meditation Chamber, communing with the Land like every Stâpân and Stâpâna before her. The time in the chamber steadied her sea legs, removing the nausea common for the first week home to many sailors. Part of why they would turn around and sign back up on a different ship was to avoid that sensation. When you were at sea, being on solid ground felt *wrong*.

So she would come in there, commune with the Land, then leave, steady as a literal rock. But she *never remembered anything that happened within.* Nothing. Not a prayer, not a stretch, nothing. She walked in the room a little wobbly, and out minutes, hours, or days later completely acclimated. Everyone who ever used the chamber felt a connection to the Land in there, but they could remember the time spent in it, even other Stâpâns. She was the only one who couldn't.

She had not shared that with anyone. The fact that she remembered that Raven was brought by the Land to her now struck her as strange. She *remembered* Raven being in the Chamber with her. She had not even noticed the difference between this time and every other encounter with the Chamber.

No. That's not true. When I returned the first time, after I died, I remembered Tib. I remembered my son. I remembered Myrgen sitting by the bier. I remembered the room. But it was so natural, such a part of me then, it was not confusing.

She got up and looked at her robe. She arched an eyebrow at the thought of donning *again* a piece of clothing she had used more tonight than in the previous year, and dismissed it. If she was going to do this, it was time for pants.

Sixteen

"The rain is to the cloud as the blood is to the ox." (The rain fills the cloud like blood.)

Myrgen heard Catriona's door open and close and he stood up, walking to the hallway to see if she was coming back to the study. He saw her heading for the stairs.

"Hey. I thought you were going back to bed." He looked her over.

"I thought I was too. But I had a dream and now I'm going to check on something."

"You want company?"

"Yes. But more than just you."

Myrgen put his hand on his chest, feigning hurt. "Suddenly, I'm not enough for you?"

She smiled and kissed his cheek. "Bring Raven to the Meditation Chamber."

He frowned. "At this hour?"

She thought about it. "He won't be any more coherent in the morning."

Myrgen shrugged. "True enough." He went off towards the Iron Archway corridor.

Catriona went upstairs to the third floor and listened to her boots echo off the walls. According to Myrgen, Tib had been cut down here, but she knew there was nothing left of him here. Haunted places rarely existed where the Land was worshipped, thanks to Summerland. If a ghost were to walk these halls, it would not be because a worshipper fell here, but because the fallen had no access to their own afterlife. She wondered if she should have Lucifer come through and collect the souls of the Mandian invasion.

The doors opened easily, despite the size of them. Built right into the mountain, they did not have the same limitations of the rest of the rooms. They covered a hole in the cliff face that she now observed seemed to be made of the same stone. It fit so completely, it was clearly part of the cliff in the beginning. When they were closed, the doors looked impenetrable, and in truth, they actually were.

She entered the chamber and was met with simple, smooth, Ashstone construction. It wasn't too warm, there was no smell save the stone itself, and the meditation area was uncomplicated with predetermined furniture. It was a small rise against a wall, nothing more. The room was lit like every other room in Ashstone.

And yet…

She looked around the room.

Raven was right. There was a throne here, and that behemoth. There was lava and ash, sparks in the air and a smell of...

The room flashed and she stood before a shelf in the stone, lava and fire everywhere. The air was hot and dry and full of sparks. There was a presence there, all around her, but nothing else was in the room. She heard a noise behind her and turned to see Myrgen and Raven coming through the doors. They stopped, looking around.

Raven scratched his forehead. "Well, this is better."

Myrgen looked at him. "It is?"

"Yes. It proves I'm not crazy."

Myrgen opened his mouth to protest but Catriona walked over. "You can both see this?"

Myrgen nodded, looking in her eyes. "Black, glassy, fire. Yeah. Not just you."

Raven looked around. "Did you find the Pillar?"

Catriona looked around the room. "I don't see anything like that. Can you?"

He shrugged. "It's probably something you have to summon."

Catriona hesitated.

Myrgen put his hand on her shoulder. "What's wrong?"

"It's just…" She waved her hand around the room. "I've never remembered anything after I've left this room. I have come here multiple times and only tonight did I realize I have never had a memory of this room until after I returned from Summerland." She looked at the shelf behind her. "Even then, it… it wasn't this."

"Hey," Raven reached out to touch Catriona.

Myrgen blocked him and punched him hard in the chest, knocking him back several steps. Raven fell and sputtered up blood. He coughed, spitting onto the hot lava around them, causing steam to rise where it hit. The air got a tinge of copper to it.

Raven tapped his chest. "…still stabbed… here… not better…"

Catriona started to move towards him but Myrgen pressed her back. "I'll check. You stay away."

"Myrgen."

"I mean it." He held up his finger to her and walked over to Raven. "Please don't touch her."

Raven gave a thumbs up and nodded.

"Are you going to be alright?"

Raven shrugged.

Catriona turned to look at the shelf. "Was this where the throne was that you spoke of?"

Raven nodded, then croaked out a yes.

"Do you remember something?" Myrgen walked over to her.

"Yes. I think I can get it, but I have to do something." She looked at him. "You're not going to like it."

"Do I need to get him out of here?"

She shook her head. "No. He can't die anyway so nothing is going to be fatal."

"Can still be hurt…" Raven shifted on the ground and tried to take a few deep breaths.

Myrgen folded his arms. "What do you want to do that I'm not going to like?"

"I need to change my eye color."

Myrgen narrowed his eyes. "Alright. I'll be right here."

She nodded and looked at the shelf. She tried to imagine a great volcanic glass throne thrust up through the shelf.

Nothing happened.

"I feel foolish."

"Why?"

"Because I'm trying to imagine myself as a god."

"Try imagining yourself as a servant."

She glanced at him and nodded. "Do you think it will work?"

Myrgen smiled. "It already has. Your eyes have been jade since the moment we came in here."

She nodded, then looked around the room. "Alright. Show me your true self."

The doors to the chamber closed, blocking off the external daylight. Lava flared and spouted on the edges of the room. A great shard of black glass pierced the ground on the shelf and a moment later, a throne half the size of Ashstone itself stood before them. On the left of it was a white crystal pillar. On the right was a kneeling stone statue.

She looked at the throne and caught a thin shimmer in the dark, like a spider thread. It blended in and she moved to find it. She walked to the throne and reached up to grab the thread. It was just out of reach so she looked down at the throne and put her knee on the seat, boosting herself up.

She wrapped her fingers around the thread. It was strong, sturdy, and went off into nowhere. She tried to discern where it was attached. She looked at the statue on the side. "Where does this go?"

The statue stood and pointed to the darkness around them. The wall beyond the flames turned translucent and showed a tower fallen amongst wild foliage.

Myrgen stepped towards the wall. "Persephone?"

Catriona followed the thread the other direction. It went to the Pillar. The Pillar changed as she focused upon it. A tall tower stood in the middle of a great forest. It rose easily a day's walk into the sky.

Raven pointed with the hand not clutching his chest. "That is Sovereignlumen."

Catriona and Myrgen both turned to face him.

Myrgen looked beyond her to the Pillar. He nodded. "That's where you almost died the first time. There's a healer there."

"But you can't go there anymore."

Raven shook his head.

She looked again at the tower in the crystal. "Fine. Myrgen, I need you to prep the army. Get them ready to go to Bordeaux. Raven, I'm going to get your answers for you."

"What do you want me to do?"

She looked down at Raven. "You will find the Giver and put her in the trap at Persephone."

She turned her gaze to the Pillar again and stepped into the Fae realm.

Myrgen and Raven started to protest but Catriona disappeared. Myrgen closed his mouth and walked away from the throne and Pillar. Raven struggled to get to his feet.

"Wait. Aren't you going to help me?"

Myrgen looked back. "You murdered the woman I love to achieve your own ends. I'm walking away without your spine in my fist. That *is* helping you."

He walked to the doors. The fire fell away and the room settled back to normal. Myrgen pushed on the stone and they opened. He strode from the room without a backwards glance.

Raven gave himself a moment to let his breathing start working again. Then he realized he was in the heart of the Land. He closed his eyes and drew healing from within the soil. His hand was covered in blood from where Myrgen ripped his stitches, but he managed to concentrate enough to pull the flesh back together. He had no idea how long he stayed there but eventually, his breathing became normal and the bleeding stopped.

He sat back on the stone and shook the feeling back into his hands and feet. He took his time and when was able to stand, it was dawn. He walked out of the Chamber and climbed onto the battlement wall. He looked over the woods of Zara, then leapt off the wall.

He caught the earth sled as the wall fell away behind him and moved quickly towards York. He needed to get Lauriel. The Fae wolf was far smarter and clear of thought than Raven. He might have an idea about what to do next.

He got to the top of the pass and stopped in the trees. He could hear animals to the west, and started moving towards them. He found the Inn and watched the children gathering vegetables and feeding the chickens. He decided not to introduce himself but rode his earth sled quietly through the trees, going too quick to be seen.

The plants in the garden sprung to full growth at his passing, and he smiled at the astonished look on the children's faces. He returned his attention to the way to York. He had left Lauriel at Persephone and he needed the Fae wolf's counsel.

Capture the Giver? Put her in the trap? Why would Catriona request such a thing?

She still looked and sounded the same, but this order felt like one she never would have given before. She seemed to have some sort of bigger picture though, and she was investigating his grandfather. Maybe… maybe there was an answer only she could get. And maybe that answer needed the Giver in the trap.

If she needed the Giver in the trap, he would find a way to put her in the trap.

James looked at the glittering castle on the mountain. Brilliant lights swam above like sea serpents with glowing rainbows on their backs. The ground was starting to get a dusting of snow upon it, but it was still warmer than he expected. He looked behind him as the sky lightened with pre-dawn. The path from his parent's home stretched through the woods, wide and easy to travel. James frowned.

"That's not a good sign."

It was still spring for at least another month, but the temperature and the path proclaimed summer. The rivers around the country would be swollen with melting snow. There would be flooding in York because of this, especially since there was no foliage to block it. Still, with the greenery that was springing up from Persephone, that may have changed. Maybe the flooding was exactly what York's countryside needed to finally shake off the curse of the Soulless War.

He had expected the trek to Gloriana's realm to take longer, and knew his mother would likely be worried. He hadn't said he was going to see the Midwinter Queen. He hadn't told her anything after letting her know about Gwen. He didn't explain what happened afterwards with Alexander. He felt his mother would not have understood that she had raised two Fae children. He had such a normal childhood. He remembered playing with the animals and Gwen, exploring the hillsides near their sheep farm, and tending the sheep. He remembered visiting town with his parents and people asking about his brothers and eventually his sisters. He always thought they were silly because it was just him and Gwen.

He sighed, pulling his jacket closer at the neck. He was ill prepared for the change in temperature. He had never had trouble functioning in even the coldest conditions so the fact he was noticing the frigid air meant he was entering Gloriana's influence. He glanced at the trees, thinking he might stuff his shirt with leaves to insulate against the chill, but any deciduous trees were bare and the rest were needles. Not helpful. He rubbed his arms, cupping his hands to breathe on them, stepping a bit quicker to increase his body's core temperature, all things he had seen sailors do in the northern voyages. He was surprised to find that helped.

Soon, he crested a small hill and saw the entire frozen kingdom before him. On the mountain was the castle, alone. There were no settlements around the base and he worried he would be scaling the mountain with frozen fingers and toes. Then the shifting lights in the sky revealed a road moving lazily up the mountain. He frowned again, concerned about the ease of access to the Fae Lord's home. Would invaders be able to get here if they wanted to?

He started down the hill and stepped through the crust of the snow on the road. He sank up to his knee. As he pulled his foot out, lamenting the snow coating his pants, the lights were blocked from helping him escape. He looked up and his gaze outlined a gigantic ice troll. Long claws and spindly appendages grew from a thin, wiry torso. It was over nine feet tall, with glowing blue eyes. The whole thing looked like glacial ice chiseled by someone who didn't like ice. The effect was a mean one.

It grabbed James' head and pushed his face into the snow. Ice crystals stabbed his eyes and he closed them against the assault. His nose was smashed to his face, forcing him to breathe through his teeth. His breath should have melted the snow but this was Fae snow and it did not change. He packed it together by pushing it with his tongue, giving him a very small air pocket.

The troll wasn't doing anything else, just pinning him. If it cut him, he wasn't sure what he could do, and he was sorting through options when he heard something else walking up.

"I have news for the Queen." His voice was muffled in the snow and he raised it to be heard. "It's about her daughter."

The troll eased up and lifted James' head, and then body, from the snow. He dangled in the air, held up by the troll's grip on his head and neck. A smaller creature of ice, wearing livery complete with a jaunty hat and feather also carved from ice, looked at him. It had a frosty tone of authority.

"What did you say, boy?"

James gasped, grateful for the air. "I have news for Her Majesty. It concerns her daughter Gwen."

"Who are you?"

"Her son."

The guard looked him up and down, then peered into his eyes. He straightened, frowning. "Wait here."

The guard turned from him but the troll did not release him. James arched an eyebrow. "Uh, sure. I'll be right here. But don't dawdle. I got places to be."

The guard sneered over his shoulder. "I'm sure you do."

He walked to a snowbird and spoke to it. The tiny white bird flew off to the castle and the guard returned to the troll and James. He stood still and suddenly became like an ice sculpture. James glanced around, but nothing so much as shifted. His eyes felt like the fluid within was freezing and he remembered what happened to some eggs that were flash frozen on the ship during a freak snowstorm a few years back. They became hard rocks and were inedible when they finally thawed.

After a few minutes, the snowbird returned and lit on the guard's shoulder. It chirped in his ear and then flew off. The guard stirred and looked at James.

"Her Majesty will see you. Follow me."

The troll did not release him but instead carried him like that to the castle. He actually appreciated the ride when he realized the snow Fae could just go up the mountain instead of following the road. About ten minutes later, he was dropped before a set of very large ice doors. The guard nodded to the ice golems towering beside them. The golems opened the doors and James looked at the guard for direction. The guard walked through the opening and James followed him.

In the room was a great throne that glittered in the light of the aurora borealis above. The ceiling was crystal clear, letting in all the light from the sky. The room was immense and clearly designed to make an impression. It looked like it was carved from a single glacier. Fae in various beautiful attire were scattered about the area, chatting and looking upon them as they entered. Beautiful women tittered and gestured to him, and men scowled, looking him over for a challenge. Various legendary beasts like the ice troll and other, stranger Fae, mingled among the sycophants in livery or ornamental trinkets. Giants of frost flanked the throne, looking dwarfed by it.

Upon the throne was a resplendent blonde woman, her hair done up in extremely long braids in an elaborate sculpture upon her head. She wore furs of a dozen shades of white and the woolen coat was the truest definition of ice blue. Her eyelashes and eyes were also blue, her gloves embroidered with snowflakes and trimmed in fur. Her skin was pale white and she looked down upon them with great authority.

The guard approached the throne and knelt. "Your Majesty, I bring you the boy."

James took a deep breath, remembering the weight of the message he came to deliver, and walked past the guard. He wasn't here to start a scuffle or worry about his bruised ego at being called "boy". He took a knee before the queen and bowed his head, fist across his chest in salute.

"Your Majesty, I bear bad news. Your daughter Gwen, my twin, is dead."

Gloriana tilted her head slightly, then gestured with her right hand. Everyone in the room cleared the hall, including the flanking guards and James' escort. The doors closed behind him once the place was empty, leaving an echoing silence as the only company.

"I am sorry for your loss." Her voice echoed, and filled the hall. She stood and walked down to him, her form altering to remain the same size in his vision as she approached until she was the size of a normal woman when she was before him.

She removed her right glove, revealing a great diamond and nails that shown with almost ethereal light. She lifted his chin and looked at his eyes. She then shifted her gaze to take in his whole face.

"So beautiful. You look so much like your father."

She moved her hand away then backhanded him across the face. Her nails or ring gouged him from temple to chin, a gash almost to the bone ripping apart his face. He fell backwards, gripping his cheek. It was bleeding but he felt the flesh almost knit together badly, leaving a huge scar.

She nodded. "There. Much better. Now go."

The giant doors flew open behind him and the golems grabbed him before he could respond. They drug him outside and threw him down the mountain. He fell and landed in a snowbank, snow puffing around him. The landing was softened but not enough that he didn't feel his skin scraped on the way. The great doors above him closed, the realm's final judgment filling the air.

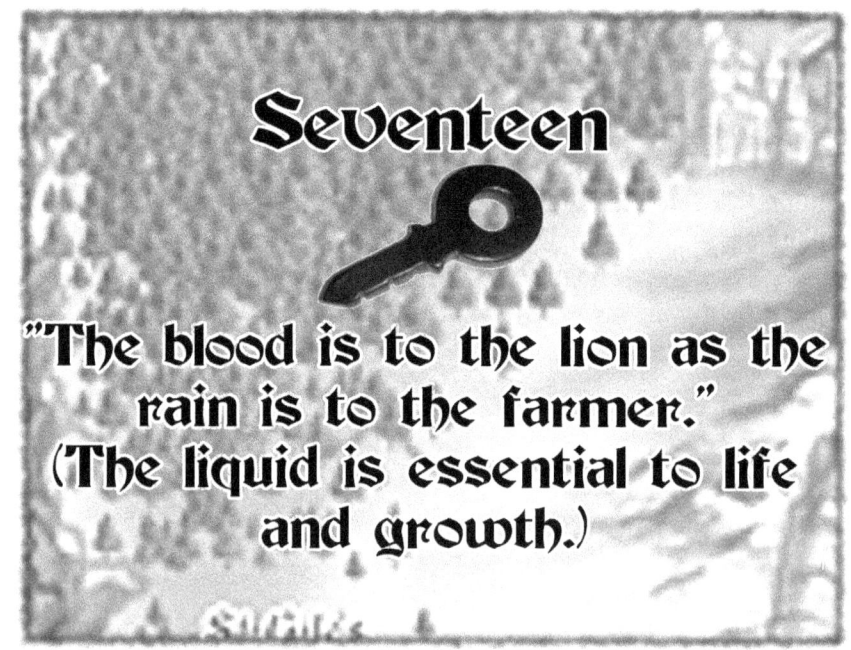

Seventeen

"The blood is to the lion as the rain is to the farmer." (The liquid is essential to life and growth.)

James lay in the snow, catching his breath. It took a few minutes, but finally, he felt good enough to move. His clothes were wet, but they were also wool so he didn't fear not being warm. He got to his feet and started the trek back home in the dark. The lights in the sky glinted off the snow until the snow went away, and once he was no longer cold, he was able to think.

Why would my likeness to Alistair be a problem? I thought…

He realized he didn't have the whole picture but he also felt like he wasn't going to get it from Gloriana. The journal was quite vague on this so he wasn't sure at all where to go. He thought he knew Alistair, but that proved untrue the moment he found out the man was his father and not his uncle. And that Gwen and James were *twins* was also confusing. After seeing Gloriana, James had no doubt they were related. Their hair and eye color were hers, as was Gwen's ability to grow hair to the floor.

He was home before he knew it and laid down in his bed just as his mother and father got up to feed the animals. The dawn light woke the chickens and sheep and he realized he really didn't have any obligations. The *Veil* would be sailing now, his parents were fine, Alistair was dead, and Gloriana wanted nothing to do with him. He closed his eyes, planning on thinking things through and fell asleep before the next breath.

Michael awoke to the sound of puttering outside. The crunch of a small shovel turning earth was comforting and almost loud in the silent area. The wall between the city and the wasteland cut off a lot of the city sounds and smells, but he could still hear the high pitched *tinks* of chamberpots against window sills, or the shouts of children playing in the streets or hawking goods. Occasionally, he heard the sound of ship bells, prepping for launch or coming into port. It was a lively, muffled place that was different from Patras, where he and Myrgen had lived for the past two years, and still pretty much the same.

He got up, slipped on his boots, and went outside. Trimelda was weeding her garden and she sat back as he approached.

"Hey sleepy head."

"Mistress."

Trimelda waved him off. "You know my name. Use it." She nodded to the outhouse. "Do your business, then get out here. I got a few things you can help with."

Michael did as directed, returning ready to work. In Patras, there had been the privilege of training with the guards and he had missed the consistency of a routine. The past couple months had been nothing but chaos, yet he had to admit he had encountered people he never expected to and he couldn't bring himself to regret it.

"Ready to go, Trimelda."

"Good. I have a few spots on the roof that are starting to wear through. I need you to get up there and replace those shingles. Later, I need that outhouse freshened. It isn't going to be all sweet air. You can do those jobs in whatever order you prefer."

He smiled and nodded. He walked back to the outhouse and opened the door to let it air out. He grabbed a carrot Trimelda held out to him as he passed her and ate it as his breakfast. He found an urn of lye that she used for making soap and brought it to the outhouse. He sprinkled some on the contents of the middens below, then sealed the urn. He knew better than to wash his hands in case any lye got on them. Instead, he "washed" them with the dirt nearby.

After wiping the dirt off, he was comfortable washing his hands before starting on the roof. He got the small ladder and the wooden shingles from a box Trimelda indicated with a nod. He climbed up on the roof and got to work. There were only a few loose ones and only a couple that were broken or missing. Michael thought it would be smarter to have ceramic tiles or clay instead of wood. The weather here was too inhospitable for wooden shingles to last very long.

Then again, that might be the point.

Trimelda seemed to always have a lesson with every task. Taking care of the outhouse was her way of saying to mind your own problems and take care of those first. It also taught him to acknowledge that, like the contents of the outhouse, everyone has problems they deal with every day so taking care of your own was just part of taking care of yourself. It was strange because he felt like he had been here for months when it had only been a couple days. James had explained he would not tell his mother right away but wait a day, but Michael had said that was a bad idea. Waiting to deliver bad news just made the recipient feel like you wanted something from them first. It almost always led to resentment.

Michael didn't know how long James was going to be gone either. His family owned sheep so he might be hiking the hills all over Glarren by the end of the tenday. Sooner if his family was already off to let them graze. He looked off towards Glarren. The little house was enough of an elevation that he could see rolling green hills and a few houses with smoking chimneys set amongst them. There were forests coming right to the edges of the water that reached up to a tall mountain at least a tenday away.

The Wall of York was much closer and he could see the tops of tall homes and hear the sounds of the city better up here. Smells of smoked fish wafted up to him as well. The scent made his stomach growl and he looked down to Trimleda's garden to ask if she was hungry.

The sight of it put the thought from his mind.

"Trimelda, why do you grow your food in a spiral?" He gestured to the pattern that surrounded the house and wrapped until it stopped at the edge of the wasteland.

"I don't grow it that way. It does it on its own. According to the Legend of Saint Clara, she walked the spiral so a mage named Raven could gather as much soil as possible that her feet had touched. It was used to stop the progress of the Soulless back during that war."

"Why does it stop?"

"Well, the account by Raven wasn't exactly coherent on that but that was the last thing she did before she disappeared before his eyes."

Disappeared... into the sky? "Did he see her ascend?"

Trimelda nodded. "At least, that's what they reported he said. I think the man was probably mad from the magic. He had to take others with him to interpret his words to strangers."

"Really? How odd."

Trimelda smiled and nodded. "Well, it's always the odd ones who make the best stories. Now hurry up, up there. We have some eggs to join with some bacon in a fitting union."

Michael's stomach didn't have to be asked twice.

James woke up to a touch on his shoulder.

"James? Are you alright?"

James looked up at his concerned mother's face. The light coming through the window was fully up. He rubbed his eyes. "I'm sorry, Mother. I guess I was tired."

"I think so. It's afternoon."

He frowned and looked at the window again. He got up and saw the shadows facing the wrong direction for the time of day he thought it was.

His mother gasped. "What happened to you?"

He looked down at his clothes. They looked like he had taken a twenty-day journey. He looked at her but her eyes were on his face. Then he remembered the cut on his cheek and raised his hand, shaking his head. "Don't worry, Mother. It looks worse..."

The flesh on his cheek was smooth, like it was twenty days old. He went outside to the rain barrel and looked in. His reflection had a hard, pink line on his cheek. He touched it and it was still sore when he pressed on it but it was the dull ache of a healed wound.

"I don't... She did this last night."

"Who?"

"Glor…" He stopped himself but it was too late.

His mother turned him to face her. "Talk."

James sighed, rubbed his palm with his thumb, and nodded. "Let's get Dad. There's a lot to cover."

"So, I walked home. I swear I wasn't out long enough for this to heal."

Orabilia looked at her husband Gavan, who picked up the empty dinner plates. She glanced at them as he picked them up.

"I haven't eaten since you told us about Gwen."

Gavan touched her shoulder. "That's understandable." He gestured with the plates. "It got dark on us."

Orabilia looked out the window. "Dawn won't wait for our grief. You should get to bed, James."

James stood. "Why don't I take care of these and you two get some sleep? I got up late."

Orabilia looked to protest but Gavan took her by the shoulder and guided her back to their room. James did the dishes and watched the animals in the back. He could see a light across the bay where he imagined he could see Trimelda's place. He set the dishes to dry and went outside. He looked to the north, to the mountain of lights. The door opened and Gavan came out.

"She went right to sleep."

James sat on the well-used chair outside. Gavan took the other one. They sat in silence for a few moments.

"Dad, what do you know of the Midwinter Queen?"

He shrugged. "She is Fae. She freezes the area, but she also preserves it. She is a consummate healer. We pray to her about those who are sick." He nodded to the scar on James' face. "If she cut you, I'm not surprised it is healed already. She probably did it just by her presence. There are stories of illnesses cured by a strand of her hair."

James nodded. "How come you and Mom never mentioned her?"

Gavan leaned on his knees. "You've never been sick. In fact, none of us have been since Alistair dropped you off with us."

James frowned. "That explains why everyone on the *Crimson Veil* was in such good shape. I was told turnover was often high on crews because some folks would contract things when they went ashore. Our Navigator refused to leave the ship because he never got sick the entire time I served. Now, I think I understand why."

Gavan nodded. "So, will you be sticking around now? I notice Ham brought you over. Is the *Veil* in port in Landon?"

James shook his head. "A little farther south, actually. Mande."

Gavan sat back, his eyebrows scrunched with concern. "Did you *walk* here?"

James nodded. "I had somethings to do in York." He gestured to the center of the country.

"What could you possibly have to do in a desert wasteland?"

James smirked. "I wanted to see where my father met my mother. I had his notes from his journal." He almost hesitated and mentioned the Soulless War, but he had only revealed that he knew Alistair was his father and Gloriana his mother. He didn't reveal their relationship was three centuries old. He wasn't sure he wanted to tell them everything.

He, too, leaned back in the seat. "You know, Dad, it was so strange. The journals spoke of his caring for her and how much he worshiped Gloriana, how they worked together and were very much in love. Her response was…" He shook his head. "I just don't understand it."

"You think she cast a spell on him?"

James shook his head. "That's not her style. Calpurnia was the spell caster. Gloriana was a potion maker."

"Then maybe it was something he drank?"

James frowned. "Maybe. It was just so *extreme.*" He waved the discussion away. "Eh, it might have been grief. Maybe I wasn't the first one to bring her the news and I just reminded her of his death. I know telling you and Mom about Gwen put me right back in the center of it."

His father put his arm around James' shoulder. "I'm glad you came and did it in person. Seeing you has helped your mother."

James patted Gavan's hand. "I was overdue for a visit anyway."

"So, how long are you staying?"

James took a deep breath. "I'm going to save that answer for tomorrow morning. Maybe I'll locate it in the night so I can tell you."

Gavan squeezed his son's shoulder in a hug, then stood. "I'm gonna head in then. Good luck with your musings."

Gavan creaked to his feet and shut the door quietly so as not to wake Orabilia.

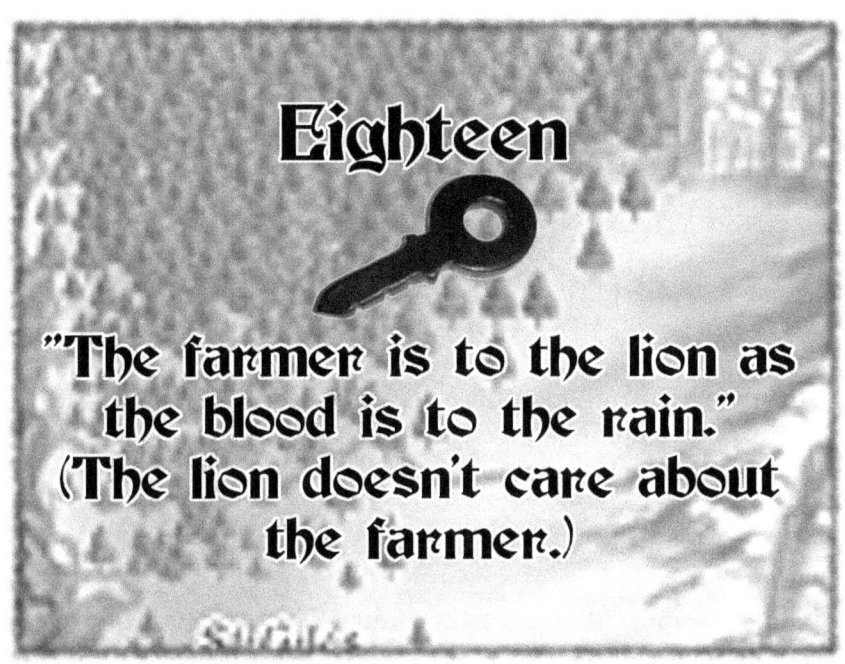

Eighteen

"The farmer is to the lion as the blood is to the rain." (The lion doesn't care about the farmer.)

When his parents arose the next day, James was packed and ready to head out. His father noted the pack setting by the front door.

"So. Seems like an answer came to you."

James nodded. "I know a woman who knew Alistair and traveled with him for years. He might have opened up to her."

"Is she the type he would open up to?"

James smiled. "She's the type who can get secrets even if you *don't*. We traveled together a bit, left her a few days back. I'm going to see if she is ready to head home."

Orabilia wiped her hands on her apron. "Let me send you with some food for the journey. You sure you don't want to stay a bit longer? I can bake some travel food."

James shook his head. "I grabbed some of that smoked fish out of the larder. It should help and we have the city right there. Besides, my companion Michael might be a full-fledged farmer by now. We may have a donkey laden with food. The woman he was staying with seemed pretty competent with a garden hoe."

"A garden hoe? Where in York can you grow a garden?"

He gestured to the opposite side of the bay near the wall. "She has a little patch of land there outside that seems to do well enough."

"You mean Trimelda?" Orabilia smiled. "We haven't seen her since the Fall."

James arched an eyebrow. "You want to come with me? You can meet Michael. He was learning from her."

"I'll get my shawl."

It was around mid-morning when Trimelda stood and dusted her hands on her own apron to give Orabilia a hug.

"Orabilia! What brings you and Gavan around to my humble home?"

Gavan set down a bag. "Brought you some wool. Figured you might be running low."

Trimelda smiled. "Thank you so much. James, I see you have one as well. You folks must have a fine harvest this year."

Gavan nodded. "Well, the thing about a sheep farm is you always have extra wool. We brought you some lanolin too. You seem to really like it."

"It helps keep my skin soft." Trimelda nodded to the house. "Come inside. We'll reunite these young friends."

She reached for the bag, but James and Gavan lifted them instead. Gavan nodded to James. "We brought them this far. We can take them the last twenty feet."

Trimelda threw her hands in the air. "Suit yourselves. Let's get you some tea."

James looked around. "Where's Michael?"

"He's inside, getting all emotional over some vegetables, no doubt."

Everyone looked confused as they followed her inside.

When the group entered the house, Michael looked up from paring onions, his eyes red. "James?"

James embraced his friend. He nodded to the onion. "You shouldn't get so attached."

Michael nodded. "Trimelda warned me not to name them. Now I know why." He washed his hands. "What's got you in a traveling mood? You heading into the hills?"

"Not quite. I'm heading back to Persephone. I need to talk to Catriona."

"You think she's still there?"

He shrugged. "She was trapped there by magic. I was hoping to have something to help break her out but I didn't find anything."

Michael raised a finger. "I just might have. Apparently, the dirt from this area has special powers. They used it in the Soulless War. I am hoping to get some from Trimelda. I think we can sprinkle it either on our clothes or on the ground at Persephone to get past the barrier."

James' eyes widened in hope. "That's genius. It might be our ticket to help her escape."

"That's my hope."

"What do we do?"

Michael shrugged. "I've been working in the garden today, getting my clothes dirty. I figure we duck into town there, get a new set of clothes with boots, and wear those to Persephone. We change into these clothes, which we have riding in a bag with the dirt. These will have the dirt all through them by that time and we can walk through. Worst case, we have new clothes and she's still there."

James nodded. "We really haven't spent any money going through the Wastes, but I'm not sure I have enough coin to buy two sets of clothes. We might just need to use these."

Michael smiled. "Well, what you don't know is that I've been making soap. I was about to head into town to sell it." He gestured to a wooden crate next to the sink. Blue and white bars of soap a foot long rested within. "Let me finish up with these vegetables and I'll head on in."

"Let me help. More hands and all that."

By the time Michael and James returned from town, it was closing in on midafternoon. Trimelda was standing up and taking their lunch dishes to the sink. She glanced at the young men.

"I'm hoping you boys ate in town."

James nodded. "The soap had sold fast. I was surprised."

Trimelda nodded. "Being on the coast with so much salt causes a great need for soap. Speaking of which," She went over to a crate and pulled out a couple bars wrapped in cloth. She handed them to Gavan. "For the wool."

Orabilia smiled. "Thank you." She looked at her son and his friend. How was your foray into the big city?"

"Good. Trimelda has a following. Her soap was known to be good. Between the portside inns and the merchant mansions, Michael's soap was sold within ten feet of the gate. The rest of the time was spent eating and looking at shops. Apparently, in Landon, shoemakers were as common as prostitutes and worked just as hard. I've never seen so many leather goods. Where do they get it?"

Gavan nodded to the north. "From Glarren, of course." He looked at their hostess. "Trimelda, it was good to see you again."

Trimelda, Gavan, and Orabilia exchanged hugs. Gavan walked up to James while the women spoke in low tones.

"We're gonna head home. Gotta feed the sheep. You fellas going to stay here tonight or are you getting a spot in town before heading through the wilderness?"

James and Michael shrugged. James glanced behind them at the gate. "I hadn't thought of getting a place in town but we just spent all of our money on new boots."

"New *boots?*" Gavan frowned at James and Michael. "James, you *know* we can get you boots back home."

James raised his hands. "I know, I know. We just wanted to be on the road sooner than later."

Gavan took a deep breath and looked to the wastes. "You still have daylight. You can ride and put a good mile between here and there by the time you make camp."

Trimelda and Orabilia walked over, arm in arm. Orabilia unhooked from Trimelda and took her son's hand. "You heading out then?"

James smiled, noting this visit was probably good for her. Her face had grown haggard from crying over the last couple days and he knew there would be more to come, but right now, she seemed to be better.

"Yeah. We have a friend trapped back there. We need to get back to her."

"Her? You left someone in a trap?" Orabilia's concern turned to anger. "Why didn't you say something instead of letting us think you might be here for the summer?"

"I never gave *any* indication I was staying. When we left, she wasn't hurt or anything. She's protected. She just can't get out. We were hoping I could get something from Gloriana to get us past the gate. Turns out," James nodded to his friend, "Michael might have a way to rescue her."

Trimelda cocked her head. "That's what you needed that dirt for."

Michael looked guilty. "I didn't realize you noticed."

"I'm old. I notice a lot. Did you remember to get your horses?"

Michael nodded behind them. "I brought them back from the inn where we sold our soap. They're rested and ready."

Trimelda walked over to the trough and hitching post out in front of her house. "A friend of mine made sure they got fed and brushed while you were off dealing with your family business. Got a little work out of them too, to pay their way."

The two horses James and Michael rode there were happy to see Trimelda and James saw why pretty quick. She pulled an apple and a sugar cube for each of them out of her pockets.

Gavan smiled. "You spoil those animals, Trimelda."

She waved him off. "Eh, they only got a short time in this world, compared to us. Might as well make it pleasurable." She petted their heads and glanced back at the group. "You boys best get over here if you want to ride out. Daylight's wasting."

They had saddled the horses back at the inn because it was easier than carrying the saddles themselves. Packs were stowed in the saddle bags and a bag of the Douglas wool was added to the mix. Trimelda used the time to talk to Gavan and Orabilia together.

James nodded to the trio. "What do you think is going on there?"

Michael glanced over. "Probably telling them she's here if they need her and that she'll take some time and visit soon."

James looked at Michael. "Can you hear them or something?"

Michael shook his head. "No, but I know her role in the village back home. As an elder, that's what she would say to someone who had suffered a loss."

The group broke up when James and Michael finished with the packing. James hugged his mother while Michael bowed in thanks to Trimelda, then they swapped. Orabilia hugged Michael too and patted his shoulders. Suddenly, Orabilia's eyes widened and she searched her belt pouch. She found what she was looking for in a pocket and handed it to James.

"Here, use this. It will help you get back to your friend."

James looked at it. It was a small waterproof pouch. "What is it?"

"Just a little something to help get you on your way. Gwen made it," her voice caught at her daughter's name, "but we've never been in a hurry. No sense letting it go to waste."

James opened the pouch. There was a green powder that sparkled even in the shadows of the container.

She nodded to the horses. "Sprinkle a handful of it on their foreheads. It will help speed the journey. Don't fall off and only do it when you are in the saddle and ready to go."

Michael looked at the pouch. "It won't hurt them, will it?"

"No, but they might need to rest when you finally stop. And they'll be hungrier than usual."

Trimelda patted the young men on the shoulders and guided them towards the horses. "Now, you boys be careful out there. Watch for bandits."

James and Michael exchanged a knowing glance but nodded anyway. A few tears and kisses later and the Douglases were on their way back to the sheep farm and James and Michael were on their way south.

"Did you learn what you needed to from Trimelda?"

Michael nodded. "Oh, make no mistake. I'd learn even more and every day if I lived the rest of my life with her. But she reminded me of the way the world feels to a Fang and Claw."

"How is it different?"

"From Augustinian beliefs? Not as much as you might think. They pray to the Saints who watch over them. We speak to the animal spirits that watch over us. You know how the religious battle for them is the Auggies who speak to the Saints, and the Emilianites who just pray to

Heaven? For us, if it could be called a 'schism' at all, is between those that feel each person gets a personal animal, and those that feel all animals watch us. But the truth is that we all believe both, instead of thinking it's one or the other."

He gestured behind them. "Take Trimelda. She never got the personal experience of bonding with a specific animal as a young girl. So, she has a bond with all animals. You saw how she was with these horses. She's like that with all creatures. She grows enough food to feed about a dozen people, and anything that doesn't go in a human mouth goes in an animal's. A lot of people are better off because she's there.

"She's a healer too. She knows more about herbs and herbology than anyone I've ever met so she makes remedies and people come and buy them. If they can't pay, they don't. If they can, they leave what they can spare. It's very equitable. Anyone who tries to take advantage of the system is studied. If they are predators, she denies them their prey. If they aren't, she helps them. She has so many things as a result of people learning to be supportive of each other, to be a community."

James smiled. He was glad his friend got to spend time with the Nubian woman. It was nice to have contact with a culture restore instead of diminish. His mind wandered to the encounter with his own culture. The memory of Gloriana's response to his news caused him to wince and Michael stopped talking.

"What just happened?"

James looked at him. "What?"

"You just winced. Since I was talking about carrots and other root vegetables, I doubt it was that."

"Oh." James shook his head. "No, not really." James told his companion about the visit to Gloriana, including the fact that the wound was half healed by morning.

"What do you think it means?" Michael had listened without interruption, letting James sort it out on his own.

"I don't know. That's why I want to talk to Catriona. She spent years with Alistair. She may have a clue."

"Well then, let's hope our trick to get her out works. Why don't we push the horses a little and get to that first resting place Raymond made? If we try, I think we can make it."

James nodded. He took out the pouch of dust and dumped some in his palm. "Does that look like enough?"

Michael shrugged. "How should I know?"

James frowned, then dumped half the pouch into his hand. He handed the pouch to Michael. "At the same time?"

Michael nodded and they counted off. Michael emptied the pouch onto his horse's head as James did likewise with his handful. Swirls of green powder sparkled around the horses' heads until they both breathed it in. A ripple of power went through them and James and Michael barely had time to hang on before the animals bolted.

Everything became a blur and it was all James could do to keep his mind on the goal. He realized this was Fae in nature and yelled to Michael, *"Focus on Persephone!"*

Michael nodded, his eyes wide in panic. The reins were in his hands but his grip was on the edge of the saddle. He closed his eyes and concentrated.

James did likewise and the two friends galloped into the afternoon.

Nineteen

"The spade is to the farmer as the claw is to the lion." (Both creatures have tools that double as weapons.)

Raymond saw a plume of dust in the far distance, dancing like a cloud in the moonlight. He rose and stood upon the wagon to elevate his perspective. He could almost hear horse hooves but that seemed very unlikely. No horse could travel that fast, even in these wastes. A groan below caught his attention and he got down with a final glance at the plume.

It seems to be going to Persephone. Either that, or to Mervolingia. I hope they can see in the dark.

He knelt between Brigit and Giles. The groan came again and he saw the dirt around Brigit's fingers move. She opened her eyes and looked at Raymond.

"… how… long…"

"It's been a full day."

She groaned again and shifted. The now-dry dirt shifted as well, cracking and dropping away as she worked to sit up. "… wa…ter…"

Raymond produced a waterskin and put it to her lips. He squeezed gently, letting only a small amount trickle into her mouth. "Swish it around in your mouth and then spit it out. You don't want to swallow the mud."

Brigit nodded and did as directed. She felt her teeth with her tongue. "Ugh… you were right…"

He gave her more water and after a couple rinses, she was able to take the water and swallow it without impairment. She nodded. "You're right. That dust just leeches the liquid right out of you."

She moved her legs, breaking the hold on them. They moved up and down like waking a sleeping limb, only much slower.

"I thought the damage was worse than this."

Raymond helped her sit up. "Oh, it was. I guess it's just the nature of Saints, being as we were in Heaven. Must have absorbed that Divine energy."

"Or it's being that close to the Giver for so long." Giles pushed himself to a sitting position.

"Giles!" She moved too fast in her excitement and pain shot through her. She stopped, exhaling.

"Are you okay?" Giles looked worried.

"Yes. Just moved a little too much a little too soon. You?"

Giles waved off her concern, choosing to stretch instead.

Raymond glanced at the sky. "The Giver?"

Brigit nodded. "Gabriel stole her, or Raphael did… Anyway, they caught her and took her to Heaven where they have her trapped in a cage. They're trying to refill the Well of Souls but she simply isn't giving up the soul creation stuff. Occasionally, they got her to cry, which they added to the Well, but she doesn't do that except on *very* rare occasions. They even tortured her to get her to cry but she didn't."

Raymond sighed, closing his eyes. "That's horrible."

Giles popped his back. "It may be worse. They were talking like they were going to bleed her if she didn't give up the tears. I think they have only held off on that because there was no turning back if they did. The Well's contents would be the last of any created."

"By the Faithful Stones… how could they do that?"

Brigit touched her chest in shock. "'Faithful Stones?' Have you converted to worshiping the Land, Raymond?"

"Saints, no. The Faithful Stones are the ones near my shack. We'll head there in the morning if you are all up and capable of walking."

Giles looked around. "Where are we?"

"The Wastes of York. Here, drink up, but spit out the first couple of mouthfuls. You don't want to swallow this mud."

Michael clung to his saddle, the panic still present in his heart but at this point, the exhaustion was finally winning. They had ridden for hours now, going far too fast to talk. Darkness had come and the animals showed no signs of slowing. He and James had managed to communicate over the rushing wind of travel, determined to let the animals run until they were done. The travel powder would not kill them or hurt them, but they would likely be unwilling to travel for several days after it wore off. With that in mind, the men had chosen to let them run as long as they wanted. There was literally nothing to get in their way.

They had shouted over the wind about the second hour into the run, checking on each other to make sure the fatigue wasn't getting to either of them. Apparently, the spell effected the riders too, not letting them fall from the saddle from exhaustion. They couldn't be *too* close to each other and risk bumping and the shouting had started making their voice sore after an hour. After that they worked out hand signals and spent much of the time in their own minds.

Michael let his mind wander to the lion that had dominated his dreams on the trip north. He knew now what it was and was ready to go where it led.

Right after we rescue Catriona.

As they passed the spot where Raymond lived, Michael saw the Lion sitting amongst the standing stones beside his house. The Lion was in front of the stone he was drawn to, he just *knew* it.

I'll return. I promise. Please, let us help her first.

The Lion nodded, as if it understood his thought, and watched them go.

"Hey!"

Michael turned to look at James.

James pointed ahead and the ruin of the tower started to come into view. Suddenly, they both grabbed their saddles as the thundering hoof sounds were replaced with softer sounds. There was a smell of grass and flowers and when Michael opened his mouth to speak, he swallowed a bug.

James looked equally confused and started flinching, his arm before him in protection. The horses slowed and the tower came into full view. There was green grass for a couple miles before the fallen towers and their protective wall, as if something spilled life onto the surrounding area. It flowed like a fountain around the ruins and by the time the horses slowed, they looked like they were back near Glarren, it was so lush.

"Is this Catriona's doing somehow?"

James shook his head, looking around. "I have no idea." He pointed to a break in the wall where water was pouring out, forming a small stream. "But maybe the spell has lost its integrity. The water is leaving. I wonder if that means we can get in now."

The animals stopped near the water and drank exactly like they had run three hundred miles in six hours. James and Michael got off the horses and both had to grab onto the saddles to steady themselves. It took another ten minutes before they could trust their legs to hold them. Michael felt like he had been vibrated for hours, which was essentially the truth. He expected to be sore but wasn't just yet.

"Are you ready?" James let go as he asked the question, testing his ability to go from sitting to standing.

Michael risked letting go of the saddle and nodded when he didn't fall to the ground under his own weight.

James walked to the hole in the wall and tried to enter there but he encountered the same barrier they had left. He looked at Michael and shook his head.

Michael nodded. "I guess we'll need that trick after all. Help me unsaddle them. Your mother said they weren't going to go anywhere for a while after we stopped."

James smiled at the horses gulping up the water. "It's a good thing there's grass now. Though there probably won't be by the time we leave again. As thirsty as they are, they'll be just as hungry."

The saddles were set aside just in time too. Both horses let out a stream of urine that rivaled the water and both men realized they had the same necessity. A few minutes later and they were ready to unpack the dirt from Michael's saddle bag.

They got undressed in turn, one standing watch while the other put their clothes in the bag and shook it to coat them. Getting redressed was gritty.

James sputtered as some dirt got on his mouth. "And here, I was worried we would have to roll around in the dirt to get it everywhere."

Michael laughed as James rubbed the dirt from the inside of his shirt through his hair. Michael got dressed and saw what James meant. The dirt was rich and still slightly damp from the air, but was a powder as well, silt that got into every nook and fold. Michael accidentally breathed in at the wrong moment and got a nose full. He coughed his breath back into working order, then nodded to James.

"Well, I guess that helps us be as protected inside as out."

James nodded. "Let's hope that's enough. Here, steady me."

James reached out with his foot as Michael lent him a shoulder for balance. It made contact with the broken wall and his foot passed the edge of the barrier. He looked at Michael.

"It worked!" He glanced around. "Now we see if the guardian detected us." He put his foot back on the ground, listening.

When no sounds came from the tower, James nodded towards some rubble to hide behind inside the wall. They climbed over the wall, using what looked like a hole made by a cannon ball as a hand and foot hold. Still, the place wasn't in as much disrepair as Michael expected after three hundred years. The obsidian towers were still intact as were the houses, with one tower broken and on the ground on its side. The thing that was likely to destroy the place now was the immense overgrowth of vegetation.

Trees were laden with early fruit and flowers bloomed on every bush. The air within the walls was fragrant to a fault and the sound of insects buzzing about with urgent bugly business made the place seem *normal*. After their previous encounter, it was confusing.

"Did Catriona do all this?" James looked around. "I don't see her. Could this be what that golden woman wanted her for?"

"The spirit of the Fang says nature wants to be this. Humans change the course of nature, but they do not change nature. It will reclaim all that humans abandon and quickly."

"*This* quickly?"

Michael shrugged. "You'd be surprised. Think of how often you must weed a garden."

James nodded. "I don't see, or hear, that gold creature."

Michael shook his head. "Neither do I." He glanced at the ground, then frowned. "Someone has been here."

James started to say something, then stopped, noticing the multiple boot prints in dirt on a stone slab not yet overgrown. He looked at the base of the fallen tower and pointed.

Michael also studied the prints and held up two fingers.

James shook his head in confusion, his eyebrows sharing the question Michael also asked himself. *Were there two people who were still alive from that era?* He looked closer at the boot prints in the dirt and shook his head. He and James exchanged a look of caution, then proceeded.

They entered the room at the base of the tower and saw a strange lump in a room off the main chamber. The room itself was overgrown but there was a lump of branches and leaves amongst the ivy. They looked closer and found it to be a sort of scarecrow, twisted branches in human form. The "neck" was broken and the body looked discarded.

They looked around the room with different eyes and both saw the battle that had recently taken place. Stone fragments of the shattered tower were flung around the room except for a swath that was strangely clear of debris. The path of this went into a second room. Shelves were damaged but the ceiling was high so whatever focused windstorm might have gone through there had limited the damage to the upper shelves. This went into a corridor with runes on the side. Here the ground was gravel made of smooth river stones that dumped into a chamber.

They walked to the chamber opening, mindful of the slipperiness of the ground. The back of the chamber had four strange ropes or something stretching a body in an X. James went back to the other room and got the broken scarecrow. He took a minute to light it on fire, then he and Michael threw it into the room near the X.

The flames lit up the mangled and rusted body of the golden woman who used to be the caretaker. Both men snorted in relief.

"Well, I think we know what that woman wanted with Catriona." Michael looked behind them. "Did you see a way out of the barrier?"

James shook his head. "But there was something in that last room. I didn't *see* it but I could *sense* it."

They looked at the Gold Wife once more, then returned to the room with the shelves. There was very little light in the room, scant stars and moonlight that came in through the open door. James shook his head.

"I can't see a thing. Can you?"

Michael shook his head. "I can see you but the fire has made me a little night blind."

James looked at the doorway and tugged Michael in that direction. They went to the bedroom where the scarecrow was and looked around. The bed was a mess of overgrown, living ivy.

"Not much here to burn. I think I may have lit up our only potential firewood."

"Maybe there's something in the houses."

The two men scoured the nearest house and found some very old wooden frames and long disintegrated mattresses. James pulled on the frame of one and it fought being torn apart.

Michael nodded. "That's good. If it's that strong after all this time, then it will probably burn well."

James tugged and the leg came apart. "I'm surprised anything is intact after three hundred years. These must have been made through magic or something."

"No, I think this environment was not conducive to any of the things that cause natural products to rot. No bugs, nor rain, no sun, just dust. It's even protected from the wind inside."

James gestured to a chest of drawers. "Let's see if anything else survived."

It took some rummaging but they found some scraps of cloth and a bit of lamp oil resin to rub on the torch. They crossed their fingers and set it to light. It did what they wanted, but it was definitely not going to last long. They rushed to the store room, minding the flame, and James led them to a back wall on the northern side.

"There's something here."

He reached out and touched the area at the back of the room. His hand went into the wall. He looked at Michael.

"It's illusion. Fae magic. C'mon."

They went through the wall. It was daylight on the other side and a tall, beautiful tower rose not far from the entry point. They looked behind them and saw a store room filled with empty shelves, dark and unwelcoming. There were windows up in the tower and James pointed.

"There's someone there."

Michael arched an eyebrow. "Are you expecting them to let down their hair or something?"

James shrugged. "Better than an arranged marriage, I suspect." He motioned to the tower like he was presenting an item on sale. "Besides, don't you want to explore such an inviting mystery? Besides, it's the only direction she could have gone. There's no other way out of that place."

Michael had to admit to himself it looked very enticing. "Lead the way, my friend."

They set the torch on the stone floor in the store room and walked towards the tower.

Twenty

"The lion is to the farmer as the rain is to the flood banks." (The rain and the lion both present imminent danger.)

Catriona looked down into the lobby as two men entered it. They moved around, gathering food and water from the Fae Lords' doors and talking. They glanced up at the top and gestured to the stairs, but did not react like they had seen her. It wasn't surprising. The walk up the stairs had taken over a day. There were resting spots along the way, comfortable benches good for sleeping, and food and water in the entwined branches that made up the railing. She had expected to go directly to the tomb of Sovereignlumen, but that was not the way it worked in this place. Even though she was the representative of the Land here, the rules set up *by* the Land servants still needed to be respected. If the Land did not honor the rules set in place by the Land, then the servants had no reason to stay.

She turned to face the man laying upon the altar. She had expected something encasing the body but then she realized this was not the way of the Fae. They did not hide their dead, but put them where their families and friends could still see them. Sovereignlumen had an ashen look to his skin, almost stone-like, but his clothes were resplendent and rich. They also looked very old. Embroidery of faeries and fantastic beasts were shot with colors and metals that defied the shadows in the upper tower. The windows were shuttered for some reason, and the ambient light from fireflies and the white stone of the tower glittered off the gold and silver thread on the body. This gave off light like a full moon but it was no wonder the men below had not been able to see her. The light moved with the fireflies, making a very serene atmosphere.

She touched the man on the altar and reached out to summon his spirit. She felt a connection to the world, to the special places and creatures that made up the Fae nation. Small Fae were scattered like embers across the world in inns and taverns. There were hundreds of Fae creatures in the Bordeaux Valley, thousands trapped in the nearby Black Forest. Hundreds more marched north from the southern reaches, led by Corrigan Starshadow himself. In the north, Gloriana Talnig wept in her chambers, alone.

But there were two missing. Calpurnia Allegheri, the Autumnal Sovereign and Embertwist Apocrafix, the Vernal Monarch, were not out in the world at all. In fact, their presence was stifled and almost nonexistent. She stepped back, releasing the feeling.

I can't summon him because he is dispersed into the world, sustaining all other Fae creatures. If I forced him to take form, it would remove his essence from them, changing them.

She knew from living with Estelle that changing a Fae destroyed it. She could not get Raven's answers like this. She looked around the room.

That also explains the fireflies. At first, I thought they were will-of-the-wisps. But they aren't. They are representative of Summer being in power.

Summer coming too soon meant the seeds didn't get enough water from the Spring rains. That could lead to drought and stunted crops. Ironically, it would also lead to flooding. The snow runoff would swell the rivers because they melt over the course of weeks or days instead of months. This would wash away the seeds not yet adhered to the soil, leading to low yield harvests and famine.

Her people needed to know what they were facing. She stopped feeling like she had to care for the whole world and returned to caring about her people. If she didn't use her powers to help them, they would be in trouble. She needed Myrgen.

"I have to get back."

James and Michael started as something splattered onto the ground. They stood, examining the item.

"It's a pear." James looked up.

Michael pointed. "It's Catriona."

She waved, then cupped her hands around her mouth. "Hello!"

James waved back.

Michael repeated her gesture. "Are you okay?"

"Yes, I'm fine, but I need to get home. How did you get here?"

"Through the storage room at Persephone."

"How did you get in?"

"That's a long story."

She nodded and waved, then started for the stairs.

James looked at Michael. "That's going to take her a while to get down here."

"Do you want to meet her halfway?"

James looked at the stairway. It had narrow stairs with no railing for about a story going up, maybe two, then the railing grew and the stairs widened. He looked around the lobby and shrugged.

"You got anything better to do?"

Clara spat. "You're right. That mud was foul."

Raymond nodded. "Unfortunately, it was the only way to immobilize you."

Brigit dusted off the last of the caked mud from Clara's legs. "Uh oh. This doesn't look good."

The trio looked at the area Brigit just uncovered. A small spur of bone broke the skin on Clara's left shin.

Raymond frowned. "How did I miss that?"

"Her skirt was wadded up over it." Brigit looked at Clara. "It's already healed. We will need to rebreak it or you won't be able to walk."

Clara looked around. "We can't stay here. We have to warn Alexander and the others."

Giles shook his head. "We've been here a day. Anything the angels had planned has probably already happened."

Clara closed her eyes. *George? George, can you hear me? You need to be careful. George?*

She shook her head. "I can't sense George."

Raymond looked at the others. "You can't pray to Heaven or the Saints anymore. Once you are cast out, you're cut off."

Brigit scowled at Heaven. "How can they expect to keep followers if they cut off access to Heaven?"

"I don't get the impression they want our input." Giles looked at Clara. "What do you want to do?"

"I… I don't know."

Raymond gestured to Giles. "Help me get her to the wagon. We can take her back to my home and reset the leg there. I have the same dirt there that we do here."

They helped get Clara on the wagon.

Once there, Giles put a hand on Brigit's shoulder again.

"You okay?"

Brigit looked at Clara, then at Raymond. "We need to get to Alexander. He needs to know he isn't dealing with me anymore. I don't want him to think he has healing powers and try to save a life only to have Gabriel withhold the ability."

Raymond handed Clara a bundle of cloth for her head. "Where do you need to go?"

"Mervolingia. St. Giles, to be exact."

Giles frowned. "I have no idea where that is, which is weird because it has my name."

Raymond nodded to the south. "It's that way. Go southwest. It's at the bottom of the Black Forest, next to the ocean."

"Wait, *right* at the base of the forest?"

Raymond nodded.

Giles turned to Brigit. "That's Cliffport. My friend Kalvin is from there. We had our covenants there. Serenity and the Haunt. The Black Forest was what the villagers called it because…" He stopped, looking uncomfortable.

Brigit leaned in. "Because?"

156

"Because we made it haunted. We trapped Fae creatures there so they couldn't attack the villagers."

"Why were Fae creatures attacking the villagers?"

Giles shrugged. "It was what beasts did when someone invaded their territory. We also had a mage who stole the abilities of different beasts to attack the region out of a personal vendetta. We needed a way to protect the beasts from him. So, we made an area where he couldn't reach them. It was really important that they not be able to leave if they went there so he would release them because he couldn't use their strength or breathe fire anymore."

Raymond gestured to the west. "It stretches all the way from the top of Mervolingia to nearly the top of Krakte. Some very interesting developments have come from that forest."

"*Eeesh.*" Clara lifted her leg and put a bag of something under it, wincing and hissing through her teeth. She wanted distraction from the pain, which was starting to become a low throb. "Why did they change the name of the town?"

Raymond helped her get the bag under the broken part. "The Soulless War took quite a toll. The Church refused to accept any petitions for sainthood in the aftermath. People found safety in the churches from the monsters, so afterwards, the Church capitalized upon this. They offered to financially assist the rebuilding of towns impacted by the war and engineers went in and rearranged everything into set patterns. Those patterns reinforced Church rule, with the Augustinian churches being the centers of the small towns where the devastation was most severe.

"As time went on, the large cities also adopted the patterns in order to get the Church funds infusing into their economy. The Church was happy to do it because it served their purpose. They said any town under a certain number of people had to choose a Patron Saint. As more towns got more funds, the Church referred to the towns by their Saint names, publishing maps with the new designations. After a hundred years, no one called them by the old names anymore."

Brigit rolled her eyes. "Ensuring that the Church had control over them all."

"It seems to have been most prominent in Mervolingia, but a few towns in Mande and Toledo are also named like that."

Giles looked around. "What about the northern regions?"

Raymond put a blanket over Clara. "Well, north of Mervolingia is still Fae country. This here is York and as you can see, it hasn't fared well."

Brigit sighed. "We would be getting prayers and suddenly, whole areas would just go silent."

Raymond nodded. "I remember. After it was all over, I was brought before Raphael and Gabriel. Michael had disappeared and Uriel was down helping clean things up. They told me I was to blame for destroying so many souls. I didn't even get to say a word before I was thrown here."

Giles looked at his old friend. "It was unfair what they did to you. It wasn't your fault."

Raymond shrugged. "I played a part. There can be no denying that."

Clara wrapped up to ward off the chills she could sense coming. "I remember coming up there and everything was in chaos. Uriel eventually arrived and when things were settled, I was assigned as your replacement. That brings up another question: Who will replace us?"

"I don't know that they will." Giles jerked his thumb skyward. "That place is going to be a mess for a while. I wouldn't be surprised if you get more visitors, Raymond."

"I'll keep an eye out for them."

"I think I should, or maybe," Brigit looked at Giles, "*we* should head to Alexander. Can you handle the trip back, Raymond?"

He nodded. "I've done this trek before. It will be fine. Remember, head south and west, but don't go into the woods."

Brigit and Giles nodded and took off.

Raven's earth sled stopped at the edge of Persephone and he went over to the horses grazing on the new grass. He could tell they had recently endured Fae magic, but the nature of the stuff was not as obvious. In general, mages put off horses and other animals but not Raven. Between his half-Fae blood and his worship of the Land, he felt kinship instead of repulsion to animals and beasts.

Lauriel!

He had left so abruptly, he didn't know where his companion would be. He felt the Fae wolf coming from inside the tower and waited with his hands on his hips for the creature to arrive. It did so with a dead rabbit in its mouth.

"Oh. Well, I suppose that is fine. Who are the visitors?"

Lauriel looked at the horses, then swallowed a bite of the rabbit while it thought of an answer.

Raven frowned. "What do you mean you don't know? Obviously someone is here."

Lauriel looked at Raven.

Raven's mouth twisted around itself in contemplation. "Can you smell where they went then? I can wait until you're ready."

The wolf finished eating and then walked to the tower. He sniffed around, following the scent into the tower. He went over to Raven's bedroom, then he went towards the trap Raven was supposed to use to catch the Giver. The room was lit by some flames on a bundle of sticks. The Gold Wife hung there, nearly disintegrated. She didn't move at all.

"Who set fire to my body double?"

Lauriel sniffed, then turned around and went back to the storeroom. He went into it and sniffed the smoldering torch on the ground. Raven picked it up and used magic to relight it. He waved it around the back wall but saw nothing. Lauriel went through the wall into the Fae realm, but returned seconds later.

"They went to Sovereignlumin? Why?"

Lauriel sat.

"Well why didn't you ask them then?"

Lauriel just looked at Raven.

"Oh. Well, I suppose catching that rabbit is a valid reason. I didn't mean to leave so abruptly. It was an accident."

Lauriel licked his mouth.

"I didn't have any way of knowing the Land would just grab me and haul me there. It didn't even bring me back."

Lauriel blinked.

"No, I *didn't* but now that you mention it, asking for a ride back might not have been a bad idea. Though honestly, I don't think she would have done it. Her request was outrageous. I'm supposed to find the Giver and put her in that trap."

Lauriel sniffed his paw.

"Because. Catriona didn't grace me with the details. I have no idea how I'm supposed to do it, either. That's why I'm here."

Lauriel licked some stray rabbit blood from his paw.

"I thought, maybe, you might know where the Giver is. Or have a way to look for her."

Lauriel ran his paw over his ear, cleaning a bit of blood from back there too.

Raven sighed. "Not really. It's not like the Fae are connected to the Giver but I didn't know what else to do. I figured you might have a few suggestions. You usually do."

Lauriel cleaned his ears and face while Raven nodded.

"So, we need a place to commune with the Giver, you say. Where would something like that exist? She hasn't been seen in a long time."

Lauriel shook his fur.

"I can see that. If the Land is Bringer, then Heaven must be Giver."

Lauriel looked at Raven.

"Oh. You didn't know that. Catriona is the embodiment of more than just the Land. She's the Death Bringer of old."

Lauriel snorted.

"Hey, you didn't see her. She was all deathy and scary. Plus Myrgen said he was the Hunter and that he travelled with the Death Bringer. He says Catriona is his companion from that time."

Lauriel looked at the ground and sniffed a bit of lost bone marrow from the rabbit.

"Hunh. Okay. So where then?"

Lauriel picked up the bone bit and chewed it.

"Hm. Yeah, I remember that guy. Raymond, right? I suppose he may have an idea about Heaven-y stuff, since he used to be a Saint." Raven patted Lauriel on the head. "You're very smart."

Lauriel licked Raven's hand.

Raven shook his head. "Not really. But I don't know if he'll have anything so we should gather some fruit from the trees outside. If they last, we can present them as gifts for his wisdom. You shouldn't drop in unexpectedly without a gift anyway. Let's go."

Raven put the torch in a torch holder by the shelves and left.

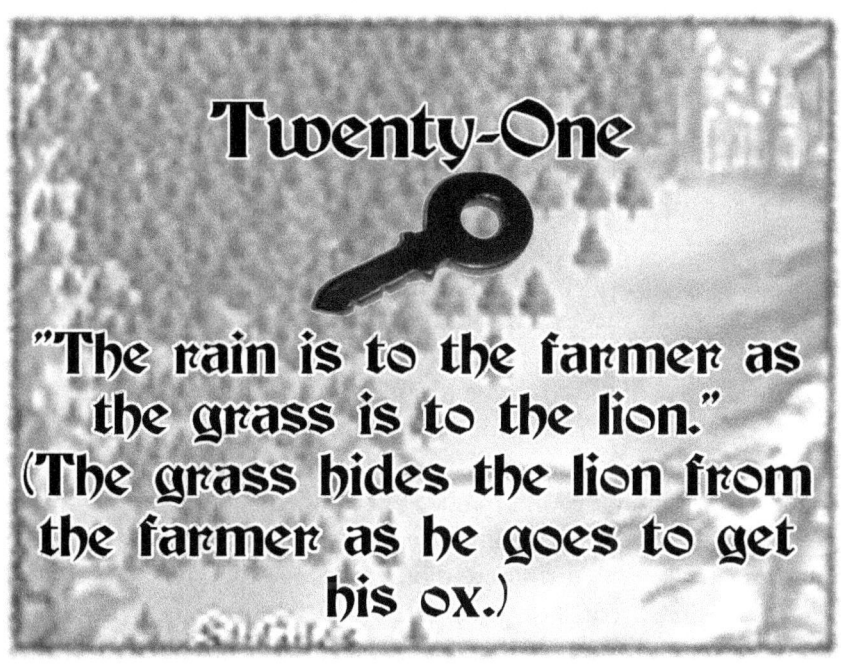

Twenty-One

"The rain is to the farmer as
the grass is to the lion."
(The grass hides the lion from
the farmer as he goes to get
his ox.)

Raven gathered some fruit from the trees outside and made a spot for them on a new earth sled he drew from the ground.

"Good thing my magic is independent of my relationship with the Land. Still, I don't like the idea of being cut off from my faith."

Lauriel jumped onto the sled and looked up at Raven.

"Oh, let me tell you, that is an interesting story." As he got the earth sled moving away from the covenant, Lauriel put his front paws on the raised steering part of the sled and Raven scratched his ears.

"So, I arrived at a dark, underground area thick with heat and the smell of lava…"

"Wow. This area looks nothing like I remember." Giles frowned at the wasteland around him.

"What did it used to be like?" Brigit wiped her forehead of the sweat from walking.

"Lush. Green. There was a Giver resting place near where we put Serenity, and there had once been a village." He looked at the sky and then around, pointing. "The village we encountered that was part of the problem was over there. We were sent from the Estate in the Southern Region up to this area. We were asked to establish a new Estate because they wanted to expand into the world. We had swollen in ranks to have almost a hundred mages at the Estate. It was the only place in the world to learn magic at the time.

"We had been carefully chosen for the mission. I had skills in the lore of the monstrous beasts of the Northern Region. Kalvin was from the area and knew the Central region. And Davvik was our connection to nature. He could change into an ox. Or an owl."

Brigit frowned. "Like a lycanthrope?"

Giles shook his head. "Not exactly. It was just the form his magic took. He was also a healer, though you had to feed the spell *čaro* in order to make it permanent. Some magic, like food or healing, goes away at the next sunrise unless you commit a part of your soul to it. Or you can use some naturally occurring creation essence, called *čaro*. The trouble with *čaro* is that it takes on properties of the thing it is left over from creating. So a poisonous plant might drip *čaro* with a destruction essence, while mother's milk has a healing essence. You never get just plain *čaro*."

He frowned.

"What?"

Giles looked at her. "Unless it comes directly from the Giver."

Brigit sighed, shaking her head. "That's why they were milking her."

"Yes. Pure, unaligned essence isn't really possible in the world unless it falls directly from the Giver."

"So the Well must be something they took from her."

Giles rolled his eyes skyward. "And that's why she can't come in contact with anything else. If it touches some other aspect, it changes to reflect that essence. So, we couldn't collect the tears or whatever because our contact with the world would make it unusable for souls."

"And they must be able to use it because they were created by it. So, they betrayed and captured their maker?"

Giles nodded. "Yeah, that's what it looks like from here. They never trusted any of us enough to confide in us. None of us know how they became the creatures they are."

They walked a moment in silence as they contemplated that information.

"What happened to the village?"

"They… rejected the Bringer."

Brigit frowned. "Rejected the Death Bringer? What… why would that be something a magical school had to deal with? Especially one so far away."

"They didn't die."

"So, they were a village of immortals? Was it that they were able to study magic or something? Were they competition?"

Giles shook his head. "I didn't say they couldn't get hurt. I said they didn't *die*. They just kept… being alive. People would get attacked by animals or monsters or suffer some accident that would kill them, but they didn't die. Eventually, they resorted to cutting up the dead, throwing them into a pit, and setting them on fire until they were ash. Even so, the ash still moved."

Brigit's eyes and face reflected the horror of envisioning that discovery. "That's… I can't even describe my thoughts on that."

Giles nodded. "The presence of something like that caused all kinds of creatures that were less than friendly to humans to flock even more to the area. The village Kalvin grew up in was jeopardized, so we were sent up."

"Was this village an important one?"

"Not to the Estate. It was just a long way from there with a lot of intervening terrain where we could designate future areas for magical settlements. Along the way, we learned there were a lot of ramifications from doing that. One area had been under the secret management of a head mage at the Estate for almost seventy years. The resulting saturation of the area in magic (because magic begets magic) warped newborns and the elderly. Some warping simply made the children more capable of learning magic when they were older. Some merely attracted magical creatures. But the ones whom it warped into monsters were the hardest to deal with because of the human toll."

"This all sounds so repulsive."

"There were a lot of amazing things about magic. When harnessed properly, it was a tremendous aid. We could protect large regions without warping by spreading the magic over larger areas, so we established three strongholds: One in the village where Kalvin grew up, one in the Haunted Woods, and one on the ruins of the village we put down who couldn't die. By doing so, the *čaro* would pool in designated areas, like farming plants. This in turn fueled our magic, which then sustained our *čaro* crops."

"You *planted* this *čaro*?"

Giles shook his head. "No. We imported items that already produced the *čaro,* then harvested it. But any magic that would have seeped into the people or the ground would simply grow in those existing sources. For example, we found a dragon skull that had fallen into a town's well. The skull poisoned all the water in the area with death magic as a result, creating a wasteland like this."

He waved his hand at the area around them.

"So, we pulled it from the well and cleansed the water table so it would start to grow things again. Then we took the skull and put it in a contained fountain so water flowed through and around it. When we needed destruction *čaro*, we simply dipped a ladle from that pool and poured it into the item we were creating."

Brigit frowned. "What could you *ever* need destruction *čaro* for?"

Giles looked at her. "Forging weapons. Dousing a sword or bow in the death water empowered it to kill. Some creatures could only be fought with magical weapons. That's how you make magical weapons."

Brigit tried to hide her disgust but Giles saw it anyway. He reached out and put a hand on her shoulder. "This is disturbing to you."

Brigit shook his hand from her. "Of *course* it is. My entire life was spent healing people and here you are, reminiscing about the glory days of forging magical weapons endowed with extra killing power."

Giles blinked. "I... I didn't think..."

"Yeah. Clearly. You know my specialty, but the single thing you chose to extoll was the destructive nature of your entire order. Special weapons, warping *children*... why didn't you brag about your sexual conquests along the way while you were at it?"

"I was untried until I was married."

Brigit glared at him. "You seriously thought *that* was the relevant statement I was making?"

Giles opened his mouth, then stopped. "I think I should maybe... not talk for a while."

"Gee. I guess you really are smarter than you reveal."

"And then I found you. And you know the parts after that."

Lauriel pulled the sled up to the house and Raven grabbed the fruit before letting the earth sled revert back into the ground. He walked up to the open door with his arms loaded.

"Hello? I have fruit!"

No response.

He looked at Lauriel. "Where could he be? There's no place to hide around here. Well, except behind those things, I guess." He nodded to the pillars around them.

Lauriel sniffed the air, then looked to the west.

Raven turned and took a few steps in that that direction. "Oh. How far away?"

Lauriel's nostrils flared and he growled.

The fruit dropped from Raven's arms.

"That's... that's not possible. She died. I saw her."

Lauriel snorted.

Raven pulled the earth sled from the ground under their feet and took off to the west, the fruit rolling away in his wake.

"It could also destroy diseases."

Brigit didn't look at him. "You said you were shutting up."

"And parasites. Parasite killing is okay, right?"

She held up her hand to silence him. He silenced.

She put him out of her mind but the concern wasn't gone. Alexander was out there, near a war zone, and didn't know that she was no longer controlling his heavenly powers. *If he tries to heal someone and Raphael or Gabriel answers the call...*

She didn't want to think about the ramifications of that granted power, especially from betrayers like the Archangels. There was too much at stake and the idea that they might grant that same destructive essence Giles was going on about scared her. Worse, Alexander would be destroyed and the resulting civil war would finish off anyone left over from the war between Heaven and the Land. They had to get there quickly, and all they could do was walk.

She felt helpless.

She focused her energy on plodding forward and picked up the pace.

Lauriel growled again.

"I see them."

Raven pulled the earth sled to a halt. Raymond set down the arms of the small cart he was pulling.

Clara sat up, wincing. "What's…"

"Clara!" Raven ran over to the back of the wagon and grabbed her in a hug.

Clara screamed in pain and Raymond rushed to the pair.

Raven jumped back as Raymond checked her leg. The wound started bleeding where the bone jutted through the skin.

"By the Stones, what happened?"

Raymond dabbed at the blood with his sleeve, trying not to touch the bone. "She fell and the bone wasn't set right."

Raven looked at Clara. "They cast you out? I just talked to you two hours ago."

"Weeks, Raven. It's been weeks."

Raven waved his hand dismissively. "Same thing. What… who set the bone?"

Raymond took a breath to speak but Clara put a hand on his.

"My entire body was broken. The mud here healed me but my skirts hid this damage. *Eesh!*" She squeezed Raymond's hand as his sleeve caught on a jagged edge, tugging the bone.

"I'm so sorry."

Raven looked at the wound. "I don't have healing powers. I never mastered it enough to help a person." He looked at Clara. "I'm sorry."

Raymond drew his sleeve back to get it away from the bone and squinted at it. "I'm sorry, my dear. It's going to hurt even more as we move now."

Clara winced, trying to hide the tears forming by looking up.

Raven put a hand on Raymond's arm. "What needs to be done?"

"She's in pain. Their bones were broken from the fall, so I immobilized them in mud until their natural healing took over. It's one of the benefits of being a saint. Your body heals better afterwards." He gestured to the bone. "But I missed this so now, we have to rebreak it and reset it. I was taking her back to my hut because she can heal there more comfortably."

"Do you have something there that will help with the pain?" Raven's brow furrowed and he looked at Clara.

"Sadly, no. But I have a bed she can rest upon and fresh water."

Raven looked at the swath of green grass that marked his travel to this spot. "I was just there. I can get you back, if you like."

Raymond looked at the swath. "So I see. Take her. I will walk quicker if I am not hauling her in the cart."

"Or we can just use the cart."

Raven moved his hands and the earth sled rose beneath the cart, the two men, and the Fae wolf. He paid attention to making it smooth so as not to jostle the patient. Then the landscape rushed by so fast, the only evidence that they had been moving was the windblown mess of Raymond's hair. Raven moved the cart to the door of the hut as Raymond rushed to open the door.

"Oh. My goodness." Raymond eyed the two fruit tree saplings that were near his front door and stepped back as they grew to full size as Raven used a spur of earth to lift Clara through the door. He set her down on the bed there, ignoring the plants in the wall troughs that sprouted and matured around them.

"Are you comfortable?" Raven moved the rest of the dirt back out to the ground outside with a flick of his wrist.

Clara winced and shifted. "As best as can be expected." She nodded to the growth around them. "I had forgotten about that."

"Huh?" Raven glanced around the room, not understanding.

"The plant growth?"

"Oh. Yeah, I guess I forgot about it too."

Raymond ducked into the darkened room, marveling. "Oh. Here too, I see."

Raven looked at him over his shoulder. "What was your plan once we were here?"

"Uh, let me get some light in here and I'll see what I can do."

Raven rose. "I can supply light. What else do you need?"

"Oh. Well," Raymond rubbed his hands on his robes, "I need to splint it and prepare it to be rebroken." He looked at Clara. "It will hurt a lot."

"Is there anything you can give her?"

Raymond shook his head. "I have very little use for something like that."

Raven snorted. "I… I am not a healer… but I do know how to make the pain go away. It will only last until sunrise tomorrow, but at least you'll be able to sleep." He looked at Raymond. "I will process it and you get everything ready to do the procedure."

Raymond nodded and Raven went to Lauriel.

"Hey, do you have any paralytic venom on you?"

Lauriel looked at him.

Raven winced. "I know that stuff. It's too potent for this. It'll stop her heart."

Lauriel ruffled his back spines.

Raven pursed his lips, nodding. "That might work. Okay. Gimme one."

Lauriel's spines rippled again and an old, long spine fell out. Raven picked it up and started to put it in the water trough but Lauriel bolted between the two.

"What? Oh, that's *not* what you meant by dilute it?" He looked at the spine. "Then what?"

Lauriel glanced at his hand.

"Won't that knock *me* out?"

Lauriel snorted.

"Hm. Okay." Raven started to put it in his mouth.

Lauriel put a paw on his foot.

"Not saliva?"

The paw was removed.

"You're right. That *would* be disgusting." He looked at the fruit trees. "One of those maybe?"

Lauriel glanced up at the fruit, then back to Raven.

"Too acidic. Got it." Raven stroked his chin. "I think I know something. And don't worry. I'll do it right."

Raven walked into the hut. He took a kernel of wheat from a nearby stalk and shucked it. The sharp case cut him and he bled a little on the grain. He glanced around, then looked at Raymond and Clara. He was propping up her leg and getting it into position to rebreak it. She was breathing through clenched teeth while biting on a rolled piece of fabric.

Raven rubbed the spine on the kernel, being very careful not to get it near his cut. The blood picked up the venom and Raven nodded. He looked around for a utensil and found a metal spoon on a table. He scooped the kernel in the spoon and took it to Clara.

"Here. Eat this. It will take the pain away and relax you enough to reset the leg."

"What is it?"

"Wheat."

She glanced at it. "Okay."

"And blood."

She arched an eyebrow. "Ew?"

"It's an... important factor for the spell."

"Oh." She frowned at him, but put the kernel in her mouth.

"And poison." He pointed at the Fae wolf. "From Lauriel."

Raymond sat up. *"What?"*

Raven waved him down. "It was the reason for the blood. It tempers the poison."

The blood touched her tongue and the spell hit. She closed her eyes and sighed. Raven looked at Raymond and nodded.

"You should do it now."

Raymond started with surprise, then reached down and yanked hard on her leg. Her dead weight countered the yank and the bone slipped back into her skin. Raymond put his hand on her knee and put her ankle under his armpit, then pulled the two apart.

"Put your hands on the wound. Make sure the bone is in place."

Raven set the spike and spoon aside and went to the wound. His blood entered the gash and he blinked. He could feel the sensations of her body and knew the poison was maintaining above her heart. It was paralyzing the pain and awareness receptors. He focused and felt where the bone was not quite lined up.

He put both hands on the shin bone and pulled the bone apart, lining up the jagged parts to align. Then he relaxed and the two pieces settled together. He reached out, summoning a branch of the pear tree outside. It came in as the bed under Clara sprouted leaves. He pulled a small stick from one branch and placed it upon her leg, right above the gash.

Sprouts of leaves grew into other sticks of new growth until the branch was as long as her shin and completely encompassing her leg. Raymond moved away until Raven felt the weave of branches was sturdy enough to brace the bones. Then he, too, stepped back.

"That was amazing." Raymond's voice shook just a little.

"Lauriel showed me how. I was hurt myself recently."

"How do I get it off?"

Raven looked at Raymond. "Oh. Well, I should probably come back. The only way to remove it is with an axe right now."

Raymond swallowed. "That would be counterproductive."

"Yes. Do you know anything about the whereabouts of the Giver?"

Raymond blinked, looking at Raven in surprise and studying his face and hair. "I...*yes*. But not as much as Clara and her companions."

"Companions?"

"Yes. She fell with Brigit and Giles. They are on their way to St. Giles. She needs to talk to someone there."

"That sounds confusing."

Raymond frowned, nodding. "Yes, I suppose it does." He pointed to the southwest. "They went that way about two hours ago. They can't be far."

Raven nodded. "Ah'll be bahk."

Raymond frowned. "Why did you say it like that?"

Raven shrugged. "That's how I always say it," and left.

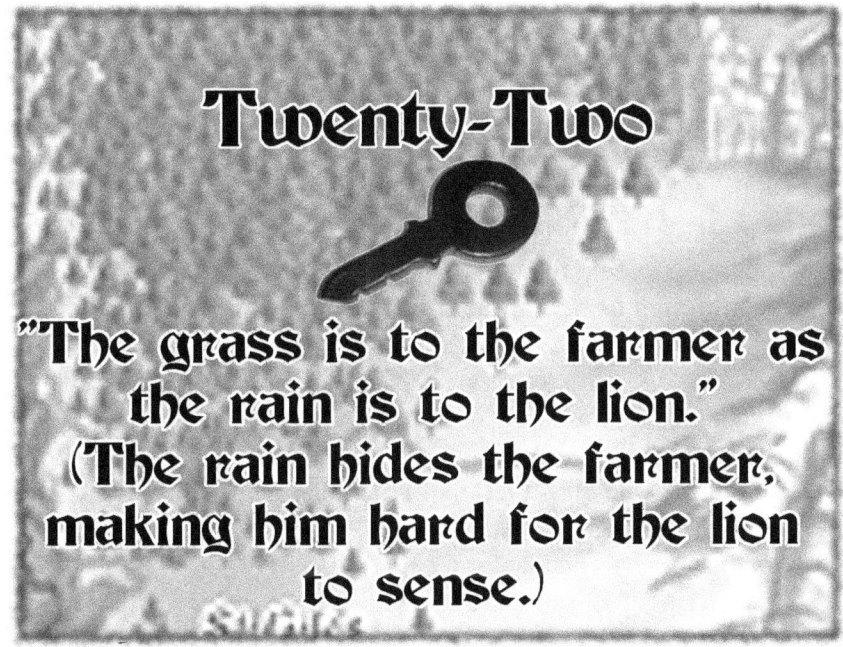

Twenty-Two

"The grass is to the farmer as the rain is to the lion." (The rain hides the farmer, making him hard for the lion to sense.)

"And that brought us here." James gestured to the vaulted tower around them. He looked up to the top of the tower. "What did you find up there?"

Catriona glanced upwards. "Not what I expected."

They had stopped to rest on the last bench before the lobby below. There was food and water at this landing but the pickings got thinner as they got within an hour of the bottom.

"You said you left Gloriana a day or so ago?"

James nodded.

"Is that why she was crying?"

James frowned. "I have no ide... she was crying?"

Catriona nodded. "I felt it when I was up there."

"Dammit." He leaned forward, his arms across his knees. "I don't understand this at all. She was my father's beloved, yet she cut the hell out of my face when she saw I looked like him. Once she did, she seemed satisfied that she maimed me, then threw me out of the realm."

Catriona glanced away.

Michael caught the expression. "You know why she reacted like that, don't you?"

James looked at Michael, then turned to Catriona. "You do?"

Catriona sighed. A cursory glance at him said why he had wanted to go to her. He thought she would be as distraught about Gwen's death as Orabilia had been, as he envisioned a mother was supposed to be. She wasn't sure how he would take this news.

"Your mother fell in love with the Prince of York. The prince came to Persephone to save his people. Gloriana worked to help. But in a battle, he was touched while rescuing a thief from the monsters. The thief felt an obligation to help the man who saved him. He assumed the man's appearance through a spell, probably expecting to get the people's help escaping."

James snorted. "Let me guess. He used the status to bed some women and Gloriana found out?"

Catriona closed her eyes and took a deep breath. "What he did was worse. He didn't... he didn't tell her the prince had fallen. Instead, when he saw her and she was... affectionate..."

Michael shook his head.

James stiffened. *"How* affectionate?"

Catriona swallowed. "She thought she was with her beloved and he didn't stop her. You and your sister were the result."

James paled, his face falling in shock. Then he closed his mouth, shaking his head. "That makes sense now. By the Fae, Alistair."

The group fell into silence, digesting the information. After a while, Catriona stood.

"I fear I must go now. I have some bad news to deliver. Seems it is the order of the day."

Michael looked at James. James stared into the wall by the final descent. Eventually, he shook his head.

"Michael, I have something I need to do and... I can't do it where you are headed."

"Where am I headed?"

"Back to Myrgen."

Michael blinked, then shrugged. He looked at Catriona. "He's right. I want to check in with him. See how he's doing."

Catriona's mouth turned into a half-frown. "I didn't come here by traditional means."

"Neither did we."

"Take my horse."

Catriona and Michael looked at James.

"I'm not going to use it."

Michael arched his eyebrow. "What are you going to do?"

James rubbed the palm of his hand with his thumb. "What should have been done by Alistair."

Catriona shifted her gaze across his face, then nodded. "We will leave you to it, then."

James looked at her. "Thank you for telling me."

She shrugged. "It's not like he could."

James sighed and sat back on the bench, closing his eyes.

Michael and Catriona took the hint and left him.

Raven saw the figures walking and pulled the earth sled up beside them.

"Hi. You're Clara's friends?"

Giles stepped between Raven and Brigit. Brigit frowned at him and moved next to him.

"Yes. I'm Brigit. This is Giles. And you are?"

"Raven."

"Raven…" Brigit's eyes narrowed in contemplation. "She spoke to you recently."

"Yes, but it was more than two hours ago. What can you tell me about the Giver?"

"Um…"

Giles shifted forward. "Why are you asking about the Giver?"

"Because the Bringer needs her."

Brigit and Giles looked at each other.

Raven leaned on the earth sled. "You know where she is."

Giles nodded, frowning. "Yes, but we don't know how to get her down here."

"Down here? You mean she's…" Raven pointed upwards.

Brigit nodded. "She's been captured by the Angels. They have her in a cage."

"Why would she be in a cage?"

Brigit shook her head. "We don't know for certain, but they are keeping her prisoner."

Raven stroked his hair. "That's a problem. I can't get into the afterlife. I wouldn't go to Heaven even if I could."

Giles gestured to Brigit. "We were kicked out so it's denied to us too."

"I wonder if Lucifer knows she's there."

Giles looked at Brigit again. "Uh… I don't know… He left a long time ago."

"Well, his *new* place is pretty nice."

Brigit and Giles eyed Raven and stepped back half a step together.

Lauriel sniffed, then looked at Raven.

"What?" Raven pointed. "Him?" He looked at Giles. "You're a mage?"

Giles nodded, arching an eyebrow at Lauriel. "Yes."

"I heard about you! The Land told me! Well, not *me* but someone near me."

"The *Land?* Why would the *Land* tell you about me?"

"It just said you could explain magic."

"Well, yes, I can." Giles straightened, a slight swagger present now.

Brigit pointed to the sled. "Isn't *that* magic?"

Raven looked at the sled as if seeing it for the first time. "Oh, well yes." He looked at her. "Oh, I meant explain it to someone else. Not me. I understand me."

Giles smiled. "Ah. I take it they were confused."

Brigit blinked. "Yeah, I can see that happening."

Raven gestured to the Fae wolf. "And Lauriel wasn't there or the whole problem would have been solved."

Brigit looked at Lauriel. "Oh. So, you speak?"

Lauriel sniffed.

Raven tapped his lower lip, thinking. "So, we need to head to Caratia so you can talk to the Death Bringer."

"Wait. You've seen the Death Bringer?" Giles glanced at Brigit, then back at Raven.

"Yeah, though I'm not sure what I saw. She said to put the Giver in a trap."

"The Giver is already in a trap."

"She meant a different trap."

Brigit's whole face argued between confusion and anger. "Why does the Bringer want the Giver in a trap of *any kind*?"

Raven shrugged. "She didn't say. I'm just supposed to do it."

"And what is *she* doing?"

"She's investigating why my grandfather put my grandmother in the trap in the first place."

Brigit shook her head. "Your grandmother... in the Heaven trap? Is the Giver your *grandmother*?"

Raven tilted his head up. "Isn't she kind of *everyone's* grandmother?"

Brigit stammered, trying to make her brain assemble words. She looked at Lauriel. "You make this stuff understandable?"

Lauriel blinked, then farted.

Brigit raised her hand, dismissing the whole thing. "I have to get to Alexander. I have to warn him about Heaven. Giles, go with this," she looked at Raven, then at the Fae wolf, "wolf and see if you can figure out what they need."

Giles grabbed Brigit's hand. "Please. Don't try to do this alone."

Brigit looked at his hand and Giles let go.

Giles turned to Lauriel. "Can we get her to Alexander, then head to see the Bringer?"

Lauriel stood and walked over to the earth sled. He put his front paws on the steering column. Giles gestured to the sled and Brigit rolled her eyes and got onto the device. Giles joined her as the size of the earth sled grew to accommodate them. Raven nodded, smiling. Everyone looked at him. Lauriel gave a low, conversational growl.

"Oh!" Raven hopped onto the sled and small walls grew around the edges to keep everybody inside.

Brigit looked at Lauriel. "Do you know where we need to go?"

Lauriel licked her hand, then powered the sled towards the war front.

James heard a noise and opened his eyes. He hadn't meant to doze off, but the bench was magically comfortable and the hike up and down the stairs had been tiring. He sat up and walked over to the railing. The lobby of the tower was empty.

Must have been Michael and Catriona leaving the realm.

He wasn't sure if he would know that or not because the only doors were the ones to the different seasonal realms. The access to the realm likewise had no door so it had to be just the feeling of suddenly being entirely alone.

That's probably best though. If either of them had any inkling of my intention…

James remembered Catriona's glance over his features. He snorted. She knew. She didn't stop him. Michael probably wouldn't have either, now that he gave it some thought. Michael let him handle his family grief while he followed his own path. He would have understood.

No point in putting it off any longer.

James went down the stairs as quickly as he dared and went before the Door of Winter. He opened it and found himself at the doors to the great throne room. Silence hung like a deep blanket of snow across the room. Everywhere, Fae creatures slumped where the stood, dormant. Even the giant guards by the doors seemed deep asleep. James pushed on the doors to the throne room and they slid open, deepening the silence by adding more space to it. He walked in on the entire Winter Court unmoving. A light dusting of snow covered them all. He looked behind him at the guards and realized their white fur also had a dusting of snow. A few flakes fell from the ceiling which was covered in clouds.

He looked around for any sign of movement or habitation but there was none. He left his footprints in the snow behind him as he explored the palace. Off to the right of the great throne, he thought he heard a sound. The air was crisp and the building perpetuated the echoes of his clothes swishing. The snow cover dampened any other sounds so he had difficulty locating the source of the sound, or even identifying it. It was a clipped, high timber that seemed to come from everywhere and nowhere at once.

He moved towards a hallway to the right of the throne and the tunnel amplified the sound. He followed it to a room with the door partially open. Inside, he saw Gloriana draped across an effigy of Alistair, carved onto the stone lid of a sarcophagus. An engraving around the edge of the lid proclaimed, "Alistair Chapton Hapsburg, Prince of York."

James took a knee in the doorway and cleared his throat. "Your Majesty."

Gloriana looked at him, sorrow temporarily overcome by surprise. "You."

"James, Your Majesty. My name is James." He looked at the effigy. "Chapton?"

Gloriana glanced back at the effigy, then nodded.

"Alistair didn't have a middle name, that I knew." James nodded to the figure on the top of the lid. "That's the real man, I take it?"

Gloriana inclined her head. "He told it to me when he asked for a token. I told him I would give him my glove until after the war. Then, I would give him my hand in exchange. He promised to keep it safe until he could return it."

James reached into a pouch on his belt. "Was it this one?"

Gloriana looked at the glove, snow white including the fur at the cuff, embroidered with a "G".

Her tears ran fresh as she rose and came to collect it. When she touched it, a figure sprang from it, and a man who looked very much like Alistair stood before her.

"My love, my beautiful snowy Queen. I had Snow cast a spell so I could be with you once again. The mission to my castle is dangerous. I don't know what I'll find there. But I know what I have *here*." He touched his heart. "And here." He touched the glove. "I am in love with you. And if we get clear of this war intact, I want to marry you. We will live wherever you choose. I will abdicate the throne if need be to be with you. I don't care.

"Gloriana, my mountain flower, you are my strength. Hold fast to the knowledge that I love you, and look for my return."

Gloriana reached out to the man but her hand passed through him. However, her eyes closed and she breathed deeply. "It's him, truly him. There is some of his essence inside this spell." She held the glove to her chest and smiled.

She opened her eyes, looking at James. The image faded as she took her son's hand. "Thank you for bringing him back to me."

She pulled him into an embrace, much to James' shock. He returned the embrace and relaxed.

When she finally released him, she looked at his face and frowned. "I'm sorry I hurt you. Here, let me heal that." She raised her hand and a glow of white-blue light emitted from her fingers.

James took her wrist gently, stopping her. "Please, don't. I need you to be able to tell us apart."

Gloriana blinked, then nodded. "I will leave it then." She stepped back as he released her wrist, glancing down at the glove. "Is this why you returned?"

"No, though I had planned to return this to you. It simply slipped my mind at our last encounter. No, I have come to do something that… should have been done the *last* generation." He took a knee before her. "I wish to enter your service, to repay the debt and damage my father did to you."

Gloriana straightened, her hands in front of her. The room grew cold for a moment, but then she glanced at the glove in her hand and the temperature warmed again.

"My Breath was taken from me in the war. One of the first casualties, in fact. We froze the air around us, killing anything that could carry the disease. My nephew came to warn us of the impending trouble, and we went to his covenant at Persephone to discuss what could be done. That's where I met my love. We all worked together, utilizing frozen specimens to study the virulence of the problem. Once we knew, we realized we could not stop it. Embertwist had closed the roads but we only had so long before the seasons changed hands and the world was flooded with the disease.

"That's when Calpurnia suggested we close them off from reality." She stepped over to a set of chairs with fur blankets upon them, motioning James to follow. A decanter of dark blue liquid rested upon a silver tray, and she poured it into two glasses. James sat after she did, taking the offered glass.

"You must understand that creating a new realm is terribly difficult. You have to access powers beyond those of the world to request a new piece be made. Calpurnia thought she could do it, but she didn't know how long it would take. She and Merrick went about doing so, using a mage spell that created a pocket place only the mage could access. The trouble with it was that the mage's pocket dimension collapsed when they died. That would release the monsters back into the world, something we all found unacceptable.

"So, she found a different solution."

James frowned. "What was it?"

Gloriana shrugged. "We don't know. She kept that secret to herself. It's possible the Elegant Solution has it, but we don't know who that is."

"Elegant Solution?"

Gloriana nodded. "Yes. Her lieutenant. The Sinister Glove of Embertwist, The Voice of Command of Corrigan, the Elegant Solution of Calpurnia, and the Glacial Breath of myself."

"I see. This is not common knowledge in the human world."

"It isn't *for* the human world, to be honest. Though we do employ the human world to do it."

"How so?"

"All our lieutenants are human. It's necessary so they can read and write what we do. That's why Alistair had to go to such lengths to make a message for me. I could never read a letter and he knew it."

"He said the snow helped him make it?"

"Snow. She was a mage who specialized in weather and image magic. She was from Yokotama and came to Persephone to learn the ways of magic here, then return."

"Could she still be in Yokotama?"

Gloriana shook her head. "I don't know. Her infant was destroyed during the war, before it was born, by the Soulless. The child was ripped from her before the disease could kill her. She survived, but only barely. Eirdrin was part giant, and they went to his people after the war to recover. Then the human Church began to attack all sacred sites of the Land and all creatures retreated into our realms. Most were sealed against anything holy or human."

"If the human world is so dangerous to the Fae, why have your lieutenants be human?"

"Because not all humans are bad, and they can communicate with other humans easily. Though it can be difficult to understand us. We are not linear thinkers."

"I'm not having any trouble."

"You are part Fae, but raised by humans. This is how we have communicated for centuries with the humans: through a bond like this."

"And do you wish me to be a conduit through which you speak to the world?" James was humble in the request, no arrogance or assertion that this should be her choice.

Gloriana thought about this. "I will have to see. We must wait and determine your place here. Come. I will show you a room where you may put your things."

They rose and she led him down the corridor to a place with a working fireplace, lots of furs, a bed, a desk, and paper, quills, and ink.

"I hope you will find this comfortable. Excuse me, I am tired and must rest. Food will arrive as you are hungry. Relax until we meet again."

She gave a small bow and he bowed deeply in thanks as she left the room.

Twenty-Three

"The rain is to the river as the lion is to the farmer." (The danger rises.)

Johner pointed to a cot. "Put His Majesty there."

The half ogres set him on the cot, not nearly as careful about the arrow in his leg as Alexander would have liked.

"Now, send in the medical team."

A half ogre grunted and stepped out. The other one stood in the doorway, facing the room with his arms crossed. Moments later, a half dog and a half spider entered the room. Both were terrifying but Alexander did his diplomatic best not to flinch. The half spider used her mandibles to cut the pant leg cleanly away from the wound and remove the shaft, then the half dog licked the wound to clean it.

Alexander flinched away from the action at first, until the numbing agent took effect. The pain in his leg faded to a dull ache. The half spider stepped back in with silk and a large hooked needle.

Alexander turned to Johner. "What do you want, General?"

"You're the royal leader of the opposing army. It would be inappropriate not to have captured you for leverage. You were in the enemy camp. The best thing I could do for your safety was to seize you."

"Then you plan to return me to the village?"

Johner shook his head. "Not if I wish to keep you safe."

Alexander flinched as the needle went deeper than the anesthesia. "What… what makes you think I'm not safe in the village?"

Johner glanced at the medical spider, who was filling the wound with spider silk to stop the bleeding. "You said before you did not order the destruction of the Fae soldiers. Someone divine did. What do you know about that?"

Alexander scratched an itch on his neck that seemed to travel all the way up from his leg. "I have no idea. I'm afraid I'm just a pawn in this."

"You are more important than that, Your Majesty. You are at least a bishop." He smiled, then took a deep breath, his posture more professional. "What do you *know* about the attack?"

"Only what you've told me. But, I can pray to my patron saint. She might know more. If this came from Heaven…"

"And the Saints will answer a human?"

Alexander shrugged, then winced at the needle poked again. "I don't know about *all* humans, but she answered us a day ago."

Johner gestured. "Proceed then."

Alexander closed his eyes and focused his attention on Heaven.

Saint Brigit, help me. I need to know what's going on.

He heard and sensed no reply. He took a cleansing breath and let it out again.

Saint Brigit, please! Hear me!

He was about to call out again when a distinctly not-Brigit voice answered him. The sound filled his entire consciousness, surrounding him and cutting off the outside world.

What is it, sinner?

Alexander blinked. *Uh, it's Alexander. I'm trying to speak to Brigit, Patron Saint of Healers.*

Brigit is… indisposed.

Alexander could hear the smirk in the voice.

Forgive me, but a Fae army is marching on my country as we speak. I need her help to stop a war.

And I'm trying to get one started.

A flash lit the valley and Johner stepped outside. Alexander leaned to look out the tent door. Johner looked up, then motioned to the guards. They entered and picked Alexander up, carrying him in a makeshift sling between them. The spider protested but the dog was already outside with Johner.

Above the valley was a glowing yellow-white figure suspended like a star. Giant wings stretched behind it. Shoulder-length hair of glowing white light framed a face of immense beauty, but the sense Alexander got was far from benevolent.

"Listen well. I am the Archangel Gabriel. My champion Alexander chose to deliver the tool of Heaven to your army. He knows how to destroy you all. He has given this knowledge to his fellow humans." Gabriel turned to Alexander, gesturing. "The war is yours, Your Majesty."

Alexander felt the half ogres tense, and terror ripped through his chest.

Heaven wanted a war. Gabriel just ensured he'd get one.

Tanglwyst looked at her ship captain. "Did you see and hear that?"

"Hear what?"

"Nothing. Never mind. Get the families organized. I need something from my cabin."

She took off towards the ship which was being loaded with the supplies from the town. She dodged the deck hands and ducked into her room. It still had the bedding for a dozen children in here and two adults, and smelled faintly of dirty diapers, even with the windows open. The sea water would cause chafing and misery, and could get the babies sick so the diapers were being washed twice: Once in sea water to get the filth off, then again in fresh drinking water to get the salt out. It meant the water supplies were going to be gone through faster than normal. The adults would have to ration their drinking use for the next two days of travel and the first week on the island.

She sat at her desk and closed her eyes.

Alex.

She could see him being carried inside a tent and felt his wounded leg. Johner was with him.

"Leave us." Johner gestured to the half Fae monsters around the tent and they scurried outside. *"How is your leg?"*

"Better. Numb, currently."

"Good. What was that out there?"

Alexander shook his head. *"I don't know. That's not my saint. He wants a war with humans."*

"But they worship the saints? Why does he want to destroy his base?"

"Now we're to questions I would like answered."

Johner paced. *"This makes no sense. Killing humans would make Heaven weaker, not stronger."*

"I know. I..."

A cacophony of howls and shrieks came from outside the tent and Johner glanced at Alexander, then tucked outside to deal with it.

Alexander turned his attention inward.

She sent panicked feelings to him regarding his injury but he sent reassurance back. Clearly, this was not the thing he was worried about.

He sent feelings about his mother. It was her turn to send reassurance and he relaxed.

She indicated concern about Johner and the Fae army but he was negative. Apparently, he did not see them as a threat anymore, despite what she had overheard through their link.

She felt that was foolish.

He felt she might be right. But they both sensed Johner was protecting Alexander and waiting.

The Fae Army. Corrigan's army. They were coming. They both believed that was what the General was waiting for.

Neither wanted to admit they were worried about the outcome of meeting Corrigan.

They held each other a moment longer, then Tanglwyst pulled back. She needed to get some things taken care of and there wasn't much time left. She promised to return and broke the connection.

She glanced around the cabin and then unlocked a drawer in the desk. She pulled out a paper and a seal. She heated the wax and sealed the note, then put it in a pouch on her belt. Then she left the cabin to help get things loaded.

Gabriel lowered his arms, his presence fading from the sky below them. The crystal pillar returned to normal glow, which made the whole room look dim by comparison. He smiled, turning to Raphael.

Raphael returned the smile. "That should get the creatures scrambling to kill each other. That king should be dead within the minute."

Gabriel nodded to the pillar. "Do we want to watch?"

Raphael snorted. "Watch the death of one single, but significant human? I would love to, but I have to ensure the war occurs. I can't count on this fool's death to be the catalyst. He might be less valuable that Brigit believed." He focused upon the pillar. "Go, prepare your champion. We have set the stage. Time to get the first act going."

Brother Robert stepped back into the church after the Archangel faded from the sky. The trick had worked. Alexander was being given credit for it, which meant he *had* been working for Heaven when he left the coat behind.

That's why he didn't want to discuss it! Those rabbit eared monsters might have heard the plan.

But now he had a duty to Heaven and the Kingdom. He needed to get the village protected.

He saw a barrel of water being rolled away from the city well and frowned. The well water was going to be needed for the army coming from Patras. They had to stop using it. He stepped out of the church and saw Gomez.

"Grande Guarde, a moment please."

Gomez looked at Brother Robert and came over to him. "Yes, Brother Robert?"

"The army of Mervolingia will be arriving soon. We need to conserve supplies. They can't drink sea water."

Gomez nodded. "I was thinking the same thing." He looked Brother Robert over a moment. "Is there any reason why you can't bless *sea* water?"

Brother Robert frowned. "The well has already been blessed so it makes it simple for me to just mutter a blessing to finish the job. The sea has its own mythos. I have to do a more vigorous blessing to get it to work."

Ais ran up to the pair. "Gentlemen, I'm to inform you that we have a second brand available. It just got finished."

Gomez looked at the barrels awaiting filling.

"Guards!" He walked over to the men, and Ais and Brother Robert followed. "Ais has a new brand. We need these barrels brought to the docks via the blacksmith shop. Brand every one."

"Aye Sir."

Gomez turned back to Ais. "You and Brother Robert head there now so he can bless the brands."

"Bless the *brands*, sir?"

"Yes. You'll burn the brand into the barrels so the sea water is blessed with a single gesture."

Brother Robert snapped his fingers. "The Sea Goddess hates fire and will abandon that which it touches. That's *brilliant*!"

Ais smiled slowly, nodding.

Gomez looked at Brother Robert. "Is that vigorous enough for you?"

Brother Robert smiled. "That should do nicely."

Tanglwyst found Catherine as Captain Nesbit spoke to the crew about the change in plans. She was handing a small girl off to two adult women. Catherine waved as they gathered the girl into relieved hugs.

Catherine glanced at Tanglwyst as she walked up. "Their daughter wandered off to play in the woods and didn't let anyone know."

"That would be so frightening in a new place like this."

Catherine turned to her. "What's wrong?"

"A lot." She filled her in on the Mervol army and their missive, and on the situation with Alexander.

Catherine stepped back to lean against a tree. This allowed her to collapse a bit without alerting the people around her. She closed her eyes. "The number of Fae in that valley…"

Tanglwyst dropped her gaze to the forest floor. "I know."

"Have you checked on him since?"

"I think you'd know if something happened to him. You *are* a loyal citizen of Mervolingia."

Catherine sighed. "True. By the Saints, this is a nightmare."

She tilted her head back, containing the tears that threatened her composure. She closed her eyes for a moment, then shook herself. A deep breath later and she was ready.

"We need to get these people back on your ship then?"

Tanglwyst put her hand on Catherine's arm. "Not you. You need to get to Patras. Now." She nodded to the main road just within sight a quarter mile through the woods. "Go towards Patras about a mile. There is an inn with stables. Give them this. It will get you home."

Tanglwyst pulled the sealed note from her pouch.

Catherine took it and nodded.

"Go now. We need you directing things from the palace. If something happens to Alexander…"

"I know." Catherine hugged Tanglwyst and took off through the woods.

Gabriel opened the door to the small room. "It's time."

Saint George, Patron to Soldiers, looked up at the archangel. The Saints had been relegated to individual rooms with no contact with each other. Only a few Saints were working the birthing floor at a time, cutting back on the number of souls being taken from the Well. This bothered George because it meant many babies would be stillborn. But the angels had given the order, and he knew they had a reason. It was a soldier's place to follow orders and trust his command.

He stood and Gabriel opened a hole in the floor. "You are to go to the human army and help them defeat the Fae menace. Do you understand?"

George nodded.

Gabriel gestured to George and the Saint found himself on a field near a large dome of thorns. He frowned at the structure, recognizing the magic behind it to not be of Heaven, then turned away from it. The sky above was clear but the air smelled of campfires. He strode towards the edge of the valley and looked out over the army camped there. At first, he wondered if this was the army he was to lead. Then he noticed the abnormally large soldiers scattered about and the ones with bird heads and realized this was the enemy.

He could sense the Fae behind him and in the forest by the road. He could now smell the Fae before him. He looked across the valley and could barely make out a village on the far side. George frowned. This was going to be harder than he expected.

It took less than an hour to get the barrels branded and loaded. The docks had multiple pumps for their dry dock and those enabled the barrels to be filled six at a time as opposed to one with a bucket at the town's well. The wagons were pulled to the blacksmith's shop where they were branded, then by Brother Robert's church to do the final touch for the contents. He smiled at the first batch when the experiment worked.

"Take the barrels a mile out of town on the road then empty them onto the ground. Be careful not to break them. We only have so many. Have the next wagonload stop before the drenched road and do likewise all the way back to the village. We need a clear path of protection for the Mervol army." He motioned to Ais and directed him to a barrel. "Have a barrel with the brand at the smithy and put the discs in it. When it's full, fill it with water and put it with the others for blessing. We need enough of those discs to have one on every soldier."

Ais nodded and returned to the blacksmith.

"What about us, Brother?"

Robert turned to look at the young farmers' sons who had remained behind to protect the village. He pointed to a new wagonload of barrels that just arrived.

"Use those to line the street from the barrier line to the docks, about a house apart. We need a barrier to protect our homes."

He walked to the barrels and uttered a blessing. A light from his hand spread out and touched every barrel at the symbols, filling the barrels before fading. The young men grabbed a barrel each and split up, one going to the docks, one to the barrier line towards Patras.

At this rate, we'll be set by nightfall.

He smiled as another wagonload of barrels lumbered up the hill.

By nightfall, all the supplies and people were loaded and the *Sulocco* had pulled away from shore. Captain Nesbit turned the ship north and sighted along the stars to move them in the right direction.

They had two days to sail before the very tricky maneuvering of a laden ship in the maelstrom surrounding the Storm King's Island. He did not relish that part.

He looked out over the families settling in to sleep amongst the lumber and sawdust. The supplies actually offered a modicum of protection and comfort to the refugees, an unexpected but grateful side effect of the stop at St. Teresa. This enabled the crew more comfortable sleeping quarters as well as families to cuddle with their children.

Before long, the storms would set in and all the children and half the adults would be sent into the hold or quarters while the rest maintained the ropes and worked to sail the ship. Water would rush through the supplies, carrying away some of the flotsam already starting to accumulate from the very small children. The men and women caring for the infants were kept quite busy with cleaning and feeding and walking the babies. The toddlers and "young runners" were an additional concern as everyone was mindful of potential death traps for them.

There was nowhere the supplies could be put that wasn't a possible playground for these children too young and restless to understand the peril. They could get into crannies the adults could not and a ship was plenty dangerous *without* the added challenges. The whole crew was wary and alert, and Captain Nesbit was grateful they only had two days travel. More than that and they would no doubt lose a couple of the young ones who would take advantage of a sleeping parent or guardian.

But for now, tonight, things were peaceful. At dawn, there would be fish nets to cast and haul to feed everyone, which would prove a chore beyond measure for the cook. With all the extra wood on board, there was no place to build a fire for the cook pot. He prayed to Calista for fair winds and following seas, then returned to the helm to rest.

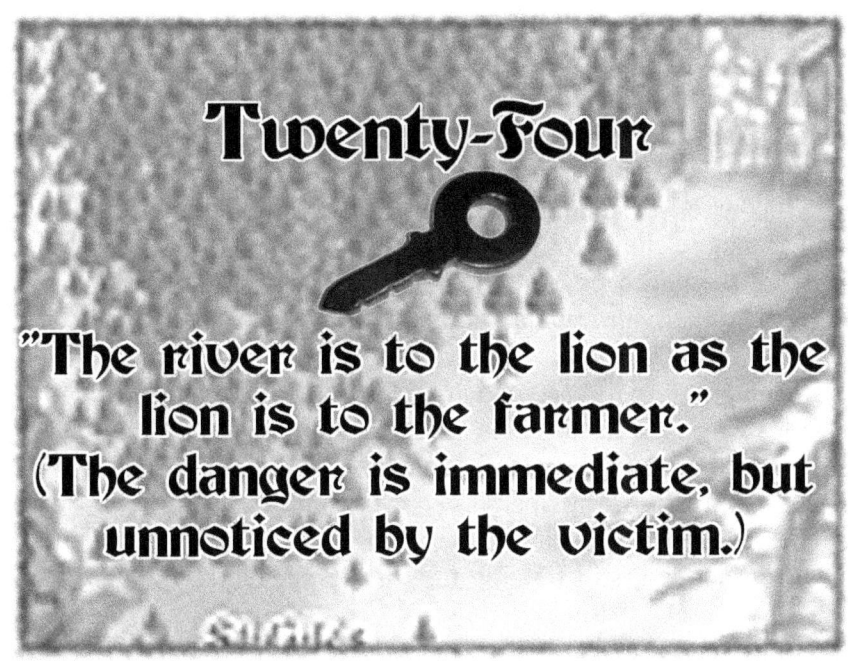

Twenty-Four

"The river is to the lion as the lion is to the farmer." (The danger is immediate, but unnoticed by the victim.)

Giles tapped Lauriel on the shoulder. "Can you stop a moment here?"

Brigit looked at Giles. "What's wrong?"

"Nothing's *wrong*. Raven, you said you need to get to the Giver. There's an old resting place of hers around here. We used it once to reach out to her."

"Resting place?"

"Yeah. She used to travel all over the area, bringing births to term and prepping fields. Life Giver stuff. And when she was done with a bout of that, she would rest for a while, away from the demands of the people. The places got infused with her pure essence. They were hidden from everyone so she wouldn't be disturbed. My mother accidentally gave birth to me in one so I've always been able to see them."

Raven lowered the protective walls and jumped down from the sled. "And there's one here? I've never felt anything in this area."

"You said you don't worship Heaven. Or rather, I guess that was what you meant when you said you wouldn't go to Heaven if you could get into the afterlife."

"No, you're right. I'm not a Heaven guy." Raven smiled. "See? Magic understands magic!"

Giles nodded, peering around. "It's so faint. But then again, it has been a long time." He held up his hand and conjured light. He sent it into the air to float behind him. He pointed to the ground. "There. Can you move the earth around it, carefully?"

"Of course." Raven focused upon the area and lifted the top two feet of soil as a large chunk for about thirty feet.

Brigit stepped back, but Giles just looked around, like Raven had lifted a rug to help him find a button. He shook his head.

"Try here." Giles pointed to another area.

Raven put the soil back and pulled another thirty feet.

Giles shook his head. "This isn't turning it up."

Brigit rolled her eyes. "Raven, can you tell what's under the ground *without* ripping the world apart?"

Giles looked at Brigit, then at Raven.

Raven nodded, still holding the dirt suspended. "Oh yeah. Easily. Why?"

"Giles, tell him what you're looking for."

"Oh. A cavern, with water and trees."

Raven nodded. He put the soil back and then touched the ground. "There's a couple of things here. One is over there. It's an old pit."

Giles shook his head. "Yeah, we don't want that one."

"The other one is there." Raven lifted considerably more soil than previously from the ground, at least five feet of depth.

Giles nodded. "That's it."

He stepped down into the cavern. From above, it was just a natural cavern with some water flowing through it. But when he entered it fully, the area transformed. Now there was also a sparkling pond and a tree growing to the sky, old and much taller than he remembered.

Brigit went to the edge and looked in. "Doesn't look like much."

Giles looked around. "What do you see?"

Raven walked over as well, holding the soil in the air behind him. "Cave. Stream. More cave."

Brigit nodded. "Yeah, that's about it."

"Do you see the tree?" Giles motioned to it.

Brigit frowned. "No."

He motioned for them both to join him. Raven put the soil on the ground behind him. Lauriel joined him at the edge. Brigit climbed down and Giles went to help her. She frowned at him as he put his hands on her hips and assisted her down.

"Really?"

He glanced around. "I was helping you... down."

"I didn't need help getting the last five feet."

"Catch me, Giles!" Raven jumped into Giles' arms.

Giles wasn't expecting it and they both fell to the ground as Brigit dodged the fiasco. Lauriel jumped down beside her, bristling.

Raven got up, dusting himself off. He looked around. "Still no tree."

Brigit blinked. "It's there." She looked at the upper branches. "That tree is definitely not visible from out there. And it really should be."

Raven looked at Lauriel. "Really?"

Lauriel snorted, spikes on his back up and sharp.

Brigit looked at the Fae wolf. "What's wrong?"

"He says this place is not of the Land."

Giles shook his head. "No. It's..." He rubbed his hands through his hair. "Honestly, it's of Heaven. You can't see this?"

Lauriel growled.

Raven slumped. "Oh."

Brigit looked at Lauriel. "What?"

"Lauriel says it's a realm. I can't go into those now if they connect to the afterlife. I've been banned."

"That's *great!*"

Everyone looked at Giles.

"No, I mean, well, not great for *you,* but great for your quest! Look!" Giles went over to the tree, his hands waving at the giant specimen. "This is here, and *bigger* than it was before. That branch up there," he looked up about twenty feet, "that branch was down here before. That means this tree..."

"Is still alive!" Raven and Giles said together. Giles ran to Raven and they jumped around together. Lauriel stood, tail wagging and joined in the revelry.

Brigit folded her arms. "So? How does this help Alexander?"

Giles grinned at her. "It doesn't!"

Brigit set her teeth. "Lauriel, can you take me the rest of the way to where Alexander is?"

Raven waved his hands at her. "No! Wait, this kinda helps everyone. If we can extract the essence, the *čaro* of this place, we can make a key that unlocks Heaven." He patted his chest. "I still can't use it, but you can. It might free the Giver if you can get Catriona there."

"Who is Catriona?"

"She's the Death Bringer."

Brigit blinked, thinking. "Wait, is she Caratian? Is that the woman you spoke of?"

"Yeah yeah! That's her!"

"Oh for…" Brigit threw her arms in the air. "No wonder she was wrong for him." She looked at Giles. "That's the woman Alexander was chasing."

Giles' face sank. "Oh." He swallowed. "That explains a lot." He shook himself out of it. "But that's not what we have right now. Right now, I need your help, Raven, to extract the essence of this place. Clearly, there's still some in that tree or it wouldn't be growing."

"But it's in a tree, Giles." Brigit pointed to the tree. "Doesn't that mean it's tree *čaro* now?"

He looked up at the tree. "Um…" His face fell as he realized she was right. The essence was altered. He sighed. "Yes, yes you're right. Come. Let's get moving."

Lauriel looked up and then at Raven.

"Maybe. But it won't work for me."

Brigit and Giles both looked at them.

"Lauriel says that sleeping here might give you dreams that can solve the problem."

Giles perked up. "Yes! *Yes.* That happened all the time back when I was here."

"Giles, we don't *have time…*"

"Why are you *rushing,* Brigit?" Giles was furious, her constant pushing back finally taking its toll. "We were thrown out of Heaven days ago. *Days.* If they were going to kill him, they would have done it by now, while we were out of commission from the fall. The only reason you *care* so much is because you don't want him to think you've abandoned him. And why would he think that, Brigit? *Because you have already done exactly that.*"

Brigit swallowed, taking a step back.

"We have a chance to make a key that will *stop* the angels from destroying everyone. We can access the Giver and possibly put her in a trap that Gabriel and Raphael can't get to because it's something belonging to the Land. It's not ideal, but it's better than letting them bleed her for souls."

"Uh, actually," Raven held up a finger, "the trap feeds a different spell and drains the victim. It's something I was going to ask for your help with."

Giles and Brigit turned slowly to look at Raven.

Raven turned upwards palms to Giles. "But, but your idea is still a valid one! We do still need a key to get her out of there, whether we then put her in a trap or not."

Brigit scowled in frustration. "Whether we…?"

Giles grabbed Brigit's arm. "Please don't kill him. We need him to get her out. And then you can kill him."

Raven nodded, nervous. "Yeah. Kill me later, I'll totally deserve it by then."

"By then?" Brigit jerked her arm from Giles. "I'm trying to stop a *war* that will destroy every living thing with a *soul*. I'm quite willing to kill you right *now*."

Raven frowned. "Gee. I thought Saints were supposed to be benevolent."

"Well I'm not exactly a Saint anymore, am I?"

"Well no, but you're not going to let that change your fundamental nature, are you? I mean, it's not like the angels aren't probably watching you right now, reveling in your pain."

Brigit stopped, stunned by Raven's words.

"What?" Giles looked up, then at Brigit. "Do you think he's right?"

Brigit's gaze wandered as she thought this over. "We're cut off from them. I guess I thought…"

"They'd be cut off from you? Why? *They* threw *you* out. It wasn't a mutual parting." Raven gestured to the north. "Could you still see Raymond after he fell?"

Brigit's eyes rolled, sadness eating away the exasperation. "Yes. I kept track of him at first, until Clara came up and assumed his duties." She turned to Raven. "And you think they're watching us now?"

Raven looked at Giles. "Do you think they can see into this place?"

"There's no reason they shouldn't."

"Wrong." Brigit's expression had changed to wicked excitement. "She has *every* reason not to allow them access to it." She looked at Giles. "You said she made this place, right?"

Giles nodded.

"Then *she* controls it, not the Angels. It's not connected to *Heaven.* It's connected to *her.* This may be the best place possible to plan. I have no doubt she is has sealed it against Heaven's supporters. In fact," Brigit looked up at the tree, "this may be a conduit directly to her."

"You think that tree reaches all the way to her?" Giles looked again at the tree.

Brigit smiled. "I do. You don't need to extract it. You already have the key into Heaven."

Raven smirked. "Because *I* can't see it."

Brigit pointed to him. "Exactly."

Giles nodded. "Okay, we'll rest here for the night, then we'll head out. That way, she can reach out to us. It's the best chance we have."

Brigit glanced at the sky, then nodded. "Fine, we'll stay. Let's hope she reaches out."

Catherine entered the Weary Traveler Inn as dark descended. The trek was not far from St. Teresa, but it was far enough to have taken some time, and as she had observed before, she was not young anymore. Sovereigna's refreshments had helped her this far though. She doubted she could have made it without them.

She swallowed past the lump in her throat. She was worried about her beloved, about her son, now about her son's beloved. She was also worried about her people, and her granddaughter. So much was happening that endangered her family, she would have either been immobilized with fear or driven to save them. She was glad to have the energy to do the latter.

The innkeep looked up from a comfortable chair by the hearth. "Welcome, traveler! Are you alone tonight or will there be others?"

"Just myself tonight. I have a letter." She handed the sealed missive to the man.

He looked at the seal. "Ah. You're on Holloway business." He opened the missive. "It says you need a room, a meal, and a horse."

"The last two for sure. I'm not certain I can spare time for the first one though."

"My lady, as tough as you may be, I would be remiss if I allowed you to travel the road at night."

Catherine realized at once she was actually quite exhausted. The trip from St. Giles in the middle of the night and not resting since, she had been running purely on that wine Sovereigna had given her. But that effect was fading as she spoke to the man. She leaned against a chair to steady herself from the onrush of fatigue.

The man caught the gesture and moved to help her into a chair. "Let me get you something. *Ren.*"

A young woman with short brown hair and one wandering eye came in. "Yesh, Shawn?" The woman also had a slight lisp.

"Get a room ready. And ask Sarah to ready a bowl of stew, please."

Ren popped into the next room and Shawn poured her a cup of tea from the decanter he had on the table by his chair. "Here. This should help."

Catherine took it and sipped carefully. It was exactly the right temperature to be drank and she did so. A minute later, another woman came from the back with a tray of food and a mug. She was about Shawn's age and blond, though both women were about the same height. Shawn, in contrast, was a tall man with a perpetually merry face. His small eyes were upturned at the ends, like his mouth, so he looked happy no matter what. Catherine found these fine traits in an innkeep. He made her feel at ease.

Another man leaned forward in his hearth chair and looked at Catherine. He nodded to her and stood, putting his tea mug on the tray Shawn served hers from. He looked at Shawn.

"I'm going to retire, Master Lowry. You have a new victim for your tales so I will leave you to tend to her."

Shawn waved and smiled as the other man took his leave and went upstairs.

After she had eaten, Ren escorted Catherine upstairs to a room. It was well appointed and quaint, and had the most important thing in the world right then: a bed. Fresh towels were on it and Ren motioned to the table by the hearth.

"There's fresh water in the pitcher if you want to wash up."

"You are a treasure, young lady. Thank you."

"Thanksh. Do you need anything elsh?"

"No, but I have nothing to give you for your kindness."

Ren waved her off. "Don't worry about it. Holloway hash an account here. Lady Tanglwysht alwaysh thinksh of that. Resht well."

Catherine nodded, then took the towels to the basin. She almost didn't use the it, but changed her mind. She would sleep better if she were clean. She barely got herself dry when she heard a small noise behind her. She turned to see the man from the lobby in her room.

The man took a knee before her, head bowed. "Your Majesty."

Catherine stayed wary. "Yes?"

"I am a scout for the Mervol Army." He showed her a symbol sewn inside his jacket. It meant little to her. "Do you need a guard and escort?"

"I…" She was about to refuse him, but realized he was undoubtedly right. "I *might*. You are a scout? How far behind is the army?"

"A day, Your Majesty."

A day? "And what do you have to report?"

"There is an army marching through the forest to the south, opposite from the King's Highway here. They will be reinforcing the Fae army."

"What makes you think they are Fae?"

"Because they are parting the forest before them and closing it behind. I saw it from the mountain passage by Caratia's border."

"The border? Why were you there?"

"I'm a scout, Your Majesty. It's what I do."

"So, you came from the other side of the valley. Have you been to St. Giles yet?"

"No Ma'am. I have seen the Fae army in the valley though. I was going to report back their numbers and strengths."

"I have come back from that area just now."

"You…m, Ma'am?"

"I have my ways. And I have a report to give as well. We will go to the army tomorrow. Leave and get some rest."

He stood and started to leave. "Your Majesty… the King?"

"Is in St. Giles. He has freed the people there and awaits the army."

The man nodded and left.

She locked the door behind him and settled in to get some rest. Tomorrow was going to be a busy day.

Brother Robert opened his eyes and saw a figure before him. He raised his arm and shielded his eyes from the light emanating from the creature. The figure stretched out a hand and touched Robert on the forehead. Then it disappeared.

Brother Robert sat up, an idea strong and compelling in his head.

Divine inspiration. That's what this is. I can stop this. I can save us all.

He muttered a thank you to St. Giles. The picture in his mind was clear and he knew exactly how to make it. He got up and rushed outside into the darkness.

Twenty-Five

"The flood is to the lion as the river is to the rain."
(The swollen river does not notice the lion any more than it notices the rain.)

"So, you know magic and stuff."

Giles looked at Raven. "You might say. In fact, I invented a lot of spells. There was the one that infused weapons with magic to fight beasts that could only be hurt by spells. One that released mental magic so we could destroy ghosts. One that helped locate Fae. One that siphoned off *čaro* and put it into solid form so it was no longer there. I made a teleportation amulet so I could travel back and forth to the estate."

"Wait. *You* created those? Why did you make them so evil?"

Giles paused. "Evil?" Then he relaxed, waving off Raven's concerns. "They weren't *evil*, my boy. They were simply magic. It's easy to believe something different is evil but I can assure you, it's simply new."

"'My boy?' Seriously?" Brigit glared at Giles. "You arrogant cretin. Did you honestly just explain *magic* to a *mage* like he was a stupid farmhand?"

Giles blinked. "Uh… oh no. I fear I did. I just…"

Brigit got up from the small fire they had built and stormed over to the area farthest from the mages. She moved around on a mossy spot, then settled in to sleep. Lauriel looked at the men and then joined her, shaking his head.

Giles sighed. "I just can't seem to make any headway with her. I fear my attraction to her is starting to suffer."

"Why does that matter?"

"Well, she'll surely need a man in her life here on earth."

"Why?"

"Because we are on earth and no one will pay any attention to her or give her any value at all if she doesn't have a man with her. She needs someone to speak for her, buy things for her, feed her, clothe her."

Raven blinked. "Wow. I see why you went to Heaven."

"Well, it was only inevitable. I *did* do a lot of groundbreaking work on divine magic. And vanquished many, many monsters. Whole lines of creatures were destroyed thanks to my efforts."

"You somehow think you're the right person for this job?"

"Of course. We have shared experiences. Why wouldn't I be?"

"Because you're a man."

Giles' brow furrowed. "I don't understand your reasoning."

"She's not interested in men. She's interested in women. You've literally done nothing but irritate her the entire time I've been around you. I'm pretty sure she hates you."

"But she can't prefer women. That would be unnatural."

Raven's eyes grew wide. "Whoa! Ho boy. Are you cursed? I'll bet you're cursed. If you did what you're saying you did, someone cursed you. Thinking women *need* men and that any woman who doesn't is unnatural is a good way to get yourself slaughtered." Raven blinked. "How *did* you die?"

"My wife went insane. She snapped after having our third child and I told her she needed to take care of the children from now on instead of bothering me in my laboratory or when I was having tea at the local inn." Giles frowned. "Come to think of it, I think she said something about being in labor right then."

"You told a woman in labor not to bother you? How did she do it? Snap your neck?"

"Shot me. With a bow *I* made for her, in fact!"

"Uh, would you excuse me for a second."

Raven got up and walked over to Brigit. Lauriel looked at him but Brigit went back to closing her eyes and pretending to sleep when he sat down.

"Brigit, forgive me for bothering you, but has he always been like this?"

"An arrogant jerk? I…," she blinked, frowning. "I don't remember him upsetting me like this in Heaven. We were all allies there. I don't understand how he's changed so drastically."

"I think I do. He's cursed."

Brigit sat up. "What?"

"Coming back down here clearly restarted it. It means it was something associated with this place, not ending at his death. He was just bragging about how he destroyed whole lines of beasts when he was alive. It's not just you he's alienating. It's anyone he meets. The longer you're around him, the worse he becomes.

"Take what he just said. He was going on about how women need men. I can easily shrug that off since I'm not a woman."

Brigit nodded. "But I had to deal with it my entire life. I was constantly being told I had no value except to men or through them."

"Well, him bragging that whole lineages of beasts were destroyed or trying to explain magic to me are more trigger points for me. I don't really get irritated by much but I can see what's happening. He's feeling me out for reactions. I'm more obscure, so he's doing a wide range of insults until something works."

Brigit sighed. "And with us not being able to die, he has all the time in the world to offend everyone." She looked at Raven. "So what do we do?"

Raven pursed his lips in thought. Lauriel cocked his head, then got up. He padded over to the other mage. Giles said something to him that made Lauriel take a step back, then he reached out and tugged on Giles' sleeve. Giles got up and Lauriel walked over to an area about four feet away from the little stream.

He stood there, staring down at the ground.

Giles came over to the Fae wolf and looked at where Lauriel was staring. Lauriel didn't move, continuing to stare. Giles looked all around, then down where the wolf was focused. He leaned closer and Lauriel backed up to let Giles stand where he was. Giles looked around until Lauriel jumped on him, propelling him into the water.

Both Brigit and Raven stood up. Lauriel raised a paw to them, then jumped on Giles to hold him down in the water. Giles struggled, fighting the wolf on his back, but Lauriel was not without his own magics. The water became dense, like gelatin and the mud stirred up became tendrils that pressed Giles under the water. Then the air was pulled from his lungs, and water rushed in, shoving past the mage's panicked flailing.

Giles tried to cast a spell, gathering divine magic to him, and the water began to glow.

The tendrils of the mud increased visibly, the particles becoming more numerous and fitting together tight and smooth, pinning him and forcing the last of the air from his lungs. A tap to his head disrupted the spell and the glow faded.

Giles stopped struggling and eventually lay still. Lauriel left him and walked back around to the others. The tendrils held him underwater for another minute, then dissipated. The mud settled back down like it was returning home.

Brigit was too shocked to move. "I... What do we..."

Raven blinked and looked at Lauriel. Lauriel walked up and sat down next to Raven.

"I think we trust the dog."

Brigit looked at Lauriel. Lauriel continued to watch Giles. After a few minutes, Giles' twitched. He started coughing and moving. He got to his hands and knees and vomited water. The water joined the stream and a flash of light destroyed it, leaving the water pure again. Giles looked up at the group.

"What happened?"

Brigit cocked her head. "You insulted Lauriel? So he killed you?"

Raven looked at her. "No. That's not why he killed him. He did it to break the spell."

"How would..."

"Whatever curse he had on him would need a divine flushing to get rid of. Or a mage of sufficient mastery to do a removal of the curse. For me to do it, it means I need to know what cursed him, then get a piece of it, etc. Judging from what he said, I suspect it was the last of something that put the curse on him so that it could never be removed by magical means."

Brigit nodded. "I see. That explains why it wasn't a problem up there. Divine magic permeated the place. But down here, *this* place is a divine source, but the whole place isn't divine so we can see if it worked." She looked at Lauriel. "Good thinking."

Lauriel nodded to her in thanks.

Giles walked out of the stream towards them. "So, is the curse gone then?"

Brigit crossed her arms. "I don't know. Say something and I'll see if it makes me want to drown you too. I imagine there was a lot of satisfaction in that."

"I apologize for being an ass earlier. I did not realize you preferred the company of women to men. I understand how that would be especially irritating. And you, Raven, I may have created a lot of spells, but I'm sure the resources of magical study have long since surpassed what I did. My companion Kalvin taught the Estate many ways to study, experimentation being one of the most useful. The discoveries from that method alone have furthered magic farther than anything I could hope to understand.

"And Lauriel, I'm sorry I said you would make an uncomfortable rug."

Brigit and Raven rolled their eyes at that. Lauriel did not respond.

"I would have killed you too, you pompous ass." Brigit glanced at Lauriel. "Thank you."

"You created a lot of spells..." Raven stroked his chin. "Maybe we can get to the base nature of all this then. My friend Merrick has been studying magic and doing experiments for three hundred years now. His library is extensive. Maybe he can help us. The trap I mentioned before fuels a spell that we know nothing about. We have no idea where it goes or who cast it to begin with. But at one point, it was fed by the embodiment of Magic itself.

"When I left it last, there was a servant of the Land as the power source. I don't know what will happen if there's no source at all. Will it draw from the world around it until something of sufficient power investigates? And how do we find out what spell it fuels? I don't know yet if it would be wise to let the spell fail since it seems to be strong enough to cover all of the Saintlands and possibly the world."

"You said the Bringer was in the trap herself?"

Raven nodded. "And it killed her."

Brigit's hand went to her mouth. "She's dead?"

"Oh no. She's back. Can't keep her down, apparently. It's just the nature of the office, I think. She's the fifth one, or something."

"Fifth…?"

Raven frowned. "And sixth, though if you don't change, I'll bet you get to keep your place in line."

Giles arched an eyebrow. "Aaand he's back. Let's get back to the stuff I understood: The spell. There's a spell with far reaching effects that has been powered by extremely strong sources. How old is the spell?"

"Unknown, but it might be older than even you. Were there Fae lords when you were alive?"

"Yes. One ran the tavern in our village at Serenity."

Raven's eyebrows arched this time. "A *Fae lord* was allowed to run a *tavern*? You do know that eating or drinking Fae stuff can be detrimental to humans, right?"

Giles nodded. "And he made deals for the payment instead of asking for money. I realize that was potentially detrimental, but we gave him the property as a gift and he had to abide by the rules of our contract for the land. That meant no permanent changes, no taking of children, etc."

Raven pointed at Giles. "That was smart. If it was a gift freely given, he had to accept it, rules and all. Which one was it?"

"Embertwist."

Raven's eyes narrowed in thought. "And it was tied to your death, right?"

Giles blinked. "Um… I didn't… yes, I think it was."

"Is that where you were when your wife shot you?"

"Yes! Was he the one that cursed me?"

Raven nodded. "Undoubtedly. You probably killed something important and he needed out of the contract."

Brigit sighed. "Or maybe that's when this spell was cast and Embertwist needed to go stop it."

Raven looked at her, eyes growing wide. He snapped his fingers. "That's it. He knew about the spell. He knew his mother was in it." He stood, looking up into the sky. "I can't call him… But I *can* call someone else." He turned to Lauriel. "Head to Merrick and ask him to meet us at Persephone. Bring anything he has on metaphysical spells."

Lauriel nodded, then leapt out of the cavern.

Raven turned to Giles and Brigit. "I need to talk to an Angel. I could summon him here but it might open this place up to angelic viewing. And we still need to get Brigit to Alexander."

Giles looked at her. "We're very close, less than two days from here. Please, let me take you where you need to be."

Raven pointed to Giles. "You said you created those teleporting amulets. Do you have one?"

Giles reached for his chest. "No, not on me." He looked between the companions. "But I am close to where we lived. I have a stash of items there. It means backtracking a bit, but if we get them, then we can go to Cliffport immediately."

Brigit frowned. "How *much* backtracking?"

"Less than a day." He pointed to the northeast. "That way. I didn't have my bearings before but now I know where I am. Please."

"Persephone is that direction. I can give you a ride. We can get there in an hour." Raven looked at Brigit. "It might be a good place to call Uriel too."

"You can call Uriel?"

Raven nodded. "I think so."

Brigit looked at the men. "I'm immortal now. I don't need to sleep."

Raven and Giles nodded in solidarity and climbed out of the cave.

The lion sat before Michael, encompassing the sky again. Surrounded by the stone monoliths, he waited.

"Clinging to the plow, the farmer does not drown." Michael *realized that he was about to let go of the plow. If he returned to Caratia, he would be back in the tumultuous river, at the mercy of its currents.*

The lion was the plow he needed to cling to.

Michael opened his eyes. He and Catriona had stopped at one of the shelters Raymond made. The horses were watered and laying down outside, asleep like their riders. He stepped outside to look towards Raymond's place and saw the Lion sitting there again. It was as huge in real life as it had been in his dream.

It looked him in the eye and Michael exhaled, nodding.

"I see you."

The lion nodded and dissipated.

Catriona stepped outside. "Trouble?"

Michael shook his head. "No, but I have something I need to give you." He reached into his belt pouch and pulled out a small, velvet bag. He emptied it into his hand.

It was a single silver piece.

He handed it to Catriona. "I need you to give this to Myrgen. He'll know what it means."

Catriona looked at it, remembering the vision she had when she first touched Myrgen's hand outside the cell in Patras. She closed her eyes and nodded, eyes wet and throat closing.

"I'll be sure he gets it." She put the piece in her pouch, then looked towards the north. "Are you heading back then?"

"Yes. I need to finish something and I don't know how long or what form it will take."

She hugged him. "For Myrgen."

He returned the hug. They saddled the horses and did not bother to finish off the night before parting ways.

Twenty-Six

"The plow is to the farmer as the air is to the lion."
(Clinging to the plow, the farmer does not drown.)

"Here. This is it."

Raven stopped the earth sled at the place Giles indicated. "I don't see anything?"

"You're not supposed to. When we were running into problems with outside forces, we put the Covenant in a separate realm. Come. What we want is this way." Giles motioned them to follow.

They walked to a still desolate area in the landscape, though the path from the Giver's resting place now spouted lush green grass. Brigit pointed to it, all but glowing green in the moonlight.

"You are going to need to cover that or people will be able to walk right to the resting place. We left it open, you know."

Raven looked back. "Oh! We did, didn't we? Well, I can run back I suppose. Nothing like realizing you left the house unlocked after you're hours down the road."

Giles shook his head. "We'll be done here long before you get there. Just stick with me." He waved his hand over a stone with a symbol carved into it.

The area around them shimmered and a whole village appeared before them. But to say it was a village was to assign provincial traits this did not possess.

The buildings looked like giant conch shells. They had cream-colored centers with blue, pink, and peach tinted edges. Brigit went up to the nearest shell and touched it.

"It's *stone*."

Giles nodded. "We met a troll on the way to this area about ten days from here. He was attacking villagers and they wanted us to kill him. It turned out that people were sneaking in to his cave and stealing his creations. He was a master sculptor, working stone like Raven there works earth. He just wanted to create. So we brought him with us and he worked on all of these. Every building is like this, and the town is laid out on a spiral, moving towards the town's operating buildings and marketplace. Come, there's a main street this way."

Brigit had expected the "main street" to be straight but it was instead as if a spiral shell was cut in half and laid on its side. The streets curved to connect main buildings all the way towards the center, like jumps from a skipping rock. Fireflies had set up nests in the upper areas of the shells, colonies as old as the buildings. Ivy with glowing blue veins decorated the sides and backs of each home, but the fronts remained free of such things. Windows dotted the faces of each place, a few fireflies dancing around the interiors.

"Where are all the people?"

Giles shrugged. "I have no idea. Sleeping maybe?"

Raven glanced at the homes. "You mean people might still be here?"

"I doubt it. Anyone who left would be unable to get back in unless I opened it for them. My companions and I set each place to seal off so the work within would not fall into the hands of anyone that felled us." Giles looked back at Raven and Brigit. "We had some pretty powerful enemies… and few untrustworthy friends."

"You mean the Estate."

Giles nodded.

Raven exhaled. "The church destroyed all the covenants they found, starting with the Estate in Mande. That's where I trained, as well as my other covenant mages. After the Soulless War, the Church decided to remove magic from the world and covenants and the Estate were destroyed before anyone knew it was happening. They were fueled by the use of those amulets I mentioned."

"I'm not surprised the Church had the plans. We gave them to a few folks in order to encourage diplomatic relations. This started the role of Divine Mages in the area. We didn't really *have* a church when I was around, but I believe it was an easy step to form an organization around the divine. With the way the divine was incorporated into the magic, thought, I don't know how they could have made them evil."

Brigit snorted. "You don't see, with what we witnessed in Heaven, how an extension of that could turn something *evil*? They're holding the Life Giver hostage and are threatening to *bleed her* for souls." She glanced above, worried for a second that they might be listening.

Raven patted her shoulder. "They can't hear you. This place is cut off from Heaven, or I couldn't come here because it's a different realm. It doesn't touch *any* afterlife."

Each layer moving toward the center of town had larger and larger conch shells until they reached the town "square". In the very center was a gigantic shell, easily the equivalent of a four story mansion. Around it at the four primary compass points were buildings about three stories tall, with small, ten foot buildings filling the spaces between. Those looked like market stalls. Some still had the names of their businesses carved into the curved shells.

To the north was a tavern and inn with a faded sign that could not be read. The door was hanging open. Brigit pointed.

"Is that where it happened?"

Giles looked and nodded. "Yeah. Walked right in there, confronted me, shot me. I was dragged out of town by nearly everyone in the room and thrown out. After they turned their backs, I died and was drawn up into Heaven."

Raven frowned, brow furrowing in confusion. "You were a mage with a lot of power and experience. How did she catch you off guard?"

"I kept forgetting to put up my protections. That's how Lauriel was able to dispatch me earlier. I couldn't remember the protection spells I used to cast. I guess that was part of the curse." Giles gestured to Raven. "I mean, how long has it been since *you* were caught without your protections up?"

"Six days ago."

Giles frowned, stopping. "Excuse me?"

"We've traveled to here, then from Raymond's, that's one day. From Caratia, that's two. That was instantaneous from there to Persephone, where I was healing for three days, so that's five. And being kicked out of the afterlife after being thrown over a balcony by Lucifer. That's six!"

Giles stammered. "Six days?"

Brigit stammered. "Thrown off a balcony by Lucifer?"

Raven shrugged, arching an eyebrow. "He undoubtedly felt like I deserved it, after killing Catriona and all that in his study. He was probably upset about the blood on the carpet."

Brigit and Giles' mouths just hung open.

"She didn't bleed as much when I killed her the tenday before."

Brigit's eyes grew and she ran her hand over her face, trying to wipe away the insanity of the man. She saw Giles doing a similar action.

"Why don't you wait here, Raven? I'm going to head inside. Brigit, what do you want to do?"

"Uh… Raven, what are you going to do?"

Raven looked at the tavern. "I'm going to check that place out."

"Brilliant! I'm going to the…" She looked at the building on the opposite end of the town square.

Giles pointed. "The records hall?"

"Yes!" She tapped her nose, then pointed at the building. "That sounds fascinating!" She bustled off before anyone could question her.

Raven watched her leave, then walked over to the tavern as Giles triggered a lock and stepped into the central shell. The tavern had a few fireflies around it, lighting the place enough to keep him from running into anything large but that was all. Shapes of tables and chairs and a wall in the center were all he could make out. He flared a fire spell, tossing it into the fireplace that appeared once the light filled the room.

The first thing that struck him was the extreme lack of dust and grime. The logs in the fireplace were neatly stacked, the tables gleaming like they were just scrubbed. Even the floor was clean. Raven had expected a blood stain at least but there was nothing to mark where Giles had met his final end.

He heard puttering in the kitchen and went back there to investigate. He smiled when he saw a trio of brownies putting together some food.

"Hello."

The brownies looked at him, confused. The one by the chef's island in the center stepped closer. "You can see us?"

"Of course! I'm part Fae myself."

"Where have you been then?"

Raven waved a hand towards the east. "A lot of places."

The brownie by the stove leaned on the piece of wood he was about to shove in the belly. "What happened to our Lord?"

"You mean why did he leave here?"

All the brownies nodded.

"I don't know. What did he tell you?"

The brownie drawing water from a pump glanced at the other two. "He said, 'I'm leaving the place in your capable hands. Take care of any people you encounter here.'"

"That was a really good impression of him."

"He also said he was going to see his mother."

Raven swallowed. *So he did know she was in there. If he spoke to her before she lapsed into unconsciousness, he may have an idea what happened. Except, I can't find him.* "What are you making?"

The brownie at the island smiled. "Chicken soup. Should be ready in a few minutes, once you aren't watching. Fresh bread too."

A ginger-haired brownie came into the kitchen via a side staircase. "Your room is ready, sir."

Raven pointed behind him. "There's actually two of us."

The brownie bowed and went back up the staircase.

"Thank you all. I'll go get the others."

The brownies turned back to their tasks.

Giles came out of the building as Raven did.

"Any trouble?"

Giles shook his head. "No. Right where I left it. It was hard going in there. My lab was…" He shifted, shrugging and wincing. "It's not like I left *in the middle* of experiments exactly, but there were a lot of things that were set to gestate or simmer. I was hard pressed not to start going over everything and figuring out what I was doing."

"Would you like some help? I might be able to tell you where we've made advances."

Giles smiled, nodding. "That would be great. Yes, I'd prefer to discover them myself, but it would be nice to have someone to collaborate with."

"Great! And I'd love to see your lab!"

Giles hesitated. "I just… we have to go through my home to get there and…" He looked around. "Hey, Brigit should have been back here by now. Let's go see what's going on."

Brigit closed the door and looked around the room. Moonlight fed through the windows in the front of the shell and fireflies ebbed and flowed in their mating dances. There were lots of shelves with various kinds of boxes on them. Some were clay pots, a few were metal, an occasional pile of rust in dotted formation. She looked closer at these.

By Heaven, they were nails.

These must have been wood.

It didn't surprise her with the insect activity. She imagined any written record would likewise be destroyed by firefly larvae. She glanced around and noticed a blue glow coming from under a door.

Is someone in there?

She doubted it. This place was long since abandoned. She went to the door and turned the knob. It opened and she walked in. Upon the desk in the room was a large box with elaborate carvings of ivy all over it. The glow was coming from within.

Brigit went up to the box but it was locked. She looked around and found a drawer that needed a very small key to open. It looked like something tried to break open the drawer and might have even attacked the desk, but the drawer remained locked. She went to the glowing box and tried to lift it. It wouldn't budge. Then she looked closer and saw the box was actually *part* of the desk! The desk was part of the floor. And the hinges were non-existent. This was a very secure spot.

A firefly floated down by her feet and she looked at it, fascinated by the grace of the bug. Its glow caught on something on one of the legs and she bent down to examine it in the faint glow of the fly. It was a spot on the wood which was a little apart from the rest of it. She touched it and it moved slightly. She played around with it and a small compartment swung open, barely the size of her little finger.

Inside it was a tiny, delicate key.

She put it in the lock and a musical tune started playing. Suddenly, the carved vines started to writhe and the drawer became unlocked and popped open. Inside was a key that matched the size and motif of the box. She wondered why the person had gone so far as to hide the key that opened the drawer so close to the box. Either they were in a hurry or…

She coaxed the firefly to the floor and found a dark stain, like something had spilled a lot of liquid in that spot. Dark, thick, staining liquid. She swallowed and stood.

Time to see what was worth so much.

She used the larger key on the box and it, too, sang a musical tune as the carved leaves unthreaded themselves. After a minute, the box popped open, still no hinges to be found. She lifted the lid.

The glow filled the room. It emanated from a bow, with a quiver of arrows lying in the center. The bow was unstrung but it had a bowstring mext to it. The whole thing looked like new, right down to the string. The quiver on top was not so pristine. The quiver was aged and shriveled and the arrows all but disintegrated. She could still see the name worked into the leather: *Anna.* The same name was engraved into the handle of the bow, creating the finger grooves.

This must be the bow Giles mentioned. I hope that isn't her blood on the floor.

She glanced around and saw something near the stain. She bent down, moving the overturned desk chair and lowering the bow to help her see.

Beneath the desk was a small impression in the blood of two small feet and a larger smear.

Like a child sitting under here and hiding.

Three more stains marked the wood, obscured by the carpet on the other side of the desk. She stood and looked but the carpet had long since disintegrated and the signs were lost.

"Anna's bow!"

Brigit turned, startled. "Uh, yes." She swallowed as Giles and Raven entered the room.

Giles jerked a thumb over his shoulder. "We saw the glow when we came in." He looked around. "This was Anna's office. She spent every day here, often with the children. She wanted to contribute once she no longer felt comfortable hunting with the group."

What did she do?"

"Secured items for people. Especially notes and gifts for their families if something happened to them." Giles motioned to the desk. "We made this for her in case she ever had to secure something for herself. She kept her bow in it." His face faltered. "I guess she really did hate me. That was an anniversary present from me. Took me almost a year to make it. It was after that she announced she was pregnant again. I would like to think she wouldn't have left it behind."

"How many children did you say you had?"

"Three. Well, four, I guess. She was about to give birth when…" Giles stopped, frowning. "What's that at your feet?"

Giles walked over to the floor in front of the desk, then behind it, searching.

"Giles…" Brigit fought her compassion. *He deserves to know.*

He knelt by the chair, his eyes becoming wet as he interpreted the stains like she had. He touched the stain under the desk, then went as she had to look at the others. He motioned for the bow, which grew brighter in his hands.

The thin thread of the rug's remains showed slight discoloration. When he brushed them aside with his hand, they fell apart, but further obscured what was beneath.

"Raven, would you please?"

Raven's brow was furrowed but he realized what he was being asked. He caused a small, controlled tornado to clear away all the dirt, dust, and stray bits of rug from the whole room. He deposited it all outside in the hallway.

Giles closed his eyes and the light from the bow flared bright as the noon sun.

The room told a horrible tale.

Shelves showed damage from weapons as well as scoring. In the wall behind the desk, a hole the size of Brigit's palm was surrounded by a dark explosion which turned to slide marks and the large bloodstain on the floor. The small footprints were preceded by smears near the main one. Nearby, the bloodstains in three much smaller quantities pooled near each other. If they were from an adult, the person might have lived. But if they were not...

The box the bow was in had interrupted splatters on it.

"Was this closed?"

Brigit nodded.

Giles looked around. "The door is intact, which means it was open. She wasn't expecting it." He sighted back to the hole in the wall. The overturned chair beside the desk seemed to explain it to him.

"A mage did this."

Brigit glanced at Raven. "Are you sure?"

Giles pointed to the hole in the wall. "This is a spell that causes a stone dart to fly unerringly at a target. It can't be dodged"

Raven nodded. "It's the first offensive spell we are taught." He came over to look at the hole. "This was done by someone with a strong grasp of earth magic."

Brigit frowned. "How can you tell?"

"The size of the dart. The better you are at controlling earth, the bigger the dart. That is as big as the darts get, and shows mastery of the art."

Brigit put her hand to her mouth. "So, that flying at someone who wasn't expecting it..."

The bloodstain was right about where someone's throat would have been were they sitting where the chair was before she moved it. The weight of the evidence blanketed the room.

Giles broke it. "We should go."

Raven gestured to the inn. "There's food and rooms..."

"I want to leave, Raven." Giles turned a painful, angry look upon the others. "We're bloody immortal. We don't need food, or shelter, or sleep."

He stormed from the room, the bow dimming. Brigit barely caught sight of more bloodstains in the hallway before the shadows caught up to them. She and Raven followed him out.

They walked in silence to the edge of the realm. Outside, Raven cleared his throat.

"I need to head to Persephone to meet with Merrick. Do you want to come with me, or head to Alexander?"

Giles' face had become stony. "How far is it from here?"

"About another hour by earth sled."

Giles snorted, frustration and anger in his breath. "I have to have been to a place to return there. Brigit," he looked at her, "I'm sorry we keep putting things off, but can you spare another hour?"

Brigit nodded, and they boarded the earth sled and took off.

Book Two

"The rain is to the flood as
the ox is to the flood."
(Neither the rain nor the ox
understands its contribution
to the events unfolding.)

Twenty-Seven

"The ox is to the flood water as the flood is to the moon." (The ox does not notice the rising flood water any more than the moon notices the flood water.)

"Luci?" Alistair's voice echoed down the corridor of the mansion.

Lucifer turned his head. "Here."

Alistair entered, smiling.

"You're in a good mood."

"James went to Gloriana, offered his services, *and she accepted*."

"This calls for a drink!"

Alistair went to the brandy decanter and poured himself a glass. "Thank you, my friend." He sat beside Lucifer on the sofa and clinked his glass in celebration.

"So tell me all about it."

Alistair did so, great pride in his voice. "The man realized there was a problem, learned what it was, then took the *right* steps to correct it. I'm very proud of him."

"To intelligent offspring."

They clinked glasses and drank again.

"Hello?"

Lucifer popped forward on the sofa. "In here, My Lady."

The First Dûcesa poked her head into the room. "Oh. You have company. I'll come back later."

Lucifer stood. "Oh, please don't. Alistair was just leaving."

Alistair looked at Lucifer, then at the Dûcesa. "I was. I've been here too long already. There's Karma to… balance…" He stood and bowed to the lady. "It was nice to meet you."

She smiled, confused. "But we haven-"

Lucifer bustled Alistair from the room. "Yes. That's because he far more handsome and charming than I am and I simply can't have him around. I lose in comparison."

The Dûcesa smiled and accepted Lucifer's invitation into the room. A servant came in from a side door and took away the dirty glass Alistair had used, replacing it with a fresh one.

"What can I do for you, My Lady?"

"The entry to the sealed realm. I have given it thought."

"And?"

She took a deep breath. "I want you to do it."

Lucifer sighed, then bowed. "It will be as you wish, My Lady."

"You don't approve."

"That's not my place. People have a way of blaming me for bad decision they make but the truth is that *they* make them. I am just the means by which their desires are carried out."

She frowned. "You must feel so *used*."

"It comes with the job."

She looked him over and then leaned in to kiss him. He let her, returning the kiss in equal measure.

"You didn't pull away."

He smiled. "I didn't want to discourage you. Had I pulled back, you may never have done it again."

"And you want me to do this again?"

"Oh yes."

"But you don't think I will."

He glanced down. "You've requested a task from me that will allow you to look upon the face and fate of your one true heart. I'm going to be left in the dust."

She frowned. "Then why help me?"

"Because you might not."

She glanced at her hand, touching his. "And that is enough for you?"

He smiled. "I've worked with less."

She squeezed his hand and stood. "Thank you."

He stood as well. "Of course. But I'd also like to make you this offer." His face became serious. "The next time you kiss me, I want it to be because you are ready to be done with this. To leave it behind."

"And if I am not?"

"Then I will feel used."

"And if I *am* ready to be done?"

He touched her face, then brushed his lips across her cheek and down her neck. His hand trailed down her face and brushed the backs of his fingers along her shoulder. Goosebumps erupted in the path of his touch and she shuddered, stabilizing herself with a deep breath.

"I will be grateful."

She looked into his eyes and touched his cheek. "I will be too."

He took her hand from his cheek and kissed it. "You should go. I wouldn't want to keep your request waiting."

She smiled. "Is that true?"

His smile didn't waver. "It is a bald and barely spoken lie, My Lady. I would do all in my power to keep you from harm, but I cannot stop you from harming yourself."

She arched her eyebrows in confusion. "'A bald and barely spoken lie'?"

He shrugged. "No idea. Sounded good rolling off the tongue though, didn't it?"

She laughed and his heart lifted.

"Go." He stepped back from her. "I have work to do."

She sobered and nodded, then turned and left the room.

Lucifer gave her time to get over the wall, refreshing his drink and then drinking it. Then he went to the wall across from the study door. He placed his hand upon it and a door formed. He concentrated upon completing the door, then focused upon the door's destination. He felt the realm he was looking for and connected it to the door. Then he made sure there was no invitation from that place to this one.

His hand slid from the door, the access created. He stepped back, then returned to his study. He sat, rubbing his face with his palms. A knock at the door drew his attention.

Alistair glanced down the hallway towards the garden, then back at Lucifer. "What happened?"

"I fulfilled a request. She left."

Alistair rubbed the back of his neck. "By the Balance, how long was I gone?"

Lucifer smiled. "Just a few minutes. She didn't come to linger."

"Then why was she here?"

"To ask a favor."

"Did you do it?"

"Yes." Lucifer gestured to the new door.

Alistair looked at it, then turned in the doorway to the study. "Wait. Is that…?"

"The access to Calpurnia's spell realm, yes."

Alistair walked back, pointing behind him. "Are you insane? This place touches every single afterlife. That's *every soul available*."

"I know."

"For a *woman?*"

Lucifer stood. "*No.* For a *choice*. She knows what is behind it. She knows what she'll be looking at if she opens it. Right now, she's *choosing* self-harm to stay here. I want her to be here because it is her *choice,* not because it is her *obligation.* She's here because she feels like abandoning Slade to this fate is wrong. She won't move on and be reborn.

"But this gives her the *choice* to move on. And if she stays after that then…"

"You love her?"

Lucifer looked away. "A bit, yes."

Alistair gestured to the house. "Is she why you built this place?"

Lucifer shook his head. "No. But doing *this* is. Giving people the choice to go elsewhere, to be fulfilled. I know what happens to them in Heaven. I just want them to have the choice."

Alistair leaned against the doorjamb. "And if she chooses the door?"

Lucifer sighed. "Then I'll be sad."

"And if she doesn't?"

Lucifer smiled and raised his glass. "Then I shall be grateful."

Alistair sighed and grabbed a glass. "You need to seal this place off." He waved the glass at the door. "You don't know how bad or how fast those monsters are."

Lucifer nodded. "I do. And I already have. Nothing can come in here without an invitation from me."

"Yeah, but once here, they can go anywhere, right?"

Lucifer sipped his drink. "I see your point." He looked at Alistair. "Don't want the First Dûcesa just wandering into your bedroom, eh?"

"I did *not* say that. I would *never* say that. I just… don't want to have to explain anything." He sat beside Lucifer. "For what it's worth, I hope she chooses you."

Lucifer smiled. "Thank you. I hope so too."

George entered the Benevolent Friar and was stopped at the door by several guards.

"I'm sorry, sir, but you aren't allowed in here." The burly guard looked George over. "This… I don't recognize your livery, sir. Are you from Toledo?"

George glanced around. He caught sight of a man in a dark corner, nondescript and easily missed in the dozen people in the room wearing Mervol insignia. Except, to George, he was obvious, and knowing who the man was, George also knew it was because he *wanted* George to see him.

George looked at the guards denying him entry. "Yes. I am. I wanted to ask about the situation. This seemed the right choice. I assume someone of significance to the incursion is here?"

George spoke with such authority, the guards drew themselves up in attention. There were several men and women sleeping in the common area, all wearing uniforms but none of them were wearing anything other than local patrol garb. There was no one here from the military.

A large man walking with a cane entered the room from the kitchen. He had long hair and was missing a few teeth. He came close and kept his voice low once he got to the group. "I'm Svein, owner of this inn. Let's take this outside."

He nodded to the porch and the group filed out. Once outside, and with the door closed, he turned to George. "Who are you again?"

"I'm George of Toledo." George glanced at the other men. "I came here to speak to someone in authority about the incursion."

The guards and Svein exchanged a look. "We're actually waiting for word back from the Mervol Army."

"Is there a way to send a message to them?"

The guard shook his head. "Our messenger has left to deliver some missives. He's due in today."

Svein shrugged. "I'd offer you a room, but as you can see, I'm at capacity. But I am up preparing breakfast. You're welcome to relax at the table out here until it's ready."

He gestured to a small table and two hefty chairs on the porch. George nodded and took a seat. The guards and Svein stepped back inside. George looked out at the valley, assessing the force he could see.

"I was quite surprised to see you, Saint George."

George took a breath, not changing his position. "I was likewise surprised to see you, Archangel Uriel. I got the impression you wanted to speak."

"I do. Your presence here means Brigit's champion has failed?"

"Not exactly. Brigit has been expelled. As have Giles and... and Clara."

"Clara? But with Raymond gone there's..."

George nodded, very slightly. "I know. It helps that the Angels have chosen not to give souls to all the births now. There's only one Saint at any time allowed on the birthing floor. The rest are in separate compartments. We have stopped being allowed to speak to each other."

"Only *one* giving out souls? How are they planning on..." Uriel exhaled in disgust. "They *aren't* planning on dealing with influx of births. They're just going to let those infants die, aren't they?"

"It appears so." George felt the weight of every death as if he could see them. "Plus, they want the Mervol army to engage that one there."

"*Humans?* Against *that* foe?"

"Yes." George hazarded a glance at Uriel. He was hidden in the dappled shadows of pre-dawn, between the lights from the windows and the moon. George leaned forward on the table, his hand covering his chin and mouth, studying the army. "I need intel about the army though. Any idea what the plan is?"

Uriel shook his head. "But let me do some recon for you."

George sat back as a sound like a bird taking off heralded Uriel's exit.

Catherine awoke to the sound of boots marching outside. The sky was barely out of dawn twilight, but it sounded like an army was on the hoof. She got up and went to the window.

She had been right. A line of young men and women were marching past the Inn on the way to St. Giles. She craned her head to see how far the line stretched but couldn't see much without opening the window. She didn't want to reveal her presence just yet. Then she remembered the scout from last night.

That will be a problem. If he takes me to the General, he'll want me to have an escort back, which won't be available until after they deal with the mess in the valley.

As much as she wanted to see Sovereigna again, she knew the delay would put Emmy in danger. She gathered her things with much haste and made it look like she had already left the room. Then she got dressed. She had just put her boots on when a knock came at the door.

"Your Majesty, are you awake?" The voice was a whisper, but managed to penetrate the door.

As I anticipated.

She tugged the blanket to hang off the end, then slipped underneath the bed, facing the door. The blanket hid the underside of the bed in shadow. It wouldn't work if the scout looked under the bed, but she found it laughable that anyone would check under a bed for the Queen Mother of Mervolingia.

Another knock. "Your Majesty? It's Sergeant Hall from the First Squadron." This whisper added authority to its tone.

She heard him mumble something to someone else, then the knob on the door turned. Light came in from a hand lamp, casting the room in light and shadow equally.

She saw booted feet come in and black clad feet and legs as well. All attempts were made to keep things quiet, from voices to footsteps. The door closed behind them.

"Are you sure it was her?"

The scout from last night revealed himself as the companion to Sergeant Hall. "I was in here personally. It was her."

"She's supposedly at the Benevolent Friar near the Papal City. We got a missive."

"Apparently she left. And the Papal City is cut off."

Sergeant Hall exhaled, exasperated. "It looks like she's not here either. When did you see her?"

"After dark."

"So you might be wrong?"

"It wasn't dark *in here*, Eddie."

Sergeant Hall sighed. "Well, apparently she left at some point. If she was trying to give the impression she was still at an inn on the other side of the valley, she probably didn't want to be recognized. I'm not saying you did anything wrong at all, Adam. You were right to tell us. She might be on a mission for the King, to be honest. We got word he was in St Giles."

"What do you want to do now then?"

"Let's send a bird on. You said she planned to head to Patras?"

"That's what she told me."

Sergeant Hall moved towards the door. "Then let's report this to the General. He'll decide what to do."

The door was opened with care and the two men left. Catherine waited a few minutes until she heard Sergeant Hall's voice outside. She crawled out and checked his location carefully from the shadows by the window. She saw both the scout from last night and a man with the same boots that were in her room talking to an older gentleman she recognized from meetings at the palace with Henri.

He's gotten old, but then, we all have.

She went to the door and cracked it enough to see out of. This was problematic, since she had a horse as part of her needs and she doubted she could get it without getting caught.

I know Aethelraed. He would listen to me.

She screwed up her courage and went outside.

The General saw her come out of the Inn and frowned at the soldiers.

"Your Majesty." General Aethelraed Rhydderch bowed.

"General Rhydderch." She bowed as well. "Aethelraed, I need to get back to Patras immediately."

"I thought you were holed up in an inn on the other side of the valley, Catherine."

"His Majesty tasked me with protecting the Princess. He also felt I might be able to take care of any potential political threats."

Aethelraed sighed. "He is right about that. Captain Richelieu has taken charge of the Princess's safety but your presence would deter any who think a Night of Long Knives is due." He turned to a passing soldier.

"Syr. To me."

A young woman in her twenties with dark hair pulled up in a braid and deep brown eyes stepped out of the line of marching soldiers.

"Yes, Sir?"

"You are to accompany the Queen Mother back to Patras, and take care of her needs until she dismisses you. Understood?"

"Yes sir!" Syrial turned to the Queen and bowed. "Whenever you're ready, Your Majesty."

Catherine smiled. "I have a horse in the stable. See if there is a second one available. I'll pay for it from my personal accounts."

"Yes ma'am." The woman bowed again and left around the side of the Inn.

"Private Kyx Syrial is one of our best hand to hand combatants. I'm running a lesser army without her so see to it I get her back." Aethelraed's smile took the edge of the harsh words.

"You'll get her back when I'm damned good and ready, Aethelraed." Catherine's smile betrayed her own chastisement.

His eyes grew serious and he nodded to a spot away from the marching troops. He glanced at the line and Sergeant Hall and Adam turned their backs to give them privacy.

"Catherine, what do you know about what we're marching into?"

Catherine sighed. *So much for keeping things light.*

Uriel dropped down beside the Inn, then moved quietly to within earshot of George. One of the two guards from before was pouring him something steaming into a mug.

"Thank you."

The guard nodded and went back inside. Uriel listened a moment but heard no one else. He glanced around the corner of the building and saw the porch was empty. He started to speak but George's hand made a staying gesture under the table. Uriel waited a moment, then heard the *klomp* of heavy boots on the stairs to the porch.

"Ah. Looks like food is ready." The guard was clearly buckling his belt again, and Uriel figured he had gone to the privy.

"And delicious. The man is an artist." George took a forkful as the other man went inside. He turned his head slightly towards Uriel.

Uriel kept his voice low. "The Mervol army marches as we speak, despite the early hour. They should make St. Giles by mid-morning. The Krakten army is entrenched in the Valley. There is a Fae army on the move to the south on an intercept course for the incursion. When they join the Army, I don't know what the human chances are."

"Do you have any way to counter them?"

"The Fae? No. We would need divine magic and I'm not sure what that would look like for this."

George frowned. "Giles was a divine mage. Did you happen to see them?"

"There is a crater to the north, near the ring of stones where Raymond lives. Someone is riding towards it but it is a single man on a horse. There was a woman nearing the base of the Caratian mountains but I saw no others."

"No sign of Clara?"

"None."

"Is it… Are we sure she survived?"

Uriel smiled. "Yes. In fact, she's already died. She can't do it again."

George glanced at Uriel, then nodded. "What do you recommend?"

Uriel shook his head. "I'm not a strategist. That was Michael. I'm a scout, a spy. But I *can* say we need to do something or the country will erupt in civil war and my brothers will get what they want."

George, took a sip of the mug. "What do you plan to do?"

Uriel looked at the valley. "I have an idea, but I need you to keep them busy. Or at least keep their attention. Can you do that?"

George gave a slight nod. "I'm certain they are watching me now."

Uriel nodded, glancing up. He knew he was imperceptible when he chose to be, which was why he was choosing so now. He had been hidden from his brothers since he discovered Embertwist was not in power anymore.

"Best of luck to you."

George nodded. "And also to you." Then sipped some more from his mug.

George finished his mug just as one of the guards stepped out with a plate of food and a mug of his own.

"May I?" He gestured to the table.

George welcomed him with a wave.

"So, what do you do in Toledo? I figured that was where you were from by your armor."

"I command armies for Heaven."

The guard's eyebrows arched. "Church Army, eh?" He gestured behind them with his fork. "What do you make of that dome over the Papal City?"

"That's something I hope to deal with here soon."

"How?"

George looked at him. "I hope that when I defeat the Fae army marching on this valley, I will break the spell." He turned back to surveying the valley. "If not, I'll hack it to pieces."

The guard nodded. "Sounds like one helluva plan."

"So, tell me what has been happening here. And please, leave nothing out."

"It all started about a tenday ago now…"

Twenty-Eight

"The plow is to the flood as
the rock is to the river."
(The plow is caught in the
ground, unmoving.)

Michael rode up to the circle of stones and dismounted. The lion sat before a monolith, waiting for him. He knelt before the creature.

"I have come. What do I do, my friend?"

The lion stood and turned from him walking into the stone and disappearing. Michael walked up to the pillar and saw the outline of a sword deep within it. It was glowing so bright, he had to shield his eyes. He reached forward to it and the stone parted, revealing a large sword of white steel. The blade was etched with an elaborate carving of an angel defeating monsters. The hilt was wrapped in gold and silver, and the pommel stone roiled with light and shadow in an endless battle.

Michael put his hand upon the sword and light burst forth from it.

Raymond heard a horse ride up to the hut and looked at Clara, who stirred and sat up.

"Could it be them?"

Raymond shook his head. "Only one horse? Besides, Raven doesn't seem like the horse type. I'll check."

He got up and stepped outside as Michael grasped the sword.

A white light burst forth from the pillar, shattering it into dust. Raymond threw his arm up to protect his eyes and was pushed back by the concussive force that burst throughout the area. The sky lit up and the only thing saving Raymond's home was the presence of the other pillars, which also turned to dust.

Michael disappeared as the world filled with light.

Michael looked at the figure before him, then to the Lion beside them. The Lion nodded to the white figure.

This is the entity I wanted you to meet.

Michael looked at the figure. "What is it?"

Long ago, this creature gave itself to protect the world from monsters that would end it. Now, we have a new threat, one he will oppose. But he cannot do it from within the stone.

"What is the threat?"

His brethren. One stands against two, but he cannot hold them. We need this soldier to fight against them. Only he can access the place they battle.

Michael walked around the figure. "He does not sense us?"

No.

"Then how will he leave the stone?"

By taking your place in the world.

"My... my place?"

The Lion nodded. *You must give yourself over to this of your own free will.*

"Why me?"

Because he is you. And you are him.

Michael frowned. He *did* feel a connection to the figure, though he couldn't quite place it. "How?"

Centuries ago, this creature sacrificed his presence here to contain a monster that could destroy all. Once trapped here, it was slain, having no place to hide. But the monster cursed him as it died to never see the outside again, until his own body released him.

"How am I him?"

You are the last of his lineage. A single member of his family survived a slaughter and escaped to Nubia. You are the last of that line.

"And what am I to do?"

You must let him out.

"What happens to me if I do?"

You will come with me.

"And do what?"

You will guide others, as I do. You have always been a lion, Zubari.

Michael blinked. He had not heard his name in over a decade. It brought with it the scent of the savannah, the sounds of the wind through the grass. He remembered the trees, and the rivers and felt the sun upon his face. He remembered the voices of his people and the feel of his mother's arms.

And suddenly, he no longer wanted to be in this world.

He reached out to the figure.

It opened its eyes and looked upon him.

And the world disappeared in a white flash of light.

Catriona turned to the north, the light filling the area. The horse, drinking from the trough where she had stopped to rest it before heading up the Caratian pass, reared and bolted away.

Michael.

Catriona ran towards the light, then jumped and leapt through the Land to the Circle of Stones.

The light tore away at Catriona, her skin darkening and burning from her. She screamed in agony and disappeared.

Her eyes opened, dots of light still making black spots upon her vision. The Land chamber around her lit up with lava and the stone golem knelt before her. She looked down and in her hand was the only thing she had shielded from the light.

A single silver piece.

Giles, Brigit, and Raven stepped up to the back wall of the store room at Persephone. Raven looked at them.

"Is anyone there? I can't see anything but a wall."

Giles frowned. "I can tell something is here. But it's hidden from me."

Brigit bowed to the man on the other side of the wall. Lauriel sat beside him.

"Are you Merrick?"

"Yes. Can he even hear me?"

"He's here?" Raven smiled. "Is Lauriel with him?"

Brigit nodded.

"Lauriel, come here, you can bridge the gap between us."

Lauriel stepped forward and stood, half in and half out.

"Merrick, can you hear me?"

Brigit saw no recognition on the man's face. "I don't think so."

Merrick waved his hand and the wall thinned, becoming translucent.

Raven beamed in happiness. "Merrick! I worried I'd never see you again! What did you find out? Oh, this is Giles and Brigit. He's the mage that started all the divine magic."

Merrick arched an eyebrow. "That's not exactly a good thing."

Giles shrugged. "It was important at the time."

Raven frowned. "Wait… Giles, can *you* get Merrick a back way to Serenity? You said you have a lab there. It *is* a covenant after all."

Giles stroked his chin. "I can make another amulet, but he had to have been there to return."

"Which means coming here first."

Merrick raised his hand. "Yeah, no thanks. The mortal realm is instant death to me now. Unlike *some* mages, I don't have an unpaid debt to a Fae Lord." Merrick knelt down and unpacked a satchel. "I brought everything I have on spell creation. What are you looking for?"

"There's a spell being fueled by creatures with great power. I don't know what it is but it's centered here at Persephone."

Merrick scowled. "Persephone? How long has it been there?"

"From what I can tell, always."

"What sort of source does it have?"

"That's the tricky part. Just about anything powerful feeds into the mechanism. Marica is in it right now."

"The Gold Wife?"

Raven nodded. "But I don't know how long she'll last. The Death Bringer was in it before her and it killed her, as you know, and she wants the Life Giver put in it."

"Wait, the *Death Bringer* wants the Life Giver put in a death trap? *Why?*"

"That's what I was hoping you could tell me."

"Well, the spell source dictates the nature of the spell so if the source changes, then the properties of the spell change." He pulled a book out and put it to the wall. It protruded from the surface and Raven grabbed it.

A loud boom and a concussion beat through the area. The entrance to the realm shifted and Raven saw Merrick's thumb just for a second.

Myrgen sat up in the bed.

Catriona's here.

He got out of bed and threw on a robe, rushing to the Meditation Chamber. He threw the doors open and saw the room was obsidian and lava. He turned the corner and saw her standing by the golem, naked, looking down at her hand.

"Catriona, what happened?"

Her face was streaked with tears. "I couldn't help him."

Myrgen searched her eyes, then looked down at what was in her hand. He took it, not understanding at first.

"It's from Michael."

He looked at her, then at the silver piece. His knees gave out and he fell to the ground, weeping and clutching it to his chest.

James heard a faint sound outside and the porcelain tea set next to him clinked, like a door was just slammed down the hall. He went to the window that overlooked Glarren and saw a flash far to the south.

That was far away. What could cause such an impact this far?

He studied the horizon, but couldn't tell from here what caused it. It did not seem to spread and James set aside the tome on Fae culture he had been reading. Humans had visited repeatedly over the centuries, including one scholar named Davvik that took great interest in the Fae Realm. He had written several tomes and sent them as useless gifts to the Fae Queen of Winter. For all his study, he didn't seem to understand Fae could not read.

Wait. That location...

He went to his desk and grabbed a spyglass from a drawer. He leveled it at the site. It brought it a little closer but he was able to make out the location.

Raymond's.

Gloriana opened the door. "Did you hear something?"

James looked at her. "Yes, and I think I know *where* it happened, but I don't know..."

Gloriana came to him. "What?"

"Michael."

Captain Nesbit turned towards shore, then looked up at the Crow's Nest. "Paxton! What was that?"

The sailor in the Nest shook his head and lowered the spyglass. "Thunder, Captain, on the other side of the Black Forest. Looks like the York Valley is going to get some rain."

Captain Nesbit nodded and focused upon the trip to the island. He silently thanked Calista the thunder had not come from their destination.

General Aethelraed Rhydderch looked up at the sound of the boom. The sky lit up and he frowned.

Sergeant Hall squinted at the light. "Looks like we might get a storm. That's gonna cause problems setting up camp."

Aethelraed shook his head. "According to the Queen Mother, the Krakten army has taken over the entire valley. We'll be housing in the village. It's been cleared out of civilians."

"If it's full, where are we going to engage?"

Aethelraed looked at the report Eddie was handing him. "That's what we're here to discuss."

He glanced once more at the northern light as it faded, then returned to the battle plan.

Corrigan looked up at the sound. The light on the horizon barely peeked over the tree tops. He gestured to a winged Fae and it launched to the sky. A few moments later, it returned.

"A light in the north, but not on the battlefield, Sire."

"What was the light?"

"No idea, Sire. It faded."

Corrigan didn't like the sound of that. He raised his hand. The trees parted all the way to the Valley.

"Signal the troops to run."

The Fae nodded and conveyed the order.

Alexander sat up. Johner threw aside the tent flap, stepping in.

"What was that?"

Johner shook his head. "I don't know, but it came from the north and was distinctly divine. I take it it wasn't you?"

Alexander shook his head. "No. I haven't heard from Brigit in a while and that angel definitely wasn't speaking for me."

Johner set his jaw. "This is not good. Heaven has already indicated it was not going to let this war end without several deaths. Your presence here is supposed to be a deterrent to attacks. My scouts say your army is on the southern road, and should make the edge of the valley by mid-morning."

Alexander nodded. "Let me know what you'll need from me."

"With the Krakten Queen your captive and you ours, it compels negotiation rather than bloodshed. I know you made peace, but the rest of the world does not."

"What can we do then?"

Johner shook his head. "I don't know. There are too many variables right now. Let's see what the General of your army says."

Uriel saw the flash and dread filled his heart.

Michael.

He looked up at the sky. Now was the best time to try it. He willed himself to Hell.

The oppressive air and stench of sulfur made him cover his nose and mouth. Waves of heat rose around him, with smoke obscuring his view. He didn't see or sense Lucifer anywhere. He went right, away from the fires that purified souls and moved to the door that entered Hell from Heaven. Lucifer had long ago taken up residence here but it was still a part of Heaven and one Uriel needed right now.

He opened the door to the back way into Heaven. He entered a small room with another door on the other side. The room had not been here before, any additional security unnecessary since only an angel could enter Hell. He hoped only an angel could open this door as well.

It was sealed.

Uriel sighed, then looked the door over. He may have been blocked from it normally, but he had learned a few tricks from Embertwist over the years. The idea of a locked door to him was absurd, even if it *was* created by another angel. They were bound in their thinking of the superiority of Heaven and refused to consider anyone else might have a better way. This was their weakness.

The door was outlined but there were no hinges or handles. Regardless, it was still a door and a door had a nature. Uriel waved his hand and completed the door by giving it hinges and a handle with a keyhole. This did nothing to change the fact it was a door and in fact made it more so. He didn't have the key to the door because he did not build it, but luckily, *they* did not have the key to the door either because they did not build that part. It was a win-win, though he highly doubted his brothers would think so.

Uriel turned to mist and slipped between the cracks by the hinges. The rooms George had mentioned went left and right along a corridor, with this door indistinct from the others, outside of the presence of a handle. He turned the handle white so it would be camouflaged within the background. The hinges were on the inside so he did not need to hide those. He turned from his creation and moved along the main hallway, blending into the clouds that made up the floor.

The doors had names upon them, denoting the Saint within. He saw none that were unmarked, which meant that the rooms were made as a response to the Saints being ejected from Heaven. George indicated the Saints did not do this, which meant Heaven had become a prison. He didn't doubt they would prefer this to being cast out, but then again, he might be underestimating what his brothers were doing to them. Forcing a Saint to choose which infants would live and die must take a horrible toll on people whose only purpose before this was to help others. Now, he doubted they were even able to listen to prayers from their followers.

He found the hallway to the Pillar room and saw Raphael and Gabriel watching the Pillar with intensity.

Good.

He flowed to another locked door, the one he knew only Raphael and Gabriel were allowed to open. Again, he completed the door by giving it a threshold, creating a space beneath it. He glanced back into the Pillar Room but nothing had changed. He flowed under the door into the room.

The Giver of Life lay against the bars of a golden cage, rife with Heavenly light. She was very thin, with skin that was translucent from wear and depression. She had cuts on her arms and legs that were not healing. Her golden hair was sparse and coating the bottom of the cage, drifting down the shaft beneath her as it fell out. Her eyes were closed and he worried she was already dead.

He drifted to her. "Giver?"

Her eyes creeped open, taking considerable effort to do so. "Who…?"

"I am here to release you."

He looked at the cage. There was no door. It was a cage already and did not need a door to be complete. Adding a door would change its nature from a prison to a home and that was not within his power.

She looked at him, her eyes almost glistening with tears, but she didn't have enough left of herself to produce them. She closed them again, and Uriel feared he was about to lose her.

The Well.

He slipped into the hallway and down to the Soul area. The Well of Souls was at the far end and a single Saint, Jude, he believed, sat in tears, dripping a single, tiny drop into the viewing pillar before him. He was mixing his tears with the soul fluid on the feather, diluting the essence, but enabling him to let more children live. Uriel admired his efforts.

He dipped his own feather into the well. He had to be careful not to take too much because he could not turn it to mist and preserve it. The feather came back with a dark, silvery pearl of significant size. Uriel swallowed, aware that this much fluid missing was going to be detrimental to the babies on earth. He had to return it to the Giver if he hoped to spare her long enough to free her.

He went back along the wall, the feather with the drop carefully balanced not to bump anything. He covered the pearl of essence as it slipped under the door, counting on its fluid nature to let it spread over the whole feather to get into the room. It worked and he brought the feather to the Giver's lips and poured it in.

The Giver's eyes snapped open and she took a deep, wracking breath. Her skin got black veins throughout her body and she started flickering, vibrating. Her body twisted, eyes turned black, and her hands were armed with large claws. Her hair became a violent mass of tendrils. She gripped the cage bars and they exploded into dust beneath her grasp. Free at last, she pushed past Uriel and tore the door to the next room apart.

She strode into the Soul room and snatched the Well from its stand. Downing the rest of the souls in a gulp, she then threw the Well against the stand, shattering it. Jude fell backwards, then scrambled out of sight as the Giver grew to titanic proportions. Raphael and Gabriel ran in as she fired lightning and ice from her hands, destroying every part of the room. Then she turned to the angels who had held her captive for centuries.

"I am not your prisoner. And I revoke all I have given you."

The angels' wings suddenly burned from their backs, their faces and bodies contorting in pain.

Then, with a flash, she was gone.

Twenty-Nine

"The rock is to the plow as
the yoke is to the ox."
(The plow anchors the ox
against the flood.)

Brother Robert set down the small pot he used to smelt the gold. The next step required the blood of a criminal to empower the amulet. He didn't understand this part.

Why a criminal for a holy artifact?

He closed his eyes and prayed for guidance. The artifact was designed by Saint Giles, so it must have something to do with his purview. He was the Patron Saint against monsters, but not all monsters were supernatural beings. The Krakten Queen was all human and she was a complete monster.

The Queen.

He left the jeweler's shop and went to the town jail. He knew she had been captured. Her blood would be appropriate for this endeavor. He slipped inside and saw Gomez asleep at his desk. Brother Robert continued past him since he didn't want to explain his need for the Queen's blood. Gomez was honorable, but he wasn't necessarily *pious*. He might not serve Heaven as fervently as Robert did.

Robert entered the cell area and realized his efforts would be unproductive. A sizable hole was in the back of the cell and it was empty.

She's gone.

He ran back into the other room and shook Gomez. The guard started awake.

"Huh? Brother Robert? What…"

"The Queen is gone!"

Gomez stood and rushed into the cell area. He fell back against the wall.

"No. This is… I have to talk to the King." He rushed from the jail into the street.

Robert frowned. There were no other prisoners so he could not use their blood. The gold was cooling. He needed to handle this now.

Robert returned to the jeweler's shop, closing the door before he heard guardsmen shouting and running up from the dock area. He looked around the shop.

The shelves were a mess, gift boxes ripped open in his need to gather as much gold as possible. He had taken all the gold from Rowena's stores but it had been insufficient. He had needed more. So he had rifled through the finished pieces in her display case and tossed them into the smelting pot. When that still wasn't enough, he tore apart the finished orders on the shelves.

Wedding rings for the three couples getting married this month were sacrificed. A toddler's tooth, the one from the child who burned to death under the spell, was thrown in to release the gold, then discarded. Effigies commissioned for the fallen were part of the amulet now. Only after every item Rowena had made for the town was melted had there finally been enough. Luckily, she was a master craftsman and knew how to add alloys to make the gold hard enough to wear and not bend or distort. Those enabled the amulet to be brought to this, final, step.

Robert felt a pang of guilt and remorse at the destruction of irreplaceable property that was not his. He looked down at his hands.

He was the criminal.

He took the knife he had grabbed to cut Sovereigna, and cut the back of his forearm. It bled and he managed to drip it in time. Steam rose from the spots where the fluid hit and he squeezed until it covered the entire piece.

A light glowed from the piece, like the vision said it would if it was properly crafted. He waited a moment before releasing it from its mold to give it time to cool and solidify, but he need not have worried. The infusion of divine magic had done its job and made the entire amulet whole.

He took it out and put it on. The weight was heavy and he felt the power of the amulet infuse his will. He closed his eyes and focused upon a section of land above the Fae army's position. Suddenly, he felt the air of the outdoors hit his face, the newly risen sun warming him. He opened his eyes and saw the army below.

There was movement between the town and the forest and he saw a large half ogre moving in front of the Krakten Queen. Robert's eyes narrowed and he teleported to right in front of the creature. He grabbed it and willed them to the area above the war.

An explosion of black goop coated him upon return to the grassy area. Everywhere around him, the sludge from the ogre covered the ground. He looked behind him and realized what he could do. He needed to make a line in the defenses, one the monsters could never cross. He teleported to another half ogre near a tent, then returned with it to the area closest to the Black Forest, spattering the trees and grass with the monster's corpse. Part of the creature's armor remained, a pool of the sludge in a curved part of it. Robert dragged the armor behind him, linking the second burst with the first one.

The goo dripped from him and he felt the power of Heaven course through his veins. Blood still dripped from his arm, joining the Fae sludge, but he felt strong.

The vision had been right. He *could* stop this war.

General Rhydderch came to the first barrel of water and called for a halt. A man in a guard's uniform stood at attention beside it. He bowed, his fist to the opposite shoulder in salute.

"St. Giles City Guardsman Richard Englebert, Sir."

"Guardsman, what can I do for you?"

Richard gestured to the barrel. "Brother Robert has blessed the water in every barrel on the road as well as every barrel in town. We have three more wagons with six barrels each that have been blessed that are awaiting your instructions."

Aethelraed frowned. "What is the King planning with these?"

Richard stepped closer, holding out a scrap of paper. "His orders, Sir."

Aethelraed took the paper and unfolded it.

General,

I have extended the holy water line to protect our troops on their entry into the valley. Thanks to Heaven's support, the King can infuse a line with divine energy that the Fae cannot cross. It does not impair humans.

I have seen this work already. It has kept St. Giles free of enemy presence for a while now.

-Grande Guarde Gomez de Santander

Aethelraed looked at the guardsman, then handed him the note. "Is this true?"

Richard read the note, then nodded. "I've been witness myself, General."

"Interesting."

"There's more, I'm afraid." Richard moved closer and kept his voice very low. "The King has been captured by the Fae army. On the other hand, we have the Krakten Queen prisoner."

"And an exchange has not been made yet?"

"Not to my knowledge, Sir."

Aethelraed looked at the three wagons of water, and the line stretching all the way to town. He looked to the right, down the road to Cliffbase and the Papal City. The public did not know Catherine was no longer at that inn, and only the townsfolk of St. Giles would know His Majesty was in town, and only a select few were aware of his captured status now. If word of any of that got out, Catherine would not get back to Patras in time to save the country from civil war.

He needed to buy her time.

"Take the wagons and spread the barrels half a mile apart as far towards the Papal City as you can. Lieutenant," he turned to a nearby officer, "take the army and line the road as far as we can go. Keep the men spaced no more than an arm's length apart. And have each of them wet their uniform sleeves and chests with water from the barrels. Guardsman, are there any more barrels or wagons?"

"No more barrels, Sir. About six more wagons."

"Load half these barrels lining the road to town onto those wagons and get them down the line heading towards the Krakten border via the Papal City fork. Take them as far as you can, and provide a way for the soldiers to wet their uniforms, like a mug or bowl. As the barrels empty, return them to town to get more water."

Richard nodded. "We also have a bunch of these." He reached into his tunic and pulled out one of the holy discs. "They, too have been blessed. They line the road as well."

Aethelraed smiled. "Then grab *all* the barrels, and get that line made."

Raven dropped to his knees as the contact with the world caused Merrick to turn to dust before their eyes. The book fell with him and Lauriel yelped and crossed back into the Fae Realm. The wall became solid again.

Brigit looked at Raven. "What just happened?"

Giles looked up. "Something… an earthquake maybe?"

He and Brigit ran outside. They saw nothing.

Giles looked around. "I don't feel any aftershocks."

"And the towers are just as broken as they had been when you disrupted the barrier. Could it be a repercussion from our entry here?"

"I don't know."

He put up the shield to protect them in case it was a supernatural attack. He scanned the skies while Brigit looked to the grounds.

"The houses are still intact so it wasn't an earthquake." She looked at the broken tower from whence they came. "And the foliage hasn't moved."

"Then what was it?"

She looked north. There was a faint glow, suddenly gone in the rising sun. She shielded her eyes, trying to catch the glint again.

"What?"

"I thought I saw something." She pointed. "There."

Giles looked. "Isn't that where Raymond has Clara?"

Brigit shook her head. "I don't know. I'm a little lost at this point. I have no real idea where I am."

"Let's go check on them then."

Brigit frowned. "You go. I have to get to Alexander."

"Right." He looked back over his shoulder towards where Raven was. "You go to Raven. I'll check on Clara."

She nodded and he disappeared.

Giles appeared in the crater where they had fallen and he looked around for Raymond. The cart tracks went east so he walked to the top of the crater and looked in that direction. He saw a swath of green and teleported to it. The tracks ended and the green path started at the same spot.

Raven.

He jumped up, but couldn't see much farther than a few hundred yards. He looked up, then teleported.

In the sky where he came out, he saw the country of York in all its splendor and sadness. Most of it was a wasteland but the lower part here was turning lush and green, with several straight lines where Raven had clearly ridden his earth sled.

Near the middle was a large circle of rubble and a small dome. He ignored the wind as he plummeted towards the ground and teleported to the ring.

Michael the Archangel stood in the circle, his wings stretching to the side. His release had been too long in coming and he did not know if he would be too late to help save the world from the Soulless. A man stepped forward from a domed hut outside the circle of rubble.

"Michael?"

Michael looked at the man closer. "Raymond? What are you doing here?"

"Your brother cast me out of Heaven. He blamed me for the Soulless War."

"Were you to blame?"

"I played a part, it's true. But I was not the only component. What happened to Michael?" Raymond shook his head, irritated. "I mean the man who was just here."

"He left." Michael looked around. "Where are the Soulless now?"

"Gone. The mages and Fae got rid of them." He motioned to the north where the wasteland persisted. "But they did a ton of damage. We are recovering now, though." He pointed to the east and south where strange swaths of green interrupted the terrain. "Something has happened at Persephone that has changed it. I don't know what it is."

"Are the Mages still there?"

"No. The Church destroyed them."

Michael sighed, then looked up. "It's time I put a stoAUGH!" Searing pain erupted from his back, like lava flowing across his skin. He arched, dropping to his hands and knees. He could feel his wings being seared from his back and he concentrated upon them. They were being destroyed, so he sped up the process.

Seconds later, though it felt like hours to Michael, his wings exploded, showering the circle with bone, feathers, and flames. He was still trying to bear the pain when a deluge drenched his back in soothing, cool water. The pain stopped, and he sat back on his legs, shaking from the ordeal. He opened his eyes and saw Raymond holding a bucket with water in it that had bits of grass floating in it.

Someone knelt before him and looked into his eyes.

"Do you know where you are?"

Michael winced. "Giles?"

Giles smiled. "Michael?" He looked around and saw the sword. "By Heaven, you broke out."

Michael nodded. The pain was coming back, but it wasn't from where his wings were. It was his face and arms. He looked at his hands and the blackened skin upon them. He looked up at Giles.

"What happened?"

Giles shook his head. "That is the question of the day." He looked at Raymond. "Is there any room in there?"

Raymond shook his head. "Not for him, not with Clara still hurt."

Giles nodded. "Then we'll do it a different way."

He put his hands on Michael's and disappeared.

Thirty

"The lash is to the hand as the lion is to the farmer."
(The whip is forgotten, lost in the flood.)

Drake and Anika walked right past the Sinister Glove of Embertwist without noticing her. The Glove smiled.

Nice to know I haven't lost my touch, even in death.

She glanced past the fountain in the main square and noticed a black tower in the early morning light.

Hello, what are you? Obviously, there's a new kid in town, but this is a weird choice for a house.

She went to the door and saw a confused man standing out in front. He turned to her as she walked up.

"Merrick?"

He blinked, then squinted. "Glove?"

They hugged, then stepped apart.

"Where am I?"

"You're in Summerland. You're dead."

"What? No! I can't leave her."

The Glove shrugged. "That's not a decision you get to make, I'm afraid. I didn't."

"What happened to you?"

"I was shot by a holy ballista bolt. You?"

"I... I don't know. I was handing a book to Raven and..." His eyes grew wide. "No..."

Merrick turned behind him and ran up the stairs in the tower.

The Glove ran after him. The tower was black, like it was made from a single piece of obsidian. She followed him up the stairs to a room like the ones in Sovereignlumin. He looked around, then cast a light. The room had a hundred book shelves with books on them, but they all looked the same. He took one down and it was blank.

He stumbled back, crushed. "No... all my work..."

She looked at the tomes. "So, you can't recreate them?"

"No. Some of them were discoveries, only possible because I made a mistake. I can't reproduce those. Three hundred fifty years..."

He looked at the book, then around at the nearby desk. A quill and ink bottle sat there. "But maybe it isn't a total loss."

He ran over, bumping the table and toppling the ink. It ran out and he waved his hand and returned it to the bottle. He smiled at the Glove.

"At least I haven't lost all my gifts." He sat down and started writing.

"Wait, what are you doing?"

Merrick didn't look up. "I'm writing down the last thing I looked at. I was researching a spell for Raven. There was some spell being fueled by something at Persephone. It didn't make sense, of course. Raven. But I might be able to remember the things I saw."

"And then what?"

He glanced at her. "And then what... what?"

"After you get the spell written down, what do we do with it?"

Merrick blinked. "We have it written down."

Merrick went back to writing and the Glove sighed. His presence here was not comforting nor encouraging. That meant two of the lieutenants were no longer with their Fae Lords and two Fae Lords were out of commission. This was a problem and the Glove was not even sure she had sorted out all the ramifications. She needed someone to talk things through with.

She stepped back outside and saw the mansion on the hill, faded light in the ghostly interior. She didn't know how she was going to do it, but she needed to talk to whomever was there.

"Did you hear that?" Lucifer set his glass down and stood up.

Alistair joined him and they walked out to the garden. A woman with short, silver hair, dressed in black, was standing in the grass near the garden wall.

"Hey! Hey you! In the house!"

Alistair folded his arms across his chest. "I take it she can't see or hear us?"

"Nope. But she obviously knows this is here." Lucifer looked at Alistair. "You know her?"

"Oh yes. That's the Sinister Glove of Embertwist. Second finest thief in the world."

"So, hide the silverware? Or don't bother?"

"Don't bother. But what's she… ah Balance." He shook his head. "This isn't good. How can we talk to her?"

Lucifer waved his hand and a door closed on the hallway to the garden. The Glove started, spooked, then straightened and came to the wall.

"Hi there. Wait. *Alistair?*"

"Hi Glove. What happened?"

"I died. That's not the worst of it though. Merrick's here."

"Merrick?"

Lucifer looked at Alistair. "I take it that's not good?"

Alistair shook his head and looked at the Glove again. "Did he say what happened?"

"No idea. He was handing a book to Raven. That's all I got."

Lucifer arched an eyebrow.

Alistair glanced at the gesture, then returned his attention to the Glove. "How is he?"

"Disoriented. It's not surprising when you die suddenly. He was dead before he knew it had happened so he's still in a living mindset. He focused upon his work, making sure it wasn't lost. I think he needed to do something normal and familiar for a bit. I'll check on him in a day or so. See if I can get more out of him."

Alistair turned to Lucifer. "He's Calpurnia's caretaker. Probably her Lieutenant."

"Does that mean someone can just go in and kill her now?"

Alistair shook his head. "I don't think so. It's not like they are unprotected in there. I can go look in on her though."

The Glove leaned forward. "You can go to them?"

"I can go just about anywhere. I'm Karma."

"Please do so then. I need to know what's going on."

"What am I supposed to check?"

"I don't know. I..." She dropped her hands to her sides, looking around. "I don't know what's happening. It just feels like..."

Lucifer folded *his* arms. "Like someone's picking you guys off."

The Glove started again and looked at Lucifer. "Who the hell are you?"

Lucifer snorted a laugh. "Appropriate phrasing. I'm the owner of this fine establishment."

She frowned. "Establishment? Is it like a tavern?"

"No."

"Ok. So, can you help or not?"

Lucifer looked at Alistair again. "So, what do you think? Can she be trusted?"

"Oh hell no. Your only safe bet is that she can't enter this place. Yet."

"You think she'll find a way to bypass this?"

"If anyone could."

Lucifer shifted his gaze to her. "So, you're saying that if we don't allow her in, she'll still get in anyway, but won't understand what she's looking at and might go in, say, the *wrong door?*"

Alistair rolled his eyes and nodded. "I see your point." He spread his hands in defeat.

Lucifer looked at the Glove. "I'll grant you access to do what you need, but I will revoke it instantly if there's a problem."

"Understood." She started to climb the fence.

"No. You don't."

She stopped.

"If I eject you from this place, you are ejected from the afterlife. All of it."

"So, I go back to being alive?"

"No. Your soul becomes mine."

The Glove stepped back from the wall. "I'm not part of your," she waved her hand at the house, "whatever."

"No. You aren't."

She swallowed, then exhaled slowly, thinking it all through. "Done."

Lucifer reached out his hand to her and helped her over the wall.

Brigit put her arm on Raven's shoulder. "Are you alright?"

Raven looked at her, his eyes red and wet and filled with horror. "I can't feel Lauriel."

Brigit's eyes went wide and her fist went to her mouth. She looked at the wall, touching it. "It's solid now. I can't…"

The wall cleared and Lauriel lifted his head. He was laying on the ground, blood coursing from his chest. A chunk of his body was gone, like it had been lopped off and disintegrated. He was barely moving.

Raven leaned against the transparent wall, his face contorting into a nightmare of pain and anguish.

"NO! No! Lauriel!"

Brigit reached out. "I… I don't know what to do…"

Raven pounded on the wall, screaming. The wall started to go opaque at the edges and Raven got to his feet.

"Lauriel!"

Beyond them, near the tower of Sovereignlumin, two figures appeared. Raven saw them and screamed, shattering the wall to the tower.

Alistair turned at the sound and squinted. "What's that?"

The Glove turned. "I don't know."

Alistair moved towards the lump of flesh far away, then turned to the Glove. "Wait here."

He appeared next to Lauriel. He stepped back, then looked up at Raven screaming and pointing. He looked down at the Fae wolf and knelt beside him.

"Lauriel…"

Raven was sliding to his knees, screaming and crying. A woman Alistair didn't know was beside him, also in tears. She was bent over Raven, trying to comfort him. Alistair looked down at the wolf again.

I am really getting tired of wearing my friends' blood.

Suddenly, the Glove was beside them. She looked at Lauriel and touched the animal. "You can go anywhere?"

Alistair looked at her, his face wet with his own tears. "Wh…"

"Can you go anywhere?"

"I… I think so…" He nodded. "Yes."

"Take him to Gloriana."

Alistair's eyes grew wide, then closed. He nodded, then touched Lauriel and the Glove and disappeared.

The Glove and Lauriel were suddenly surrounded by cold and ice. She looked around but Alistair was nowhere to be seen. A pair of guards turned to look at the Fae wolf and they gave a shout. Several people came running to the area and surrounded the animal. A couple touched him and his breathing slowed. The Glove reached out to touch him but her hand passed through him.

Of course. I'm dead.

She had never thought that ghosts would be in the Fae world, but then again, ghosts were something human and there were very few of those in the Fae world. In fact, she knew of only two others and one of them was also dead.

"Get the Queen!"

A finely dressed male Fae cleared the others away. The two who touched Lauriel stayed. His clothing looked like it was made of glacial ice, that impossible blue that is equal parts cold and deep. A few moments later, Gloriana strode up, beside her, a young man the Glove knew as a sidekick of Alistair's. He looked at the animal as Gloriana knelt beside it.

"Lauriel."

Gloriana nodded. "What has happened to you, my precious one?"

Lauriel's eyes did not move.

She turned to the young man. "James, you know this creature too?"

"Yes. How did he get here?"

Gloriana shook her head. "I don't know. But we need to get him where I can work on him."

A table of ice rose gently beneath Lauriel and they all went into the palace. The Glove looked around but no one seemed to notice her. She frowned.

Am I hiding?

She concentrated on being visible but it didn't seem to change anything. She frowned and followed Lauriel into the palace. The courtyard was a flurry, everyone rushing to get things for the medical emergency. The young man spoke to Gloriana and she waved him away, her focus upon the wolf. He bowed to her back and went to the door where Lauriel appeared.

He knelt and touched the blood, then looked around. He stepped to the doorway and was gone. The Glove walked to the same place and felt the sensation of elsewhere. She smiled and also willed herself to Sovereignlumin.

She came out beside the Door of Winter. James strode to the closest door outside and looked around, then to the next one, the one that led to the gateway to Persephone. The Glove followed him.

"Alistair?"

Alistair turned from the people at the gateway. "James?"

Alistair opened his arms to James, who promptly punched him as hard as he could across the face. Alistair stumbled back, hitting the opening and stepping through it into Persephone.

"You changing maggot."

The Glove raised her eyebrows at the insult. She had not heard such a phrase in all her time as Embertwist's Glove.

Alistair shook his head, trying to recover.

Raven looked between the two. "Where is he?"

Alistair rubbed his chin and moved his jaw around. "Gloriana. The Glove suggested it."

Raven collapsed into sobbing. He held Alistair's hand. "Thank you. Thank you."

James looked around. "What happened?"

Raven shook his head. "I can't... I can't..."

The woman beside Raven looked at all of them, including the Glove. "We were here talking to Merrick. He had some magic tomes on spell creation he was going to share with us. Then, there was a loud *boom* like thunder, but like it struck right next to us. Everything felt..." She searched the debris on the floor as if it might hold the answer.

"Divine." Raven's voice was thick with phlegm and sorrow and was hoarse from screaming. "It was a divine pulse. Large enough and close enough to push the realm of the Fae back about an inch. Merrick was handing me a book and I saw... his... thumb... on this side." He swallowed, getting his voice under control again. "Then he just turned to dust. He said he couldn't come here at all. Three hundred years."

James frowned. "Three hundred years shouldn't turn him to dust. There should be bones or something."

Raven shook his head, wiping his face dry with his palms. "Mages who use longevity potions don't age normally. It takes from both ends." He held up his hands. "The time when there would be no trace becomes closer as the life becomes longer. It's where the life magic comes from. You take it from the last part where you ever existed."

Brigit looked at the book. "Does that mean his works disappear too?" She opened it and showed that it was empty.

The Glove sighed. "That's what he meant."

Brigit looked at her, though no one else did. "What who meant?"

"Merrick. He's in Summerland. His tower is filled with blank books and he said all his work was gone." She looked at Raven who was searching the area like he couldn't see her. Then she looked at Alistair. "Who all can see me?"

Brigit raised her hand, as did Alistair. James and Raven looked at them both.

James looked where Brigit was targeting. "I take it there's someone there?"

Alistair nodded. "The Sinister Glove."

James turned eyes of ice upon Alistair. "I'll not hear your words, changer. You *raped* my mother."

The Glove's eyes narrowed. "Is that why he couldn't enter the Gelid Hold?"

Brigit repeated the question in the silence.

James nodded. He looked at Brigit. "How do you know about the Gelid Hold?"

"I don't. The Sinister Glove asked it."

James looked around. "I'm the Glacial Breath. Why can't I see her?"

"Because she's dead." Raven looked and sounded broken.

"But she's here." James pointed to Brigit. "And you can see her."

Brigit nodded.

"Why?"

"Why what?"

"Why can *you* see her?"

The Glove rolled her eyes. "You're dead too. Aren't you?"

Brigit looked at the Glove and nodded. "I'm also dead. Or rather, I was."

Raven moved to his knees. "Wait. You can see her. And you can see into the realm of the Fae. So you haven't been denied that place."

Brigit closed her eyes, shaking her head. "That explains why Giles couldn't see in until magic was involved. Of course the most notorious Fae slayer would be barred from that realm. Or anything Land-based."

The Glove studied James. His loyalty was evident, which would be required of a lieutenant, and he was endowed with some Fae connection because he *felt* a little Fae. "Who is your mother, James?"

Brigit conveyed the question.

Alistair raised his hand, his eyes pleading James not to say.

James' eyes were as cold as his tone. "Gloriana."

The Gloves eyes flared, her face turning demonic with rage. *"You changing puke!"*

Brigit winced. Alistair cringed.

James didn't take his eyes off Alistair. "What did she say?"

Brigit sighed. "I don't think I should repeat it."

"You changing, pusillanimous, mephitine lusus naturae. How *dare* you touch one of the Fae Lords?"

Alistair got to his feet. "Glove, please."

James punched him again. "Get out of here, Alistair. Now."

Alistair gestured to the Glove. "I need to take her back to Summerland."

258

The Glove crossed her arms across her chest. "No you don't."

"I saved Lauriel. No one else could have done that."

Everyone went quiet.

Alistair folded his hands together. "Please. I've been trying to make amends for that since it happened. I can't go to your mother. So I've done all I can to try and set the scales even."

James rolled his eyes. "I'm out of here."

The Glove reached out. "James, wait."

Brigit reached out. "She asks that you wait." Brigit looked at the Glove. "Are you sure you can get back to where you need to go?"

"Yes. I can hear it calling to me."

Brigit turned to Alistair. "Why don't you take Raven upstairs? See what's keeping Giles. I'll talk to these folks."

Raven nodded and walked out. Alistair looked back at James and the Sinister Glove, then followed.

"Thank you." The Glove bowed.

"Thank you." James bowed.

Brigit smiled, then looked at the Glove. "What did you need to say to him? I'll translate."

"I think the lieutenants are being targeted. When I was killed, I just thought it was a fluke. My time had run out. But then Merrick showed up. I was killed with a divine ballista bolt from the Papal City. Now, Merrick is killed by a divine pulse? Calpurnia and Embertwist are in torpor and Cal has never returned from that state." The Glove spread her hands apart, like she had more to say, then dropped them, realizing that was it.

James waited for Brigit to finish, then nodded. "I'll send word to Corrigan and Johner. I want to get back to Gloriana with this news. I really feel uncomfortable being away from her at this point."

The Glove bowed.

James stepped back into the Fae realm and walked past the Glove. She turned back to Brigit. "Thank you for helping."

"Of course." Brigit furrowed her brow.

"What is it?"

Brigit looked behind her, then back at the Glove. "Tell me about your afterlife, please. Tell me about Summerland."

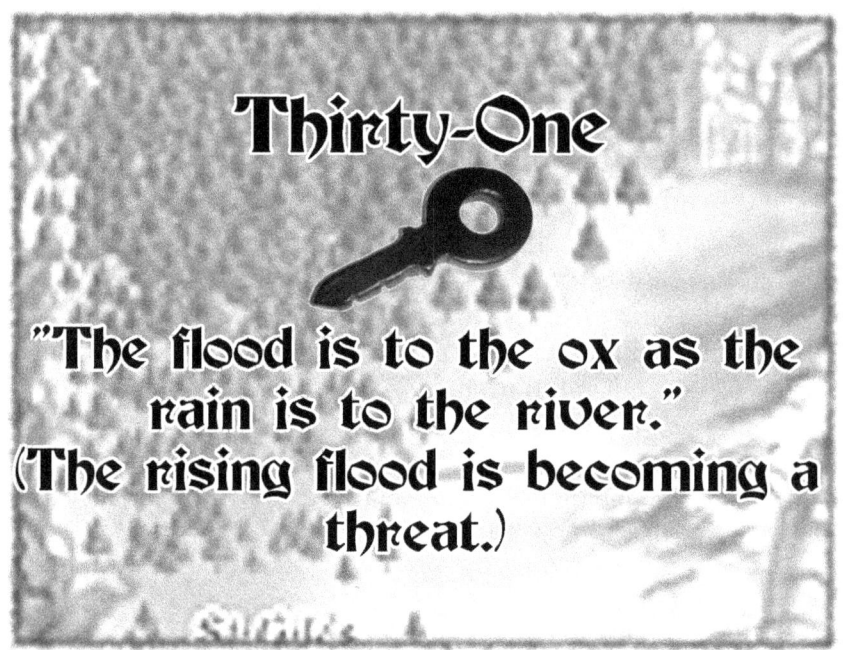

Thirty-One

"The flood is to the ox as the rain is to the river."
(The rising flood is becoming a threat.)

Raven stepped outside with Giles and leaned hard against the broken tower base, looking to the ground.

Giles put his hand on Raven's shoulder. "I'm so sorry, Raven."

Raven swallowed. "I'm going to leave now." He pushed off the wall and staggered towards the nearby barrier.

"I have a pool that might save Lauriel. It has healing *čaro* in it."

"A *divine* pool? Yeah, no thanks." Raven turned to Giles. "I think you need to go on without me now. I don't think I want to be around you anymore."

Giles snorted, trying to scoff. "That's just the grief talking. I'm a mage. You're a mage. We're the last two here."

Raven glared at him. "And why *is* that, Giles? Can ya tell me? Oh wait, I know this one. Because *your church murdered all my friends.* That's right. And in your name, to boot." Raven pointed to the broken tower. "Do you know the name inscribed upon the boulder the Church used to bring this tower down? Here! Have a look!"

Raven punched the ground and instantly, the towers around him were on fire. People were dead or dying on the ground and another Raven was grabbing a bunch of people and going underground with them by pulling the earth around them. After he disappeared, Giles saw the red hot boulder with his name and symbol upon it. Etched into the side in white letters was a prayer.

Saint Giles, defend us against the minions of magic.

Giles sighed. "I didn't help them. I didn't answer that prayer."

"It didn't changing matter, Giles." He waved at the chaos around them. "Invoking your name was all it took! *Your name* has been used every time I've tried to fight back. It's in every church to repel my kind. Your kind." He walked away, the illusion remaining around them.

"Where are you going? Brigit will want to know."

"Well, let's see. I can't go to my familiar because he's in the Fae realm. So if he dies, it will be away from me and I will be truly alone. So I'm going to see if I can prevent that. But don't you go worrying about me, Giles. I'm gonna go where I need to be from here on out."

Raven stepped over the low wall and knelt down. A ball of stone encompassed him and he disappeared.

Brigit's eyebrows raised and she leaned towards the Glove. "And you can just live your life, doing what you want?"

The Glove nodded.

"But you were an infiltrator. A thief. What do you do there?"

The Glove smiled, shrugging. "Well, I don't *steal*. I haven't been that kind of thief for a thousand years. But the infiltration thing is still correct. I could turn into anyone."

The Glove waited until Brigit blinked and transformed her appearance to mirror hers. This was magic the Glove had learned in the course of her life, so it wasn't taken from her in death. Brigit sat back, then moved forward, looking over the woman before her.

"Who is this?"

The Glove frowned. "It's you."

"Extraordinary! I haven't seen myself since before I died." She reached up and felt her face. "I look so different. I was a young girl when

I went into the service of the Angels. I spent so much time in the gardens, I became a fast expert regarding the healing properties of the plants. But I was only one of many. Lots of holy women at the Keep could heal."

The Glove frowned. "Then why were *you* made a saint?"

Brigit reached out and touched the Glove's face, comparing it to her own. "Oh, I refused to put up with the lies of the patriarchy. I was also an artist, thanks to some horrible headaches I used to have regularly. I turned the pain into paintings and we sold them to fund the Keep. This gained notice and people began to come as pilgrimages to the Keep for healing and to study the art.

"There was a fountain that fed our gardens that I suspect had some Giver Resting Place powers or something. People came from all over to be cured. But then a bunch of 'holy men' showed up and said they were from the Church created by Raphael. They said that Heaven wanted them to build a great palace here and a great golden city around it. They *tried* to kick us out of the Keep! But we were a scrappy bunch of ladies, let me tell you. We fought back and they started laying siege to the place. But we had food, water, and everything we needed.

"Then a wounded soldier was left behind at our gates. We don't know if he crawled there or if he had friends who did it. We brought him inside and I used the fountain water to cure him. He changed sides, then and there and fought against his old unit. More and more wounded ended up inside the gates than out and eventually, the army defected. The Church had no fighters.

"So, they compromised with us, had us in charge of the Keep and built around it. That was fine with us for a long time. They tried to bully us into things though. The Mother Superior put me as our spokesperson, since I was the one who healed the first soldier. Then the Church realized we were making money off my paintings and suddenly, they were very supportive of me. They touted me as Brigit the Healer.

"The Mother Superior shrugged and let that happen. It only spread our fame, which brought more pilgrims. When the Church tried to make us do things, I would 'come down ill' and be unable to bless people or produce a painting. This method worked for a long time.

"But the Church was playing the long game. Our order didn't grow. No other women ever came to be a part of us. We found out later that any woman who tried was accepted and sent to another place 'to be trained'. The siege became a different one. A sick person came in, in pain and crazed. He had been bitten by some animal. He foamed at the mouth and was deathly afraid of water. He was also highly contagious.

"We were dead before we could fight it. I was one of the last to go. As the Church members strode in to take over the Keep, I was ascended to Heaven. They were horrified, frightened, and arrogant. They tried to stop everyone from saying anything, but that was stupid. The place was lousy with pilgrims. The word spread fast. The men tried to silence the rumors and the one who ordered the siege stood before the fountain and declared it a lie.

"A pillar came down from Heaven in a bolt, forming right out of the fountain. It proclaimed in some language anyone could understand, even if they couldn't read, that this was the Word of Heaven and whosoever's name appeared on it was a Saint. Church officials tried to chisel the stone but it didn't take and broke the tools. The evil bastard who sent the diseased person into our midst to kill us all was torn apart by the pilgrims. The next man they sent was smarter and made it a holy site. Then they just built the city around it and eventually, the palace as well, burying the fountain and the pillar."

The Glove tilted her head. "Does the Pillar still get names?"

"Yes. The Church refused to acknowledge Clara but we knew she was real and that the Pillar has her name on it. She was the last Saint made though."

"She still here, I take it?" Giles pushed off the wall when Brigit looked at him.

Brigit turned around to face him. "Yes. Where's Raven?"

Giles looked down at his feet. "He left. I get the feeling he won't be joining us on the rest of this trip."

Brigit got to her feet. "What the…?" She ran past Giles.

Giles glanced over the area, still unable to see the Glove. That's when she noticed the fire. She frowned as she saw the flicker of flames outside in the anteroom of the broken tower. She stepped out into the chaos of Persephone under attack.

Giles walked up to Brigit. "It isn't real. It's a spell."

"A spell?"

"Yeah. I, I used to do it all the time. We would investigate an area and I could call forth the memory of the incident in a place." He gestured to the attack. "This was what brought this place down."

"Can you stop it?"

Giles shrugged. "Probably, but it will bleed itself out at sunset." He looked at her. "We need to go. You have a kingdom to save."

Brigit looked at the Glove, who reverted to her own form. "Thank you. Can I reach out to you?"

The Glove shrugged. "I have no idea. But it wouldn't hurt to try."

Brigit bowed and turned to Giles. "Get us there."

Giles took her hand and disappeared.

The Glove closed her eyes and returned to Summerland.

Raven opened his eyes and looked around the meditation chamber. He saw Myrgen and Catriona huddled together and he walked to them. He took a knee before her and bowed his head.

"Forgive my intrusion. I have a request."

Catriona turned tear-streaked eyes of emerald on Raven. "What do you need?"

"There was… a divine pulse. My… Lauriel was caught in it."

She sat back, despair filling her face.

Myrgen looked up at him. "Lauriel too?" He rubbed his eyes with the heels of his hands. "How many more is this going to claim?" He looked at Raven. "It killed Michael."

Raven's eyes screwed closed in sorrow. "I am so sorry."

Catriona squeezed Raven's shoulder and Myrgen embraced him, sobbing. Raven joined him in the embrace for a moment, then pushed back.

"Lauriel is with Gloriana. She's the Healer of the Fae nation. But he was…" He couldn't bring himself to speak the words.

Catriona saved him the trouble with a thorough study of him. She looked at Myrgen. "Stay with him. I'll see what I can do."

Her eyes turned to jade and she was gone.

Catriona arrived in the hall of the Midwinter Queen. All discussion trickled away to silence as she entered and looked around. She looked at one of the bystanders.

"The Fae wolf. Where is it?"

The ice troll woman pointed an elegant finger towards a passage in the left side of the room. She strode down it, listening. There was a sound coming from a chamber and the Queen of Winter screamed in frustration. A blast of ice spears embedded in a wall across from a door. Catriona looked in.

"Your Majesty?"

Gloriana looked up, her hands on either side of Lauriel's frozen head. James looked up.

"Catriona? What are you doing here?"

"I'm going to try and help."

Gloriana looked her over. "James, give her your coat."

James took off his long, fur and wool coat and helped Catriona into it. As she buttoned it over her naked body, she looked at the damage to Lauriel.

"Now leave us."

James glanced at them both, then bowed and left, closing the doors behind him.

Gloriana looked up. "So, which capacity are you here in?"

Catriona stepped to look at the Fae wolf. "Let's see which one works. What have you tried?"

"I have frozen him so he won't deteriorate. He's in hibernation. But he can't heal this way. I can try a restorative, but it needs time to work, and he's already a breath away from dying. If I unfreeze him without him being healed, he's done. Anything else would change his nature."

"Service?"

Gloriana shook her head. "He's a mage's familiar. It took special rules being made for that to even happen and one of them is that Lauriel can serve no others."

Catriona sighed. "If he dies?"

"He may go to Summerland, to wait for Raven."

Catriona frowned. "Who will never arrive. He's been banned from the afterlife."

"He's…" Gloriana rolled her eyes. "Well, that doesn't surprise me." She looked at Lauriel. "So, what can we do?"

"Well, death is not an option. So I guess I'm here in the other capacity." She lifted Lauriel in her arms and turned to Gloriana. "Be ready, my Queen. Gather your forces."

Gloriana closed her eyes and bowed to Catriona. "As you command."

Catriona stepped from the realm of Ice into the meditation chamber. Raven ran to her and Lauriel. Myrgen and Raven took Lauriel from her arms, barely able to lower him to the ground without dropping him. She looked at Raven.

"You need to leave the chamber."

"No."

Myrgen put a hand on his shoulder.

"No." Raven knelt beside Lauriel. "And if you dismiss me, I'll return the way I got here. I'm not leaving him."

"I don't know if you…" She wasn't sure what to say.

"Yeah yeah, you're the Land. Duh. Why do you think I'm here?"

Catriona huffed a laughed, then looked at Lauriel. "Be whole."

Essence flowed from Catriona and the heart of the Land into Lauriel. His chest filled in, stitching sinew over newly formed bone. His front right paw had been cut off and tucked under his body but it had shifted when he was originally moved. Now, it regrew, fresh, new claws and soft pads. His fur became lush and fine on his chest and foot. His lower jaw had also been cut away, more than half of his mouth had to be restored. When it was, his teeth were sharp and golden like summer wheat.

The essence stopped flowing and he thawed in the hot room. He twitched and blinked.

Raven stroked his fur. "He's here… I can feel him again."

Lauriel rolled to a laying down position, looking up at Raven. He put his paw on Raven's leg. Raven hugged his neck, poking his hands and tearing his shirt on the Fae wolf's hackle spines. He leaned back and rubbed the Fae wolf's ears.

Myrgen put his arm around Catriona's waist and she squeezed his hand. "You did it."

She turned to him. "I had to save someone."

Raven finished rubbing Lauriel's ears, then stood and turned to Catriona. "Thank you."

Lauriel bowed, then stepped forward to put a forepaw out as Raven also took a knee.

"I can't repay what you have done here. You have given me back the only thing left me. But I can assure you I will not rest until we have defeated the foe that did this. It has taken so much from so many. I'll not let it take another thing unscathed."

"Thank you, Raven. I understand your oath. But you have your friend back. I don't want you throwing your lot in with us on the high of gratitude."

"It's not that, though I appreciate that you aren't just commanding me to kill myself repeatedly for killing you. The truth is that I have spent too long adrift. I've wandered, and studied, and served all over this world. But I believe I have a purpose here.

"I've served the Land all my life. And during that life, I have stayed out of human conflicts. The Mages Code taught us long ago that mages have too much power. Influencing politics was wrong, because a mage was a weapon that would encourage other mages to be brought in as well."

Catriona nodded. "Except there *are* no other mages."

"Even fewer now. The Church decided to use magic to fight us, even though we never fought them. We may have made the rules, but we aren't the ones who broke them. I'm saying, My Lady, that I'm going to be fighting back for all the mages that fell before them. It's up to you if you want to direct my energy."

Catriona took a deep breath. Holding Myrgen's hand, she put her other one on Raven's shoulder. "Tell me what you know. We have a war to fight."

Thirty-Two

"The ox is to the farmer as the rock is to the river." (The ox is higher ground, and the farmer climbs onto the ox.)

Lucifer looked up as the Glove walked past the open study door. "Ah, you're back! How did it go?"

The Glove frowned, leaning against the doorjamb and folding her arms. "Not entirely like I thought it would be."

He sat forward. "Oh?"

"It was more active than I planned. A lot more running about. And lonely. I wasn't expecting that part."

"Lonely?"

"Yeah. The Fae can't see me."

"Ah. Because they have no souls."

She cocked her head. "Is that actually it? I had a fleeting thought like that but," she shrugged, "I figure you would know a lot better than I." She pointed to him. "Oh, and I may have a convert."

"You ministered to some poor, unsuspecting Fae?"

She smiled. "Not entirely. Saint Brigit."

"Ooh! How did you manage that?" Lucifer smiled, his eyes glittering, and he clasped his hands and rested his chin on them.

"She was on earth. She talked to me about Summerland."

Lucifer's smile left. "On earth?"

"Her and Giles at least. Who knows how many more might be down here?"

"Yeah. Who knows?" He blinked, restoring his attention to his guest. "Would you like to sit and tell me about it?"

The Glove nodded. "I thought you'd never ask." She glanced at his decanter and glasses. "Which is the good stuff?"

"Here, my friend, it's *all* the good stuff."

He rose and listened as she told about the incident with Merrick and Lauriel. He settled back after she finished that part, finishing off his drink. He refreshed both while she told the rest.

"'Changer'?"

She glanced away. "It's… derogatory. Fae die if their nature is changed. So, if Gloriana tried to save Lauriel's life by replacing his wounded parts with ice or by turning him into an ice wolf, he would be destroyed. Thus, she would never do that." She sipped her drink. "Anyway, the term is the harshest insult a Fae can give. In general, the reason Fae like humans is because they are so different and confusing. They are like puzzles. And humans can be many, many things at once.

"But Fae also fear that changing ability. Calling someone a changer says they have no integrity. I've only ever heard the term uttered by Fae-held Humans or half-Fae humans. Apparently, the human part is the essential aspect. It means from that point, you always expect the person to lie, and you can't trust them."

"And James called Alistair that."

She shrugged. "So did I, but he is one. I'd recommend against you trusting him, but he can't really do anything to you, you being the ruler of Hell and all."

"Not ruler. *Caretaker.* The place exists. I take care of it. That's all."

"Then why do you have such a bad reputation?"

Lucifer pointed at her. "That's a damned fine question!"

The Glove yawned. "Wow. I'm tired. How can I be tired? I'm dead."

"No idea, but listen to your body. Shoo. I should retire myself."

They stood and he saw her to the door of the study. She turned. "You know, you remind me of Embertwist."

269

He arched an eyebrow. "Is that a good thing?"

She smirked. "I'll have to get back to you on that."

The Glove yawned again and waved goodbye.

Lucifer tidied up and then headed up the stairs at the end of the hallway. He knocked on the door at the top on the left. He heard a mumble and opened it, peeking in.

"Was that a come in?"

"No. That was a go away." Alistair stared at the crystal Pillar in the room.

Lucifer opened the door fully and stood in the doorway. "The Glove told me what happened."

Alistair shifted a glance at Lucifer. "Did she?"

"You okay?"

Alistair looked back at the Pillar, then pushed away. "Lauriel's okay. Catriona healed him. Turns out she's a little more important than we thought. She doesn't *serve* the Land. She *is* the Land."

"Like the actual deity?"

"Apparently. Regardless, she saved Lauriel. Remade him from his own stuff. Just essentially fed Essence of Land into him and let him regenerate."

"Essence of Land, eh? Is that a new perfume?"

Alistair snorted. "I think it will be very popular in certain circles."

Lucifer nodded. "So. What do you think that means?"

Alistair walked over to a bowl of colorful foods. "What? That she's the Land?" He shrugged. "No idea. But I worry it means more than any of us think." He pulled out a juicy, tropical fruit called an *ahm* and tossed it to Lucifer. "I mean, if the Bringer is the Land..."

Lucifer caught the fruit, nodding. "Then maybe the Giver is Heaven? That's not a far leap. Heaven was created from the stuff in the Well of Souls." Lucifer looked over the offering. "Don't these have a huge pit in the center?"

"Usually. But not here."

"What are these called?" Lucifer took a bite.

"*Ahms*. The Rhamidal always had them. But the pit was always fifty percent of the fruit so I just summon them without it. If this wasn't all my imagination, I'd assume there was a huge pile of *ahm* pits near the Yantap palace."

Lucifer chewed and swallowed. The flavor was exquisite, undoubtedly better than they were in real life. "You seem to be adjusting to this place."

Alistair shrugged. "I did my time in self-pity. Time to balance that back out with some indulgence. I never realized how much I do that, but I do. I guess Karma wasn't wrong to choose me."

"So, do you have Karma's knowledge?"

Alistair looked around the room. "Probably. Somewhere. I haven't found any notes or anything, if that's what you're asking."

"Is it possible you only know what *you* know and the knowledge died with the previous incarnation?"

"By the Balance, I hope not. If so, then whatever that spell is down there, it's gonna end. It doesn't have the same source it once did and now, those sources burn out. Anything that goes in there is going to die. And we still don't know what will happen when the spell fails."

Lucifer finished off the *ahm* and walked to a basin of water to wash up. "I have an idea. Maybe the Giver knows something. I'll go ask her. We know Catriona doesn't because she dies and comes back. Her memories are lost. But I don't think the Giver has ever died or changed."

Alistair sat upright, setting aside the *ahm.* "What do you need me to do?"

"Let me see how she is. I'll see if the war is keeping my brother angels occupied. If so, I'll get her out and bring her here. They can't get here."

"Why not? You did."

"I knew where it was."

"How?"

"The previous Karma and I were lovers."

Alistair blinked. Then bobbed his head. "Yeah, I can see that. Hurry back."

Lucifer went back down the stairs to the first floor, then opened a door hidden in the wall. The room on the other side was hot and smoky, full of darkness interrupted by glows of lava. He went to a large throne and moved behind it. He reached into the glowing mountain of souls and grabbed a handful. Then he walked to the shaft below the Giver's cage. He was concerned that she would not survive down here. But that was no longer affordable. He needed to get her out of there. And now was the time.

Uriel opened his eyes and looked around. He didn't recognize anything. He tried to move and was able to get to his knees. His flesh crackled and he looked at it. It was roasted, burnt black in most places. He looked to the right and saw Gabriel likewise burnt and barely moving. Around them was the scaffolding of Heaven, with all the raw Giver removed. The factory was gone. The walls and floor were solid air, built with them by air spirits long ago to hide the Well from the world to keep it safe. That was all that was holding them from the ground miles below.

He slowly turned.

All the structures Raphael and Gabriel had built recently, to house the Saints and keep them from convening, were destroyed. The blast had gone through that area and there was nothing left. He thought maybe they all fell to the ground, but there were black smears that indicated otherwise. He could feel his old injury stronger now and tried to look around for Raphael. His neck cracked like an autumn leaf.

A noise behind him drew his attention and he tried to see what made it.

"Uriel?"

"Lucifer?"

He felt a hand upon his shoulder and the pain caused him to scream. He was rolled onto his back. Lucifer knelt beside him, looking him over in a panic.

"What happened?"

Uriel swallowed. "Giver… out…"

Lucifer looked beside him, nodding. "Yeah, I can see that. Where's Raphael?"

Uriel moved his head slightly. "I don't… know… Help…me…"

Lucifer looked him over, then reached into his pocket. He pulled out a perfect ball of glowing silver white. "Eat this."

Uriel opened his mouth and swallowed the soul. His skin healed from the edge of death to less burnt. Lucifer gave him a few more and the blackness went away, replaced by horrid scars. He ate another and the skin became smooth. His eyes cleared of pain and his breathing eased.

Suddenly, Lucifer lurched back and tumbled from the ledge where the cage once was. The souls spilled out onto the floor. Raphael grabbed about ten and shoved them in his mouth. They worked instantly, giving him wings again. He glared at Uriel.

Uriel started to get up and Raphael grabbed him, hauling him from the floor. He threw him across the room. Uriel slammed into the wall where the Well had stood.

"What did you do?"

Uriel shook his head trying to orient himself. "I just… I gave her a drop of her own essence." Uriel looked around, blood trickling from a cut on his cheek from the impact with the wall.

"From that *filthy* thing?" Raphael pointed to the place where the Well explosion had gouged furrows in the wall. "That thing was tainted with pure corruption. That was nothing short of poison to her. How do you think we kept her in there all this time? The cage was made of that corruption."

Uriel tried to stand. "You were poisoning her?"

Raphael turned and picked up four souls. "We figured out a way to strain the corruption from the Well. But it depleted it. There was nothing else we could use it for but we could *use* it. So, we made the cage to keep her in. We figured we could siphon souls from her to refresh the Well, and we *did*. Every time she saw you, she cried when you left. But you stopped coming. Why, Uriel? Did you figure it out?"

Raphael took the souls to Gabriel and poured them into his mouth. The angel healed to the scarred level, wincing and working to stand.

"What?" Uriel pushed away from the wall. "No. She… She missed me?"

Raphael walked over to Uriel and helped him to his feet. "Here. Lean on me."

Uriel did and Raphael walked him over to Gabriel, pointing. "Look what she did to your brother."

"I'm sorry, Gabriel."

"You are, huh?" Raphael looked at Uriel.

"Yes."

"Then you'll help us catch her and rebuild this?"

Uriel looked at Raphael. "What? No. She's gone."

Raphael grabbed Uriel's arms, causing him to cry out. *"Yes! By your hand."* Raphael threw Uriel to the edge of the floor. "You've betrayed us for the last time, Uriel!"

He gathered a bunch of sunlight in his hands then threw it at Uriel. It wrapped around him, hurling Uriel off the edge. The light formed into a bolt that hurtled to earth. An opening in the ground yawned and a gold statue of a woman disintegrated as he arrived. Cords wrapped around Uriel and snatched him from the air, pulling him spread-eagled. A light flowed from him right before the ground closed over him.

Raphael turned to look at Gabriel. "Can you stand?"

Gabriel tried but couldn't.

Raphael turned to the room where the cage was. He found three more souls and brought them to Gabriel. This healed all but his wings.

They turned to the pit that led to Hell and jumped down.

Lucifer dropped into the pit and landed in Hell. He hoped the few souls he left behind on the platform would distract Raphael for a few minutes. He looked around and wiped the sweat from his brow. He went to the pile of souls and grabbed another handful. Then Raphael landed with Gabriel in the pit. Lucifer turned to face them.

Raphael and Gabriel stepped out from the shaft that led to the Giver's cage and Lucifer ducked into the shadows, willing his outfit to black. Raphael looked through the heat shimmers and Gabriel pointed at the glowing pile of souls.

Raphael went to them and picked up a handful from the mountain. "Looks like my brother was hiding more than yours was."

"That must be how he was uninjured."

Raphael glared at the pile. "No. He would have had to be right here when she broke out in order to heal himself that fast, and I did not hear him scream. Plus, his clothes were intact."

Lucifer stepped between the heat shimmers to the door at the other end of the room, the one that went to his mansion. The door opened and he slipped through it. It was closing silently when fingers wedged inside. Gabriel, fully restored, pulled the door open.

Lucifer scrambled backwards and ran up the stairs. The stairs turned to a spiral staircase, which slowed the other Archangels with their newly restored wings. Lucifer ran down the hall and looked around. The fragrant air of Summerland wafted in from the gardens, and the smell of a summer storm came from Sovereignlumin. He heard the *clank* of feet ascending the staircase, accompanied by yelps as the hot metal scored their hands.

He ducked into the study and ran to the desk. He pulled a quill and dipped it in ink, writing as fast as he could. The message was enough and he hoped the Dûcesa would understand. He folded it as Raphael and Gabriel entered the room.

"Nice place you have here." Gabriel circled towards the desk.

"It works for me."

"It works for a lot of things." Raphael looked around the room, appraising it. "Connected to all the Afterlives?"

"You might say. What do you want, Raph?"

"That's quite a lot of souls downstairs."

"Yeah, about that. What do you say you take those and rebuild Heaven?" Lucifer was getting flanked and he was having trouble keeping his eye on both angels.

"We will. We definitely will. But I can't believe you hoarded them all this time. You let all those babies die. You could have been ensouling humans all along."

Lucifer set his jaw. "Humans benefit from having souls with memory. Art, literature, creative thinking comes from a soul with experience. Those had none. Back when you used to walk the earth, I would add some to the Well when I was up here alone. Then you grabbed the Giver and the place was always under guard." Lucifer looked at Gabriel. "Why did you let him do that?"

"I owed him for saving me and Uriel from the Bringer. Because I understand the sacrifice he made for us."

"Sacrifice?" Lucifer tapped his own chest. "It was *my* daughter, not his."

"Only because he couldn't have one! He tried, everywhere! He even tried with your wife! He thought Persis was his own."

Lucifer turned to Raphael. "Is this true? Is this why you fought for her?"

Raphael straightened. "It didn't matter, did it? It didn't stop her from being *murdered* by the Bringer."

"She was in pain, Raphael. She couldn't *run or play or think.* Just *writhe.* How could you say you loved her when she was suffering and you did nothing to stop it?"

"I tried." Raphael pointed behind him and up. "But she *denied* us. She stopped Persis from being able to live *without pain.* I *owed* the Giver that much suffering, as much as she inflicted upon our daughter, Lucifer."

"It wasn't her area. It wasn't her purview to heal someone touched by the Death Bringer."

"No." Raphael held up a finger. "She was just like her. They are the same thing. She could have created a new" he waved a hand dismissively, "*whatever* to fix her. She didn't. She let a beautiful young girl suffer and die instead of just help us. She didn't deserve to walk the earth and as soon as I found out where she was hiding, I captured her and held her."

Raphael shook his head, looking like he was holding back stomach bile. "I will find her again, and I will trap her just like I did before. Only this time, I'm going to put her in a trap she can't get out of. I'll put her in a trap no one can spring her from because there's no other entity stronger than her."

Lucifer's eye grew wide. *The trap. He's going to use the trap to kill her.*

Raphael saw the understanding in Lucifer's eyes and hit him with a bolt of sunlight. The blast threw him back against the hearth and he slumped to the floor, vases and sculptures falling from the mantle to crash at his feet. One fell on his head, driving him to the ground where he lay still.

Raphael looked at Gabriel. "Come. We have work to do. The first thing is to harvest those souls."

"Where are we going to put them?"

"We'll make something. Or maybe we won't. We can just leave them there." Raphael looked back at Lucifer. "He won't be using this place again."

They stepped out into the hallway and looked back the way they came. The hallway had large double doors that looked out onto a forested area with a tall tower.

Gabriel nodded to it. "What is that?"

Raphael shrugged. "Undoubtedly a heathen afterlife."

"Can he really have access to all of them here?"

"I don't know. But there's one way to find out. I'll bet one of these places is where the Giver is." Raphael nodded to the tower. "Check that way, I'll check this way."

They walked to their respective ends. The door in front of Raphael closed. He tried to open it but it didn't even rattle when he hammered on it. He looked at Gabriel.

"Anything?"

Gabriel shook his head. "Maybe it closes off when he's dead." He looked around, then tried the door they came from, then another. "Nope. Not opening."

Raphael looked around. "He has to have a way into Heaven here. He brought us through Hell. Open that one across from the room he's in. I'm going to try something."

Gabriel nodded and Raphael stepped back from his door. Then he fired the sunlight bolt at it. The light went everywhere and even Raphael winced back from the power he was pouring into it. He let it flow for several seconds, then stopped to examine the damage.

There was none.

"What the…?" Gabriel opened the door across from the other one. He looked at Raphael. "It's just darkness."

Raphael turned to his cousin and saw Lucifer step to the door of the study. He flipped a black card with silver writing on it into the hall and it fluttered across and into the door Gabriel stood before.

Then the door to the study shut and sealed.

Thirty-Three

"The tree is to the farmer as the air is to the ox." (The tree is the farmer's salvation.)

Catriona looked at Raven. "You can't get anywhere in the afterlife then?"

Raven shook his head. "No where."

She frowned. "I can probably change that."

"Whatever you prefer. It won't enable me to get into Heaven."

She sighed. "True. But at least you know you can go home afterwards."

He bowed and she touched him. Red-gold light bathed him. "There. The way to Summerland is open to you again."

He straightened, smiling. "I can feel it. Thank you."

Lauriel snorted.

Raven looked at Lauriel, then at Catriona.

"What?" She smiled.

"Lauriel says your eyes are clear. You're much nicer when your eyes are clear."

She glanced at Myrgen, who shrugged.

"He's right. You are nicer."

"That doesn't help us free the Giver." She pursed her lips, then bowed to the Fae wolf. "But thank you, nonetheless. Now, about this mage. What can you tell me about him? Does he know anything about the trap?"

"I don't think so, but we can go to his realm. He has shown it to me."

They stood and Raven held her and Myrgen's hands.

Nothing happened.

He opened an eye. "You gonna take us there or what?"

Catriona frowned. "I don't know where it is."

"Oh. Then let's just go to Persephone and I'll take us from there."

She nodded and the world grew bright. The left onyx tower was struck with two giant boulders at once and blasted apart into dust. Catriona and Myrgen ducked and Raven yelped.

"Oh! Sorry!" He raised his hand and the scene vanished.

"What was that?" Myrgen looked Catriona and himself over for damage but there wasn't even dust upon them.

"The Battle of Persephone, when we lost this place. Merrick was in Sovereignlumin, Snow and Eirdrin were visiting his giant family. Antoine was gone. Wilge was in the keep with the babies. Everyone else who lived here died. Constance and Pander were in that tower when it was pulverized. All Wilge's staff. Our friends. Tarbo and the apprentices. The spells were supposed to protect the towers so everyone ran inside them. Then that happened." He waved a hand at the spot where the tower had been.

"What took them down?" Myrgen looked at the houses with holes in them, like pieces of stone were hurled across them.

"Giant stones that were enhanced with holy magic."

Catriona closed her eyes and shook her head. "Of course. Enough." She opened her eyes. "Take us to this place of Giles'."

Raven strode to the wall and hopped over it. Catriona and Myrgen joined him.

"Hey, wait. You just dispelled that vision." Myrgen pointed to the courtyard.

"Yes."

"Did you cast the spell to show that?"

"Yes."

"Can you show us who made the trap?"

"No. I wasn't there for it. I had to experience some part of it to do that."

"Oh."

Raven took their hands and they dropped into the earth like it was water. A second later, they emerged from it next to nothing. She looked around. Grass grew under foot. "You've definitely been here. Where is this place?"

Raven pushed aside a curtain of air and another realm opened. Catriona and Myrgen stepped in. "How did you get access to this?"

"It's a covenant. While we were here, I attuned to it. But you two haven't. You had to come in the front door, so to speak."

Myrgen inhaled. "What is that? Fresh bread?"

Raven smiled for the first time since Lauriel had been hurt. "Oh! That's right! Come! I have someone to introduce you to."

Giles and Brigit arrived in a cavern and she looked around. "Where are we now?"

"The Haunted Covenant. I have something I need to show you."

"Giles, why do you keep not taking me to Alexander?"

He raised his hand. "I… this might be important. Come here." He walked to the next room of the cavern.

She followed. "This had better be good."

"It just might be."

He gestured to a pool that glowed with white and silver light. Inside it was a man covered in red-black skin. He was asleep in the pool.

"Who is that?" She kept her voice low so as not to awaken him.

Giles took a deep breath. "Michael."

"What? How did he get *here?* I thought he was in a sword."

"He got out. And then fire from nowhere struck his entire body and burned away his wings."

She went to the pool. She reached in and touched him. He didn't stir, but continued to sleep. Then she frowned. "Is… Is that my necklace?"

Giles stepped over to look at the pool. In the bottom was a translucent blue stone with silver flecks throughout it, wrapped in twisted wire and hanging on a silver chain. "Is it? We found it in an abandoned keep. It had a lot of healing *čaro* in it so we brought it here."

"Abandoned? You mean it wasn't... No one was there? They didn't repopulate it?"

Giles glanced away. "It looked like they left everyone where they fell. We saw skeletons that still had clothes on them. The flesh was all gone though."

She walked to the other side and climbed into the pool. She reached down and picked up the necklace, holding it under the water. "I made this. It was my sacred stone."

Giles stood behind her, out of the water. "Why was it sacred?"

She smiled, turning it over. "I found it when I had my first powerful headache. I picked it up and the headache went away. After that, I had this vision of a radiant, colorful sphere. I knew everything about it. It was beyond beautiful. It took me a while to paint it and I used dyes on a piece of wool. I wore that as a cape for a long time, until I outgrew it. Later, it was on my bed at the keep. Whenever I wanted to paint, I removed the necklace. The pain would take over and I stayed like that until I got a vision of what to create next. Then I put on the necklace and did so."

She looked at Michael, covered in burns, then released the necklace back into the pool.

"It's doing more good here than anywhere else. Come on. I still need to go to Alexander."

The Giver dropped into the crater and curled into a ball. The rage was thinning, replaced by pain and nausea. She looked around. The sun was harsh here and she felt unwavering heat pounding down on her. One thing about Heaven, it was temperate. Her eyes hurt and when she tried to move, jolts of agony exploded in her gut. She cried out, wincing.

She felt a hand on her shoulder and started, fear overcoming the pain momentarily. A brown man with long brown hair and an impressive amount of facial hair knelt beside her.

"Are you hurt?"

"I'm... sick...They were poisoning me."

The man glanced up and then back at her. "Can you vomit?"

She shook her head. "Not without consequences."

"What consequences?"

She was wracked again with pain and this time, the nausea won. She threw up.

The bile was green-black and glistened like oil. Then tendrils of growth spiraled out from it. Branches formed from those, and veins from those, spreading out in a fractal pattern, like a swamp frost. She touched it and it swirled. The black broke apart, releasing all the colors it was holding hostage. The colors separated into a glowing rainbow that threaded like blood through the veins.

She propped herself up on her elbow to watch the pattern change and flow.

"That is strangely beautiful."

The Giver looked at the man, then back at the pattern. "Yes."

"It's also rather disgusting."

She laughed and was hit with another wave of pain. "Ow. Yes, I suppose it is."

"Did it help?"

She looked at the man and pushed herself up. "Yes. It did."

"Do you need to do more?"

"Yes. But I think I want to direct it. Can you help me stand?"

The man rose and helped her to her feet. The gut pain was still pretty severe and she breathed through gritted teeth.

"Where are we?"

The man sighed. "Where everything that leaves Heaven goes. The Wasteland."

The Giver looked at him, frowning. "Wasteland? I left no wastelands."

He shrugged. "It wasn't your fault. It actually undid a lot of your work. I'm Jude, by the way."

She smiled, leaning on her knee with one hand while her other held her stomach. "I'm the Giver."

Jude nodded. "Yeah, I'm pretty aware of that. How long were you up there?"

"Long enough for this to happen." She nodded to the crater. "Did I bring you down with me?"

Jude patted her shoulder. "Don't worry about it. I was looking to quit that job anyway."

"What was your specialty?"

"I was the Patron Saint of Hopeless Cases. It was why I volunteered to do the ensouling. I realized, even though the Well was almost empty, one of the babies that were born might actually be able to save us. You never know with human potential."

"Then it looks like you'll have a use for those skills. But right now, I need to do something about this poison."

He nodded and helped her to the edge of the crater. She straightened and lay eyes on the wasteland of York for the first time. The horror in her eyes translated to her voice.

"How far does it go?"

He gestured as he spoke. "To the Glarren bay on the north. To the west, almost to the Black Forest. To the east, to the wall and the sea. And to the south..." He stopped, frowning at the greenery spreading in strange paths. "Uh... apparently to right over there. Erratically."

She tilted her head, looking at the strange patterns of growth. She focused and grew larger, titanic in height. The patterns were indeed erratic but seemed to show a very distinct history of... something. She took a knee and reached out, touching the ground between the closest trails.

The green-black flowed from her hands as she drew in the ground. It filled in and blended at the edges. Then she blew on it and it again broke into the glowing rainbow, this time in flowers. She breathed, smiling.

"I can fix this." She looked at Jude. "I can fix this." She closed her eyes and spread her arms wide. "There is new growth to the south. That feels like *her*. But the rest has nothing. But *there*," she pointed west, "that feels like me."

She opened her eyes and looked at the crater. "This is where things fall from the sky?"

"If they fall, yes. I don't know what happens if they just leave."

"Were you cast out?"

Jude narrowed his eyes. "I jumped. You looked like you were gonna explode, and I didn't want to be there for that. I more or less aimed for this spot."

"Well then, let's start here."

She thrust her hands into the ground and a crack formed where they struck. The crack rushed through the crater to the north and she pulled the earth apart, widening the rift. Water blew upwards from the aquafer and began filling the crater. She walked to the eastern edge and did the same. Water started pouring from the east as well.

The pain in her body started to ebb, then surge, and she gripped the ground to steady herself.

"Are you alright?" Jude had his tiny hand upon her calf and she could barely hear him.

She winced, smiling. "Not yet. But I'm going to try."

She looked at the crater and the small spiral of colors in the now growing water. She tilted her head as inspiration came to her. She reached out to the west and grasped the essence that felt familiar there. There was a lot of it, and it felt very creative. She used that to fuel the energy she was putting into the area.

The forest expanded, new trees a hundred years old punching through the ground. She felt fields germinate, grow, and go to seed in a minute. The trees spread in the same fractal pattern as the slime had until she got what she wanted.

A tree finally grew at the edge of the crater and she used her power to ring the crater with them. When the circle met up with her, she plucked a seed from a branch and threw it into the center of the lake. It sank to the bottom and when it touched the soil, it grew a thousand feet into the air. Water cascaded down from it in a beautiful rainbow shower, sparkling in the light.

She smiled. "I like that. I like that a lot."

She twisted her hands and the tree wrapped itself into a spiral that cut its height in half, but the result was the water from the lake flowing up it.

Jude looked up. "Wow. So, will it just keep climbing until it reaches the top?"

She frowned. The water stopped a little way up the tree, barely making it through the first wrap of the spiral. "It doesn't look like it. It needs a source."

She winced and closed her eyes. She felt something on her cheek and touched it. It was a tear.

That should work.

She put the tear on the top of the spiral tree and it gushed down in a waterfall, following the trunk to the rapidly forming lake. The top likewise became a geyser, shooting mist into the air to form a continuous rain.

Jude laughed. "You did it!"

She smiled and leaned on the ground, breathing heavy. Jude patted her calf again.

"You need to rest now."

She shook her head. "I can't rest while this is here."

She grabbed the tree beside her and shook a host of seeds from it. Then she scattered the seeds in every direction. For miles, the seeds flew and when they hit the ground, they burst forth in new forest growth. She flung more out and the growth spread. Then she threw them a third time and blew on them. The seeds carried towards the north, setting down within sight of the edge of the Glarren bay.

She felt all of them take root and grow. Some even flew south. She could feel the forest stretching in every direction and taking hold, the pulse of energy from the original forest flowing through their descendants.

She collapsed, shrinking down to human size again. She closed her eyes and went unconscious.

Thirty-Four

"The ox is to the farmer as the ground is to the river." (The ox is starting to falter as the river erodes the ground beneath its feet.)

Giles and Brigit arrived in the church in St. Giles. She looked around and saw the window of saints' symbols on the wall above the altar.

"I'll look for the priest. He can tell us where Alexander is."

Brigit nodded, frowning at the symbol. "Giles, what does that look like?"

Giles looked at it. "A bunch of markings. It's just art. I thought you wanted to find Alexander."

She looked away. "Right. You're right. I'll check outside. You look around in here for the priest."

They split up and Brigit went outside. To the left was a road leading to what practically looked like a faire with all the colorful tents. Then she remembered they were fighting a Fae army and she looked the other directions. In front of her was the main highway of Mervolingia. She could see the Mervol army heading east on the road, with some of them lining the road into town. A red haired man in a non-army uniform spoke to some other men in uniforms. She glanced to the right and saw a street heading down to what smelled like a pier.

She went forward towards the guards.

Giles looked around, but found no one. He entered the priest's bedroom but there was no sign of anything. He went back into the chapel, glanced out the open church door, and saw Brigit heading towards some guards on the edge of town.

Obviously, she hasn't found him. I wonder where the priest is?

He went to the doorway and was going to call out to Brigit to wait for him when he noticed the font by the door was practically dry. He heard a creak to the right and saw a door a few buildings down move.

Ah. An inhabitant. I'll ask them.

He walked past the Guards office and the Barracks to a jeweler. The door hung open just slightly and the hinges creaked as it swung in the light sea breeze.

The lock is broken. Did someone break in here?

The door was slightly ajar and he pushed it open.

Boxes and fabric littered the place, and the display case had been broken and ransacked. A few stones were still in settings, but other than that, the shelves and counter were bare. He went behind the sales counter and into a back room.

On a table was a carving of a symbol. It was made in soap and the single casting of the item rendered it unable to be used for the same task again. A jar of powder lay on its side, spilling out the contents, and a light dusting of it coated the mold. Giles noticed blood on the mold as well, and a knife on the counter. A smelter's pot lay on the ground, its remaining contents splattered across the floor and furnishings like it was cast aside. A few drops of gold had burned holes in the rug.

Giles looked at the mold but it was too distorted to figure out what it was. He glanced around for a book with a drawing but there was nothing open on the counter. Since the thief had not cared about the remaining gold in the pot, Giles felt certain he or she would not have put the recipe or design away and left the rest out for anyone to find.

He leaned his elbows on the table and stared at the evidence in front of him. This *felt* familiar. He rested his head on his hands and his eyes fell upon his amulet. He looked at the mold again and stepped back. He moved his hands and mumbled a spell.

Instantly, a heavy man with white hair and beard appeared before him. The man was wearing priest's robes and a pall with the church window symbol on it.

The priest removed the melting pot from the burner and was about to pour it into the mold when he stopped. He stood very still a moment, then leaned on the counter. He looked at the carving knife and grabbed it, then rushed out of the room.

Giles looked at the mold on the table in the vision. It was hastily done, but still a valid carving. Whatever he was making wouldn't be very thick or sturdy but he didn't apparently need it to be more than he needed it *now*. He tried to sort out the lines and make a pattern but the light in the room was not good.

Giles waved a hand over the mold and the lines within it brightened. He recognized it instantly.

It was his traveling medallion.

Except it *wasn't*. There were a bunch of symbols that didn't make sense. He studied the pattern, then duplicated it in the air above it. He pulled certain pieces apart and set them to the side. It took a few moments of overlapping lines, but he figured out what he was looking at. The symbols of several saints were being invoked. His was the first he figured out. Then Walburga, Raphael, and Nicholas the Wonderworker.

Those were the symbols on the window in the church.

The priest came back in and leaned on the counter before the mold. He cut his forearm on the back and dripped enough blood on the mold to thoroughly coat it. Then he grabbed the melting pot, and emptied it into the mold. Steam and the stench of burning blood bit the air. Then there was a flash of light. The priest threw the pot aside and reached out for the medallion.

Giles expected it to be hot but it wasn't. The symbol popped out of the mold and the priest grabbed a chain that was open, as if something used to be on it. He closed his eyes.

Black tendrils of icor shot into the priest and Giles raised his hand, stopping the image in place. He walked around it, looking at the claws on the ends of the hands grabbing the priest. They were stabbing into his body, including his face and the back of his head. His eyes were partially open and even held in place as an image, the eyes swirled like ink in water.

He stepped back from it and saw that the shadow tendrils didn't stop moving either. This was corruption, writhing and controlling the man. Giles had seen it before, a long time ago. It was responsible for the Black Forest.

Giles dispelled the image and ran out the door.

"Brigit!"

Brigit looked at Giles running towards them, then back at the men. "...Brigit."

The red-haired man frowned at Giles, then returned his attention to her. "Pleased to meet you. Now where did you come from?"

Giles was suddenly right next to all of them. They all jumped back from him in alarm. Brigit grasped her chest.

"By the Pillar, Giles, warn a person next time."

"What should I have said? 'Incoming?'" He turned to the redhead. "When did you last see the priest from the church?"

"Brother Robert?" He looked at the other two guards. "I... I think last night? No. Yesterday afternoon. Why?"

"I think he has done something horrible. He has created an amulet that teleports and, well, he made it... wrong."

"Amulet?" The guard captain arched his shoulders, danger in his eyes.

"Wrong?" Brigit's eyes widened and filled with worry.

"Yeah. I have no idea where he got this recipe but it has an infernal component that I didn't have. I don't know what it does but the fact that it's infernal can't be good."

The guard captain narrowed his eyes. "How do you know that?"

"I created the original." He pulled out his amulet.

The ginger punched him in the face and Giles went down hard.

Brigit snapped back out of the way. When Giles hit the ground, she looked at him, then at the ginger.

"What are you doing?"

The ginger nodded and the guards picked up Giles. "My king was prey to one of those things. I'll not let it destroy us."

She sighed.

Gomez eyed her. "Are you going to interfere?"

"No. I've wanted to do that myself for days."

Thirty-Five

"The plow is to the ox as the
rock is to the flood."
(The plow is trapping the ox
beneath the water, as the
flood rises over its head.)

Lightning? Here?

The First Dûcesa looked at the flash out the window. She stepped outside and looked around.

No thunder. Then what was *that?*

Another flash went off and she saw it was coming from Lucifer's mansion. She started towards it, the other people in Summerland oblivious to it. She got to the house where Catriona and Myrgen lived and saw someone running up to the mansion. She vaulted the wall and banged on the door but it wasn't open. She was shouting and the Dûcesa could almost hear her.

The Glove was panicking.

The Dûcesa ran to the mansion as well and likewise climbed over the wall. The Glove looked over at her, then got a look of horror on her face. She ran over to the Dûcesa.

"No. You can't be here. No. Leave."

The Dûcesa's eyes went wide. "What is it? *What's happened to him?*"

The Glove was pushing her away. "You need to go. You need to go."

The Dûcesa pushed past her and the Glove grabbed her wrist.

"Don't go over there!"

The Dûcesa yanked her arm from the Glove and ran towards the door. The huge flashes of light were brutal and she brought her arm up to shield her eyes.

The hallway on the other side of the glass door was a battlefield. Scoring on the white walls had turned them black. Two white creatures were fighting dark figures. The Dûcesa tried to see what was what and had a hard time determining what the combatants actually were.

Then a blast struck one of the dark creatures and it slammed into the door. It turned to look at her.

Blue eyes and black hair looked up at her, and her heart stopped.

Slade.

She put her hand to the glass panes in the door and his face changed to one of recognition. He mouthed her name.

Famira.

"Slade!"

She pounded on the door but it didn't move at all. She might as well have been punching the Land.

A blast of light hit the glass and Slade returned his attention to the fight. He jumped on the white creature he had been fighting and grabbed the remaining wing on its back. He wrapped his arm around it and dropped, breaking the bones within it. The creature cried out and Slade twisted the thing apart. Blood and feathers flew everywhere, painting the walls a different color.

The Dûcesa looked around for something to break the door and was blindsided by the Glove. She twisted, trying to throw the tiny woman off her, but the Glove was wiry and terribly strong.

"You can't do that."

The Dûcesa growled. "I have to help him!"

She got some leverage and flipped the Glove onto her back and knocked her head into the floor, then she scrambled to a large rock. She grabbed it and tried to lift it but it wouldn't move. She looked up and the

Glove was standing on the rock. The Glove kicked her, tumbling her backwards. She hit the wall beside the door.

The Glove was on her then, and pulled her arm behind her, pushing her face against the glass.

"Look at what is happening. *Look!"*

The Dûcesa looked sideways into the hallway. Slade was attacking, but now the Dûcesa realized she recognized some of the other things fighting too.

Prince Alistair. Several soldiers from the Yorkish army. An infant still dragging its umbilical cord.

And one, single Child.

Everywhere that Slade touched, blackness flashed across the white creature. Every time he did, it grew more and more worn and damaged.

The Dûcesa relaxed, sorrow and fear filling her. "The Last Child."

The Glove let go and stepped back. "Yes. Lucifer sealed off the place. If he hadn't, those things would pour into the afterlife and devour every. Soul. Here."

The Dûcesa sat up slowly, her hand on the glass. Tears fell from her eyes as she watched her beloved battle the white monsters. "What are they fighting?"

"You're kidding me, right? Those are the archangels."

The Dûcesa frowned, remembering. "There was one on our side, during the war. I never saw him but I heard about his fight." She raised her eyes again. "Where's Lucifer?"

"Trying to keep all these doors closed, I imagine. This place touches every afterlife. Every soul would be forfeit if that thing got out."

Lucifer. She put her hand on the glass and pushed her will into reinforcing it.

"Help me."

"Help you?" The Glove looked at her. "Help you what?"

"Protect the other realms."

"We don't need to help him. He's revoked our membership. He's sealed off."

"If our membership was revoked, we couldn't be in the garden."

The Glove stepped back, looking around. "You're right. What can I do?"

"Go to the other side, the Sovereignlumin side. Brace the door there."

The Glove nodded and ran off.

Hang in there, Lucifer. You can do it.

Raphael felt the wing rip from his body and he screamed in agony. He had to do something or he was going to die. He knew he could recover if he finished the fight. The mountain of souls below would restore them. But they had no weapons and there was nothing in the hallway to improvise one. He looked down upon the wing and feathers coating the floor.

Gabriel still had a wing attached, but it was hanging limp. Had they not consumed the souls they had right before coming here, the battle would have been over instantly. Gabriel hurled a body against the wall and it bounced off, hitting the floor. Then it crawled to its feet again. Gabriel stepped back, and bumped the broken wing on the wall, causing him to wince.

Then, he gritted his teeth and grabbed the broken wing. He tore it from his body, and ripped it apart. Then he held the broken shard of a bone and ran it through the head of the soldier. The soldier fell and didn't get back up.

Raphael looked down at the wing on the floor, then at the blue-eyed monster that had ripped it off. He still had the other one in his hand. Raphael grabbed for the wing on the floor, but the man whipped it away from him using the one he held. He stood before the child, protecting the it.

Of course. The Last Child. If I can destroy that, I take away the power it has to refresh these creatures. I've been shooting at drones. I need to take out the queen.

Raphael bull-rushed the blue-eyed one and propelled it back to the far end of the hall. It slid and hit the door hard, dazing it. He picked up the wing near him and broke it, creating a shard of his own. He jumped up and stabbed it into the infant that was chewing on Gabriel's other wing. The infant burst apart, and stopped moving.

One of the other monsters backed away and Raphael shot it into the open doorway. Another one, not in a soldier's uniform joined the first one.

294

They may come back out, but not this second.

Raphael set his light to the makeshift sword and it glowed. He rolled to the other soldier fighting Gabriel and stabbed it through the neck. The two angels leaned against each other, recovering for a moment. Raphael looked at the Child, who still stood by the door, not engaging. His eyes swirled like ink in water.

The two angels stumbled towards the boy, moving in for the kill. They circled him. Then, they leaped, each one grabbing an arm and pinning him to the ground. The Last Child looked up at them, eyes flicking between the two.

"Hold him."

Gabriel shifted his hold to pin the Child's shoulders down. Raphael raised his bone shard high above his head and made it glow. Suddenly, it caught fire and the Child's eyes finally showed fear. He opened his mouth and screamed. Raphael plunged the flaming shard into the chest of the Child.

The Child burst forth into thousands of hornets. They flew at the angels and stabbed them repeatedly. The angels cried out in pain as hornets crawled into the open wounds on their backs, stabbing them in the blood and muscles. They crawled in through their eyes and ears, and stung their tongues and throats. Their skin writhed and rippled with the black bugs, stingers perforating their skin from the inside. Raphael felt his integrity going. The muscles disintegrated beneath the onslaught and both he and Gabriel rolled on the floor, trying to prevent their further infestation.

Raphael stabbed himself with the flaming bone, trying to get rid of the hornets. Over and over, in the gut, until he stopped feeling the pain. He felt a coolness come over him and the stinging dulled. The heat of anguish ebbed. He looked down at his hands and they were turning black, like the rest of him. His blood went away and he turned his head to look at Gabriel. Gabriel was still rolling around, screaming and slapping at his skin.

Raphael reached out and touched him and Gabriel looked at him. As he watched, Gabriel's eyes turned to swirling with black, like ink in water. Gabriel stopped writhing and slapping and then everything turned dark.

The Glove could still hear buzzing on the other side of the door, but these doors were opaque. She didn't know what was happening in the hallway, but whatever it was, it seemed to have finally stopped. She checked that the door was still solidly closed, then scurried to the opposite side of the house.

The Dûcesa sat there, her hand against the glass, looking into Slade's eyes. He wasn't speaking, just touching the glass. The Glove looked in and saw the hallway and the dead angels by the door.

"Where's the Last Child?"

The Dûcesa didn't look away from Slade. "He broke into hornets. That's him, flying all over the place."

The angels squirmed with tiny monsters, and started disintegrating, turning into black sludge. It bled out onto the floor. After a moment, the two bodies burst, spraying the hallway with black icor. The hornets flew around, looking for an escape, even flying towards the glass doors.

A rumble started deep inside the mansion. Slade looked down as the floor began to shorten. The open door and the study got closer and closer to them. He looked at the hall and got to his feet, leaning on the glass door. The Dûcesa also rose, keeping her hand to his. The door on the end of the hallway reached the other side of the Soulless door and stopped. The hallway continued to shrink until Slade was at the door too.

I love you.

She repeated the words back to him. He turned and stepped into the door.

All the hornets went with him. Then the walls stripped off the outer layer like a snake shedding its skin. The entirety of the hall folded into the room and the door closed.

The garden door clicked open and the Dûcesa looked down at the handle. She pulled it open and the Glove walked in with her. The hallway was back to normal. Outside the Soulless door was a black card with silver writing that said *please come in.* The *come in* had been crossed out and replaced with *leave.*

Everything was clean and crisp again and Alistair came running down the stairs at the end of the hall.

"Lucifer!"

The study doors opened and the caretaker of Hell leaned heavily against the doorjamb.

"Is everyone okay?"

Alistair put a hand on Lucifer's shoulder. "I heard the door to Karma slam and couldn't get it open."

"Yes. I closed everything. I couldn't risk those things getting even a single part out."

"Are you sure they are all gone?" The Dûcesa had a silent strength in her body, even though her cheeks were streaked with pain.

Lucifer nodded. "I built this place with no loopholes. If I allow you in, you can come in. But if I revoke that, you can't stay." He looked at the Glove. "That isn't a challenge, miss. Please don't test it."

"After *that* display, I won't!" The Glove grinned. "Did us holding the doors even make a difference?"

Lucifer smiled. "Yes. I was starting to worry that I was going to lose that bet. They were so full of soul stuff, they had it to burn. They burned it. Then I felt your pressure on the respective doors, all three of you. And I remembered I wasn't alone. That helped a lot."

He reached out and squeezed the hand of the Glove and then Alistair, then put a hand on the Dûcesa's shoulder.

"Are you okay?"

She shook her head, smiling and wiping her wet cheeks. "No. But I am glad to see he has not changed completely. He knew me."

"Do we need to drink?" Lucifer looked at everyone.

Alistair nodded. The Glove almost jumped on it, but then she saw the look in the Dûcesa's eyes.

"I'm going to walk her home first."

The Dûcesa nodded. "Yes, I fear I am not in the mood for celebration."

"As you wish, my Lady." Lucifer bowed, and the Glove noticed his hand had not left his side the entire time. He looked at the Glove. "Do you want us to wait?"

The Glove shook her head. "It might be a long walk."

He nodded and Alistair took up residence at the bar as the women left the room.

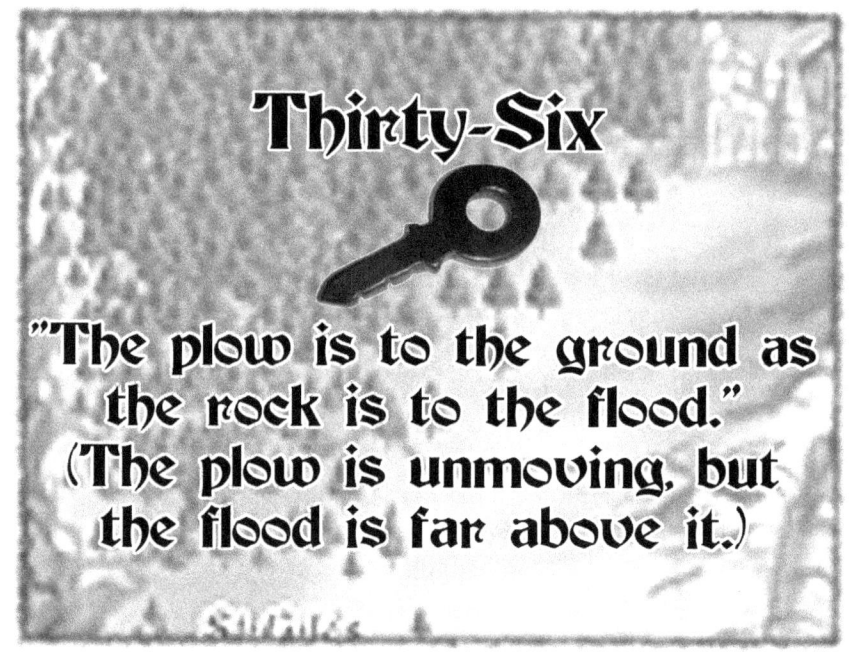

Thirty-Six

"The plow is to the ground as the rock is to the flood." (The plow is unmoving, but the flood is far above it.)

Catriona felt something tug at the edge of her consciousness. She looked at her companions but they showed nothing different.

Myrgen bowed to the Good Neighbors in the Tavern, accepting the fresh bread. "Thank you! It smells delicious."

The Good Neighbors bowed in return, then handed a warm loaf to Catriona. She bowed and accepted it.

Myrgen leaned to her as they handed Raven a loaf too. "We need some of these at Ashstone."

"You think we don't have them? Who do you think repaired your clothes?"

His brow furrowed. "Anika?"

"After she went to Summerland?"

"The dog?"

Catriona smiled and took a bite of the bread. It tasted better than it smelled and it smelled like the finest bread ever baked. She had no idea she was hungry until then. Now, she was starving.

Myrgen groaned in pleasure. "This place seems really dangerous. We should take these guys home with us. For their own safety."

She nodded. "I'll make a place for them in the kitchen."

"I'll build them a house of their own if I must. It will be my life's work."

Raven walked over with two rolls and handed one to Lauriel. "Good huh? And you were worried we were wasting time here."

Catriona swallowed. "I was wrong. Please forgive me."

Myrgen pointed at her with a piece of bread. "She was wrong. Please forgive her."

She smiled at Myrgen's comment, then looked around. "So, this realm is cut off from the world?"

Raven nodded, poking some stray bread into his mouth.

"And you could attune to it because you are a mage and it is designed for your kind?"

Raven swallowed. "I almost un-attuned to it after I left Giles, but hadn't gotten the chance."

"I'm not sure that would be wise. You may need a place to hide out or study." She licked her fingers of crumbs. "But we need to free the Giver. Is there anything in here that can do that?"

Raven shrugged. "The only one who could answer that would be Giles."

She nodded. "Then I fear I must seek audience with him. You said he was heading to the Mervol war front?"

"Yeah."

"Then that is where we shall go."

Myrgen put his hand on her arm. "That's where Alexander is."

"It was inevitable that we would meet again. He is Heaven's Champion. I am the Land's. This battle is one I knew was coming."

They all bowed thanks to the brownies and went towards the exit. As they approached, Raven opened the rift. He was about to step out when Lauriel grabbed his pants and pulled him back. He stumbled and fell.

"Lauriel, what are you doing?"

The Fae wolf looked at the opening. Catriona and Myrgen looked out on either side.

There was a huge, ancient forest around the opening. It went on and on, shrouding the area in dappled sunlight.

"What in Sovereignlumin is that?" Raven sat forward, staring.

Lauriel growled.

"How did we get in the Black Forest?"

Lauriel shook his head.

Myrgen looked at Raven. "Could this be some contingency Giles threw out to protect this place?"

"You mean have it open into the Black Forest when that's not where we entered?" Raven shrugged. "That's not how I was taught that spell works."

Catriona craned her neck to see outside. "I'll be right back. You wait here."

Myrgen turned concerned eyes on her and grabbed her hand. "Wait. What if it traps you out there?"

"I'm not Fae, Myrgen. I don't think it will trap me. Besides, we need to find out what happened here. Raven," she looked at him, "can you conjure that image thing you mentioned before, at Persephone, to show what happened here?"

"No. It will just show what we did inside this realm. Cut off, remember?"

"Alright. Wait for me."

She stepped out and Myrgen reluctantly let her leave. She looked around, nodding. She pointed to the ground with both hands.

"This. This is what I felt." She looked at the others. "I felt a tug in there. This must have been what it was."

Myrgen frowned. "What? It didn't just grow in the two minutes we were in there."

She knelt and touched the soil. "Yes. It did. Look around. There's the grassy path we left as we rode here. And there are no leaves on the ground, no mulch. The place smells the same as when we left. No, this literally grew in the two minutes we were in that place."

"Is it really the Black Forest then?" Myrgen looked at Lauriel.

Lauriel nodded.

"Does that mean you can't leave this area now?"

Raven looked at the covenant behind him. "I don't think so. I mean, if I step out *there*, I can never leave and being immortal, that would be a problem. But this is a dimension. It is separate from out there. If I had one of those amulets, I could leave. I just wouldn't live through it."

He frowned. "Except…"

Catriona and Myrgen watched him for a moment.

"Giles said he had an amulet that could teleport him. He designed the one Alexander had. But he said it never caused anyone any harm. Hmmm…" Raven looked at Lauriel. "He *did* ascend straight up. It may be there."

"What may?" Myrgen looked at Lauriel, then at Raven again.

"Writing!" He ran off towards the giant shell at the center of the realm. Lauriel ran with him.

Myrgen watched them run off, then turned to Catriona. "I'm coming with you."

"How can you be sure you won't be trapped here?"

"I'll risk it. A lot less chance of me choking him if I go with you." Myrgen turned to shout at Raven. *"I'm going with Catriona."*

Raven waved acknowledgement without slowing.

Myrgen stepped out of the realm and it closed behind him. He looked around. "What are you thinking?"

"This forest just grew here, in two minutes, trees hundreds of years old. What are the ways that could happen, and it still have the aura that traps Fae?"

"Well, we know mages can cause plant growth." He gestured to the path of grass that led to that spot. "And Raven said Giles made the Black Forest. Sounds like Giles decided to trap Raven, to keep him out of play."

"Then why would *I* feel it and not him?"

"You're the Land. You knew something was happening. Something that would alter the face of the world. Something that affected a significant segment of your constituency." He frowned. "What do you think?"

"I think someone *created* something with a divine aspect in moments. Someone who could affect dead soil as old as these trees. Someone who did what it took me being drained to accomplish, and I didn't grow things from a forest a day and a half from this spot."

"Why not?"

She furrowed her brow. "There are two possibilities. One is that I am the Land, like Raven and those in that chamber think, but that I am too weak now to grow much.

"The other is that… the Bringer of Death wasn't part of the *growth* cycle. She was… *I* was part of cycling down the season, harvesting both plant and animal as well as humans. It's not my *purview* to be in charge of making things grow."

Myrgen exhaled, running his hands through his hair as he percolated that thought. "You think she's here."

Catriona nodded. "I think the Giver made a forest grow while we weren't looking."

"You think she just sneezed out a forest?"

"I'm not going to envision that because that would mean I was standing beneath her mucus, but perhaps. I don't know her process. I honestly don't even know mine. I just have memories of harvests and reaping the lives of those leaving the world."

"So, where do you think she is then?"

Catriona looked around. "Guess I'll climb this tree and see."

"And if you fall and break your neck?"

She smiled. "Then I'll see you in Caratia."

Raven ran up the hall to the room at the top. It was locked, of course. Raven studied the runic pattern. It was complex and ancient. In fact, it was *overly* complicated. It was like looking at a wish written to thwart a leprechaun. The truth was that you didn't need to be really, really specific. The trick was making the leprechaun no longer able to grant wishes. By doing that, you changed his nature and killed him.

He studied the lock and the instructions and then, warped the lock not to fit any of that criteria. It became a padlock on the outside of the door. He tickled the lock under the chin and it opened to laugh. He removed it and went in the door.

Inside he found an actual domicile, something he wasn't expecting. He thought this would be the lab, but it wasn't. A quick inspection of the rooms showed no lab at all.

"Lauriel, where did he go?"

Lauriel sniffed and ran to a wall. Raven looked around and realized this was the actual entry to his sanctum. Now he was in a tougher place. Only the magic of the mage whose sanctum it was could open this door. Raven knew this. He stared at it and shrugged.

He needed to conjure the image of the last time Giles was here. This was during the time frame Raven had been in the area, and he had a chance to have it work, but he needed the magic to believe the person doing it was its master.

Raven looked around and found a ring that radiated magic used by Giles. There was so much stuff in here that had that particular caster aura, he was practically the only thing that *didn't*. Still, this would work. He put on the ring, conjured the image and watched.

Image Giles stepped up and waved a hand over the wall, then it opened and he went in. Raven replayed the image and did the exact same thing with the ringed hand in the exact same place. The door opened and Raven smiled at the ring. He went down the stairs and discovered that, apparently, the entire dome part of this shell was Giles' lab.

He looked around. Giles had been right. Several experiments had been ruined because they were left to simmer and burned away. Others had evaporated to powder or simply to nothing. Books were everywhere and Raven ran to them. His face brightened as ink was still on the paper.

"I was right. He didn't die so they never erased!" He turned to Lauriel. "That's fantastic!"

Lauriel wagged his tail.

"Okay, what we need now is smelting materials."

Lauriel cocked his head.

"Um, a mold with a carving. A pot or cauldron with a bit of melted metal in the bottom. Stuff like that."

Lauriel nodded and sniffed.

"I don't expect it to necessarily be right out in the open. I have no idea how long it was since he made it."

He looked at the walls of books. There were twenty or so but when he opened them, many were blank.

"These were obviously written by other wizards." He turned them to look at the spines. "Probably from the Estate."

Lauriel growled and Raven looked at him.

"Really?" He walked over to a couple books open side by side. He scanned the books, then nodded.

"You're right. These *are* different hands. So, either the mage who wrote them is still alive, or a mage didn't write them. You think maybe Giles had a scribe?"

Lauriel arched an eyebrow.

"Well, I don't know. We were taught to use *Amanuensis* as our first spell. It enabled us to copy something written exactly. Of course, now we know why. New mages could scribe books and the books would last *their* lifetime instead of the mage's who had written them before. But a lot of knowledge was lost over the centuries, especially now that there are only two in the world. Merrick's library will be a huge loss since I never write anything down."

Raven looked at the two writings. He sighed, flipping one of them with a finger. "This one is so old. We have refined this formula. That's not even how you make that any more. It's like the arcane lock spell above."

He looked at the one next to it. "And this one…"

He frowned, studying. "This one… *By the Fae!*" He looked at Lauriel. *"This is it! This is going to change everything!"*

He grabbed a piece of paper and wrote something on it. "Take this to Myrgen and Catriona. But don't leave the area."

Lauriel took the note and ran outside.

"What do you see?" Myrgen's neck was craned almost to breaking.

"There's a hollow, to the north. And a new river. Wait… *three.* Three new rivers. Oh! That's a *lake*."

"Any sign of *her*?"

Catriona looked down at him. "Other than the presence of a new forest, three rivers, and a lake? What exactly are you wanting me to look for?"

Myrgen nodded. "Fair point."

A rustle behind him caught his attention. He looked and saw Lauriel at the opening of the dimension. He was barking and jumping around, but Myrgen hadn't heard anything. Lauriel was holding a paper. Myrgen walked over and reached out, but hit a barrier when it got to the rift. He winced and shook his hand in pain.

"By the Stones!" He looked at the rift. It was still open but he could not enter it. "Apparently the mage has to be present to let us in. Can you hear me, Lauriel?"

The Fae wolf nodded.

"What do you have there?"

Lauriel tried to flip the note but it bounced back. He growled at it and then pick it up carefully, displaying the written part to Myrgen. He read it, then sighed.

"Fantastic. Catriona, I have good news and bad news."

Catriona landed next to him. "What?"

"Well, Raven has found a version of the memory spell that doesn't require the person to have been in the area. We can find out what happened at that trap in Persephone.

"The bad news is that we can't get Raven out of there and we can't go in."

She rolled her eyes. "Fantastic. There's more bad news. Persephone is now within the Black Forest."

Thirty-Seven

"The ox is to the farmer as
the meal is to the lion."
(The farmer cannot get to his
ox to save it.)

Gomez looked at Brigit. "Are you going to come quietly?"

"Can I just savor this for a moment?" She smiled at Giles' sprawled form.

"Aren't you worried about him being hurt?"

"If he doesn't wake up in a few minutes, then I'll worry."

"I'm afraid him waking up out here would defeat the purpose."

Gomez took the amulet and the bow from him and nodded to the guards, who picked him up. Brigit followed them to the jail. Giles was manacled to the bars of a cell that had the wall demolished. Gomez turned to one of the guards. "Watch him. Let me know when he wakes up."

Giles groaned and stirred. The guard pointed. "He's waking up."

"Thanks."

Brigit looked at Gomez. "Sir, I need to get to Alexander."

"He's captive in the Fae encampment. We don't know where. We can't get to him without the Mervol Army. And it's Gomez."

Brigit bowed. "Thank you, Gomez. When will they be here?"

Gomez nodded to the men down the road. "They're down there. We're waiting for them to get here We sent someone to tell them about Alexander. Then they started heading east on that road. My messenger hasn't returned yet."

"I can help with that." Giles sat up, rubbing his face.

Gomez turned to him. "How?"

"I can go get him with my amulet." Giles held up his hand. "Wait! Before you attack me, I need to tell you something." He pointed to Brigit. "She's Saint Brigit."

Gomez looked at her. "What?"

She took a deep breath. "We were kicked out of Heaven. That's what I need to tell Alexander. I'm not the one answering his prayers now."

Gomez swallowed. "I have no idea how to get you to prove it."

Giles stepped through the bars, the manacles clanging to the ground. The two guards gasped. "Look, we need to get to Alexander. We need to get him this information. Heaven is in turmoil and their intent is to start a war that kills humans."

Gomez rolled his eyes, then closed them. "If their intent is to kill humans and turn them against the Fae, this is the war that will do it." He looked at Giles again. "You said 'we'. So, you're a Saint too?"

"Apparently, this town is my namesake."

Gomez folded his arms across his chest. "You're going to need to tell me a lot more about this amulet before I trust it. Alexander barely survived the one he had."

"I suspect it was made with the same recipe your Brother Robert used then. You said my eyes were clear before."

"Yes. Alexander said his eyes swirled with a blackness that looked like ink in water when he or anyone used the amulet. Tanglwyst confirmed that."

"The recipe I saw had a corruptive element. That would probably explain that. There might be a reservoir the amulet draws from that feeds the corruption. When I made ours, I created a link to our safe places. With the recipe corrupted, it might connect to a place that feeds it."

"Tanglwyst said there was a room connected to the amulets that it would take the holder to in times of danger. She said they were beneath the Papal City."

Brigit frowned. "How old are these amulets?"

307

"We're not sure. But the symbols on them are the same as the rose windows in the church. Or on these discs." Gomez produced a blessed disc from his vest.

Giles looked it over. "And you said this amulet had the same symbol?"

"I never saw it but both the Lady and the King confirmed this."

"Why would it bring them to this town?"

Gomez was confused. "What do you mean?"

Giles gestured generally towards the church. "That window is very specific and the reservoir is in the Papal City. I wonder why they connected it to this town here."

"Oh, those windows are in every Augustinian church in the world."

Giles flicked a glance at Brigit. "Every church? For how long?"

"Centuries. We spent a long night talking about all of this. According to Tanglwyst, she found a book that indicated they were made after the Soulless War, but there was no information on how to make them or where the recipe, as you called it, came from."

"I have a suspicion. Come, I can show you."

They all walked to the jeweler's and Giles replayed the entire thing with his memory illusion spell. Gomez was unsettled by the display but got past that very quickly as the mystery unfolded. The other guards looked ready to run.

Giles gestured to the work area after it finished. "What did you see, Captain?"

Gomez frowned. "There was no book. The recipe wasn't written down."

"Exactly. We can go to the church and see what happened, if you like."

"This is just magic, like the Queen did." The guard on Gomez' left pulled out his sword.

Giles furrowed his brow, looking at the man. "It's divine magic. What do you think you're going to do with that?"

"All magic is evil." The man lunged at Giles, but his blade was turned aside.

Gomez and the other guard grabbed the man. *"Elander, stop.* He might be able to help us get to the King. And possibly rescue him."

"At what cost? How many more will die under *his* magic?"

Giles looked around. "What has happened in this town to set this man so furiously against magic?"

Gomez looked Elander in the eye, drawing his attention. "We need to investigate this. Did you see what happened there?"

Elander swallowed, distrust and murder in his eyes as he looked at Giles. "Magic killed my nephew."

Gomez put his hand on the man's shoulder. "I know. I'm so sorry. Asher was a good man. But do you see what this thing can do? It can show us what happened."

"Unless it's a lie."

Giles shook his head. "Let him go."

Gomez and the other guard let Elander go.

"Now. You want to stab me? To kill me to get revenge against me for the death of your nephew?"

Elander set his jaw.

"Do you? Because you are blaming me for magic done by a Land entity that resulted in a death. To your narrow, stupid mind, *all* magic is evil! So do it, you petulant infant. Go ahead and try to kill me."

Elander lunged at Giles and Giles closed his eyes and let him run him through.

Elander shoved the sword through him and then pushed it harder. Giles cried out in pain and fell backwards a step. Elander gripped his shoulder, hatred in his eyes. Then, he seemed to realize what he had done. His expression changed to one of immediate remorse and regret.

"I-I'm sorry..."

Brigit ran to Giles. "*What in Heaven were you thinking?*"

Giles looked at her and then at Gomez. "Am...u...let."

Giles took the amulet from his pouch and when Giles touched it, the whole group teleported to a cave. They landed in a pool of glowing white water.

Elander let go of Giles and staggered back. Giles looked down at the sword and Brigit nodded and pulled it out. She dropped it in the pool and turned back to him.

"You're an idiot."

Gomez looked around. "Where are we?"

"It's a healing pool. It's in a secret place. This is one of those safe places Giles mentioned before."

The guardsman pointed at a creature in the pool. "By the Saints, what is that?"

Giles leveled a gaze at the man. "What does it look like?" His voice had steadied in the pool and Gomez saw his wound was closing.

"An…angel…" The guard looked at the pool. "Is this its blood?"

Brigit rolled her eyes. "No. It comes… from me. He was wounded in an attack from Heaven. Like you were told, I'm Saint Brigit."

Gomez nodded. "What can you show us?"

Giles stood and Elander looked at the wet robe covering the mage's wound. "Is it…?"

Giles spread apart the rip in the robe. The flesh had no damage. *"Now* will you listen to me? Because if we are to save your king, we need to stop doing this testing crap."

The men nodded and Giles returned with them all to the back room of the jeweler's. He took another moment to clean the blood from the room, then cleaned and mended his clothes with a wave of his hands. He walked out with the others following him and strode to the church.

One of the guards leaned in to talk to Gomez. "What is he doing?"

Gomez shrugged.

They all entered the church. Giles looked at them when they all got in. "We need to figure out how he got that recipe. If we can sort that out, we'll know who started the war."

Elander shook his head, finally coming out of his shell after stabbing Giles. "We know who started the war. The Queen of Krakte."

Gomez looked uncomfortable but said nothing.

"You think the Queen of Krakte gave a priest a recipe for an amulet that was of divine construct but corrupted?"

Elander glanced for support at the other guard but was denied. Giles looked back and forth between the two and then proceeded. He went to the altar and walked around it. He closed his eyes and cast the spell that showed the room's memories.

The first images were of Giles and Brigit looking around and then Giles leaving a few minutes after Brigit. Giles stopped the image and pushed it back farther in time. They saw Brother Robert running out of the church and Giles pushed it back farther. There were prayers and discussions with townsfolk before he went to bed.

"It was after this that he went and made the amulet. I believe it came to him in a dream."

The other guard glanced at his friend. "So it could have been the Queen?"

Giles shook his head. "No. Dreams are the realm of the Divine. The Fae can't give anyone dreams. They give illusions, but not dreams."

"Could it have been the *illusion* of a dream?"

Giles looked at the guard. "You have a Fae army right outside this town. How many Fae have come near this place?"

All three guards nodded.

Giles returned to the memory. He watched with careful eye, then turned back the time again.

"How far can you go back?"

"About a week. If I don't find anything before-"

The discussion ended as a bright, all-encompassing light filled the room from a memory. Giles rolled the memory back a bit more and Gomez saw Robert watch Alexander and Tanglwyst returning from the dinner with Sovereigna, after Catherine arrived. Brother Robert went before the altar and knelt in prayer.

"St. Michael, St Giles, I have a weapon to use against Heaven's enemies. A coat that will slay any Fae that touches it. Help me decide what to do. Help me please."

"I remember this." Brigit nodded to the man praying. "That was right before the three of us were expelled. He included an angel in the prayer so Gabriel heard it too and came to check on it. It ended with us being cast out for not fueling the war."

Giles turned to Gomez. "A coat?"

"That's a really long story but the short answer is that corruption you mentioned takes on a physical form that can destroy Fae on contact. Anyone with a Fae grandparent will die if they are teleported. Alexander had a coat that had some on it."

"Where is it now?"

"I don't know. He left with it but didn't have it when he came back."

"Wait." Elander held up his hand. "The king had a Fae-killing coat and he didn't tell us? Are you saying we could have destroyed this whole army all this time? We didn't have to send our families away?"

"I'm saying that the king had a coat that would slay any Fae that touched it and that Fae arrows are capable of being shot from the Benevolent Friar and hit a messenger bird here."

The bright flash of light stopped all conversation.

"Where is the weapon?"

The priest stuttered. "Th... the k...King went to the Fae encampment. He was wearing it. It was a coat that had something on it that destroyed Fae on contact. He wasn't wearing it when he returned just now."

"I see."

The light persisted for a few minutes, then it went out. The priest looked around, unsure of what he had encountered. Suddenly, there was a ruckus and screaming from the Fae encampment. Robert went to the window and Giles and the rest followed. There was nothing out there.

"What's he looking at?" Elander and the other guard were at a different window.

Giles looked at the priest. "I'm not sure. The spell doesn't extend to where the incident originated, but I suspect it's a fire."

"Why?"

"Look at him."

Everyone turned to look at the image of the priest and saw the fire reflected in his eyes. Light flickered across his face, the movement being the only change from the stained glass coloration already present.

Gomez nodded. "The main pavilion caught fire. We saw it."

"Caught? Or was *set* on fire?"

Gomez looked at the other guards. "We don't know. But when Alexander went back the next morning to get the coat, that's when they captured him."

Brigit's brow furrowed in worry. "How long has he been there?"

"Tomorrow morning will be a full day."

Giles folded his arms. Brother Robert went to the front of the church, wringing his hands as he stepped outside. "Have they made any demands?"

Gomez shook his head. "We had the Queen of Krakte prisoner but, well, you saw the state of the jail."

Giles frowned.

Brigit looked at him. "The cell had the back wall destroyed."

"That isn't a very secure location then, is it? And you expected to hold me there?"

Gomez shrugged. "Habit."

"Where is the Queen now?"

Gomez looked at Brigit. "No idea. I'm certain she's not back in the Fae encampment or Alexander would be back here. The Fae General is an extremely honorable man. If they took Alex to get the queen back, he wouldn't keep him hostage once she returned. Also, they had made peace the night before. She released the Lady Tanglwyst back to us and the peace was to be announced this morning. Then all this happened." He gestured to the illusion.

"If they made peace, why was she in the jail?"

"Because my men didn't know that. And because she is responsible for the deaths of several people in the village." He flicked his eyes at Elander and Brigit and Giles nodded in understanding.

"Could she be staying away in order to get Alexander killed?" Brigit's worry was not assuaged by the conversation.

"Meaning they don't know she's out?" Gomez stroked his chin, thinking. He nodded. "That might be the only way this makes sense."

He looked at his men and straightened. "Elander, Karl, find out how much holy water is available. Robert was blessing it in the barrels because he can't just bless the sea. That means our source may bleed out. I'll see what's going on with the army."

The guards nodded and bowed, then left. Gomez waited until they were gone, then motioned for the saints to step away from the windows.

"That amulet you have is different how?"

"Oh, well, for one thing, it doesn't have an infernal component. My amulet draws from the covenants it is attuned to. Those were established centuries ago. Their magic is pure and diverse to keep the balance. Robert's amulet *created* an attunement point and the infernal provided that attunement point. It was the only way to make an arcane connection strong enough to power the amulet that fast. I was able to do it and can make one about as fast as he did but the big difference is the source of the magic."

"You can make more of these?"

"Yes."

"How can we tell they will be safe?"

"You aren't sick and I used it on you."

"I'm not a Fae. I doubt we could tell if it was corrupt."

Giles motioned to his eyes. "No 'ink in water'."

Gomez nodded. "Then let's see what we can do about rescuing my King."

Thirty-Eight

"The plow is to the ground as the river is to the flood."
(The plow breaks free.)

Giles and Gomez teleported next to General Aethelraed, causing the older man to start. Two guards drew their weapons and stepped in front of the General. Gomez bowed.

"Hello General."

Aethelraed stepped forward between the guards. "Gomez! After not hearing from you and the King, we feared the worst."

"Turns out you were mostly right. The King is being held captive in the Fae encampment. We do not know where."

The guard on Aethelraed's right stepped forward. "Where did you come from?"

Aethelraed arched an eyebrow at the man, who was immediately chastised for speaking out of turn, then looked back at Gomez. "In truth, that is a fine question."

"St. Giles."

Giles perked up. "Yes?"

Aethelraed flicked a glance at the man, then sent a bewildered one to Gomez.

Gomez cleared his throat. "We should probably speak in private."

"Daine, you have the com." The General motioned to a shady spot away from the bustle of water activities.

Gomez made sure they were out of earshot, then turned to Giles. "This is Saint Giles. He is here to help."

"Alright. What can you do?"

Gomez and Giles looked at each other.

"Gentlemen, this isn't the first time I've dealt with magic. Now quit wasting time."

Giles pointed to the town. "I can go fast to places."

Gomez blinked at the odd phrasing.

Aethelraed nodded. "What are the parameters of your movement?"

"Line of sight, familiarity with the area, and a few touchstones."

"Frequency?"

"All I wish."

"Item or inherent?"

"Item."

"Can anyone use it?"

Giles smiled. "I would prefer they didn't."

"Capacity?"

"Not sure but there is probably an upper limit."

"More than three men?"

"Yes, sir."

The General nodded to the line the men were making. "Can you get those barrels of holy water around the valley by nightfall?"

"Around all over or someplace specific?"

"Perimeter. And the men with them."

Giles nodded. "Yeah, I can do that."

"Would you be so kind?"

"Show me where you want them."

Aethelraed waved to a man carrying a satchel of papers. "Collings. Bring me that map of the area."

The man rifled through his satchel and handed over a folded piece of paper. The General unfolded it and laid it on the ground. He pointed to a road.

"This is where we are, at the fork in the King's Highway. This is St. Giles, and this is the Papal City. This is the Krakten border." He touched several points on the road that went to the Papal city from where they were. "I would like these distributed along this road."

Giles nodded. He gestured to the map. "May I?"

The General nodded and Giles picked it up. He disappeared for about thirty seconds, then returned. "Okay, I see what you mean. I can do that."

"What did you do just now?" Gomez looked at Giles.

"I went up to see if this was anything like the real thing. It is pretty good, except there's now a forest on the Krakten border. It looks as if the Black Forest just extended itself across the top of the valley."

The General flicked his eyes up. "Show me."

Giles linked arms with him and disappeared. Gomez looked up and saw a couple of dots in the sky. He glanced at the Fae army creatures he could see but they were just the troll ones. He wondered if the rabbits or eagles saw them.

A few seconds later, the General and Giles were back. The General looked a little shaken but nodded. "Yes, the Black Forest has grown. We went up high enough to see it, then moved again to see more. It has taken over York."

Gomez' eyes went wide. "The Wasteland of York is now a forest? How?"

Giles shrugged. "I might be able to find out, but I want to handle things here first. General, what do you want me to do?"

Aethelraed took a deep breath and motioned for Daine. The soldier came over. He was tall and had a beard that looked like it existed just to prove that, given enough time, he *could* grow one and have it cover his face.

"Sir?"

"This man is going to help you get the men and barrels distributed. Go with him and make sure the men understand to listen to him and do exactly what he says while he transports them. Maintain the distribution orders."

"Yes, sir." Daine looked at Giles and gestured to the barrels. Giles followed him.

"Gomez, I need a word with you." Aethelraed turned his back to the army as Giles took his first load of water and men away. "What do you know of this Giles?"

"As much as you do from church, Sir. I have no idea if he is the Saint but he is doing magic and it can operate inside a church, something the Fae can't do."

"Magic, inside a church. What is this world coming to? But enough of that. I saw more than the forest. While he had me in the air, I saw the Fae army has entered from the south. A scout told me that they were advancing and the trees were parting for them. There were no passages through the woods to the south. I believe that means the Fae army reinforcements have arrived."

"That may be a problem, Sir. With Alexander still their prisoner…"

"That's why the presence of the Black Forest interests me so. Gomez, if we can drive the army into that forest, we can stop this and any future attacks. Krakte will be free of the Fae."

"If the forest has expanded as you say, they are already contained. The Krakten capital is halfway between Glarren and Mervolingia. Every half Fae is already trapped. Only the humans can leave now." Gomez nodded to the army in the valley. "This constitutes the last of the Krakten army that is free and they are now stranded here. Could you tell if they have noticed this or not?"

"No. There are tents almost solid from the border to the edge of the city. With the Fae Lord present now, all eyes will be on him."

"What's your plan?"

"We soak our men in the holy water and move the barrels forward, tightening the noose. They will be hemmed in before they realize it."

"And Alexander?"

"That's where your new friend comes in. He does reconnaissance and figures out where the King is. Then he snatches them when the Army realizes they are trapped. Right now, he'll be a prized prisoner and the Fae Lord will no doubt want to toy with him. This aids our plan."

Gomez nodded. "I'm sure Johner will not allow him to come to harm. He is a royal hostage."

"Johner?"

Gomez explained who Johner was and how he knew the man. "I can vouch for his honorable nature. He's already saved the Lady and the

King, and he serves Corrigan. I believe the two are cut from the same cloth."

"Once your man is back, get him on this task. We need our King safe."

Elander went into the City Guard office but didn't see Gomez. He did see the exquisite bow Giles had been carrying and grabbed it. He found it odd there was no quiver with it. He pointed it and drew it to test the pull. A blue-silver arrow formed on the bowstring as he did so and he dropped the string back into rest.

He blinked, then drew the bow again. The arrow formed again. He returned it to rest and it went away. He smiled, nodding. The bow was practically nondescript and could easily be part of the arsenal and not be detected. He grabbed a quiver and put it on his back just for show, then tried to unstring it to further disguise it. The string would not do so.

A permanent bowstring that shoots magic arrows.

He glanced around to make sure he wasn't observed and left the building. He went to the Wise Wench and climbed up on the roof, nodding to the guard up there.

"Agythe. How are you?"

"Tired as hell, Elander. Been up here all night."

"You look it. Get out and get some sleep. I've got this watch."

Agythe clapped Elander on the shoulder. "Thank you, man. Thank you."

After Agythe was gone, Elander looked over the scene. He was barely as high as the husk of the royal pavilion, and the rest of the tents were still impressive. Many were the size of small houses. They were so close together, their ropes were a web of support that allowed for specific walkways but no crossing between tents. This made chaotic passages that would be impossible to navigate in the dark.

Elander craned his neck, trying to see any sign of Alexander. He doubted he could do anything to from here to help the king, but at least he could bear witness.

He settled back and waited.

Brother Robert leaned against the porch post of the Benevolent Friar, exhausted. He had vomited an hour before, all his food from the previous night now that black sludge that covered the northern border. His eyes were so dark and thick with the poison, he could no longer see. He panted, trying to figure out where he was.

Maybe I'll just rest here for a few minutes.

The smell of food permeated his brain fog, and it caused him to retch again. He kept thinking he would have nothing in him, but each time, a belly of sludge came out. He knelt and sat back on his heels.

"Saint Giles, Saint Michael, hear my plea. What am I to do now?"

Robert felt a sword sprout from his chest, then felt nothing.

Saint George stepped out of the shadow of the Benevolent Friar and went to wipe his sword on the clothes of the creature he had just slain. Unfortunately, the man and the sword were covered in some sort of crude, thick oil sludge, like lampblack and water. He rolled the creature on its back and saw the eyes swirling with corruption.

Giles and Michael indeed. This is Raphael and Gabriel's work.

He wiped the sludge on his cloak instead. The oozing fluid pooled on the grass and refused to be absorbed by the ground. He looked and could see a trail leading from the hill off to the north. The sludge seemed to slide and pool at the bottom of any rise or into any depression.

A man in messenger attire walked onto the porch and saw George. He bowed in greeting, then saw the man at George's feet. His eyes grew panic and he ran inside, calling for the guards. The men from before ran outside, swords drawn. The one in charge walked down the stairs and over to George, sword pointed at him.

"What is the meaning of this? Did you attack this man?"

"That's no man. Look."

The guard hazarded a glance, then grew more curious. "What is that?"

"I know not, but he has left a trail of the stuff." George nodded to the north as he sheathed his sword.

The man knelt down, then covered his nose and mouth with his sleeve. "He smells like rotten eggs."

"Yes. That is the scent of the infernal. This is likely a demon."

The man stepped away. "How did it get here?"

"It walked. Was that the messenger I have been awaiting?"

The man looked at George, then back on the body. "Uh, yeah. Charles. *Charles. Come out here.*"

The messenger came back outside and glanced around the guards. "Yes Ulrich?"

"This man has been waiting for you. Do you have word from the Crown?"

"Sort of. I have word from a scout. The Mervol army should be in St. Giles by now."

A splash and a chorus of grunts accompanied the sudden arrival of three soldiers, a barrel of water, and Giles.

"George?"

"Giles!" George walked around the body and greeted his friend. "Watch your step."

Giles looked down as the soldiers maneuvered the barrel into place.

"Ugh. Wait…" He squatted near the body. "Oh no. This is Brother Robert, from St. Giles."

"Who is that? And how did he get here?"

Giles grabbed a stick and moved aside the man's tunic. He hooked the tip on a cord and tugged an amulet from inside.

"This. It's an amulet that allows you to teleport, like mine. Can be used by anyone so long as they have a clear line of sight or have been there before. It has the side benefit of being deadly to Fae of any breed or percentage." Giles stood, his arms dropping in frustration. "Such a waste."

"Yours does this to people?"

"No. This was built wrong. The side effect of which is that black stuff there. A fellow told us of a coat that could kill Fae. It was touched by that stuff. This is Brother Robert, man of the Church in the town on the other side of the valley."

George looked at his cloak and removed it, covering the body. "We'll have to figure out what to do about this later. You have soldiers with you."

"Yes."

"Come." George walked over to the hill, out of earshot of the people on the porch, who were now talking with the soldiers fidgeting with a barrel.

"Tell me everything since you left Heaven."

Charles gathered the guardsmen and went to help the soldiers. He nodded to one, motioning to the stables. Once they were away from the soldier with the barrel, he spoke.

"Adam, what are you doing here?"

"I was conscripted. They wanted a person who could scout. Aethelraed actually summoned me from Cliffside a few days ago, after your first missives. I was to meet them at the crossroad inn and report back." Adam leaned in to Charles. "I saw the Queen Mother today. She's on her way home."

Charles sighed. "Good. Did anyone else see her?"

"Aethelraed sent Syr with her to make sure she got home okay."

"Good choice. So, what's all this?"

Adam explained, keeping a wary eye on the man who was talking to George now. "So, who's that guy?"

"Some Toledan. Showed up early this morning."

"Before or after the forest?"

Charles frowned and looked where indicated. His eyes widened in surprise. "When the hell did *that* happen?"

"Dunno. We noticed only a half hour ago, but it wasn't here when I went through from Cliffside."

"Do you know the guy who was killed?"

Adam shook his head. "But did you hear what he said? That the amulet lets you move like he did, *and* it's deadly to Fae."

"Yeah. Think of how useful that would be getting messages to the Queen Mother and back. It could really impair the nobles who are spoiling for a coup."

"Yeah, but isn't it dangerous?"

Giles was squatting by the bottom of the small hill, taking a sample of something on the ground.

"Maybe. We can ask about it."

"And if they say no?"

Charles shrugged. "Then we find someone willing to take a suicide mission to take as many Fae out as possible."

Adam nodded. "Maybe they can figure out a way to purify it."

"Yeah."

Adam looked at Charles. There was something unspoken for a moment. Charles stepped farther back, out of sight of the strange foreigners. Adam joined him.

"Look, if it looks like they plan to destroy it, we need to take it and get it to the General. This is a decision that will affect the whole kingdom. We can't let outsiders make that choice for our people."

Adam nodded. He hazarded a glance at the two outsiders. "Hey. They're leaving." Adam stepped out from behind the Inn. "We can grab it now."

"What if it's dangerous?"

"I've got an idea."

Adam pulled out a leather pouch. He walked over to the barrel. He dumped the contents of the pouch into a different pouch and then gathered water in the leather one.

"This is holy water. My pouch is waterproof. Seams sealed with wax and everything."

They went over to the body and Adam used the edge of George's cloak to grab the amulet and tug it over the body's head. Charles held the pouch open and Adam deposited the amulet inside. Then they re-draped the body. The guards and other soldier watched but didn't interfere. The two looked at the group and they all nodded approval.

"Saints and angels protect us."

Adam nodded and they joined the others.

Thirty-Nine

"The plow is to the ox as the
lion is to the farmer."
(The plow is now the threat
to the ox.)

The First Dûcesa lay in her bed. She was done crying now. That had taken a long time to accomplish. The Glove had left her after putting her to bed, but sleep had not taken her.

This was her own doing.

Had she slept, she might have dreamed.

Dreaming could lead to seeing Slade again, whole, to believing she could touch him, or feel his arms around her.

Dreaming could lead to moving on.

She got up and went to the front of her house. She could see the mansion. The lights in the garden were still there, as they were every night now that she could see them.

She walked through the village, silent as Death herself. She went up the hill to the garden wall and climbed over it. She tried the door and it was open. She could not see Slade's hand print on the glass, but the entire room had been pulled away. All trace of the battle was gone.

Sound echoed down the hallway from the study. She could hear Lucifer's voice, as well as the Glove and Alistair. They sounded serious, but also like they were recovering and trying to joke.

They're good friends to him. Unlike me.

The door was open only a crack, as if to give her privacy should she return. She walked down the hall and stood before Slade's door. She put her hand on it, closing her eyes to listen. She heard nothing but the sound of glasses clinking and light conversation.

She looked at the study door.

He said I was welcome there. Any time.

She turned towards it, reaching out for the door to push it open.

Then her mind flashed upon Slade's last moments in the battle. She closed her eyes and opened the door to the Soulless room.

Lucifer stood, feigning interest in the exploit the Glove was telling Alistair, and leaned on his desk. He let the story finish, then covered a yawn. This had the desired effect and both the Glove and Alistair yawned as well.

The Glove stretched. "It's late, isn't it? It feels late."

Lucifer nodded. "It might even be morning in some parts of the world or midday."

Alistair stood and the Glove followed.

"I'm going to check on the Dûcesa. I couldn't get a read on her when I left. I heard her crying after I put her to bed."

Lucifer nodded, then frowned. "Actually, you should just let her rest. Yesterday was pretty hard on her."

Alistair nodded. "Yeah. It was rough on a couple people, I believe."

The Glove sighed. "I'll head out then. I'll let you know how she is tomorrow. Maybe I'll even bring her by."

"I'd love to see her tomorrow if you can manage that."

The Glove smiled and left. Alistair looked for a long moment at Lucifer.

"You okay?"

Lucifer's lips flattened. "A large part of my life is gone now. Something that was once beautiful and kind and loving, but has now been consumed by monsters. I'm gonna need a minute."

"I'm sorry about your family."

Lucifer waved a hand. "That is a conversation for another day. We have to figure out what to do about Uriel."

"Uriel?"

"Yeah. Raph threw him down into the Karma trap. I thought I mentioned it. Anyway, I need to get him out of there before he's destroyed but I have no idea how."

Alistair rubbed his eyes. "You know, I don't *actually* sleep. I can do some research into this. Focus a bit more."

"Would you mind? I need to get something figured out. And I need to find the Giver."

Alistair nodded. "I'll talk to you later."

Lucifer nodded and Alistair closed the door.

Lucifer lifted his hand, and glanced at the invitation under it.

I'd love to chat with you, if you don't mind. Would you join me in my home for dinner?

~L.

He passed his hand over it, revoking it. Then he walked over to the fireplace and threw the paper and ink into it. He watched as the fire consumed it utterly. Then he went over to the study door and opened it. He looked across at the door to the Soulless.

He walked over and put his hand on the knob. The metal was cold in his hand and he held it, just held it, until it was warm. Every thought of turning it and seeing inside broke him.

If I never look, then she's still here. She's moved on or just seeing the underworld.

But he knew that wasn't true. He felt her open that door. He felt her dissolve. He knew he needed to revoke her invitation because now, she was a danger to every soul here. He knew there was only one other person who could have opened this door. He did it that way on purpose.

Leave it closed. I don't need to see that. Just imagine she's happy and in Slade's arms. Raph and Gabe were destroyed because they were outside that room. She wasn't. She went in. She's fine. Slade was no different than when he went in before. There must be a time lock or something. Maybe she is standing in there, her arms around Slade. Or, maybe she's right inside, unable to move.

He twisted the knob.

And if she is? If she's right inside the door? Then what?

I can pull her out.

He pictured him rescuing her, and her turning to him. She would apologize and hug him, thanking him for saving her. Then she would kiss him, and while their mouths were connected, she would dissolve into soulless matter…

Lucifer eased the knob closed again. He backed away, putting his back against the wall by the study, the open door letting the firelight from the dimming fire splay upon the Soulless one. He slid down to sit on the floor, staring at it.

A tear found its way onto the back of his hand and he didn't look down. He let the rest fall, dotting his clothes with emotion, and eventually, he simply let go, and sobbed.

Forty

"The ox is to the farmer as the lion is to the farmer." (Because of the plow, the ox is swept away, lost.)

Giles pointed to the sludge trail coming from the north. "There's more of it. This is horrible. Why doesn't it sink into the ground?"

George frowned at the pool of the stuff at the base of a small rise in the area. "This area is near the Papal City. Maybe the ground here is blessed?"

Giles shook his head. "This was from a divine source. That wouldn't interfere." He stood, looking up the hill. "No, this is something else. Damn! I wish I could ask Raven."

"Who's Raven?"

"Another Mage. Someone with Land ties."

"Why can't you ask him?"

"I... upset him, I think."

George frowned. "You *think*?"

Giles rolled his eyes at George. "It wasn't my fault. A bunch of church-mongers destroyed his home in my name."

"Ah. And you don't know where he is?"

"Oh, I know exactly where he is. He's in my sanctuary in Serenity. I felt him the moment he entered."

George just looked at him.

Giles closed his eyes and exhaled. "Fine. I'll go see him. I need to yell at him for entering my sanctuary anyway."

"That might not be the best approach."

Giles frowned. "A warrior is coaching me *against* confrontation?"

"A *soldier* is coaching you against confrontation with someone whose *home was destroyed* in your name."

Giles nodded. "Right. Right. Okay. I'll head out. What are you going to do?"

"I need to communicate with the General you mentioned."

"Oh. He's clear on the other side of the Valley. Wait here and I'll take you there when I get back."

"Alright. I'll get briefed from these men and see what the plan is."

Giles nodded and disappeared.

Catriona stiffened and fell back against a tree. Her eyes flared jade.

"Something has happened to the First Dûcesa."

Myrgen felt something in his hand and he held it up for both of them to see. It was a dark, translucent stone with so many gold flecks in it, it looked like a gold stone with a dozen black ones. He swallowed and looked at her.

"My heart is racing at what this means."

She nodded. "Mine too. It's…" She fumbled for the proper descriptor but failed to grasp it.

Myrgen nodded. "Yeah, like that. What do you want to do?"

She looked at the stone. "If I touch that, I get those memories. It might be the most complete set we've ever had."

"Does that mean it might know what happened to Magic?"

She swallowed. "I have no idea. But that's an awful lot of gold flecks."

"Yeah."

They waited in silence for a few moments, then Catriona held out her hand.

Myrgen took it, kissed it, then put the memory stone in her palm.

She was able to close her hand before the memories overtook her.

Images flew at her, ancient and overwhelming in number. It was like being force fed all the knowledge in the world. She felt like she was drowning. Finally, she screamed and collapsed on the ground. Her eyes were dark jade and Myrgen steeled himself in case she lashed out at him. Her screaming continued, lost in the trees, and a lifetime passed before she stopped.

When it did, she released her grip on Myrgen's hand. He shook it out, keeping his eyes on her.

"Are you in there?"

She looked at him. "Yes."

"Okay, *that's* gonna take getting used to."

"What?"

"Your voice is… unusual."

She nodded. "Yes, I imagine it might be. It'll shake out soon, Hunter."

Myrgen bit his lip, nodding. "Yeah. I'm sure it will. Here, let me help you up."

She did and stood, leaning against the tree. She looked at the rift to the pocket dimension. "Interesting."

Myrgen looked at it. "What?"

"I can see the Giver's touch here. In everything. Except…" She turned to the north. "Up there. Something is… different." She then looked east, but said nothing before she started walking.

Myrgen looked at Lauriel. "Tell Raven we'll be back."

Lauriel nodded and watched them leave.

Corrigan nodded to the scout brought before him. "Give your report."

The two eagle scouts saluted, and the one on the left proceeded. "A monster has drawn a line of poison across the northern border. It is fatal to us."

"Poison?"

"Yes, Sire." The eagle fidgeted. "It appears to be the same poison that was on the clothing the human king left behind."

Corrigan frowned. He turned to Johner. "This is the toxin you said that a mere touch could destroy even the strongest of us?"

"Yes, Sire." Johner looked at the scout. "How far does it extend?"

The scout's expression became even more grave. "The entire top of the valley. Reports came in last night of patrols not being at their posts. No one could find the soldiers. This morning, the reports are arriving from the entire line of the valley."

"Sire!" A rabbit scout ran up and bowed. "Sorry to intrude, but the Black Forest has expanded!"

"What?"

Corrigan and the rest stepped outside. The rabbit scout pointed.

Johner turned to the eagle. "Fly. See how far it extends."

The eagle leapt into the air. Johner looked at the other eagle scout. "How many have been reported missing?"

"Over a hundred."

Corrigan looked at his lieutenant. "That many? How?"

"The Human king might know the answer."

"Then get him. Bring him to me."

Johner bowed as the eagle returned.

"It goes all the way north, nearly to Glarren."

Johner glanced at Corrigan, then left.

"Sire."

A troll soldier came in, carrying another half-troll. The half troll was injured with burns like acid. The entire side of his face and an ear were scarred and pitted.

"What happened to this man?"

"He is an earth troll, Sire. He went to see what was happening on the border to the south. A group of three men and a barrel appeared out of nowhere, splashing the contents onto the ground. It was holy water."

Corrigan straightened. "Take him to be healed. I will deal with this."

The troll left and Corrigan sat in his throne, waiting.

Forty-One

"The tears of the farmer are as the rain to the flood." (The ox gave its life to save his master who hurt him.)

Giles appeared in his sanctuary and saw Raven poring over a tome. "You broke into my sanctuary."

Raven looked up. "You weren't using it." He stood, holding out the book. "But this is interesting. Your writing is still here."

Giles cocked his head and walked over to the book. "Hunh. Why didn't it erase when I died?"

"My guess? You didn't actually *die* before you were taken up into Heaven."

"But, I was stabbed earlier today. I didn't die then either."

"If you were in Heaven for as long as you say, you probably just absorbed so much Life energy, it's taking a while to wear off."

"Raymond says he's also immortal."

Raven pointed at Giles with the book. "Ah, but when was the last time he *tested* that? After a while, I imagine he just accepted it and moved on. It's probably been *years* since he attempted suicide."

"Is it the same with you?"

Raven shook his head. "Doubtful. I was denied access to any afterlife if it was touching Hell."

"You're a Land worshipper though."

"Doesn't seem to matter. Don't know what that means."

"Oh, speaking of things that are baffling, there's some black sludge in the valley with that army. Won't soak into the ground. Do you know why?"

"It's anti-Fae. Anything that is against the Land doesn't get to enter it. That's why Augustinians put their dead on shelves. The Land just spits them out otherwise."

"What are you doing in here?"

"I was looking for something… Oh! That amulet spell you mentioned. I wanted to have a look at it. Then I found this spell."

Raven pointed to the spell on the open page.

Giles nodded. "The memory spell. Why did that catch your fancy? You obviously know it."

"That's the thing. I *don't* know it! The one *I* know says you can only recall things you *witnessed personally* or was in the vicinity for. This spell doesn't have those constraints. There is an early version of it that has that requirement but you improved upon it. We were never taught that."

"Oh." Giles stroked his chin. "Oh yeah, that's right. I made this spell and tested it on the Estate by going there. I was required to write it down. These experiments changed it but I never went back there."

"Why not?"

"Falling out."

Raven nodded, understanding.

Giles looked around. "Do you need a place to study?"

"You got a spare alembic?"

"There are houses. They can have labs if you want to have a home here."

Raven sighed. "Well, apparently there's a forest right outside this place. One I can't get out of. My father's Fae."

"Why would that matter?"

Raven blinked. "Uh, this is the Black Forest. I can't leave it."

Giles snorted a laugh. "I *made* this place. I know what the spell is. I can get you out of here."

Raven sat up straighter. "Without the destruction of what makes me Fae?"

"Yeah. At least I think so. No, wait. I can. I can get Fae out of here. I have to be the one to do it, but that's the loophole."

"Oh. I see why it became a prison after you left."

"So, where do you want to go then?"

"Probably just out of here."

Giles got up. "Okay. Let's go then."

Raven put his hand up to stop Giles. "I know my soul isn't going anywhere, but I don't want to become goo. Where's the amulet spell?"

Giles looked around and found his notes under another book. "Here. Check it out for yourself. Oh! And I have investigated the other amulet design. I know what's wrong with it. It has an infernal component."

Raven frowned. "Oh. Well, that would be a problem."

"Yes. Especially since it's coming from Heaven."

Raven shrugged. "Lucifer is part of Heaven, you know. He's an angel too."

"Uh, yeah." Giles pointed to himself. "Saint."

"Yeah, but how often did you see him?"

Giles opened his mouth, then closed it again. "Come to think of it… never. In the entire time I was up there, I never saw him. I kinda forgot he was part of Heaven's paradigm." He looked at Raven. "So, are we good now?"

"Huh?"

"You left and were very mad at me before."

"Oh that. Well, here's the thing, Giles; We have a conflict coming up between Heaven and the Land. I'm a Land Worshipper. I was never going to be on your side."

"I guess I just hoped we would stay out of it, like we were taught at the Estate."

"I have 'stayed out of it' for over three hundred years. You have been a direct part of it for longer than that. What do you have to show for your participation?"

Giles thought about it. "My wife is dead. My friends are gone. I can't die. There's no one left to teach things to because I have no idea how to even find someone with the Gift now. My entire life has been taken away and the world changed by monsters."

Raven tapped his nose. "Exactly. You just described me. The only difference is that in my case, the monsters are simply creatures and not betrayers. It has literally made no difference. So how much do you really want to sit this one out?"

Giles was silent while Raven went over the spell to make the amulet. After a few minutes, he nodded.

"Well, it looks like there's nothing here that can harm me. And I'm already trapped in this place if I leave so, I'm going to take a chance with you. Where do we want to go?"

Giles bit his lip. "I think I need to show you the other amulet."

"Why?"

Giles stammered. "Uh… to… show you that I'm legit?"

"If I die because I travel with you, then we'll know. But if what you say is true, then I can *only* leave if I'm with you. Either way, I'm out of commission for this battle if I don't take a chance. In that respect, it doesn't matter where I go to test this."

Lauriel entered the room. He looked at Raven.

Raven nodded. "Did you see where they went?"

Lauriel sneezed.

Raven looked at Giles. "Okay, let's do this first. We need to head to Persephone. We need to find out what happened there with the trap."

"The what now?"

"I'm pretty sure I mentioned the trap."

"You probably did and I wasn't listening."

"Lauriel, I need to go with him. We're going to use his amulet."

Lauriel lowered his head, growling.

"I know. If that happens, you go to Catriona."

Lauriel growled again.

Raven took a knee and hugged his friend. "It could kill you."

Lauriel snorted.

"Good point." Raven stood. "Lauriel's coming with us."

Giles nodded. "Okay."

He put his hand on Raven and Lauriel, and disappeared.

George returned to the men. "I need to speak to your General. You are a messenger. How long does it take to get to the crossroads where these men came from?"

"About two days, sir."

Adam gestured to the hill. "We can just wait for your friend to return. He can do it instantly."

"Yes, but he also has his own missions. Right now, he's on one."

Charles frowned. "Wasn't he already on a mission?"

Adam shook his head. "This was the last barrel we had. They now dot the perimeter." He looked at George. "Do you have any idea what the plan would be with these?"

"That's why I want to talk to your General." George looked at the valley, teeming with Fae. He could see the pavilion of a noble rising in the center. He nodded to it.

"That's likely Corrigan. He's in the center, in order to be surrounded by his people. That other pavilion, the one near town, there's something wrong with it."

Charles pulled a spy glass from a pouch and held it to his eye. "It looks burnt."

"May I see that?"

Charles handed the glass to George, and he looked at the area. "You mentioned your King was being held captive?"

"Yes, sir."

"What does he look like?"

"Blonde, tall. Human."

George gave the spyglass back to Charles. "Then we may have a problem."

"What?"

"It looks like they are taking him to the Midsummer King."

Forty-Two

"The rain is to the flood as the tears are to the farmer." (The rain helps the flood grow, just as the tears and loss help the farmer grow.)

Johner stepped into Alexander's tent. "The Midsummer King is here and requesting an audience."

Alexander nodded. "Has the Mervol General sent word yet?"

"No. But he is doing something. We're not sure what. Corrigan would like to ask about them."

They left the tent, Alexander's hands tied in front of him with silver cord. Though it was almost like a decorative chain, it was unyielding. He walked to the road that connected to the town and saw a woman sitting in the middle. She stood when she saw him.

"Alexander!"

He turned with Johner.

"Who is that?"

Alexander shook his head. "I have no idea."

She ran towards him. The surrounding ogre guards blocked her but Johner stopped them. She bowed thanks to him and went to Alexander.

"Finally. I'm Brigit."

Alexander glanced at Johner. "Have we met?"

"No. I mean I'm *Saint* Brigit."

Alexander frowned. "What…?"

She bowed to Johner. "You must be Johner. Gomez said you were an honorable man. I have some very important information."

Alexander raised his hands. "How are you down here? I mean, I recognize your voice, now that you said your name. But you were in Heaven."

"That's part of my information. Giles, Clara and I were kicked out."

She quickly explained the goals of the angels and how the saints had been fighting that for years.

"But they caught us and cast us out. We've been trying to get to you ever since. You need to know that Heaven does not care about anyone down here at all. They only care about the souls coming back to Heaven.

"There's more. The Queen is not in the jail anymore. Is she here?"

Johner frowned. "No. If she were, your king would be unbound."

"Then unbind him."

All three turned as Sovereigna walked from the northern walkway. Her guard was with her.

"Your Majesty." Johner inclined his head.

Alexander stepped over to her. "Sovereigna, what are you doing here?"

"My duty, young man. I know you were trying to spare your mother and I more pain, but I got to the forest and could not enter. I could not abandon her son." She looked at Johner. "Please release him."

Johner touched the silver cord and took it away. "You are free to go. It is inappropriate for you to be captive if your hostage is free."

"Thank you." Alexander rubbed his wrists. "Brigit, what do we need to do to stop Heaven's plan?"

"Make peace and make it public. Right now, they are placing barrels of holy water along the road to stop you all from retreating. I don't know what the plan is past that."

Alexander looked at the others. "I originally planned to line the streets of the town with holy water and symbols to repel the Fae. They must be taking that idea and running with it. I knew I could connect the symbols through the divine energy from Heaven. Now, I'm not so sure if you're down here. An angel spoke to the valley and town earlier, trying to say I wanted to kill them all in here."

Sovereigna glanced at her guard. "It's worse than you think. There is a line of that toxic substance all along the northern border. I went into the woods, and saw some man drag a Fae body oozing the stuff along the upper road. He threw it into the tree line and disappeared. I checked the body as it dissolved."

Alexander swallowed. "Someone else has an amulet?"

Johner stiffened. "And they are using it to make a border."

"There's more. The forest has... *grown*." Sovereigna gestured to the north. "It goes a lot farther now. I felt a rumble and climbed a tree. It goes on for miles along the Krakte southern border."

Alexander frowned, eyes wide. "How?"

"I don't know. But anyone thinking they can flee into the woods with be killed by that toxin. We have to warn everyone."

"This way." Johner motioned towards the Midsummer King's pavilion.

Elander saw the armored man gesture to the center of the new reinforcements and set his jaw.

So even with the queen returned, they aren't letting him go. And now they have the Saint as well.

He nocked an arrow out of habit and drew the bow. If Alexander wasn't going to be released, then Elander *had* to create a way for him to escape.

"For King, and country."

He let the arrow fly.

Johner felt the threat coming. Movement from a rooftop caught his eyes and he saw the arrow flying. He realized it was going to hit Sovereigna and stepped in front of it. He knew no human arrow could penetrate his armor. He put his back to the man and put his hands upon Sovereigna's shoulders.

Then the arrow, bright with blue, holy light, punched through his chest plate and burrowed into the queen. They stood, connected, for a few moments. Blood burst from her chest wound, spraying Alexander, Brigit, and Johner. He turned to Alexander and reached out to him, then the two collapsed on the ground.

Corrigan turned towards the screams as he felt a part of his realm die. He ran outside his pavilion and saw Johner and the Krakten Queen fall to the ground, an arrow through them both. He screamed in anguish but his guards grabbed him and took him to the ground, covering him with their bodies. The report from the scout had said there was a line of death poison on the northern border and the other scouts reported the surrounding valley road now was protected with holy water.

He looked at his people, at the monsters that were here to destroy his race. Heaven wanted their deaths. More than that, Heaven wanted them *all* to die.

So be it.

Corrigan threw his protectors from him, his regal light emanating from his armor. He gathered all his power of summer to him. The glow turned the eyes of every creature from him, shielding themselves from his judgment. He pulled on the light, the warmth of the sun. He pulled on the strength of the army, and all who fight. That light covered every Fae in the valley.

Then, he drove his fist into the ground.

All the light surrounded the Fae, and they were drawn into the soil in an instant. The tents and fires disappeared, and in a single clock's tick, all trace of the Fae incursion was gone.

Gloriana arched her back as the power of Summer flowed into her. She cried out in surprise more than pain.

James ran into the room as the glow of summer dimmed in her eyes. "Your Majesty?"

She hung her head, realizing she was on her hands and knees.

So be it.

She rose, James helping her to stand. She walked to the throne room, haste hidden by her gown. She sat upon the throne as the front doors opened. The creature before her bowed, then knelt without a word. His presence here meant her sister could not claim him. This confirmed her fear. She nodded.

"Tooele," she said to the man before her, "close the roads."

Appendices

Appendix A: Characters of the Saintlands

Aggie- Innkeeper of the Fair Winds Inn and Tavern in St Marguerite. Husband of Flora, brother-in-law of Martin.

Aislyn Cortright- Nubian woman in St. Giles.

Alan Moriarity: Catriona's son. After his Naming Ceremony, Victor Tiberius Morstadora.

Albreda Wulftorhüter- Noblewoman of Krakte. Her and her husband Reinmar are inventors.

Alexander Angloume (ANG-loo-may): King of Mervolingia, Alexander succeeded the Throne after Charles. Alexander is also the Duke of Anjou, the family lands of the Angloume house.

Alistair MacGlarren: In service to Gloriana, the Midwinter Queen, Alistair is also the bloodline heir to the throne of York. The original Black Sparrow, he retired from this position after succeeding in learning about Tanglwyst's pirate operations. He stopped when Catriona, his former lover, found out. Alistair is also the father of James and Gwen. Since his death at the hands of Duncan McVryce, he has been serving Karma in the afterlife.

Allen Hobbs- Royal Patrolman for the Bordeaux Highway between St. Giles and Cliffbase.

Anika Zapolya- Dûcesa of Caratia. Holder of the Heartstone.

Antoinette: Cook in the mornings at the Patras Royal Palace.

Archbishop Alonzo de Patrone: Archbishop of Patras.

Artemisia: Mythical name of the Moon and mother of the Sea Goddess Calista.

Bartolemaus Johner- The Voice of Command (Lieutenant to Corrigan Starshadow).

Black Sparrow: Notorious pirate who attacked the Tanglwyst Trading Company. Taken out by Catriona Moriarity.

Brigit- Patron Saint of Healers. Alexander's personal patron saint.

Bringer- Short for Death Bringer. An entity of Power that has been missing for centuries. Counterpart to Giver.

Calpurnia Allegheri (cal-PUR-nee-uh AL-uh-GAIR-ee) the Autumnal Sovereign - Fae Lord of Autumn. Currently asleep in the tower of Sovereignlumin.

Catriona Moriarity (CAT-tree-OH-nah MORE-ee-AR-it-tee): Stâpâna of Caratia. The Stâpâna is the Protector of the Land's People in the country of Caratia, the second highest rank in the country. The Stâpâna is chosen through a secret ritual known only to those in Caratia. Lover of Myrgen.

Cecelia de Firenze- Simultaneously the proprietor of the Brew Ha House in guardianship of the Caratian Pass to York, and the head of the kitchens at the Royal Palace of Patras, respectively.

Ce'Nedra van Oppal- Innkeeper of the Black Cat and Anchor Inn in St. Andrew.

Cipriano- Annibal Cipriano Malatesta, King of Mande.

Charles Maximillian IX: Former King of Mervolingia, ruler and instigator of the St. Michael's Day Massacre.

Clara of Weltonshire- Patron Saint of Barren Women. Hero of the Soulless War, her holy footsteps blessed the soil where she walked. This soil was gathered by Raven Grasshair to corral the Last Child so that he could be captured and banished by Calpurnia. Although Heaven accepted her as the new Patron Saint of Barren Women (displacing Raymond non Nonattus after his ejection from Heaven), the Papal Council never acknowledged her.

Corrigan Starshadow the Midsummer King- Fae Lord of Summer.

Diane de Poitiers- Mistress to King Henry II. Murdered Henry in a jealous rage and then committed suicide due to being fed Cyprian Herb by him.

Dominic D'Medici (DOM-uh-nik dee MED-ee-chee): Fiancé of Gwen. As Acting Chancellor of Mervolingia, he is in charge of all funding and expenses for the entire kingdom.

Don- A general title of noble station. In Augustinian countries, it means Lord.

Drake Zapolya: Dûce of Caratia. The ruler of Caratia can be either male or female and is chosen directly by the Land through a ritual involving several trials and finally culminating in a ceremony in the town square of Zara.

Duncan McVryce: A notable member of the Back Streets of Patras, Duncan has played a role in several events involving members of the Royal family, the Augustinian church and Tanglwyst's interests.

Ealusaid (EL-uh-SASH)- Proprietress of the Benevolent Friar on the road to the Papal City.

The *Enigma*- Catriona's ship, it houses a Fae spirit named Estelle, that is the daughter of Corrigan, the Midsummer King. Estelle is wife to Octavius.

Entivia "Boots" Malatesta- Horse in the Stable of Assassins owned by Giovanni Sangiardo.

Embertwist Apocraphix the Vernal Monarch- Fae Lord of Spring.

Estelle Starshadow- Daughter of Corrigan and wife of Octavius.

Father Benjamin: A priest in service to Marco Giovanni, he was killed helping Catriona escape her captivity in the breeding pens of the Giovanni estate.

Felix Benivieni - Official messenger for the Royal Palace in Patras. Childhood sweetheart of Sylvaine Rochefort.

Flora- Innkeeper of the Fair Winds Inn and Tavern in St. Marguerite. Wife of Aggie and sister of Martin.

Fuccochio, Benivito (foo-KAH-chee-o)- Clothing designer in Florentine, Mande. Known for his fairness and incredible designs, his patrons are catalogued by the royalty and nobility of Mande.

Gabriel- Archangel. Patron Saint of Autumn.

Gillian Malatesta- Princess of Mande and daughter of Cipriano.

Giver- An entity of power being held captive in Heaven. Counterpart to Bringer.

Gloriana Talnig the Midwinter Queen- Fae Lord of Winter.

Gomez de Santander: Head of Alexander's personal guard, Gomez began as a guard at the Giovanni estate.

Gweneviere "Gwen" Douglas (GWEN-eh-veer DUG-lus): Handmaiden of Catriona, Gwen has the distinction of being her most trusted companion. Daughter of Alistair and Gloriana, twin of James.

Hamish Ó Caoindealbháin (HAY-mish oh CAY-lin)- Chief Ferryman for the Office of the Ferrymen in Kilgarren, York.

Helen Brightwater- Chatelaine for the Sanctuary Vineyards, held by the Tanglwyst Trading Company. Wife of Matthew Brightwater.

Henri de Porthos (OHN-ree dee POR-thos)- Chief Bookkeeper for St. Andrew. Beloved of Ce'Nedra.

Isabella D'Medici- Lawyer for the Tanglwyst Trading Company and cousin to Dominic D'Medici. Wife of Othon of Burwick.

James Douglas- Captain of the *Crimson Veil.* Brother of Gwen.

Jess Beck- Goatherd in Caratia. Husband of Rae.

Johannes- Bo'sun on the *Enigma.*

Karma- Entity of Balance. Worshipped by default in Yndia.

King Henry II: Father of Francois I, Charles, Alexander and Margaret, husband of Catherine, Deceased.

Kyri de Holloway- Daughter of Tanglwyst. Lives in Pardua, Mande, in the Storm Catch. Proprietress of the Storm's Catch Inn and Tavern.

Last Child- The last child left from the original children resurrected before the Soulless War. These children were returned by the Land to walk the earth, but their souls were already returned to Heaven with their deaths. As a result, they searched the world, draining life and destroying souls in their attempts to get one of their own. The Last Child hid away in Clara's basement and escaped because he convinced Mephistopheles to turn against Lucifer and serve him instead. Mephistopheles took him through the ground, thereby destroying all the farmland in York.

Lauriel- Fae wolf. Caretaker and responsible party for Raven Grasshair.

Lawrence of Cleves- Keeper of the Watch on the *Enigma.*

Lucifer- Archangel. Caretaker of Hell.

Marco Giovanni: Mandian Count and head of the Apolodorus family, Giovanni almost married his cousin to secure a large financial conglomerate but murdered his son and then committed suicide the tenday before his wedding, leaving the Apolodorus fortune to his oldest child. Father of Dominic.

Marica the Gold Wife- First creation of a mage entirely by magic, the blacksmith Hephas used a life spell to animate a metal statue he forged. The Land granted this and infused the Gold Wife with the ability to work earth magic. Unfortunately, Hephas only wanted her to speak to him, but he worded the spell poorly for the sake of rhyming. As a result, only one person at a time can understand her.

Martin- Proprietor of the Fair Winds Inn and Tavern in St. Marguerite, along with Flora and Aggie.

Matthias Lovas (muh-THI-us LO-vahs)- Stable Keeper of Ashstone in Zara, Caratia. Killed in the Second Mandian Invasion protecting Victor Tiberius Morstadora.

Merrick Blackburn- Mage at Persephone and hero of Soulless War. Beloved of Calpurnia, he watches over her as she recovers from the spell she cast to capture the Last Child.

Michael- Archangel. Patron Saint of Summer. Lost in the Soulless War.

Michael - Myrgen's Nubian Slave. A very large man who is fiercely loyal to Myrgen.

Michelyne- The Third Dûcesa, her name was only discovered after she died and was asked what her name was by the inhabitants of Summerland.

Miguel (MIH-gel)- Anika's cat from before she became Dûcesa.

Monique Delorme- Proprietress of the Wise Wench Tavern in St. Giles, and author of the Wise Wench Tavern Book.

Morgan Wolf - Vicar in St. Marguerite, and Myrgen and Tanglwyst's brother.

Myrgen "the Grey" de Sablonierres (MUR-gun dee SAB-yon-air): Former Chancellor to Mervolingia, he was accused of the regicide of King Charles. Wandering the world in search of his path, he is Catriona's lover.

Nicolai Moriarity - Husband of Catriona Moriarity and father of Tib. A guard in the Patras Palace. Dead by poison.

Nigel - King Charles's Castellan before Myrgen.

Nina Richelieu – Guard in of the Royal Palace at Patras, she is Gomez' second in command.

Octavius - First mate of the *Enigma* under Captain Catriona Moriarity, husband to Estelle.

Osondrea- Scribe for the Sanctuary Vineyards belonging to the Tanglwyst Trading Company.

Othon of Burwick- Former personal bodyguard of Tanglwyst. Husband to Isabella D'Medici.

Persephone- Covenant tower of Mages in York that was the war effort against the Last Child in the Soulless War. Also seen as the name of the entity that was the source of magic under the Covenant.

Pope Gregory - Head of the Augustinian Church.

Preston Cowley- Manager of the St. Giles Home Office for the Tanglwyst Trading Company. Married to Steve.

Princess Isabelle - A Mandian Princess of marrying age

Princess Marie-Elizabeth - The daughter of Elizabeth and Charles.

Queen Elizabeth of Krakte - Queen of Mervolingia, married to Charles Maximillian IX. Mother of Marie-Elizabeth. A school friend of Tanglwyst's along with Adriana Cappelletti.

Queen Elizabeth of York- Queen of York, and friend of Alexander.

Queen-Mother Catherine D'Medici - Mother of Charles and Alexander. Married to Henry II.

Rae Beck- Goatherd in Zara, Caratia.

Raphael- Archangel. Patron Saint of Winter.

Raven Grasshair- Mage from the Covenant at Persephone, son of Corrigan, in sworn service for Calpurnia. Ward of Lauriel.

Raymond non Nonattus- Patron Saint of Barren Women, expunged. Cast from Heaven after granting babies to a dozen Glarren women after they converted to the Augustinian faith. The women rejected the faith and returned to worshiping Fae once their children were born.

Reinmar Wulftorhüter- Krakten inventor and husband of Albreda.

Richard of Kent, Sir- Noble knight in service to the Covenant at Persephone. He and Raven went on a quest to get Clara's name in the Saintly Record. This quest failed, but exposed the corruption in the Papacy. His death at the hand of Inquisitors sparked the Emilianite movement.

Rowena of Avalon- Jeweler in St. Giles.

Sinister Glove of Embertwist- Lieutenant to Embertwist.

Slade Stormchest- Stâpân to the First Dûcesa. Died protecting her from the Last Child right before it was banished into the void by Calpurnia's spell. The Last Child touched him instead of her and was then taken by the spell as he turned into a soulless.

Sovereigna Shwartzwald- Queen of Krakte, Elizabeth's mother, Marie Elizabeth's maternal grandmother.

Sovereignlumen the Eternal- Father of all Fae and beloved of Magic.

Svein (Sven)- Proprietor of the Benevolent Friar and husband to Ealusaid.

Sylvaine Rochefort- Widow of the Lord Rochefort who terrorized the families of St. Andrew. Childhood sweetheart of Felix.

Symonne- Proprietress of the Drum and Nightingale Inn and Messenger Service, guardian of the Caratian Pass to Mervolingia. Wife to Tomas.

Tanglwyst de Holloway (TANG-gul-wist dee HALL-oh-way): Owner of the Tanglwyst Trading Company and Catriona's secret partner. Sister of Myrgen and Morgan Wolf.

Thessius- Glarren member of Catriona's crew on the *Enigma.* Former First Mate to Ramirez on the *Crimson Veil.* Quartermaster on the *Enigma.*

Thomas the Diminutive- former Stâpân of Caratia, only one of two members of this order to resign the post without dying.

Tomas- Proprietor of the Drum and Nightingale Inn and Messenger Service, guardian of the Caratian Pass to Mervolingia. Husband to Symonne.

Trimelda Daniels- Dreamwalker for the Fang and Claw. Caretaker for Clara's Way and Clara's Bed. Clara's Bed is the monument to the Soulless War that is held in trust by the Crown of York. Couples who are seeking to get pregnant went here to conceive. As such, this became a royal honeymoon spot for post-coronation copulation.

Tristram Wulfschlager - Captain of the *Righteous*, one of Catriona's ships.

Tulio d'Or- Bandit king that holds the Contested Forest.

Uriel- Archangel. Parton Saint of Spring.

Urien Atreides - Husband of Tanglwyst de Holloway, a Latian Merchant who owns The Atreides Trading Company, which along with the Tanglwyst Trading Company controls 73% of the Mervol - Mandian trade.

Ûr- Caratian form of noble address

Wilgefortis- The wife of Raven Grasshair, she was also the Baroness of Canterbury in York and the Seneschal of Persephone during the Soulless War.

William- Navigator on the *Enigma*

Xannu (ZAN-noo)- Proprietress of the Open Lotus Incense and Bath House in Rouen.

Zachary Crow- Stable hand for the Benevolent Friar and adopted son of Svein and Ealusaid.

Appendix B: The Augustinian Calendar

The world of the Saintlands has four seasons, and those are the purview of the Fae Lords. Embertwist Apocraphix, the Vernal Monarch, rules over spring, Corrigan Starshadow, the Midsummer King, rules summer, Calpurnia Allegheri, the Autumnal Sovereign, reigns over fall and Gloriana Talnig, the Midwinter Queen, rules winter.

The combat these lords, the Church originally invoked the Archangels against them. These were sufficient but as Heaven gave the Church the Saints, these former humans were invoked in addition, adding to the strength of the protections against Fae trickery. The saints were originally celebrated upon the day of their ascension and delivery by Heaven into the Rolls.

However, 300 years ago, the Church, in the aftermath of a great war, decided to write down a formal calendar, honoring saints for their purviews instead of their date of ascension. This was to battle non-church beliefs, unify the masses and establish lines of Church control.

Pope Richard I told the cardinals to which he assigned this task to begin the year prior to the apex of Gloriana's control, so as to get ahead of the rise of her power. The Cardinals discussed it and Cardinal Cosimo of Pardua offered up Genevieve, invoked against disasters, to start the year. Richard approved and the calendar was begun.

Genevary became the first month and the months were divided into 31 day sets with 10 day tenday. In the center of the month, the 16th, is the Devotional Day, where all work stops for a day to pray and invoke the saints of the month. This strengthened the divinity in the realm, repelling anything not Heaven related. Although the new calendar reorganized the role of Saints during the year, many days are still known by the saint who ascended upon that day, though the Archangel's days were established during the Augustinian Calendar.

Months

1st: Named after Saint Genevieve, **Genevary** 16 honors Sebald, Martin of Tours, and Raphael the Archangel. Genevieve is invoked against disasters, which abound in the Saintlands during the winter. Sebald once burned icicles in a poor woman's home to produce heat. Martin of Tours cut his cloak in half to give to a naked beggar. Raphael brings the heat of the sun and dawn to battle freezing cold.

2nd: Named after Saint Vitus, **Vitusary** 16 honors Medard, Catald, and Barbara. Vitus is invoked against storms, but is also the Patron saint of dancers so balls abound in Vitusary. Medard is invoked against bad weather because he sheltered the beautiful queen Angelica, granddaughter of Saint Marie Angelica, when she fled the intrigues of the Mervol court during a storm. Medard gave his own tent so she would be safe and dry. An eagle sheltered him from the weather, creating an umbrella for him as he rested. Catald cured the ill and is invoked against plagues, which often abound from bad weather. Barbara was saved when lightning struck her attackers during a siege.

3rd: Named after Saint Florien, **Florias** 16 honors Vincent, Jude, & John of Nepomuk (bridges & flooding). Florien is invoked against floods, a common problem in the Saintlands the third month. Saint Vincent Ferrer is the patron saint of builders, often put to work during this time. Jude helps the hopeless. John of Nepomuk strengthens bridges during floods to save the towns.

4th: Named after Saint Elmo, **Elmos** 16 invokes Fiacre (gardeners), Phocas (market gardeners), and Uriel the Archangel. Elmos starts the sailing season, so Saint Elmo, patron saint of sailors marks this month. Fiacre and Phocas bring the first harvests from winter, began indoors or in warmer climes to feed the masses while Uriel protects the people from the lies and trickery of thieves.

5th: Named after Saint Walburga, **Walpurgisnacht** 16 invokes Valentine, Rose of Lima, & Theodore of Sykon (reconciling the unhappily married). Walpurgisnacht 1 allows the young and amorous to pursue each other unhindered and as such, this month marks the beginnings of many marriages. Valentine honors true love. Rose of Lima honors florists and flower growers. Theodore, known for his counseling skills, reconciles the unhappily married, reminding them of the way they felt their first month of marriage.

6th: Named after Saint Wilgefortis, **Vilgfort** 16 honors Felicity (women wanting sons), Monica (wives), & Marie Angelica (nun who married). Felicity is invoked by women wanting sons, usually royals, due to her miracle of delivering sons whenever she was a woman's midwife. Monica honors wives as she was Heaven's example of a perfect wife and Marie Angelica was a nun who married for the sake of the world. A vision held that Marie Angelica would have a daughter who would alter the church and though she was a nun, she was persuaded to leave her vows to fulfill this vision. Her daughter, Tanglwyst Angelica, inherited a powerful shipping company which was destined for the hands of a corrupt Church. Her sacrifice honors all women who must abandon their own dreams for the sake of a greater good.

7th: Named after Saint Maurice, **Maur** 16 honors Elizabeth (war), Clara (savior in the Soulless War) and Michael the Archangel. This is the season of war, and thus, the people invoke Saint Maurice to keep their soldiers safe while away from home while Elizabeth is invoked to find peaceful resolutions to wars. Clara was a woman whose role in the Soulless War enabled the plague to be destroyed through the spreading of soil she had walked upon, preventing the plague from crossing it. Michael fought the creatures of Hell to preserve the faithful during the great wars.

8th: Named after Saint Francis, **Franco** 16 honors Hubert (hunters), Andrew, and Sebastian. Saint Francis honors all animals and those who tend them. Hubert honors the hunters. Andrew the fishermen and Sebastian protects archers.

9th: Named after Saint Thomas Aquinas, **Aquin** 16 honors Ivo, Augustine, and Albert. The season of scholarly pursuits, Aquin honors those who devote themselves to study. Ivo honors lawyers. Augustine honors theologians and his ideals of Heaven are the basis for the Augustinian Church. Albert honors scientists and herbalists.

10th: Named after Saint Benedict, **Benedine** 16 honors Gabriel the Archangel, Giles, & Margaret. As this is a time of darkness descending upon the land and things turning cold, people were often creating tales of ghosts and fear. Those who had died in the wars of the summer or in the professions of the year were often "seen" wandering the desolate places during this month. To counter these tales of fancy, the church brought in their strongest saints against fear and superstition. Saint Benedict fought his greatest fear, being homeless, and opened his home as a shelter. As such, he is their patrón saint. Giles protects against night terrors. Margaret defends against those being attacked by devils, enabling their escape. Gabriel the Archangel heralds Heaven's will, driving away doubt and fear.

11th: Named after Saint Ferdinand, **Ferdin** 16 honors All Saints (Fer 1), Eloi, and Anne. To celebrate the survival of the month of fear, All Saints Day was noted as the first Church holiday. It also honors those responsible for the greatest achievements of humanity: Ferdinand for Engineers, Eloi for jewelry and metal smithing and Anne for pregnancy.

12th: Named after Saint Brigit, **Brig** 16 honors Cosmas & Damian, Raymond, and Roch. A most notable saint, Brigit was one of the first saints ascended to Heaven after giving her life to heal others. Her blood created a fountain by which those who were ill or damaged could be restored. This fountain is in the center of the Papal Palace in the Papal City. Cosmos and Damian are conjoined twins who became doctors. Raymond honors midwives. Roch is invoked against epidemics.

Weekdays

Day 1: Honorasday: named from Honoratus, for bakers.

Day 2: Bernaday: Named after Saint Bernadette, shepherds.

Day 3: Rufinasday: Named after Saint Rufina, potters.

Day 4: Simproniday: Named after Four Crowned Martyrs, stonemasons.

Day 5: Julianusday: Named after Saint Julian, boatmen.

Day 6: Vincentsday: Named after Saint Vincent Ferrer, builders.

Day 7: Wencesday: Named after Saint Wenceslas, brewers.

Day 8: Genesday: Named after Saint Genesius, Actors & Comedians.

Day 9: Columbasday: Named after Saint Columba, poets.

Day 10: Dismasday: Named after Saint Dismas, undertakers.

Appendix C: Religions

Augustinian (AHG-us-TIN-ee-uhn)

The Augustinians believe God made the world and made Heaven. God set up the ability for Man to ascend to Heaven body and soul by doing good works. If a human is good enough and helps enough people, they can become a Saint. Each Saint in the Augustinian Rolls was once a human and their name appears in the Heavenly Roster when they ascend. The Heavenly Roster is a book kept in the Papal City on the Official Altar in the center of the Cathedral under constant guard.

In the 1300s, the Church stopped acknowledging new names in the Roster after The War of the Soulless which they blamed upon the heathen religions. The reason cited for this denial was the War made it difficult to believe all the reports of ascended Saints. At the time, it was unknown by the populace about the Heavenly Roster but after the declaration and an investigation by nobles outside the church, this information was revealed to the public. Regardless, once the Pope responsible passed away and the scandal was uncovered, the new Pope acknowledged the updated Rolls and the new Saints were canonized.

The main Tenant of Faith in the Augustinian religion is the Saints are the world's connection to Heaven. It is only by praying to the Saints that one can communicate with Heaven. It is against the Laws of the Church to pray directly to God, bypassing his appointed representatives, to make requests, though one can offer praise unto Heaven without invoking a particular Saint. However, if one prays to a particular saint for guidance or assistance and they receive it, it is against the laws of the Church to not acknowledge the Saint who answered the prayer.

Emilianite (uh-MEEL-ee-uhn-ITE)

After the War of the Soulless and the Scandal of the Unacknowledged Saints, a group of followers broke away from the Church. Citing corruption in the dictations of the papacy, it was determined that apparently the Church could communicate directly to

Heaven without the help of the Saints since they refused to acknowledge the Saints received in the Rolls. They called these Saints "the Abandoned Children" and called themselves Emilianites, after Emilio, the patron Saint of abandoned children.

The Emilianites believe that man cannot be trusted with the will or intent of Heaven through a conduit, for that can be hidden or destroyed. Instead, they believe man can be more assured of correct information if he prays directly to Heaven. If Heaven wants the Emilianites to pray to a Saint, they will communicate that Saint's name to all the Faithful. Until that happens, the Emilianites will pray directly to Heaven. Since the Scandal of the Unacknowledged, no Emilianite has ever noted a Saint's name being given to them. As such, they continue to offer prayers only to Heaven.

Land Worship

The Maker split in two, creating the Heavens and the Land. Both are sentient and great entities unto themselves. Heaven holds the Well of Souls and deals with all things ethereal such as dreams and thoughts, ideas and concepts. The Land deals with all things physical, be it body, plant or liquid. If it can be held, it is the purview of the Land.

When the body dies, the Land takes it into itself and dissolves the flesh, leaving the soul. The soul is filtered and cleansed of the sins of its life and when all the sin is gone, the soul that is left is returned to the Well of Souls. The Land interacts with the people on a daily basis, feeding them, clothing them, healing them. They trust the Land and count on its gifts for life.

Calista's Call

Oceanus, Father of Waters, was alone and lonely. He wandered across the world without drive or direction. Sometimes, to relieve his boredom, he would slice through a mountain or sink an island he made but in the end, he was aimless and alone. Then, one night, he heard a stirring song. It beckoned him from across the Land and he fell upon a beach, kneeling before the singer. A beautiful maiden of silver hair and glowing pale skin sat naked on the beach, her voice filling the night. He crept up behind her and she saw him and screamed, then grabbed her clothes and fled to the sky.

Every night, he went to the beach to fall upon the shore, begging her to return. He brought her gifts from the sea and faraway lands, creatures and stones, wood and plants. Eventually she peeked from behind the curtain of night and slowly emerged, a little more each night, until she fell in love with Oceanus and they made love upon the beach. They created a daughter of rich blue skin like her father and glowing white hair like her mother. They called her Calista and the salt from their tears of joy at the sight of her soaked her, making her touch turn water into salt water.

Calista watches the sea and keeps her secrets and those of her followers. She is a fickle goddess though, and prone to fits of fury that can seem unprovoked. When she is happy or dealing with honorable people, her hair is the white of sea foam. Mermaids gather the honored dead and if a sailor is a good follower, Calista recognizes them and grants them the ability to live underwater as merfolk in her cities. Her dolphins and sea mammals guide ships through treacherous areas and are always signs of her pleasure.

But she has her primal side as well and when dealing with the dishonorable, she sends her teeth to rend them. Her hair turns bloody red and her sharks and sirens call the evildoers to their destruction. If there is an argument in ship at sea and sharks arrive on the scene, it means someone in the fight is lying. If a criminal is sentenced to death at seas, the sharks will take him, but if the criminal is remorseful, they take him to the depths where he becomes a Marked One and serves Calista for as long as they breathed air. Sirens call the unjust to the sharks' maws so if one hears a siren's call, the heavier the sins on their soul, the harder it is to resist them.

If a body is rendered with fire at death, Calista will know them not and shall cast their spirit out of her mouth to walk the earth forever.

The Ancient Ones

Sovereignlumen was a good king. He loved Magic so much, that he mated with her, and fathered the Fae. The Fae were everywhere. They were the merfolk in the sea and the harpies in the air. They were the pixies and dryads in the trees and the white-furred talking animals in the snows. All the magical creatures, great and small, frolicked in the love of their mother and father. The Fae loved humans and played with them, guiding them to good places and punishing the lazy or wicked with their games and tricks.

But then a sickness came, one that threatened all the magical creatures. Dark men captured the Fae, torturing them to find the sources of Elemental magic. Sovereignlumen roared and rode to war against these dark men and felled them. In the battle, he was mortally wounded and returned home to die. He gave to his four eldest his power, divided as to their gifts.

To his youngest son Embertwist Apocraphix, he gave the powers of Spring. The Vernal Monarch is the quintessential thief and like a thief, it comes in the night, stealing the cold of winter and revealing the living things beneath her skirt. To his oldest son, Corrigan Starshadow, he gave the powers of Summer. As the Midsummer King, his paladin nature marches forthright towards the good and just.

To his oldest daughter, Calpurnia Allegheri, he gave the powers of Autumn. Calpurnia so resembled his beloved Magic, she channels the gifts of change and harvest during her reign as the Autumnal Sovereign. To his youngest daughter, Corrigan's twin, he gave the power of Winter. Gloriana Talnig, the Midwinter Queen, uses the cold to stop disease and preserve and heal, but also to punish the wicked and delay the unjust. The children split and went to different parts of the world to preserve their realms from the followers of the Dark Men, but each season, they return to Sovereignlumin, the great Tower That Watches All to transfer the power of the seasons.

Karma

Karma is all about balance. For each act, there is an equal and opposite reaction in a person's life. As they get closer to the end of their life thread, they can find themselves bound by the threads they have thrown. Negative acts cause sticky threads, positive acts throw stabilizing threads. If a soul has cast more sticky threads than stabilizing, they can be caught up in the negative and it will strangle them. Thus are many of the symbolic gods of Karma multi-limbed creatures.

The Primordial Egg

The Primordial Egg twitched and cracked and from the shell, four Dragons emerged. They opened their mouths and breathed forth the world. The Earth Dragon formed land and grass, ore and metal, wood and dale. The Water Dragon formed oceans and rivers, lakes and streams, snow and ice. The Fire Dragon breathed the sun and stars to warm the world. And the Air Dragon gave life and the moon. As all things came from magic, all creatures upon the world were magical, and all things communicated with one another in the combined tongue of the elements.

But then, a threat loomed on the face of all and it tried to conquer the magic in the world. It's flashing sword and violent means crushed all but its own belief, slaying the dragons in the world. The Elemental Dragons Rose against it, but to destroy the threat meant to destroy all they loved as well. Instead, they seized their followers and sealed them away in special places. The Earth Dragon hid the giants and Dwarves in the mountains. The Fire Dragon hid her faithful in the ash and lava. The Water Dragon took her children and gave them the ability to breathe water. And the Air Dragon took his children to the sky, to the place between life and death.

At first they spoke aloud to one another, but monsters found their hiding places, so the Dragons broke the world and spoke only in secret languages so none could find their whereabouts. The Earth Dragon spoke through entrails and omens, the Water Dragon through storms. Fire claimed its own hypnotic power and Air spoke through the dead. Together, they all keep the legends and the magic safe, making certain that only those who wish to keep magic in the world can find them.

Fang and Claw

The practice of having an animal choose to join with a person's soul to guide them is standard practice in the followers of Fang and Claw. They also believe in the consuming a part of the animal allows for that animal's superior quality to enter the consumer.

As a rite of passage, warriors of the tribes will hunt a dangerous animal with which to partner. Shaman may not be led by a dangerous animal, but by a wise one such as Snake or Owl. And those who become the Seers find themselves in the company of spiders.

Appendix D: Countries

Caratia (CUH-ray-SHEE-uh)
Capital City: Zara
Native tongue: Caratian (CUH-ray-SHEE-uhn)
Dominant Religion: Land Worship

Glarren (GLARE-uhn)
Capital City: Kilmory (kill-MORE-ee)
Native tongue: Glarren
Dominant Religion: The Ancient Ones

Krakte (KRAHK-tuh)
Capital City: Austra
Native tongue: Krakten
Dominant Religion: Augustinian, Emilianite, the Ancient Ones

Latia (LAH-tee-uh)
Capital City: Cheryb (SHARE-eeb)
Native tongue: Latian (LAH-tee-uhn)
Dominant Religion: Calista's Call

Mande (MAHND)
Capital City: Vincenza
Other Cities: Pardua, Florentine, Calais, Aquila, Balona, Trieste, Naplles, Genoa
Native tongue: Mandian (MAHN-dee-uhn)
Dominant Religion: Augustinian

Mervolingia (MER-vole-LIN-jee-uh)
Capital City: Patras
Other Cities: Rouen (ROO-en), St. Giles, St. Andrew, St. Marguerite
Native tongue: Mervol (MER-vol)
Dominant Religion: Augustinian, Emilianite

Nubia (NOO-bee-uh)
Capital City: Leeus Brul (lee-OOS bruul)
Native Tongue: Fangspek
Dominant Religion: Fang and Claw

The Papal City (PAY-puhl)
Capital City: None
Native tongue: Mervol
Dominant Religion: Augustinian Church Seat

Toledo (toe-LEED-dough)
Capital City: Tuscan
Native tongue: Toledan
Dominant Religion: Land Worship

York (YORK)
Capital City: Landen
Other cities: Canterbury, Kent, Oxford, Cambridge
Native Tongue: Yorkish
Dominant Religion: Emilianite

Yndia (YIN-dee-uh)
Capital City: Yantap (YAN-tap)
Native tongue: Yndian
Dominant Religion: Karma

Yokotama (YO-ko-TAH-mah)
Capital City: Kūki doragon
Native Tongue: Yokotaman
Dominant Religion: Dance of the Air Dragons